SHARP GLASS

By Sarah Hilary

Fragile

Black Thorn

Sharp Glass

DI Marnie Rome series

Someone Else's Skin

No Other Darkness

Tastes Like Fear

Quieter Than Killing

Come and Find Me

Never Be Broken

SHARP GLASS

SARAH HILARY

MACMILLAN

First published 2024 by Macmillan
an imprint of Pan Macmillan
The Smithson, 6 Briset Street, London EC1M 5NR
EU representative: Macmillan Publishers Ireland Ltd, 1st Floor,
The Liffey Trust Centre, 117–126 Sheriff Street Upper,
Dublin 1, D01 YC43
Associated companies throughout the world
www.panmacmillan.com

ISBN 978-1-0350-0509-3 HB
ISBN 978-1-0350-0510-9 TPB

1 3 5 7 9 8 6 4 2

A CIP catalogue record for this book is available from the British Library.

Typeset in Arno by Jouve (UK), Milton Keynes
Printed and bound by CPI Group (UK) Ltd, Croydon, CR0 4YY

Visit **www.panmacmillan.com** to read more about all our books
and to buy them. You will also find features, author interviews and
news of any author events, and you can sign up for e-newsletters
so that you're always first to hear about our new releases.

For Julie Akhurst

PART ONE

1

I heard a cuckoo this morning. The sound came through the pipes like everything from the outside world. Everything except him. He comes down the cellar steps into my darkness, bringing the scent of laurel from the garden. If there is a garden. A cuckoo. I don't know what's up there – out there – only what I can conjure in my mind's eye. But a place so far from everywhere is bound to have a garden. He carries it on his clothes: bright air that lights my darkness for a second, the time it takes him to remind me that darkness is all I have. Sometimes, to spite him, I grow a garden in my mind's eye, stuffing it with colour, scent, birdsong. Other times, there are only barren fields and a deadwood forest, cliffs falling away to nothing, to the end of the earth.

Have you ever taken a wrong turn late at night? Set out on a journey whose destination was very different in the daylight, not safe necessarily, but not deadly? Would you have turned back if you'd seen how the land lay, caught sight of the fire burning up ahead, tasted its ash on your tongue? Or would you, like me, have kept going? Needing to see, to be certain?

Three days ago, I drove through the night to get here, the last ten miles in the kind of darkness that only falls when you're far from a city. *A special quality of darkness.* No stars or moonlight, only my headlights to guide me along lanes where neglected hedges hauled at the car.

'Madwoman,' I muttered, hugging the steering wheel.

Who starts work in the middle of the night? Only a madwoman or someone whose bills are stacking up; the past few weeks had been a nightmare of last-minute cancellations. I'd have leapt on this latest job, whatever the cost. *A flagrant disregard for the small print,* my old dad would've called it.

'You have arrived at your destination.'

The house was a black square against the night sky. Detached out here, miles from anywhere. My headlights set pale eyes staring from stone walls. No light inside, but I hadn't expected any; the front-door key was stashed safe in my pocket. The boot of my car groaned with corrugated paper, bubble wrap, parcel tape, everything I needed to get started. Perhaps I should have paid better attention to the exterior of the house, but it was the contents I cared about as I cut the engine and climbed out into the night.

The house has seven rooms and a cellar. The cellar, I was told, was empty. For the seven rooms, I'd ordered packing boxes to be delivered ahead of my arrival. Clare Miranda, my client, said she'd arrange for a neighbour an hour's drive away to be here when the boxes were dropped off. These details seemed important at the time.

The house is unoccupied. Ms Miranda has never lived here, as far as I know. For years, her message said, she rented to holiday-makers. Now she wants to sell. On paper, it was an ideal job. Few personal items, no risk of anything precious being lost or damaged in transit. I'd spend a couple of days clearing and packing, sleeping in one of the three bedrooms in the sleeping bag I'd brought with me. On the fourth day, transport would arrive: a team to load my boxes into their van. For everything else, a skip was being dropped off. I love a skip. The word itself is perfect, meaning I can skip a lot of the packing, making me want to skip with joy. *A flagrant disregard for propriety and small print* (thanks, Dad), but no nearby neighbours to be scandalized, no one to bear witness to how I do my job or the peculiar pleasure I might take in doing it. On paper, it was perfect. Three days alone, away from the rest of the world. Worth driving through the dark to get a head start. That was my excuse anyway. Tonight I'd build boxes and make inventories ahead of tomorrow's hard work. I was bristling with purpose as I stood with the soft screech of owls behind me, claws skittering in trees I couldn't see, before he hit me over the head and delivered me into a deeper darkness than any I'd known before.

My cellar is a box inside a box. I know this from the way sound travels and because all houses are the same. Boxes inside boxes inside boxes. Houses are my business. There is nothing you can teach me about houses.

Three days ago, I scratched the first initial of my name into the cellar floor. I scratched a *G* but now I wish it was gone. I'm afraid he'll see it, or someone will. Whoever comes looking for me when I'm gone, searching these boxes for the hidden thing that was me.

My thoughts unravel, running to my car – *Is it parked outside or has he driven it away, drowned it or burnt it? If he's burnt it, I'll kill him –* and all the packaging in it, bubble wrap and corrugated paper to reduce the risk of breakages. My insurance policy promises every reasonable care, but I tend to go beyond *reasonable*. A better word to describe the care I take would be *extraordinary*. People trust me with their precious things. Even so, accidents happen. You certainly can't assume they won't. Look at me, at his mercy. It took him less than a minute to lay waste to my best-laid plans.

He can't have burnt my car; I'd have smelt smoke on his clothes. I didn't see another vehicle when I parked up, but how else did he get here, an hour's drive from the nearest town? He has a car. I see it in my mind's eye: a black pickup with chrome bull bars. Parked out of sight, around the back of the house. Clare Miranda was a ruse, a lie. The whole job was a lie.

He put a mattress on the cellar floor. It terrified me three days ago, conjuring all manner of humiliations. But it's just my bed. Blankets, too. He thought about my comfort, perhaps. It's so hard to know what he thinks. The human brain plays tricks when it's trapped. In the absence of sensory stimuli, it overcompensates; I'm seeing eyes in the cellar walls and in the steps leading to the door he keeps locked. Eyes like glass, cold and watchful.

My cellar has wine racks built into its walls. Empty, but I can smell fermented fruit, cork, paper labels, green glass. One of the first things I did, three days ago, was search every shelf for a bottle – *a weapon* – finding only cobwebs gluing to my fingers. The wine racks help me to imagine a family up in the house, sitting down to supper together. 'Pass the peas, will you?' Small children swinging their feet under the table, an apple-cheeked wife in an apron. And me, all the long way down here, held prisoner by their doting father, her loving husband. His secret, best kept under lock and key. For a second it warms me, the thought of being that special. Until I remember why I'm here.

Three days. That's how long I've been his prisoner.

I pick at a thread on the mattress, working it loose. He hasn't touched me yet. Except that isn't true – he carried me down here. Picked me up from the ground outside, held me in his arms. Did he sling me across his shoulder like a firefighter or a coal man, emptying me down into the darkness? He knows my weight, the shape of me, what I look like asleep. He's the first person in decades to know that. Since I was a baby in Mum's arms or on Dad's lap.

My mind skips backwards, away from the cellar where it can only scrabble, hitting walls. The past feels safe, which is another kind of madness. My past is anything but safe. It nearly killed me. But right now I'd be better off back there. I close my fists at the thought of him carrying me down the stone steps, locking me up. Why? I'm not young or pretty. I'm thirty-eight and what I know about men could be written on a wine cork. He can't be attracted to me. It's years since I snagged the eye of passing men, even those who'll look at anything, who'll *stick it in an empty vase*, as my old mum used to say. My mind skips away. Anywhere but here in the darkness pricked by those watching eyes.

Three days since I drove through the night, into his trap. I was meant to be packing this house. That's my job. I'm a professional packer. I'm neat and methodical and very, very careful. When I'm not locked up in a stranger's cellar.

I packed a pair of Sèvres vases not so long ago. Porcelain and ormolu, Louis XVI. Cobalt blue, snaked all over with gold, ugly as sin. Not my idea of beautiful, but beauty's in the eye of the beholder. Maybe he finds something to covet in my dimpled knees, the thin skin at my elbows. I shudder, curling myself smaller, a bony comma on the mattress. I need to take care; it's too easy to lose track of myself, locked up like this.

Upstairs, I imagine him sleeping. If I squeeze my eyes shut, I can see the pictures. Twins in bunk beds, flushed faces, tousled hair. His wife curled as I am, her arm around his narrow waist. The pictures are a lie, I know. He's alone up there, just as I am down here. But it helps when I imagine him with a family, doing whatever things a family does. Did he try to be normal once, like me? He's young, could still learn.

'You'll learn,' were the first words he spoke to me.

Not on Day One. On Day One, he was so silent I started to think he couldn't speak, that I'd never hear another human voice again. By the end of Day Two, I was begging him to say *something*. But on Day One, I did all the talking, waking down here in his prison.

'What're you doing?' Panic lifting my voice. 'Why'm I here?'

Silence from the top of the cellar steps, his back to the light, dark head and shoulders hiding everything, just a thin margin of light squirming behind. How slim he is, built like a swimmer or a dancer, narrowing from the span of his shoulders to the shadows at his feet.

'Why're you doing this?' I asked all the idiot questions, the ones you hear in films or read in books. It sounded fake, even to me. 'What do you want?' When his *want* was pressing into my knees, drilling like the mattress springs, hard and unyielding.

Three days.

Has no one missed me in that time?

This isn't how it was supposed to go.

In the dead end of his cellar, I remind myself of all the plans I've ever made and how few came to fruition. Lists of tasks, goals, steps. Maps to places I never reached. Escape routes, exit plans. Contingencies. Pencils worn to stubs, notebooks filled to the very last page. You can only plan so much, I've learnt. Sometimes you have to take a chance. Be spontaneous.

Thanks to spontaneity, I've been his prisoner for three days. I'm not supposed to be a prisoner. I'm a professional, a packer. I'm meant to be the one in charge of houses, of boxes. How I wish I had my shoebox of treasures down here. Just to hold, keep close. I've not been without it since I was a girl.

It has been twenty years since my first packing job: a two-bedroomed flat with a bay window where I climbed a stepladder to take down heavy brocade curtains. It took a whole day just to wrap and pack the owner's glass collection. I wish you could've seen my pleasure as I tucked the last paperweight into its box, fitting it with the others, snug as a jigsaw. There is nothing you can teach me about packing, about neatness. It's only people who puzzle me. Their attachment, for instance, to broken things. *Sentimental value* is such an oxymoron. After fitting the paperweights into their crate, I took out my shoebox and set it on the table by the bay window. The window looked naked without its curtains. From the owner's glass collection, I'd separated a thimble with a chipped base, lethally sharp. It only takes a little damage to turn glass into a weapon. Wrapping the thimble in a wisp of tissue paper, I tucked it into its new home. Now the owner's collection was flawless, ready for transit. And my shoebox had another treasure.

Above me, floorboards whisper with the sound of him walking

from room to room. My car is full of wasted paper, cardboard, bubble wrap. Well, not quite wasted. My shoebox is hidden under it all, safe. At least I hope so.

Three days. His prisoner.

Footsteps. He's alone up there. His apple-cheeked wife doesn't exist; my fantasy, not his. His fantasy isn't a clean kitchen or a neat, nuclear family. It's me rotting down here until I give up my secrets or learn my lesson or attempt whatever it is he's waiting for me to attempt. Escape? That would be an excuse to lose his temper, show his real face. He's so calm and quiet, looks clean, smells clean. But his life is mess, squalor. Why else take a stranger and hold her prisoner in your cellar?

Not a sentimental bone in his body.

I can't help him as I've helped my other clients, by losing an item or two in transit; nothing of value, just a light skimming of the detritus that shackles us to the past. Boxes of baby teeth, old birthday cards, empty make-up trays. A damaged glass thimble. My job helps people to move on. Three days ago, I came here to help Clare Miranda do that. Thirty-five boxes, a skip and me. Other people's mess is a mystery to me. Is that the lesson he's teaching? *You'll learn.* I've only ever known order, inventories. How to tidy, declutter, downsize. I don't understand mess, but perhaps it's where life's really lived. Or perhaps he's the one who needs to be taught a lesson. The damaged one, the dangerous one.

The floorboards fall silent above me.

This house. How can I get it to give up its secrets? Every other house has shared its secrets, but not his. On the cellar floor, I trace the curve of the letter I scratched there. *G* for *gone*. For *good*.

This is not how this was supposed to go.

2

His key grinds in the lock. A blade of salt air slips under the door. Salt does such damage, people have no idea. It ruins glass and wood and cloth and stone steps. He's standing on the stone steps with the light behind him so his face isn't there, I can't see him, just the long sway of his arm as he drops the bag down to where I'm crouched at the edge of the mattress, tugging at the loose thread, afraid to let go.

'Please.' Despising myself for breaking the promise made in the night to never beg, to bare my teeth at him, bear everything. 'Please.'

'I'm not going to hurt you.' His tone suggests he's said this before. It's possible I've forgotten; the blow to my head may have left a black hole where all manner of things are lost. Threats, promises, explanations. That's plausible; I find myself wringing my hands.

'I told you. I'm not interested in you like that.'

The light finds him for a second, his frown like a stitch holding his face together, keeping him from the brink of whatever he's prepared to do. I can't afford to think like that so I fill my head with places I have packed: houses, flats, a narrowboat moored on

11

a canal. Strip away the trappings and we all hoard the same things: broken spectacles, rotting rubber bands. He's no different but for the fact of me in his cellar. I'm his exception to the rule.

'Thank you,' I manage, 'for the food.'

He steps back, swings the door shut, locks it. I listen for the sound of him going into another part of the house but hear only silence. He moves like a cat, noiseless, weightless. My brain rejects this, summoning the sound of boots, the scent of cordite. In my mind's eye, he's a soldier, a sniper. Sometimes I think my brain is a bigger threat than he is.

The cooler bag sits in the darkness, a foot from my mattress, zipped shut. If the past three days have taught me anything, there will be food and water enough to keep me well. Hot soup in a flask. He keeps me stocked with toilet roll, face wipes, towels. Cares enough to keep me alive and clean. If I'm lucky, the cooler bag will contain a couple of paracetamol, which I'll suck slowly like sweets, savouring the bitterness.

The scent of salt lingers in the cellar after he's gone.

Salt comes from acid, from the air we breathe, which is full of acid. Carbon dioxide, sulphur and nitrogen all degrade the fabric of houses – *there's soup, in the Thermos* – producing salts that sit in walls and under floors. *Chicken soup, with noodles.* Rain meets carbon dioxide and forms carbonic acid that washes away – *bread rolls, the kind you buy par-baked and finish in the oven* – to melt stone and brick. *The bread's warm. I hold it in my hands. Stone degrades.* I cannot get that phrase from my head. It rattles like a loose tooth. I bring the bread to my lips; this is how he will break me, by little acts of kindness, with warm bread. *Stone degrades.* Baby teeth in a box, glass eyes in a jar, dentures in a tumbler of dead water. Whatever people won't be parted from without the help of a professional packer like me. I think of my plan, imperfect as it was. Everything packaged, put away. *A place for everything and everything in its place.* How I hate leaving a job half done.

People will pay strangers to pack their houses. The rich, of course, who don't think about what they possess, have forgotten most of it or remember only for tax purposes, their treasure stashed in safes or bank deposit boxes, too valuable to be left lying around, not worth the insurance premium. But at the other end of the scale are those who die with no one left to organize their house clearance. Murder victims whose homes are empty once the detectives depart, treading black powder in their wake, leaving tacky finger marks from the gloves they wear. Professional cleaners are called in if the crime scene is gruesome, if there's decomposition or excessive blood spatter. Or is it splatter? *The bread is going cold.* The victim's loved ones are left to clean up. Some move house even if they succeed in getting all the blood from the carpets. I need to stop thinking about this but I can't, my blood and brain matter on this mattress, the slow stickiness of my dissolve if he never returns, if I sink into horsehair and metal springs, blackening as the seasons change, reduced to a scratch of salt in the air.

I'm out of breath. The cellar shifts the way old rooms do or because I'm hallucinating, because it's been three days and no one knows I'm here. No transport team, no skip, no one. Just me and him.

Box it up and put it away.

Breathe. Eat.

Very few houses are entirely new. Most have old or restored

13

parts. Wood floors, fireplaces, exposed beams stolen from ships . . .
The narrowboat creaking on the canal. I'm going out of my mind.

Be patient.

I learnt my patience from houses. Houses can wait years –
centuries – for the right people. Keeping secrets, keeping mum. I'm
patient. But I'm not sure he is and this is *not* how it was supposed
to go.

The bread is cold but tastes fresh. I must eat everything he gives
me. It's crucial to keep my strength up, for this fight.

The Facts As I Know Them

- Three days ago, I arrived at an address in a remote part of the Peak District in the dead of night where I was knocked unconscious and locked in this cellar.
- My captor is male. In his late twenties. Tall, slim, strong. He hardly speaks. Sounds educated. Smells clean, wears dark clothes, jeans and jumpers.
- He is very calm, but that's a lie. Underneath, he's angry. Driven. Dangerous. Believe me, I know.
- The cellar where he keeps me is dry, only just warm. I have a mattress to sleep on, blankets that feel new. I'm grateful for the camping toilet; he could've left a bucket.
- He brings hot food, water to drink and to wash with. Packets of chewable toothbrushes, the kind they sell in airports, little blocks of plastic bristles studded with dried paste.
- I'm free to move around. He hasn't tied me, just trapped me. He's careful whenever he comes into the cellar, keeps his distance. He must think me capable of turning a toothbrush into a weapon. He must think I'm the dangerous one.
- He won't tell me why I'm here.
- He doesn't use my name. I left my bag at home. Driving licence, bank cards, phone – everything that might identify me is back in the flat I left in such a hurry to come here in the dead of night three days ago.
- I thought I knew what I was doing.
- He's not broken me yet, but isolation and imprisonment can break a person's mind. Believe me, I know.
- I don't know his name.

- He hasn't touched me, gives no indication of being interested in me sexually. Not that it would be sex, if he did. It would be violence, rape.
- The flat with the bay window. The narrowboat on the canal. The bedroom that became a shrine.
- Lists calm me; I make lists when I get agitated.
- Three days ago, in response to an email commissioning my services, I drove to this address to pack an unoccupied seven-room house. My client, Clare Miranda, was paying a premium for the work to be done in three days. Most removals teams can pack a house within hours, but a professional packer works more precisely, employing her judgement and discretion. I didn't question my client's need for a professional packer for her unoccupied holiday cottage. Perhaps I should have done.
- No one knows I took this job. It was a private arrangement. The nearest neighbour is an hour's drive away, with no reason to come here.
- Glossop is the closest town, outside the borders of Greater Manchester. I don't remember passing any houses or seeing even distant lights during the last hour of the drive that brought me here.
- The nearest landmark is Bleaklow: peaty, boggy moorland marked by a cairn of stones and the preserved crash site of a reconnaissance aircraft from 1948. I looked this up online the day I accepted the job. I like to be thorough. Just not thorough enough, evidently, on this occasion.
- The local landmarks have sinister names: Snake Pass, Higher Shelf Stones, Blackstone Edge, Saddleworth Moor. Each of these warnings I ignored.

- A spate of cancellations forced me into a corner. Now I consider those cancellations; they too seem sinister.
- If this was his plan, it has a flaw.
- I am not who he thinks I am.
- When he finds that out, everything will change.

3

The garden here is immaculate, at least in my mind's eye. During his mother's time, I like to think, it was a blaze of flowers; she had an eye for colour, his mum. Kidnap victims are advised to keep reminding their captors that they are human. I'm supposed to tell him about my family but I can hardly talk to him about my mum, can I? So instead I imagine his. Since he's human, too. Not just me. The pair of us are human.

Day Four.

The cellar's cold. I can't stop shivering. Luckily I was dressed for packing when I arrived, in old jeans and a flannel shirt. Had I come to visit his mum, I'd have worn a dress. Except I threw all my dresses out, along with my make-up and high heels; there comes a point when you have to stop kidding yourself. The last dress I wore wasn't red but it was the kind of green that screams red. That dress was a punch, a poke in the eye. His mum would say I deserved what I got for going out dressed like that. Mine said it often enough. Dad, too. Are his parents alive? He's younger than I am. Do they know what sort of son they raised? What part did they play in the man he's become?

Silence from upstairs.

My skull aches with listening, my eyes stretched wide. The silence doesn't mean anything. On Day Two, I imagined it meant he was gone. He hadn't spoken a word to me at that point. Easy to think it was his plan all along for me to die down here with only the scraps of the last meal he left me, a slow painful death.

Day One was confusion, from start to finish.

But Day Two was the worst day, so far.

Thinking him gone, I panicked, mapping the dark with my fingers brick by brick, searching for air coming in or a weapon to help me escape. He's too careful; I knew that about him before I knew anything else.

On Day Two, climbing the steps to the cellar door, I lay with my cheek to the knife edge of light out there, hoping for a snatch of birdsong or the scent of something other than myself. It's true what they say: you end up longing for your captor, craving his company. I've lived most of my life alone and liked it. But it's different down here. Down here, there's no escape from myself.

Now it's Day Four and I know his silence doesn't mean anything. Even so, it gnaws at my fingers and toes. Soon, I'll start calling for him. What name will I use? He hasn't told me his, or asked for mine. I'd rather my silence brought him than my noise. Calling for him would be a humiliation.

Whenever I hear his key in the lock, I tell myself, *This time I'll look at him. Square in the face, in the eyes. I'll make him look at me.* Each time, I'm too afraid. The light hurts, my eyes stinging with tears as soon as it hits. And not just the light. He's too alive, crackling with it, and with his hatred of me. No matter how well he hides it, I know it's there.

I've seen enough to describe him to the police or a sketch artist. His hair is blue-black, cut short, its ends fizzing with light. His eyes are a darker shade of the same blue, flinty and full of sparks. His skin's unblemished, thin over razored cheekbones and at the bridge of his nose. He's beautiful, like an Old Testament angel standing at the top of the cellar steps. I look away every time. He makes me feel awful. Literally *full of awe*. He'd hate that green-red dress as I came to hate it, despising my heels and the snappy boxes of eye-shadow, sticks of lip gloss. He'd bundle it all into a bin liner and throw it in the rubbish as I did. Enough of me. *Enough*.

Is this why he leaves me alone? To let my imagination build him into a bigger monster? Another man would use physical violence but he knows my imagination is my own worst enemy. How does he know that?

Day Four. He's not coming today. It doesn't matter how hard I wish or want. He's staying away. They say hating someone is like taking poison and waiting for them to die. He isn't taking any poison today. I've made him ill enough already. Too much of me. Mum always said I was too much. Dad, too.

Day One was confusion.

Day Two: panic.

Day Three: acceptance.

Day Four is misery, memories.

In the cellar's darkness, I recall the steps that brought me here. The long drive through the night, bats flying at the car, landing in leathery thumps. A moth hit the windscreen in a *pfft* of powder like my fingerprint in my mum's compact when I was a child and curious about everything, putting my hands everywhere and my nose, 'Keep this out, madam!' nose stinging and fingers too, tucked into the pockets of my pinafore dress. To please her, I learnt to be neat and orderly. Became a packer, in charge of precious things.

Box it all up. Put it away.

All my own precious things were put away, out of reach of my clumsy child's fingers in that too-big house where we could, if we chose, avoid one another for months on end. My parents didn't avoid me nearly enough, their attention swooping, landing without warning. 'Who're you hoping to attract looking like that? Is the circus in town?' Half the time it wasn't intended to wound but to make me laugh. Dad always said I didn't laugh enough. Standing at the threshold to my room, frowning in at me: thirteen and freshly unhappy. Wearing one of his fancy waistcoats with a velvet tie; his work wasn't going well, that's when he'd put on his nattiest clothes to cheer himself up. Peering around my room, which was neater than usual because whenever I felt out of control I tidied. I'd been feeling out of control for months.

'Who are you?' Dad rocked on his heels. 'And what've you done with my daughter?'

As if I'd ever been chaotic, as if I'd have dared. I smiled because he wouldn't leave until I was joining in with the joke but I didn't know who I was or what I'd done to his daughter or even who *she* was.

Like now, whoever this woman is locked in this cellar. Not me. He can't have meant to take me. I'm a mistake. When he finds that out, the fun and games will start. What my old dad used to call *fun and games*.

Day Four.

The cellar is cold, the house clenched with silence. Sitting on his mattress, I press the palms of my hands to his floor. I hate remembering Dad. I've worked hard to put all that behind me. Down here, I can't hide from the pull of the past. I scuff my hands at the floor to make the feeling go away. In a minute, I'll get up to use the camping toilet, grateful he didn't leave a bucket.

I conjure his mum in her garden in a cotton sundress and canvas apron with pockets at the front for secateurs. She's kneeling by the flower beds but when I look more closely I see a trench has been dug there, six feet long and three feet wide, deep. So that's no good. No more mind's eye for me.

I finish on the toilet and wash my hands in the basin he provided, using bottled water, before drying them on the clean towel he left folded at the foot of the mattress. He thought of everything. It makes me shiver and want to scream.

Whose plan was this anyway?

The only way out is through the solid door at the top of the cellar steps. He carries its key in the left pocket of his jeans. He's very careful with the key, with everything. But he's made a mistake, all the same. I'm a mistake.

Who is he? What does he want? I only half know the answer to that and I hate a job half done. He's in pain. I see it spilling from his eyes, staining everything. He's out of control. I know how that feels, how dangerous it is. It makes me want to tidy, put his mess into boxes.

He's as trapped here as I am, although I resent that cliché. Only one of us is locked up for starters. But he's lost, in grief or guilt or anger. Needs to move on like my clients whose baby teeth and birthday cards I lose before hanging curtains in their new house, making beds, filling bathroom cabinets with toiletries, tampons, suppositories.

My work is made of intimate acts. I know my clients inside and out, their secrets and their desires. Better than I knew myself at the age of thirteen.

What have you done with my daughter?

Silence from above but he's up there. He isn't leaving. Perhaps I know him without even being aware of it. I know his cellar, intimately. That's a start.

4

How an estate agent would describe my cellar: 'Deceptively spacious and unspoilt, the perfect project, full of original features.'

How I describe it: *Airless, windowless, packed with the smell of myself. Secret, hidden, torturous. A prison.*

Four days ago, I woke with an unfamiliar pain in my head, lying on this mattress in his cellar. I've since come to think of it as *my* cellar but that day it was his. His cellar, his mattress, his lump on my skull. Perhaps I should have started there, at the beginning of this captivity. But Day One was confusion; you'd have been forgiven for thinking me mad.

I lay for a long time struggling to make sense of what'd happened. Bats flying towards my face – I raised an arm to shield my eyes. Through the crook of my elbow, I saw a wavering rectangle of light high above me. For one terrifying second I thought I was underwater, began jerking my limbs, clawing hands over my head in a bid to swim towards the light. The mattress was a sea or river or, worse, a *canal.* The light was the surface where air was, where life was. I had to reach it or die. My lungs laboured in my chest. *I'm going to die.* I must've looked very funny flailing about on the mattress, gasping for breath. My old dad would've laughed if he'd seen me. But there was no laughter from the top of the cellar steps. It wasn't until he'd closed the door and locked it – a sharp sound from the tumblers, like glass breaking – that I realized he'd been standing on what I took to be the dry land I was so desperate to reach.

Day One. It feels so long ago now. I remember wobbling my way around the cellar, bumping into stacked bottles of water, the cold shock of a basin, blankets tangling my feet. Out of breath, a rat running around a maze, nostrils quivering. When I sat back down, I thought about what I'd seen. How he'd stood with the door open so I didn't wake alone or in darkness. Thirsty, I fumbled for a bottle of water, gulping from it, wetting the front of my shirt. Panting from my circuits of the cellar. I'd found wine racks, a camping toilet, a child's hurricane lantern with batteries screwed into its base. The lantern was dim, putting a puddle of light on the floor and walls as I raised it over my head. I found a stack of books, another of toilet rolls. I didn't like how well stocked my prison was, didn't like it at all. Had I started this story with Day One, too much of it would've been spent listening to me screaming.

The steps to the door, I avoided. Old and uneven, no banister rails, a sheer drop either side to the floor. It was hours after first waking until I felt steady enough to attempt the steps. In any case, I knew he'd locked the door; I'd heard the tumblers. I'd no real idea who he was but I knew he didn't make mistakes. *Like me,* I thought but the cellar mocked me – a pretty big mistake, whichever way I looked at it.

This is not, I thought, *the way this was supposed to go.*

My vision wobbled on and off like a faulty bulb. I looked for a light switch but logically any switch would be at the top of the steps so that curtailed my search. In the dark, I sat gulping water, thankful my wrists weren't tied, that I was alive, that I had water. As soon as my head stopped spinning, I was making a list of things to be glad of: the toilet isn't a bucket; he hasn't touched me; he's a stranger and not someone I know.

That last thought terrorized me. Maybe I was concussed. Because all the time I was trying to swim to where the light wavered and he was waiting – all that time, I was sure I knew who was standing there, watching me.

A stranger whose face rippled, their breath coming in clouds. A heavy weight in their hands that put the taste of metal in my mouth and the thought in my head of its weight swinging down on me, again and again and again.

I was wrong, thank God. *Thank God*. Nothing that's happened since has been as frightening as that thought, as that memory. *Nothing*.

5

His key in the lock, light slicing under the door. My heart in my throat. Each time he opens the cellar door, he's different. The food is the same but he's changing. I see it, feel it, taste it. The pair of us are not the same people we were four days ago.

Day Four. We're still in Day Four, just.

At the edge of my mattress, I arrange myself, neatly. It's my only defence against him; there is something unassailable about neatness. He takes his time opening the door. My mind's eye puts a crack in him, thinner than a hairline, of hesitation. He only ever opens the door to toss me food. My stomach's confused, hunger and fear slogging it out. Fear is my constant companion down here. I hardly notice her any longer.

'Grace Maddox.'

Not food. I freeze, ice in my veins, growling in my gut. *Shut up,* I tell my stomach.

'What . . . ?' My mouth's dry, my tongue gluey.

Four days of near silence have not prepared me for this. Was it his intention to catch me off guard, lull me into a stupor with hot soup, warm bread, long silences?

'Who is she?' I ask.

'You.' He stands at the top of the steps, silhouette sharp against the light. Pale shirt, dark jeans narrow in the hip. His voice has no discernible accent but he's educated, intelligent. 'You're Grace Maddox.'

He takes a step down into my darkness. 'You've been here days now. You have to tell me what I need to know.'

Another step. His hair's cropped short, black and bristling on his head just as I conjured it in my mind's eye. Old Testament angel.

'But my name's Gwen! *Gwen Leonard*. I've never even heard of Grace Maddox!'

'You're lying.' Another step. 'You're Grace.' Hands loose and empty at his sides. 'You're a professional packer.' Light lies along the bone of his cheek, drawing shadows like spears from his eyelashes. 'It's why you're here.'

A fourth step. One more and he'll be closer than he's been since he put me down here. 'You're wasting time.'

'You've made a mistake.' I swallow against the thickness of my tongue. 'Look, I'm sorry but that's the truth. I don't know who Grace is.'

Fear pokes her elbow into my ribs, telling me to shut up. My silence is part of the neatness, my only armour. Speaking gives us away.

'Who is she? What did she do to you?'

'I've food and water enough for months.' He comes to a halt on the steps, the ghost of a graze on his right cheekbone, scuff mark from a fist or a fall. 'You need to talk to me.'

We consider one another through the darkness. He's very good at keeping me alive. *For months.* He could do it.

'I'll be found.' The base of my spine is slick with sweat despite the cellar's chill. No one's missed me in four days. *And whose fault is that, madam? Other little girls make an effort to make friends.* 'I'll be found!'

'I hope not.' He retreats a step, in the direction of the light.

'What if I *am* Grace?' It blurts out of me. 'What then?'

He doesn't stop. Silence floods down the steps until I splutter in it, reaching out my hands. 'What did she *do*?'

At the top, he turns to look at me. He's made a mask of his face, its high angles hiding everything. He hesitates, as if on the brink of a decision. 'I buried the last person who lied to me. You should think about that.' He steps out. The key grinds in the lock, light dying behind the door.

My stomach shouts at me. Fear shouts too and her voice is louder, drowning out the noise from my gut.

Four days. For months. How long until someone comes looking for me? What if they never come? He's calm today but he won't stay calm. He is capable of anger, I see that now. He's capable of anything.

I buried the last person who lied to me.

Who? And where did he bury her? I'm guessing it was a woman or a girl. In the garden up there, the one I've been conjuring in my mind's eye? Is that where he'll bury me? Did she have a car? He could lock me in the boot of mine, drive it into a river, weight the car with stones and drown me slowly, a black burst of bubbles against my face.

Stop it. Think. At least the questions have started.

I nod dumbly into the darkness, telling myself how lucky I am to have a roof over my head and food to eat, this blanket I'm clutching, someone who cares whether I live or die, who wants me even if it's for all the wrong reasons.

You have to tell me what I need to know.

I have what he needs. *Me.* I press the tip of my index finger to the stone floor and make myself whisper it aloud: 'I have what he wants.'

Now it's starting.

The real business of why the two of us are here.

You're a professional packer.

We all have secrets. I've found them at the backs of cupboards, the bottoms of drawers. Love letters, sex toys, diaries, old bank notes stuffed into the toes of stockings, forgotten. My stomach growls and I pet it with the palm of my hand. He'll bring food, eventually.

Four days. For months.

He needs me to believe that threat. These past few days have been about proving he has the patience to wait for what he wants. But he doesn't really want to wait. He wants answers so he can move forward. He made the cellar habitable but he won't want to keep me here longer than necessary. The threat has to *feel* real but it isn't. I know all about those sorts of threats.

You're wasting time.

Time matters to him. He wants to move on but he can't, without the answers he's decided can only come from Grace.

You're Grace Maddox.

He won't be told he's made a mistake. He's like me, a planner. We don't like to be told we've made mistakes.

The cellar is chilly but not cold or damp. It's often too dark but I have the hurricane lamp by which to read the books he left. I reach for one: a blonde in a blue gown gazes limply from the cover while a man in a ruffled shirt glowers behind her. Two of the books are Penguin classic crime: green covers, black letters. I wonder at the impulse that made him put books down here. Vanity? A way to say, 'I'm not a monster'. But only a monster locks someone in a cellar and refuses to let her go even after she's told him he's made a mistake, taken the wrong woman.

I buried the last person who lied to me.

I thumb the pages of the romance for some clue to her identity, trying to summon the memory of news reports, missing persons. There have been so many, too many lost women and girls. I cannot lay my finger on the one he might have taken. In any case, I know that's not why I'm here. I'm making up stories to scare myself, a way of saying, 'It could be worse'. Setting the romance aside, I draw my blanket more tightly around me.

From the top of the cellar steps, light winks like eyes, like the eyes in my bedroom in the too-big house: *I see you.*

'Grace Maddox,' I whisper into the darkness. 'Where are you and what did you do?'

The Facts As I Know Them

- Four days ago, I reached a remote part of the Peak District where I was knocked out and locked in this cellar.
- My captor is male, educated, clean. He's let me see his face. He is capable of anger, has threatened me with a long captivity.
- He calls me Grace Maddox. I've told him I'm Gwen Leonard, that he took the wrong woman. He says I'm lying. He says he buried the last person who lied to him.
- He hasn't touched me yet, gives no indication of being interested in me sexually. Not that it would be sex, if he did. It would be rape.
- Their too-big house. Her bedroom that became a shrine. The narrowboat on the canal, the dark mouth of the lock, a creak of footsteps coming towards me.
- Lists calm me; I make lists when I get agitated.
- He keeps his distance, afraid of Grace who can fashion a toothbrush into a weapon. He's right to be afraid of her. And he's right to say I'm lying.
- I am Grace Maddox.
- Of course I'm Grace Maddox.
- Can I convince him I'm not?
- Four days ago, I drove to this address in order to pack an unoccupied seven-room house.
- Except that's a lie, too.
- I came here to find a killer. My first girl's killer.
- I came knowing it would be dangerous, prepared for it to be deadly.

- The cellar was a surprise; I hadn't planned for that. Not the way it was supposed to go.
- The nearest town is Glossop. The nearest landmarks are Bleaklow, Snake Pass, Higher Shelf Stones, Blackstone Edge, Saddleworth Moor.
- For the first time in four days he hasn't brought me food. Like a fool, I ate everything he gave me for my last meal. Warm bread and soup. I'm hungry. At least I have water. And my blanket.
- I've searched this cellar several times since he put me down here. But it's time to search it again. To search me again: who I am and why I came. Now that I know what he's after. Now I know it's me.
- I'm Grace Maddox and he . . . ?
- He's going to be sorry.

6

Day Five. A second day without food. He's punishing me, hasn't unlocked the door since he warned me how long he'd wait. *For months.* He's not so good now at keeping me alive. I hear him from time to time, enough to know he hasn't left. I'm listening for a car or voices, a bin lorry, anything. But I knew how it would be. Peace and quiet, no neighbours to disturb my work. *A flagrant disregard for small print.* Thanks, Dad.

Box it all up, put it away.

My very first house move was made in a panic. Bag packed, one-way ticket, the awkward elbows of a goodbye. The train took me from my parents to start a new life ninety miles away, stopping at seven stations between their house and my new home. At the pen-ultimate stop, a jolt of brakes shook my bag from the overhead rack, dropping it down into the aisle. That evening in the tiny bedsit, I found my alarm clock broken into bits. White plastic painted with pink flowers, I'd fallen in love with the little clock, begging Mum to buy it for my eleventh birthday. She didn't – *You, madam, can't be trusted with breakable things* – so I saved up and bought it for myself. The train journey broke it into pieces. I always packed more carefully after that.

The cellar is dark. I'm saving the batteries in the lantern. I wish I'd saved some food. My water's running low.

From the bedsit, I moved into an attic where the roof was pitched like a tent; I could only stand upright in the very centre of the room. That's where I learnt to fit things together, make optimal use of minimal space. Jigsawing, we professional packers call it.

The cellar's ceiling is flat. Pipes run through it carrying the sound of him living up there. He doesn't play music or watch television or listen to the radio. He lives like a monk. A monk with a woman in his wine cellar.

In my twenties, I moved to Manchester where I lived alone in the converted laundry room of an Edwardian block of flats in the artisan quarter of the city. The conversion was below street level, which meant dust coated the windows and traffic fumes seeped in. The flat flooded from time to time as my bathroom was home to a manhole cover.

This cellar hasn't ever flooded or I'd be able to smell it. The strongest smell down here is me, worse than ever after two days without washing; I'm saving what's left of the water to drink.

After the laundry room, I moved into a bigger flat in an unfashionable part of the city. That's where things started to go wrong. Partly because its size reminded me of my parents' house; I rattled around its rooms, scaring myself. Small places are safer. When I found the narrowboat, I thought I'd hit the jackpot. The slimmest, neatest place of all. Lying low on the water with its porthole windows ringed in brass. I've always loved close spaces.

Who is he? What does he really want?

Someone else would be broken by the fact of this cellar, its prison-like proportions. But not me. Neatness is a balm and his neatness is in evidence everywhere down here. It ought to oppress me, conjure thoughts of rituals, burials, disposal. But I've lived with neatness all my life and there is nothing he can teach me about oppression.

The narrowboat would have been my dream home, if things hadn't taken a turn for the worse. All fun and games, right, Dad? Until someone gets hurt. Until someone is killed.

The narrowboat was moored on the worst stretch of the canal, an open invitation to drug dealers and God knows who else. Rapists, Mum would've said, murderers. At night, the canal is a dirty snare of distant street lights, stars. That's where it started, that's why I'm here. That night on the narrowboat. Six days before he trapped me. I add the time on my fingers: eleven days since the narrowboat. Five since he put me down here.

Day Five.

He's running water, cooking a meal. Dark and meaty – a steak? My mouth waters. He knows I can smell the food. He's starving me while cooking food I'll never taste. Worse, he's making me remember the narrowboat. And before. My childhood. Mum and Dad. Things I've fought to forget. Then I realize: there's no smell of cooking, meaty or otherwise. Hunger is putting pictures in my head. I suck a breath and hold it in my mouth until it sours.

I wish I knew his name.

We're together in this place where neither of us can see the sky, not really. He's starving me but he's also hungry. I sense it, taste it. He's down here with me even when he's not. Whether he likes it or not, or knows it or not, we're in this together.

7

From overhead a skitter of chair legs says morning more reliably than any clock. Day Six?

My stomach growls. He hasn't been back since he threatened me with burial, with months more of darkness. He's making an effort to be noisier than usual, letting me know he's up there, waiting. I've learnt to listen to the house, its sighs and groans. All houses speak. People think old houses are the worst but new houses are unsettled, untrustworthy. This house isn't new, too silent much of the time. When the weather is bad, it rattles with rain against its windows and wind in its chimney but I block it out, listening for the noise he makes as he moves around. He's working in the garden, I think. Breaking things up or pulling them down. *I buried the last person who lied to me.* I think I hear him working to a rhythm, swinging, landing blows. I make myself imagine normal things like manual labour, an honest day's work. I'll do anything not to think about what he's really doing up there.

Come down here, you coward.

Let's get started.

Six days, the past two without food. But he'll be back. Down into my darkness, bringing the sharp stink of outside. In my mind's eye, he's built a bonfire a safe distance from the house. I can't smell any smoke but I believe in the bonfire. Autumn, the end of summer, school starting again – a safe place away from the house and my parents. I love the smell of autumn.

Box it all up, put it away.

My shoebox should be with me, down here. For the first time, I think about begging. Not for food but for my shoebox. All my life, I've put things into boxes. To begin with, it helped me make sense of their shapes, the ways in which they connect. And it kept the things safe, too. Tucked out of reach of clumsy hands. My old mum taught me that: there's nothing that can't be made safer by putting it in a box. The past. Our memories. Tiny glass caterpillars, slim gold pendants. Everything kept separate and secret. My fear of water. His threats. The stranger on the narrowboat and the bedroom that's a shrine.

The chair skitters a second time.

My eyes track him across the cellar's ceiling. He moves to the kitchen sink, runs a tap. Pipes hiss, water whispers. I listen for the *pop* of the gas ring as he lights the stove to heat my soup but it doesn't come. Always the same routine until two days ago. I need him to have a routine, be predictable. Not knowing what he might do next scares me. There was so much comfort in that *pop* from the gas ring.

I'd told myself this was just another house, the latest in a long line, rarely a surprise in store. Just sometimes: a chocolate box full of bullets, or a set of knives hidden in a corset, slim and wicked where bones should be. I've laid my hands on so many secrets. I'd like to lay my hands on his. It's what I came here to do, after all.

Find her killer. My first girl's killer. Put a stop to him.

There is no bonfire but I'd like one. Nothing like fire for clearing the way, for cleansing. One of my houses burnt down to the ground before I'd finished packing it. Rotting carpets and curtains, a broken bathroom suite. Boxes of shoes with the shape of the wearer's toes still in them. Beach buckets half filled with sand. Empty album sleeves curling like old house tiles. I'd almost finished the clearance on the night of the fire. When I returned, what was left of the house was wet and black, dripping from the hoses. Kids, they decided, climbing in through a missing window, setting candles on the floor. The sand in the beach buckets was fired to glass by the heat of the fire.

My dead girl's little glass caterpillar is in my shoebox, waiting for me to hold it again. It breaks my heart to think it will never be missed.

To understand the caterpillar, you need to understand the doll's house and the Noah's ark. My matryoshka: Russian nesting dolls, each with her own name. I'm not ready to talk about any of that.

Footsteps. The grate of his key in the lock is the best sound in the world. I sit at the edge of the mattress in the spot where the light will land when the door opens. I'm determined to look into his eyes. *I'm ready for you.* He hesitates, as if sensing my determination. I have the advantage, for once: the sound of the key always alerts me to his arrival.

Come on. Open the door. Show yourself.

He doesn't. After a long moment, I hear the sound of the key again, locking me back in. Then his footsteps, in retreat. My fingers search for the mattress's loose thread, stomach churning with anger and emptiness. That's why he did it. *You'll learn.* Testing me.

Expecting me to be behind the door with a weapon, ready to dart past. Giving him an excuse to stop me, hurt me. Is he such a coward he needs me to force his hand to that? He's afraid of something. Himself, the cliff edge of his anger, how easily he might tip into violence, the idea he's a monster . . . But does he really expect me to make a gift to him of the excuse to hurt me? I imagine his hand on the collar of my shirt, hauling me back as he flings me down into the darkness, stone steps breaking my bones. Is that what he wants? To thwart an escape plan? If so, there's a flaw in his thinking. I've no intention of escape. Where would I go?

Down here, I make sense.

Down here, there is someone who wants me.

So let's get started.

The Facts As I Know Them

- Six days ago, I was knocked out and locked in this cellar.
- I came to find a dead girl's killer. I have her glass caterpillar; I kept it because its nose is chipped.
- Five months ago, I packed her bedroom. Moved it to her parents' new house.
- I lived with their grief for three long weeks. I can taste it in my mouth even now.
- He's starving me. Two days without food, without water. I'll die if he keeps this up.
- He doesn't want me dead. If he wanted me dead, he'd have starved me from Day One.
- It's nearly Day Seven. Is it?
- Nearly twelve nights since I set foot on the narrowboat. Saw things I should never have seen. Did things I should never have done. Too late now.
- I came here looking for answers but he's looking, too. He thinks I'm the one with the answers.
- One of us is wrong.
- Which one?

8

Escape is the last thing on my mind. At first all I could think of was survival. Day One, Day Two, Day Three. Survival and escape felt like opposing ideas. Above all else, I need to stay alive. I'd hoped to catch a killer. Instead, I'm the one trapped. Funny the way things work out.

Day Seven.

No food, no water, no him. When my mind turns to escape it does so with a reluctance that would strike anyone else, I'm sure, as strange. Sitting on my mattress, I see in my mind's eye the actions of another prisoner who climbs the cellar's steps to beat on the door until her hands bruise. Every hour without fail: soaping the steps in the hope he'll lose his footing and fall, digging with a battery at the walls, breaking her nails in a bid to prise a gap between the bricks. Launching herself like a banshee, screaming and smashing her way free. Not me, though. I sit here, starving quietly. Uncomplaining.

I want him down here with me. He needs to understand the mistake he made. He needs to pay.

Day Seven. He's up there, I'm down here. Like an inversion of my place in the too-big house where my parents dictated how much space I took up. My bedroom was an attic conversion. I'd been put away, out of sight and mind. When a family loses a child, they often move house to make a fresh start. As a child, I used to daydream about my parents leaving me in my attic, alone. I have always lived alone. Even when I lived with them. *Alone.*

The narrowboat moves into my mind, the slow lurch of it on the water. A hallucination. Is it? Starvation will do that, break your mind into little shimmering pieces. Or perhaps the boat's a memory, breaking free from its moorings because he's starving the sense out of me, warping my reality.

When ice creeps across the canal, it freezes everything. Anyone who's lived by water knows this. Droplets of moisture become studs, turning windows into the hobnailed glass of old poison bottles. *Not To Be Taken.*

Thirteen nights ago, it was cold on the narrowboat but not yet freezing. My breath was white. In the blackness outside, the water curled, muscular along the length of the canal, swallowed by the mouth of the lock. A box of matches rattled in my hand. The stove was full of twisted bits of paper, knotted pellets of wood soaked in lighter fluid; it would've been a good fire. But the matchbox was damp, dead. Footfall on the canal path, the skid of boots. I'd latched the inside of the cabin door but it wouldn't hold if he put his shoulder to it. I'd seen his shoulders, the shadow of his shoulders, moving past the porthole windows. *Box it all up, for God's sake. Focus.*

Day Seven.

In the cellar, I count the steps, fixing my gaze on the fifth from the top, the furthest he's come since the night he carried me down here, as if he fears what'll happen if he descends any deeper into my

43

darkness. He's right to be afraid. But so am I. Breaking things up in the garden, digging a ditch deep enough for a body. Did he do that? Or is hunger making a fool of me? I fold my right hand into a fist and fit it under my ribs in the grumbling pit of my stomach. *Shut up.*

The hardest house I ever packed belonged to my dead girl's parents. An Edwardian villa if you're an estate agent, a semi to anyone else. I didn't know the Franklins, their instructions were passed to me by their solicitor. Their semi was in a market town at the foothills of the Peak District. The town made its money from the silk trade: luxury and slavery intertwined. The Franklins were a young couple, I was told, only moving a matter of miles to another semi of a similar size. Moving because their family was broken beyond repair. I almost didn't take the job when I heard it was just the two of them, Tess and Clark Franklin. I've always preferred to pack for families. A family home is special. You can learn a lot from families, the way they fit together, the shapes they make. I've always been fascinated by families.

Curling onto my side on the mattress, I feel the stab of its springs in my ribs. The cellar warps around me, as if it is made of rubber rather than stone. I'm starving. Dirty and thirsty and afraid.

The Franklins wanted me to recreate their daughter's room in their new house, insisting I take dozens of photographs in order to replicate every detail. They called it a bedroom but it was a shrine.

Elise Franklin died a year ago, when she was thirteen. She was murdered. Her parents didn't tell me that, Google did. Her killer has yet to be found.

At first, Tess and Clark were reluctant to leave their old home, but it became too painful to be there, in rooms where she'd once sat or slept or ate or smiled. In the end, they compromised on the shrine: her old room reproduced in the new house. That was months ago now. I count on my fingers: five months. Five months since I packed Elise's bedroom, since her parents moved to a new house a short distance from their old home. Five months since I built the shrine to their dead daughter and made a promise to Elise to find her killer.

Thirteen days since the night on the narrowboat. Seven since I drove out here, only to be trapped. Threatened. Starved.

Day Seven. Is it?

In the cellar an hour's drive from the Franklins' new home, I stare into darkness, thinking of murder, of killers. Harder not to think of these things with him up there and me down here. I pick at the loose thread on the mattress, recalling the details of the house move, the way grief altered the shape of the rooms, collapsing her father's face, making her mother stoop like an old woman. Just sometimes the mood lifted, a flash of light finding its way inside, in the shape of a happy memory: Elise winning a silver trophy for gymnastics when she was nine. Not real silver but I wrapped it in acid-free paper as if it were. Oil paintings need greaseproof paper, silverware acid-free. The things I know. Useless to me down here. Like my knowledge about the damage salt does, or the yards of corrugated cardboard in the boot of my car. Has he been digging in there? What has he found? I remind myself I know more than he thinks, more than he knows. About salt and silver and little daggers of glass made deadly by damage.

Footsteps bring me upright on the mattress but there's no sound from above. The footfall belongs on the narrowboat, stealthy and dangerous. I tell myself I'm safer down here but it's a lie. I'll die of thirst and starvation. At least on the boat I had the chance to fight.

Five months since I made the shrine. Nearly three days since I last ate. I can survive this, even so. What you can't endure, you can survive. My old mum taught me that.

Elise Franklin had nothing of value in her bedroom, just old toys and new books, worn clothes. A school uniform stiff from its wrappings, bits of jewellery, old phones, odd socks. I packed each as if it were priceless. Not only out of respect for her parents' grief but because it is how I work. I'll always, for example, wear gloves, whether or not I am handling antiques. Everything in Elise's bedroom was precious to her parents. I was surprised they let a stranger touch any of it.

'You will take care, won't you?' Tess said, and I promised I would.

Every packer knows the acid in our skin can cause damage to old books or to platinum but a good packer understands that moving home is seismic, an upheaval in a person's life even when that person is dead like Elise Franklin. Our job is to absorb the shockwaves, smooth out the stress. I'm very good at it. People recommend me. I had more work than I could handle until it started to dry up. Not long after I helped the Franklins move their grief to a new house, the cancellations started coming. Sometimes, I think the heartache in that house infected me.

Elise Franklin had a green glass caterpillar, the size of my little finger. A cheap thing, the sort you might buy at a seaside gift shop, with a chipped red nose. I rolled it tight in tissue paper, tucking it into a tiny envelope of bubble wrap. A tip for packing precious things: gently shake the box as you pack. If the contents move, add more padding. Were a giant to lean in and pick up this house, pinching it between his thumb and forefinger, I'd rattle. He'd have to wad the box until I stopped. A mattress for each wall, a dozen more for the floor, stacked one on top of the other until I'm the princess and the pea, my nose brushing the ceiling. I am not a fanciful person but I am starving. He is changing the shape of me, inside and out.

Is he up there still? It's been so quiet for so long. I know where everything is in the dark down here, can lay my hands on it all. But not on him. He's hiding, untouchable, up there in the light.

Elise Franklin had a zinc mirror framed in ivy on her bedroom wall. My face was so different in that mirror, I couldn't stop staring. Nostalgia, I expect. I was Elise's age once. Thirteen. She is that age for ever now. I'm nearer forty than twenty but when I looked into Elise's mirror, I was a child again. The child who lived like a ghost in my parents' house where silence was golden and threats took care of everything else.

I'd never packed a room for a dead girl before, let alone one whose killer is yet to be found. Her ghost was with me while I worked, all her cherished things whispering, wanting me to take care of them, of her. When I first felt it, I shook the strangeness away; I am not superstitious and have no time for whimsy. But the whispering persisted. Then, on a shelf above her bed, I saw the matryoshka – the Russian nesting doll – beaming down at me. One just like it had sat on a high shelf in my attic bedroom as a child. That was when I knew: like it or not, we're bound together, Elise Franklin and I. Just as he and I are bound, whether or not he's admitted it to himself.

Five months have passed since I built the Franklins' shrine to their dead daughter in their new house, an hour's drive from where I find myself now. Thirteen days have passed since the night on the narrowboat that nearly destroyed me. Everything after that was borrowed time. In a way, it was a relief to wake down here. It made more sense than waking in my own bed.

Day Seven is drawing to a close. I can live without food, for a while longer. But not without water. Thirst will kill me. I test the dryness in my mouth, trying to calculate how long I have left.

Have I missed my chance?

Is he going to get away with this?

In another bedroom, years ago, I found a pencil case stuffed with small plastic bags. The room belonged to a boy of about Elise's age, the age she was when she was attacked taking a shortcut home from school, by a killer they haven't found. Little bags with pills in the boy's bedroom, too many for personal use; he was dealing. I didn't tell his parents or anyone else, packing the drug bags with the rest of his room, neatly and safely for transit. I still think about that boy, what happened to him. Punishment so rarely fits the crime. That needs to be different, for Elise. Her killer is going to get what he deserves. I'm prepared to die to see that done.

What else can I think about? In what ways can I keep myself sane as he tries to starve the sense from me?

I packed a gun collection once. And an art forgery: an oil painting of a red yacht under a white sky. According to the inventory, it was the work of a famous artist, worth half a million pounds. I know nothing about art but I know a forgery when I see one; I knew a drug dealer when he was masquerading as a schoolboy. All the same, I packed the painting in greaseproof paper. No one has ever accused me of a job half done.

Water knocks in the pipes. Is he running a bath, filling a kettle? I should resent whatever comfort he's enjoying while I shiver and starve. But I prefer the thought of him filling a kettle to sharpening a blade or digging a grave. How many times has he moved house? He's young but his family may be nomadic, so many families are. What was he forced to leave behind when they moved? We all have to leave behind, sooner or later. *We live by leaving behind.* Putting away childish things, growing up, moving on. How many homes did he know before this one? And where did it happen? Whatever nightmare tipped him over into this place where he's put me – for company as much as anything, that's how it feels – to lend a purpose to his life, a pattern to his days. If he knew the truth about Grace Maddox, he'd have thought twice before putting her in his cellar. I trace the letter I scratched into the cellar floor.

G for Grace. I'm her. It makes me sad.

Five months ago, I sat in the kitchen at the Franklins' new house – the one with the shrine of a bedroom – drinking tea with Elise's mum, Tess. She was sharing a memory of Elise, a funny story from her childhood, weeping as she brought her murdered child back to life. Mothers can do that: they have the power of life and death over their daughters.

Listening to Tess, I saw Elise so vividly, turning cartwheels in the garden. Without thinking, I said, 'She's solid as a seed.'

Tess looked at me oddly, not for the first time. Much of my oddness she forgave because of the special care I took with her daughter's things. It's too easy to be thought odd. I was trying to change, to be different. I'm always trying. I was such a good girl, growing up. It was a shock to discover that what my parents called *good* most people considered odd. Suspicious. Like my matryoshka, I'm different inside. But isn't everyone? Isn't *he*?

That day five months ago, Tess and I drank from cloudy glasses that'd rubbed against one another in the dishwasher. Hard water seeps into micro-fractures in glass, causing white spots, dullness. *Sick glass*, they call it.

'She's solid as a seed.'

The look she gave me.

Did I become a packer in order to explore other people's homes, other families? Probably. I've been obsessed before, it's true. Tess was not the first to look at me oddly. I doubt she'll be the last. *He* might be. But people in glasshouses and all that – he'd be on shaky ground.

Who are you and what've you done with my daughter?

'Can Grace come out to play?'

9

I have a window! I found it when I was searching my cellar again. It's on the same side as the stairs, which means it looks out into the back garden, away from the driveway where my car is parked, or where it was parked. He's probably moved it but if he's burnt it, he's dead. *Dead.*

Day Eight, I think. I'm hallucinating from hunger and thirst but my window is real. I've not seen it but I've touched it. A window in my wall, in my tomb. I found it by reaching as far as I could into the darkness, the tips of my fingers agitating after a perimeter; it's become very important to know exactly how much space I have down here. I've paced my cellar a hundred times, roughly 275 square feet. What good it does me knowing that I've no idea. But this is Day Eight (I think) and I'll spend it how I please.

With my arms outstretched, I was expecting stone or plaster but my fingers hit bluntness. Smooth, chilly. About seven and a half feet from the floor. I knew from touch what it was. Not stone, not a wall. *Glass.* A window. I mapped it with my palms. It spans less than four and a half hands across and two deep. I have small hands. Strong but small. 'Keep these out, madam!'

Don't give me that face.

My window's the size of a large letter box. Not even a small child could fit through it. In any case, it is sunk deep into the wall on all sides. No latch, no hinge, the glass dimpled like the base of a wine bottle.

My darkness swims with colours. Black, grey, brown. Red in tiny bursts at the edges of my vision. Below the window, the darkness is green. The kind that rises from swamps or marshes, gas-green. Wine-bottle green.

I have a window. I can't use it to escape. Can't smash it or see through it for a glimpse of the world outside. But it is here, in what I thought was a stone box. A little window of dense green glass.

Its discovery broke me. I staggered back to my mattress and the lantern to sit with my feet in its puddle of light and howl.

The Facts As I Know Them

- Days ago, I was knocked out and locked in this cellar.
- My captor is male. Dangerous. He's starving me. I'm confused. Seven days, or eight? Or nine?
- I have a window. I do not have my shoebox.
- He calls me Grace, says he needs me to answer his questions. I've told him I'm Gwen, he took the wrong woman. He says I'm lying. He buried the last person who did that.
- It's true, I am lying. I am Grace.
- It's also true I'm dying of thirst.
- He hasn't been inside the cellar in a long time. Busy in the garden with a hammer and a spade, wanting me to hear the noise he's making, determined to get answers out of me to questions he won't ask. He doesn't make mistakes.
- He hasn't touched me yet. If he does, it will be rape.
- The glass caterpillar. The narrowboat. Elise's killer.
- Lists calm me; I make lists when I'm agitated.
- I came to find a killer. I made a promise. She had a matryoshka just like mine. Her dad's hardly ever home; a jar of dead eyes on a table next to the bed keeps him away. Mum put it there.
- I'm losing my mind.
- No one knows I took this job. No one knows I'm here except him. I came to catch a killer but I'm the one who's caught. Trapped. Dying.
- Bleaklow, Snake Pass, Higher Shelf Stones, Blackstone Edge, Saddleworth Moor.
- I made a promise to a dead girl.
- Who does that?

10

The door slams open. He's there at the top of the stone steps. My throat and stomach are awake before I am, shouting at me to do as he says, give him what he wants, *We need water! Food!* I drag myself upright on the mattress.

Day Ten . . . ?

I've lost count since he stopped coming. Yesterday's colours were bright and sharp, heightened by starvation. Today everything's a muddy slew.

He comes down into the darkness, light sliding over his shoulders, stopping six steps from the cellar door. Further than he's ever come since that first night. No cooler bag but he has a bottle of water, a small one, in his right hand. 'Move back.' He holds up the bottle. 'I'm going to throw this.'

He tosses it underarm, the way a child throws a ball. The bottle lands on the mattress, rolls into my lap. Chilly, from inside a fridge. I struggle with the lid, my fingers numb and clumsy. He might've broken the seal. But then I'd have suspected tampering, drugs or poison. Even so, I'd have wanted it, thirst overriding every other fear. I gulp water that splashes down the front of my shirt, stomach heaving at my haste. 'Thank you . . .' It's a splutter between gulps but I mean it. *Thank you*. Merciful angel.

The cellar's shadows lean in across his shoulder, laying what looks like a fresh graze along his jawline. He turns, retreating up the steps.

I'm terrified of hearing the door lock again, of the light leaving, *him* leaving, being alone with myself. '*Please!*'

He doesn't lock the door, leaving it open until he returns seconds later with a box in his hands. He carries it down towards me, stopping eight steps away. Exactly halfway down.

A shoebox. *My* shoebox. Pale green, lidded. It held a pair of women's shoes, size five. A sticker shows a black and white drawing of a high heel, a strap around the ankle. My feet ache with the memory of those shoes.

'This was in your car,' he says.

He's dug it from the well in the boot where the spare tyre would live if I had one. Digging through corrugated cardboard and bubble wrap for my hidden treasure. How dare he?

'If you're not Grace, why do you have this?'

The lies crowd behind my teeth. It hardly matters since my face is giving me away. Hunger strips our defences, leaves us maskless. He knows the box is mine, knows I wore those shoes with a green-red dress, a slash of lipstick.

'Tell me.' His temper's white-hot, shining through his skin, the only clean thing in the cellar. 'You need to tell me.'

'It's mine. You know it's mine.'

I reach my hands out. In that moment, I want it more than food, more than freedom. I don't care if he knows it, what he knows. I want my box.

'Where did it come from?'

He doesn't mean the shoes. Long gone with the dress, lipstick. He means the contents. My treasure. He's seen it, held it. *How dare he?*

'Houses. Just . . . houses.'

'Other people's houses. Not yours.' It's hunger, I know, but I can see the anger pulsing under his skin, throwing sparks from his stare, making it seem as if he's moving even when he's not.

'Mine. And other people's.' I hold the water bottle in my lap, drawing up my knees as I gaze at him. Despite the starvation, I'm hiding it better than he is. My anger. The fact I'd kill him if I could, choke him on this bottle, push my fist down his throat. 'I'd like it back.'

'And I'd like answers.' He's holding the box carefully between both hands. If I thought he'd throw it, I'd launch myself at him, not caring if he killed me in that moment. I'd do my best to kill him.

'From Grace. She has your answers.'

'From *you*.'

'All right.' I hold out my hands. They tremble. 'Give me the box and some food. I can't think straight. You've made me sick.'

'I warned you.' A flavour of frustration under his anger. I'm harder work than he anticipated when he took me. Well, *good*.

'Yes.' I drop my hands into my lap. He wants my acquiescence. I'm wasting time. 'You did.'

He crouches to set my shoebox on the step. He does it precisely, as he does everything. The light covers his hands like gloves. His fingers are long and slender, strong. A surgeon's hands. I shudder, petting my stomach as it shouts, watching his retreat up the steps, wondering if he'll leave the door open, if he's decided I'm sufficiently subdued to be left in sight of an escape route without giving in to temptation. But he shuts and locks the door, moving noiselessly into that part of the house above me where the kitchen is. The gas ring pops. *Soup.* My stomach turns circles. I reach for the lantern, twisting its small switch. Shadows crouch against the walls, the light making everything worse for a second. Wobbling, I stand, measuring the distance to the step where my shoebox sits. My head spins alarmingly, the cellar folding around me. I wait for it to stop, sucking another mouthful of water from the bottle. My clothes feel loose and gritty, my skin grittier still. After he's fed me, I'll ask for water to wash with; I need to be clean. But first I need my shoebox.

He could have thrown it like the bottle of water. Instead he set it on the step as carefully as I would have done, with reverence for the strangeness of its contents. He's looked inside, knew if he threw the box its contents might break. He didn't want that. His restraint scares me, the care he's taking. Except he's starving me, letting me dehydrate until I'm hallucinating. He took a risk denying me water, a risk putting me down here. I might be on medication, suffering from psychosis or diabetes or anything at all. He could have killed me just by leaving me alone. How did he calculate that risk? How did he know I'd be alive after ten days in his cellar, four without food, two without water? Because Grace is a fighter with a clean bill of health – he knows that about her even if he knows nothing else. I make my slow way to the steps where my shoebox is sitting, drawing it towards me with both hands, holding it to my chest as I back away to where my mattress is waiting.

The box feels the same, its weight exactly as I'd expect, nothing missing or added to its contents. It doesn't rattle; I padded it with cotton wool and polystyrene chips. If he searched the box, he put it all back the way I do whenever I inventory the contents. The thought of his long fingers picking through my treasures makes a pulse beat in my throat. I think – again – of killing him. I'm still thinking it as the key turns in the lock and the door opens, bringing him back, cooler bag in hand.

He moves slowly, as if he knows everything is an effort for me. I tell myself he looks the same but it isn't the whole truth. He's dressed in jeans and a grey sweatshirt that shows the bruised skin at his throat and wrists. The bruises are new, not on him but to me. One on his left wrist below the bone that becomes prominent when he stresses the joint, propping the door with his elbow. An older bruise, smudged yellow, marks the hollow at the base of his throat. *Damage.* From what, or whom? I stay where I am at the edge of my bed, my shoebox in my lap. He glances at it then away, as if aware of intruding on my privacy. It's a joke, madness. I've no privacy down here. What difference does it make that he's found a box of mementoes from houses I once packed? How does that change anything? I'm his prisoner, starved, defeated. He has everything he wants. He carries the cooler bag to the tenth step where he leaves it, retreating three steps in the direction of the door.

'Why do you do that? Back away. What're you afraid of?'

'You.' He looks directly at me, his face tense.

'Grace, you mean.' I smooth the palm of my hand over the lid of my box. 'And not that afraid or you wouldn't have kidnapped her and locked her down here. There's more to it, there must be . . . Is this your house? Is Clare Miranda your mother?'

The cooler bag sits on the step where he left it. He nods at it. 'I thought you were hungry.' His voice doesn't change. 'Starving, you said.'

'You haven't fed me in four days. You know I'm starving. You're the one starving me.'

'Not four days.' A frown pinches at his face. 'Three.' He circles his left wrist with the fingers of his right hand, hiding the bruise there. 'Two and a half, really.'

'Three days,' I repeat. 'Why would you say that?' To make me doubt myself, my sanity. Or to convince himself he is not a monster.

'Because it's the truth. Eat the food.'

After the food – questions. No more prevaricating. Nowhere to hide. I want my shoebox and a full stomach and for him to be gone. *Dead.*

'Three days or four, you starved me. Left me alone down here.' I splay my fingers across the lid of the box. 'What were you doing all that time?'

He moves his head away, as if it hurts him to be standing half-way between his freedom and my captivity. As if he is the one who is trapped.

'Waiting for me to break.' I wet my lips. 'To learn.'

He nods tiredly. 'Eat the food,' he says, editing the word *please*, but we both hear it. He's pleading with me. He's had enough. Of this standoff, of me.

My chest flutters with panic. Even bruised, he's stronger than I am. My chances of success, never great, have been dangerously diminished by his starvation regime.

'Hating someone is like taking poison and waiting for them to die.'

He doesn't ask me to explain this. He retreats to the top step and sits, propping open the door with his right shoulder, a blaze of light behind him.

'You're waiting for me to die.'

'There's food in the bag. And water.'

'I can't live like this.'

'You're alive, aren't you?' He sounds emptied out. 'Eat the food.'

I wonder where his anger went between leaving me with the shoebox and returning with the food. 'Who else is here?' My eyes scare to the ceiling. 'There's someone else, isn't there?'

'No one.' He lifts a hand, rubs his eyes. 'It's just us.'

'What happened?'

'You know what happened.' He drops the hand. 'You must know.'

What's left of his anger has him caged, forcing him to sit there, pale and exhausted. He hasn't slept since I last saw him, I doubt he's eaten. It must have been a relief to bring me food. Up there in the kitchen, warming soup and bread, he can tell himself he is decent. Down here, he has to face up to what he's done. I'm his worst nature, worst nightmare. There is power in that. He should be taking better care to hide his weakness from me.

It's all fun and games.

Until now.

Sliding the shoebox from my lap, I set it aside. Finding my feet, I walk to the steps, reach for the cooler bag. It's heavier than usual or I'm weaker, an old woman bent and buckled, aching in every joint. I put my palm to the stone step, shoulders shaking, seeing spots. My free hand gropes for the handle. I stagger back a step then swing forward, aiming at his skull.

My aim's off but his guard's down and there's a second when we're evenly matched. The bag hits his raised wrist with my full weight behind it. I'm the banshee at last, screaming and smashing, scratching my fingers for his face, missing and hitting the door, feet tripping, body tipping, no banister rail, a sheer drop to the stone floor, but he has me by the arm, hauling me, saving me from falling so he can put me back down onto the mattress.

'No.' One word but it crushes me, wipes me out. 'No.'

I scream, surging up, possessed by an unholy strength. The sound I'm making isn't human, isn't like any sound I've ever heard. My head is thrown back, my throat on fire, I can hardly see as I lunge for him. He steps out of range but we're closer than we've ever been. He is impossibly pale. Dark-eyed, all angles and anger but not fury, not like mine.

'Stop,' he says. 'Eat the food.'

Again I scream, reaching my claws for him. He moves smooth as water, slipping back towards the steps. My foot strikes a thing that slithers on the stone. *My shoebox.* He scoops it up, out of my reach.

I don't stop screaming until he's gone, locking the door behind him. Leaving me in the little spill of light from the lantern where I fall to my knees and weep, but not for long. I'm too weak even for that.

Soup. There is soup in the cooler bag and bread and cheese. Apples, a banana, a bar of chocolate. A carton of milk. Two big bottles of water. I fill my mouth with food until there isn't any room for sobs or screams, my teeth glued by a paste of chocolate and starch. I wash it all down with gulps of sweet milk, bitter bites of apple. My stomach heaves but I ignore it. The food is padding, keeping me from rattling in his box.

After eating, I strip to my underwear and wash at the basin, emptying an entire bottle of water for the purpose. Wasteful but I have to be clean.

61

Don't give me that face.

By the time I'm done, the screaming has gone down into my chest. My throat stutters. Tears run down my face, outside my control. Like the tears Tess kept weeping, for Elise. It reminds me why I'm here, what's at stake.

Clean, I lie on my side on the mattress, nursing the ache in my arm. He could have hurt me far worse. He saved me from falling. He has my shoebox.

The cellar sets its cold teeth against my cheek. When I shut my eyes, obscene colours pinwheel, painting the inside of my skull. My stomach chews at the food, my bladder wants me to get up and empty it. I do as it says, taking the lantern with me. Afterwards I sit in the silence left by my screaming, as if I have washed it all clean.

He won't return. Not for hours, maybe days. After my hysteria and knowing he has my shoebox. He's left me to calm down, expects me to calm down. My arm throbs where he grabbed it. I sit upright, lifting the lantern to search for the mark of his fingers on my arm. But it is too soon for any bruise. I'll check again tomorrow. I click the lantern off, lie back down. My mouth tastes vile. I grope for the chewable toothbrushes, popping one into my mouth. Chewing makes my ears pop as if I'm underwater.

The look on his face when the banshee-me attacked him – surprise, but not only that. *Relief.* Because he hadn't killed me? Or because he recognized me. Banshee-me is Grace. Recognizably, undeniably Grace.

I stroke my arm where he grabbed me to stop me from falling. He didn't punish me for the attack, or the escape bid. He could have done that. He should have done that. Now I know his weakness. Now I know he's weak.

The Facts As I Know Them

- Ten days ago, I was knocked unconscious and locked in this cellar by a man who buries people.
- He starved me for four days, he says three.
- He hasn't touched me. If he does, it will be murder.
- Blood. Bone. Brain matter.
- Lists calm me; I make lists when I get agitated.
- I'm Grace Maddox. I made a promise to a dead girl, Elise Franklin, whose killer is yet to be found.
- Blood. Bone. Brain matter.
- He has my shoebox.
- I want to kill him.

11

Day Eleven. Or Day Nine, if what he said last night is true. I've either lost two days or it was a lie. Interrogation tactics: disorientate your opponent, alter their reality so they depend on your version, rely on you for everything. He said I went two and a half days, not four without food. That might be true. It explains how I was able to attack him, the surge of strength that came from nowhere, from seeing my shoebox in his hands. Four days or three, it doesn't matter. I'm down here, he's up there. Waiting for me to break, knowing he has my box – a new hold over me even if he doesn't understand why.

I let a square of chocolate dissolve against my tongue, luxurious, my stomach purring with pleasure. Strange how a body can adjust so quickly. A fortnight ago, I was indifferent to chocolate. Now it is everything, filling me with its bitterness. Dark chocolate, 85 per cent cocoa. He took trouble choosing it, didn't grab the nearest bargain. Everything he does is so careful.

Day Nine, then.

I consider the cellar steps from my seat on the mattress. When he returns, he will bring my shoebox. And he will make threats.

Not to hurt me, or not physically. He knows how to do that without moving a muscle in my direction; I gave myself away last night; he has my shoebox.

Rinsing my mouth with water, I tongue at my teeth, recalling the shock on his face when I hit him with the cooler bag. He did not expect that. I was supposed to be subdued by starvation, desperate to do as I was told. He lectured me about patience, how he was prepared to wait months for me to break. But he was not prepared for yesterday.

Drawing up my knees, I rest my cheek there, waiting.

The darkness is gentle with me, holding everything I need. The cooler bag has bread and fruit; I am not making the same mistake twice. This is *my* space. I have mapped it, measured it, know exactly where I am, how far from the cellar steps, how near to the lantern. I've made this space my own. I need to get my bearings, to get out of here. Cannot afford to run into another trap. My chance – when I take it – will be the only one I'll get.

Sixty seconds in a minute, sixty minutes in an hour. I'll list minutes and hours; I like making lists. Each time I reach another hour, I will pull a thread from the mattress, a way to keep count. Then I'll know how many days and nights. He won't be able to alter my reality because I will know.

Hours pass. I couldn't keep count. Too many. He doesn't come. No sound from upstairs, not even water in the pipes. Uncurling my fingers from the mattress, I set my palms flat to the floor, either side of my bare feet. I washed my feet last night, wet one corner of a towel, rubbing until the worst of the dirt came away. Now I spread my fingers, sore from pulling the threads. Counting wasn't helping today. The best-laid plans and all that.

You knew what you were doing when you came here.

'Come on!' I want to yell. But it is too deeply ingrained in me, the need to be quiet and good. *Don't raise your voice, don't give me that face.*

Fifteen nights ago I descended into hell; the narrowboat had red walls and red curtains at the window. Little spots of light from the wall fixtures. The smell of tar, of old rope. Each step contained a warning but I kept going, deeper, feeling safe there in the low-ceilinged space, thinking all the world should be like this: narrow, shallow, low on the water. Until the slide of boots on the towpath said I wasn't alone. Trespassing with a stolen key, thinking I could come and go as I pleased. Stupid to think like that, to imagine a world where trespass doesn't end in arrest, where breaking the law leads nowhere. Had I learnt nothing? *Have you learnt nothing, madam?* The canal path was pitted with potholes, hard and slippery. I was dressed for the cold, swathed in enough layers for the Arctic. That was about the only blessing I could count at the end of that night as I sat with chattering teeth, thinking of what I'd done.

At least he never saw my face.

12

A key in the lock, light licking in my darkness, his shadow at the top of the steps, empty-handed. I scream at him, 'Where is it?' He doesn't move, looking down at me, fingers loose at his sides. I fire myself from the mattress, flinging the nearest thing to hand, the lantern. 'Where? *Where?*'

He backs away, his face lost in shadow.

Don't give me that face.

'Bring me my fucking box!'

I'm up the steps, my palms striking each stone like the beating of my feet, but there's no element of surprise this time. He doesn't even have to move quickly as he shuts the door in my face, grinding the key in the lock.

'Bring me my box, you bastard! You—' Words I've never used in my life spit out of me. I slap my hands at the door, kicking at it with my feet. 'I'll *kill* you!'

He is on the other side, resting his hands on the wood as I strike it. I can feel the throb of his blood, the beat of his heart. Leaning my whole body into the door, I press my mouth to its unvarnished wood, my breath hitching, my chest tight. He is right there, inches from my mouth, from my hands. I stroke the ends of my fingers at the wood, catching the snag of splinters, a tiny prickle of sensation to appease the thundering in my blood.

With my lips to the door, I whisper it: '*I hate you.*'

On the other side, I swear I hear the catch in his breath. I circle my thumb on the wood until it warms, glowing under my touch. '*I'll kill you.*'

13

'Tell me about the shoebox.'

He is at the top of the cellar steps. Hours since I fought him. At least twelve hours. Two since I threw the lantern. I stopped counting, must have slept. The light behind him is softer than usual, as if a bulb is out in the corridor. Is it night up there? Out there. Is it a new day? *Day Ten?*

'Where is it?' I struggle upright, find my feet.

'It's safe.' He waits a beat. Then, 'Who are you?' he asks.

I suck a shallow breath into my lungs and hold it. 'You know who I am. I'm Grace Maddox.' To my surprise, my voice doesn't shake.

'No,' he says. 'You're not.'

He made this prison for Grace, furnished it for her. Fed her, kept her alive. Grace was safe. She has his answers. I *have* to be Grace.

'Why would you say that?'

'Because it's the truth. And I'm tired. This has gone on long enough.'

He's tired? I take a step closer to the cellar steps, staring up at him. He looks thin-skinned, the light punching white spaces under his eyes and between the bones in his wrist as if only fragments of him are whole, held together by what is left of the anger.

'If I'm not Grace, why're you keeping me here? Why not let me go?'

'You know why.' He moves his hand, thin fingers gripping the edge of the door. 'You must know.'

'No . . . Why're you doing this? What did Grace *do*?'

'I'm not sure.' He lifts his hand, rubs the heel of it at his eyes. There is a new shadow on his wrist, another bruise – mine from when I swung the cooler bag at him. 'Not really.'

'You did all this' – I gesture at the cellar – 'without knowing why?'

'I thought I knew . . .' He straightens. 'Are you hungry? Or thirsty? What can I bring you? Do you want your shoebox?'

Trick. It's a trick. Threats didn't work, didn't break me, so now he is trying this. Pretending he is the broken one.

'Why're you doing this?'

He says quietly, 'You're all that's left.'

It reduces me to silence.

We stare at one another. The light stings my eyes. My fingers burn from tugging at the mattress threads. My throat is raw from the screaming I did earlier, my chest tight with the screaming I'm not doing right now. I cannot think of anything to say, any action I can take to change what is happening. Not a single useful thought in my head beyond how small his life has become.

Later, when he's left me alone again, that thought slides into another: how much I could bring to his life, this broken man with so little to lose.

The Facts As I Know Them

- He's kept me in this cellar for ten days.
- He says he knows I'm not Grace. But Grace is the one he wanted, the one with the answers.
- He has my shoebox, stolen from the boot of my car.
- No one knows I'm here. It's just me and him, and he makes mistakes. He's exhausted. He says he's had enough.
- He has my shoebox.
- I am all he has left.

14

'I'm thirsty,' I tell him. 'And I have a temperature. I'm not well.'

Day Eleven. My vision's red like the inside of the narrowboat. When I woke, I thought he'd poisoned me, that the bread or milk or chocolate was poisoned. 'I have a fever.'

He props the cellar door open with his hand, leaning his weight there as he studies me. If his tiredness is a trick, he's still playing it. He is hollow-eyed, as if he hasn't slept in days. The skin under his eyes is blue. He's beautiful lit from behind, the sweep of his shoulders holding the shadow of his head, bronze-bright in my darkness. If I shut my eyes, I will see the ghost of him standing there, watching me.

'I'll bring you paracetamol.' He turns to go. 'And water.'

'And my shoebox.' A sob in my voice, undisguised.

'And your box.'

I put my head on my knees, waiting for his return. The cellar bounces back the sound of my breathing, ragged. He's left the door unlocked. When he returns, I hear the sound of his feet on the steps, stopping where he always stops, halfway down. *Halfway down the stairs is a stair where I sit.*

'I can't get up,' I croak. 'I can't.'

'You'll have to.' He places the shoebox on the step with a bottle of water, a strip of pills. 'I'm done but I'm not stupid. You hate me and you'd like to kill me. Not for putting you down here. For the shoebox.' He straightens, taking his shadow from the floor. 'I'd like to know why, if you'll tell me.'

'Why should I? You won't tell me anything. Why *this* box?' I gesture at the cellar. 'Why Grace?'

He hesitates before sitting on the step, curling his left hand around the back of his neck, holding it there. He is wearing the grey sweatshirt that shows off the bruises. I don't trust it, or him.

'I had a . . . friend,' he says finally. 'Friends. One of them was . . . Luke.'

Luke. I know that name. Read it in a diary, heard it in a conversation between grieving parents. *Her* diary. *Her* parents. Elise Franklin, my dead girl.

'What happened with Luke?'

'I thought you knew.' He half raises his head, blinking at me. 'Grace Maddox knows. At least, I thought she did. Now? I don't know. It's possible I was wrong about that, too.'

'What did she do? Grace.'

He measures me with his gaze. Then he moves a foot in the direction of the shoebox, careful not to touch it. 'Why does this matter so much?'

We're trading secrets. He is all angles, strategy. *You'll learn.*

'It's mine. I haven't many things. Down here, especially.'

'The items in the box . . . You said you found them in houses. Whose?'

'My parents' house, for one. Will you let me go, now I'm not who you thought I was?'

'Where would you go? To your parents' house?'

'As a last resort, maybe.' I think I say this out loud but perhaps not as his silence stretches like his shadow until he stands, looking down at me.

We stare at one another. From the open cellar door, I smell rain. The light is soft, pink at the edges from the fever.

'If you're not Grace, who are you?'

'I told you. Gwen.'

'Gwen who?'

I swallow, convulsively, trying to remember the name I gave him days ago when I denied being Grace. 'Leonard. Gwen Leonard.'

'I gave the job to Grace Maddox.' He nods across his shoulder. 'The house packing. I employed Grace, not Gwen.'

I want him to go away, leave me alone with the pills and water and my box. 'Maybe I am Grace and I'm lying to stop you hurting me.'

'One of us is lying.' He turns, heading up the steps. 'Take your pills. I'll make you food. You can tell me about the shoebox when you're ready.'

As if the tables have turned and now I hold the power. Me.

'I need red meat,' I say to test this theory. 'I'm sick of soup.'

'I'll grill you a steak, shall I?'

He's joking but it's better than before, a foothold in his new mood. He is at the door. The key is in the lock. Not in his pocket, in the door. I can see it.

'If I die down here,' I tell him, 'you'll have to bury me.'

He shakes his head. 'You won't die. You're too strong.'

15

He returns with ham sandwiches, 'The closest thing to red meat,' down the steps – all the way – handing me the plate before retreating to sit on the third step from the bottom, his feet on my cellar floor.

I eat the sandwich slowly, watching the way he sits with his wrists on his knees, hands hanging. He is wearing ancient deck shoes, their leather full of cracks and salt stains. His feet are bare inside the shoes, naked like his neck where the light rubs at his skin.

'I checked your car. It's good to go; you have half a tank of petrol. There's a shower upstairs, or a bath if you'd like. The water's hot.'

'You're letting me go?' I swallow, my throat protesting against the wad of bread. 'Just like that?'

'I'll wait for the police. You can call them from here if you prefer. I've a phone you can use. It's unlocked. But I thought you'd want to go.'

Real remorse in his voice and his eyes. He won't last two minutes with the police. These past few days have taken everything he had.

'Tell me about your friend Luke.'

He shakes his head. 'There's nothing to say.'

'Tell me and I'll stay.' I put the sandwich aside, my fever gone. 'I won't call the police. I'll help you make sense of this. Whatever you need.'

He stares at me, uncomprehendingly. He doesn't understand what I'm offering. Thinks I'm mad, that he's driven me insane with this incarceration. I see his guilt so starkly. He is all broken edges, nowhere for him to hide.

'Whatever you need,' I repeat.

'You can't *want* to stay—'

'Not down here. But upstairs, in the house. I can stay in the house.'

'*Why?* Why would you do that?'

'You said it yourself, I'm all you have left.'

As I climb to my feet, he straightens and stands, retreating to the seventh step. He's afraid of me, properly afraid. 'Don't be,' I tell him.

He blinks. 'Don't be what?'

'Afraid.'

We eye one another. He has the light behind him. I have only darkness. The thought surprises a laugh from me.

'Come on. It's what you wanted. Someone to help you.'

'You can't stay.' He backs to the top step, eyes on me the entire time. 'Your car is outside. I'm leaving this open.' The door. 'You need to go.'

I shrug, sit back down on my mattress. He stares at me, a flicker of the old anger in his eyes, then turns and walks away.

The light washes down the cellar steps cleanly until it reaches my feet again. Alone in my cellar, I eat his sandwich. By the time I have finished, my eyes have adjusted to the light and I am ready for what comes next.

16

He is in the kitchen at the front of the house, not a large room but a long one, with views out to the gravel path and flower beds. My car isn't there. He lied about that. I remember where I parked it and it's gone. He must have heard me coming up from the cellar but he continues washing plates and cups in the Belfast sink. The kitchen door is propped open. I'm drawn in that direction against my will, the lick of cold air so sweet, so tempting. I want to stand out in what's left of the day. He knows this, thinks of me like an animal, trapped so long it will make whatever escape it can. He is still dangerous.

I set my shoebox down on the counter next to the range. The kitchen is full of colour; I have to keep blinking to take it all in. The range is black but the kettle's the colour of thick cream. The windowsill is lined with pot plants, green and tawny. The tea towel across his shoulder is printed with blue birds with red beaks. The toaster is yellow, the bread bin white. An oak table is crowded with breakfast things: a glass coffee pot, half a loaf of bread on a wooden board, a short-handled knife, a carton of milk. Two of the cooler bags he uses for my meals are stacked on top of one another in a recess that looks like a pantry, its shelves filled with tins of soup, vegetables, fruit.

He's rolled his sleeves back to do the washing-up. His forearms are narrow, sleek with muscle under the suds. When he rinses a cup and places it on the rack, I see the squareness of his wrist. I want to stand and watch him with the lick of air at my feet and the scent of bread in the kitchen, lemons in a bowl on the counter, their waxy sharpness taking my breath away.

After a while, he finishes and washes his hands under the tap, shaking the wet away before resting the heels of his hands on the broad lip of the sink. His head is bowed. 'Please go,' he says.

'What will you do, if I go?'

'I told you, I'll wait here for the police. It's over. It was madness and it's over.' He turns to face me, unflinchingly. He is not brave, I know that, but there is something courageous in the way he stands letting me look at him. 'I'm sorry. I know that's . . . My apology isn't worth anything. What I did was unforgivable. I won't deny any of it. To the police.'

'You said you don't know why you did it. If that's true, how will you explain it, to the police? To anyone?'

'I've no idea.' He pushes away from the sink, tidying the line of washed mugs with a nudge of his thumb. 'But that's my problem, not yours.'

'Who's Clare Miranda?'

'My mother's maiden name.' There is a white, wrenched look at the edges of his mouth, as if I'm pulling these truths from him by force. 'This was her house.' It hurts him to answer my questions. 'Please leave.'

'It's miles from anywhere. That's what you said in your email when you hired me. No neighbours. Why did you warn me about that?'

'I don't know.' He is fit to drop. Of the two of us, I'm in better shape. 'I can't remember.'

'You can't *remember*? What happened?'

He starts to roll down the sleeves of his sweatshirt. 'Something's gone wrong with my head. I'm having . . . an episode of some kind.'

'A breakdown?'

'Possibly. I don't know, not for certain.' From the way he flinches, it hurts him to make this admission. 'I only know I can't remember. What I did or why I did it.'

'You knocked me out and put me in your cellar. If that helps.'

He sets his teeth. 'It was a mistake. I mistook you for Grace Maddox.'

'You wanted her in your cellar. Grace.'

'Yes . . .'

'You must know *why*.'

'I don't. That's the truth.' He finishes with his sleeves and straightens, eyeing me. 'You need to go.'

Is it the truth? Can I trust him? I want to tell him I'm Grace, that he was right about that. But I can't be sure this isn't a trick.

'You owe me something. *Eleven days*. You owe me.'

He accepts this with a nod. He is holding his right wrist so tightly it'll leave a mark. I think for a second he's holding himself back from attacking me but when I look again, it's more as if he's trying to convince himself he's solid.

'What if I want to stay? If that's the price I'm asking?'

'You can't.' A thread of panic in his voice. 'This needs to be over.'

'But it's not over, is it? Not for you, until you remember why you put Grace in your cellar, learning whatever lesson you had in mind for her. *You'll learn*. What was that about?'

He moves his head as if I've hit him. 'Go, get out.' He points at the door. He is different again, more like the man who put me down there. 'I'm warning you.' He lied about my car but he's telling the truth about the warning. His eyes are spilling over with darkness. 'Get out.'

Fear runs through me, fast and hard. His stare swings in the direction of my shoebox – my weak spot, we both know it – and that's when I move. Not towards the door but at him, my fist filling with the first thing it finds. He reaches for the shoebox, the tea towel swinging at his shoulder so that for a second the kitchen is a riot of blue birds with red beaks.

I stop him. *Me*. My fist is full of knife and it goes into him, I feel it go in, puncturing his skin, jarring as it hits his hip bone. He grabs for me but his hands are empty, his eyes full and wide with shock. I pull the knife back, wanting it, a weapon. *Mine*. His legs fold under him, falling.

Scooping up my shoebox, I push past him to the door. My fingers slip for a second on the handle but it's easy, so easy to get out of the house and into the garden where I'm blinded by daylight, the stinging roll of a gravel path under my feet, long grass switching at my shins. At the gate I stop, gulping fresh air, cringing as everything hits at once. The freedom and fresh air, scents caught on his clothes – laurel and stock, rosemary and cow dung – crowding in to slap and scratch at me. I'm out. I'm free.

Run, run, run!

Beyond the gate lie fields and stone walls, distant trees where a low sun burns. My right hand, heavier than my left, is dripping. I stare down at the knife, red trailing from the silver to stain my leg. His blood on me.

No, I told you. I'm not interested in you like that.

A breeze from behind. I turn to face it, seeing the house for the first time. Grey stones scaled with white. Two chimneys tall and chilly against the sky. Four windows looking back at me. He lured me here, wanted me here. I still don't know why, not really. But I know why I came here.

Revenge is too small a word. It cannot contain his questions, or mine. *Vengeance* is better. Biblical, epic. But why? Where did it come from? And where will it go, without me?

PART TWO

1

Dan opens his eyes to darkness and pain. His first thought is *Good, you deserve it*. He expected to wake alone, or not to wake at all. When she stabbed him, as the blade went in, he knew he would die alone and he deserved that, welcomed it even. He hadn't known how to make this stop, only that it needed to stop. But he isn't dead. He is lying on a narrow bed in a room with flowered curtains drawn at the windows. *Night*. He feels the press of it against the glass. He tries lifting his head but sickness swarms in so he lies still again, struggling to make sense of where he is and what he's feeling. He is in the back bedroom of his mother's old house, lying under clean sheets. He has to dredge these facts from the very back of his skull, a place of blood and bruises.

She stabbed him.

The knife went deep, hitting bone. He gathers up the pain – messy, everywhere – and packs it into its proper place, above his left hip. When he tries to touch the wound, he finds his wrists restrained at his sides.

She belted him to the bed frame.

He can picture the belts she used. Leather for his right wrist:

oxblood with a brass buckle. Canvas for his left wrist: woven red and green. She's done a good job, his fingers cannot make any kind of impression against either belt. His legs are free but the pain in his side puts paid to that. She found the belts in a wardrobe upstairs; a half-formed picture in his head of another purpose: a high rafter, exposed ceiling pipe. *Suicide is a hostile act.* He fishes in the murky pond of his memory, comes up empty-handed. He is wearing loose-fitting chinos, a white T-shirt. Not what he was wearing when she stabbed him.

She stripped him, dressed him, put him to bed.

Pain makes a fresh grab for his attention. He moves his head against the pillow, squeezing shut his eyes. Fabric softener, fresh sheets . . . She made the bed. This room isn't used, designed for guests, an en suite bathroom in the space behind his head. The bed wasn't made when he moved in here, twelve days ago. Is it twelve days? She put clean sheets on the bed then put him in it – a half-memory of being hauled from the kitchen. She is stronger than she looks. She dressed the knife wound. While the pain is bad, it isn't appalling.

You knew she was strong, remember? He blinks through the blackness at the ceiling. *What does she want?*

That's easy. Revenge. What he did to her was unforgivable. Whatever retribution she has in mind, he deserves it. He dug two graves when he started down this path and if one of those graves is hard and narrow and has his wrists belted to it, whose fault is that but his own?

2

Two days ago, Dan was talking to his mum here in this house. He was twelve years old and his sight was failing, blank holes wherever he looked. In the garden where he was sure he'd find Dad baking potatoes, he saw a red snake wound up a white stick but it was just bindweed around a bamboo cane. He couldn't find Dad anywhere. It wasn't until he was standing at the window of Mum's room (empty, gathering dust) that he remembered his parents were dead. So whose cars were parked at the back of the house?

Every time he solved one mystery, another took its place. Like the girl he kept glimpsing in the garden, balancing with her arms outstretched. Or the phone that kept *thwapping* messages. Not his phone, he'd thought, until he found himself unlocking it without thinking. None of the texts made sense. He didn't recognize the names of the people who had sent them. He carried the phone outside, walking a long way with it, thumb tapping the screen every time it threatened to fade and lock until he had the idea of deleting the password, leaving it unlocked. It was dark by the time he registered the ache in his shins. He'd walked miles, had to find his way home by instinct.

The house was silent, its doors shut. He looked again for his parents before remembering once more that they were dead. That was a bad day, rotten right through with fear and confusion. In the kitchen, he found a stranger's food in the fridge, dozens of bottles of water stacked on the pantry floor. He searched the bedrooms in case there were others here – some niggling idea this was a holiday home, he was trespassing – but none of the beds were made, just a sleeping bag on the floor in the back bedroom. He lay on it, looking at the ceiling. When he woke, the phone had powered down, needed to be charged. He started to search the contacts for names he knew. When he looked back up, it was morning, another day. His hand held indents from the phone.

He knew he was hungry from the pain in his stomach but he didn't stop to eat, going outside to search the cars parked there. Then he remembered Dad needed his help emptying the bath upstairs. Only when he got there the bath was already empty apart from the corpses of bluebottles.

He knew he was losing his mind; he'd known it for days. A terrible thing had happened. But when he tried to get hold of it, his sight failed. Blank spaces, missing time. Through it all, the sound of water slapping along the hull of a boat, the white shape of torchlight moving across its surface, shadows crouching, uncurling. A canal? A narrowboat.

Only one thing made any kind of sense. Scribbled on a scrap of paper: *Grace Maddox*. Stuck to the fridge door with a magnet. He didn't recognize the handwriting but when he made himself write the name down, it looked the same. His handwriting, then. *Grace Maddox*. If he concentrated, he could keep hold of that, just. To begin with anyway.

It was hard to be inside the house. Easier outside, although his memory played the same tricks there. He spent an afternoon weatherproofing the shed – sanding, painting – only to find himself standing inside the ruins of its walls, bruises on his fingers and throat where he'd brought down part of the rotting structure on himself. A whole afternoon caught up in the delusion of industry, making himself useful not to his father but to his friend, Luke.

Later, bruises throbbing, he stood to watch a rainbow climb across the sky. A supernumerary rainbow. The girl in the garden watched with him, her face upturned, eyes shut. When he asked her what a 'supernumerary rainbow' was, she slipped backwards and disappeared.

Later still he found himself searching the boot of the smaller of the two cars parked at the rear of the house. From under a sea of cardboard and bubble wrap, he fished for a green shoebox.

When he removed the lid, it was like looking at a puzzle. Everything was wrapped, packed tightly into compartments built into the box. Two layers to the box, each with seven compartments separated by sturdy walls of wood like a tea caddy or a jewellery box. He was searching the compartments when rain started coming down in spots.

He was suddenly afraid of mud, of losing everything in the mud, grey and stiff, treacherous. He set the shoebox aside, searching the car for a pendant hidden under the cardboard and bubble wrap. Nothing, just carpeting, gritty against his fingers. He kept saying, 'Sorry, I'm sorry,' without knowing why.

Eventually, he carried the shoebox into the house, stopping in the passage outside the kitchen because there was another thing he had forgotten, more important than the rest, if he could only remember what it was.

Time, which had been slipping from him so fast for days, slowed to a crawl. He felt it unravelling, each strand separate and static.

As he reached for the light switch, a bulb blew, the shock of it bringing him back to her and what he had done – the cellar, Grace, his mistake – the horror of it soaking through him like fever.

3

Sleep isn't possible but he hovers near the edge of it, dipping down from time to time until he opens his eyes to daylight threading through the curtains.

He can feel the wound above his left hip. Pictures the knife she used, its short sharp blade. His brain is a soup of everything he once knew about anatomy: lower left quadrant; abdominal wall, abdominal cavity; solid organs, hollow organs. He is in one piece, for now. This is not a hospital. She is not a nurse. At least he doesn't think so. He reminds himself he has no idea what or who she is. Other than a mistake. His victim. He gropes under the fear for a proper sense of threat but there is only relief. That she stopped him, stopped this. Time ticks by until the grinding pain in his hip erodes this relief, carving it into a shape more like anger. Why did she stab him? He was letting her go. Anyone else would have left. It would be over, if she had left. Finished.

Finally, the door opens and there she is.

Washed and clean, her cropped head like pewter, the same shade as her cool grey eyes on his face. He makes himself meet her gaze, not cringing even when she comes close. He scared himself, the man he became in the cellar. But she's not afraid; the knife in his hip, her hand thrusting it home; nothing scares her. It strikes him he's made a bigger mistake than he thought. Whoever this woman is, she is dangerous.

She has brought an empty plastic bottle, places it on the bedside table before turning to open the curtains. The light lets in shadows that settle along the line of her jaw. She is different up here. Younger and softer and harder, all at once.

'I'd do this for you but I expect you'd prefer to manage it yourself. A bucket won't be possible in here.' She reaches for his right wrist, unbuckling the belt. 'I'd like you to have your dignity, since you did the same for me.'

She frees his hand, putting the bottle into it, under the clean sheet she's used to cover him. Then she walks to the window, turning her back for the time it takes him (a long time) to unfasten his fly and fill the bottle. The sound is thunderous but he is too relieved to be humiliated. 'Thank you . . .'

She belts his wrist back to the bed frame before taking the bottle to the en suite bathroom, emptying it down the lavatory and flushing, running water to wash her hands and rinse the bottle while he lies listening, waiting for her return. She puts the sheet back, examines the wound in his side. That is fairly unspeakable but he takes care not to make a sound, partly because he is afraid to betray fear but also from shame, after everything he put her through.

'It's not good. But it's not as bad as it could be.' She twitches the sheet back over him. 'I found painkillers in that kit you bought.' She eyes him. 'You should eat first, though.'

If she found the first aid kit, then she found the other items in the same carrier bag. Things he can only have bought in that rush of rage (was it?) when this plan landed on him like a tiger, fastening its jaws at his shoulder. He still cannot believe it of himself. After he laid her out cold on the mattress and locked the cellar door, he tied a knot in the neck of the carrier bag, pushing it to the back of a drawer in the kitchen's dresser, telling himself he would never use it, ever. His hands were shaking. Everything he did that night was an effort, a battle with the tiger that sank its teeth deeper into his shoulder. Some sort of psychotic episode? Maybe. But he cannot imagine her accepting that excuse, or any other.

'Thank you,' he tries. 'For stopping it. Stopping me.'

She gives him a curious look before she nods. 'I understand.'

She doesn't. How can she? But he is grateful for her lack of questions. His head is thumping, his whole body hurts. He'll have to answer her questions soon but even this brief respite is a relief.

'You need to eat,' she says next. 'And I'll bring you a hot drink.'

When she leaves the room, he tries lifting his head from the pillow, testing the extent to which he can move the rest of his body. Not much is the answer. Certainly not enough to make the discomfort worthwhile. Only his wrists are tied to the bed but his feet feel impossibly heavy. Moving his left leg sends pain spiking through his hip. She has fastened the belts in such a way he cannot push himself onto his elbows, or curl his shoulders from the mattress. A tiny margin of movement in his wrists – she could have used the next notch if she'd wanted to hurt him – but not enough to get purchase on either belt. Just trying exhausts him. He is shaking by the time she returns, with a tray and a knife. The same knife she stuck in him; he recognizes the handle.

She's cleaned the blade, its steel shining under the light. He shuts his eyes then opens them, needing to know what she's going

93

to do. His mind fires images, each bloodier than the last, of all the places she will put it, where she'll cut him and how deeply. His skin recoils from the soles of his feet to the lids of his eyes. He bites his mouth shut to stop himself begging.

'I'll have to let you up,' she says matter-of-factly. 'To eat.' She sets the tray on the bedside table. 'I could feed you but you won't be able to swallow easily so it's better if you feed yourself.' A sandwich of some kind sits on the tray with a glass of water but it's the knife she takes up in her hand. 'I brought this because it's too soon for either of us to expect trust. I don't want to hurt you any more than I have. I hope you feel the same but in case you don't . . .'

The blade is smooth and white in her hand, like an extension of her fingers. *She is made of knives.* Fright thumps through him.

He manages a nod. 'I won't try anything.'

'You won't get the chance.' She places the knife on the window-sill before unbuckling the belts, one after the other, retreating to the window where she takes up the knife and nods. 'Eat. And take the painkillers.'

Dan draws his body up the bed, vigilant of the pain that was fairly indiscriminate before he attempted an upright position and is now thrashing his left side into agonized submission. He is light-headed, wonders how much of his blood she washed off the kitchen floor (she will have washed it, he is certain of that). He needs to inspect the dressing. Presumably she improvised with whatever was in the first aid kit. No stitches means infection is more or less inevitable. A wet red stain is spreading on the white T-shirt where he has bled through the dressing. When he's upright, he reaches for the tray but his body resists his attempt to twist at the waist, spasming enough to drive home what a bad idea it was to

94

move at all. *Too soon.* If he'd had surgery, stitches, it would be too soon. He has an open wound in his abdomen.

'I'm going to bleed all over the bed if I do this.' He looks at her, at the knife in her hand. 'I don't need food. Water, yes, but—'

'First rule of warfare,' she says coolly, 'sleep and eat whenever you get the chance.'

'Pretty sure the first rule is not to die. I'll bleed – badly – if I sit up. You might not be able to stop the bleeding.'

'I stopped it before.' She shrugs. 'I'm not afraid of a bit of blood.'

'Evidently.' He sets his teeth, swallowing the anger. 'But if I eat, I'll almost certainly vomit. You will only have more work to do.'

She frowns, considering him. Then she nods. 'Lie down.'

He does as he's told. The wound is leaking, he can feel it. He has to fight to stop himself wadding the sheet and applying pressure. 'Did you wash it? Because if there's dirt in it—'

'Of course I washed it.'

'—I'll die.'

'You won't.' She belts his wrists back to the bed, firmly.

'Why did you do it?' Dan asks.

'Why did you?'

'I made a mistake. But I didn't stab anyone.'

'You didn't need to. You were starving me to death.'

'I wasn't, in fact. I just forgot you were down there.'

'That's meant to make me feel better, is it?' Her eyes go to the wet red hem of his shirt. 'I'll bring another dressing.'

She leaves the room, returning with the first aid kit.

He recites the Snellen chart in his head to keep from shouting as she unsticks the old dressing and applies the new one.

Afterwards, she feeds him ibuprofen, a mouthful of water. She stays in the room, standing by the side of the bed, until he is capable of speech.

'I need stitches.' He blinks at the ceiling, balling his fists. 'If you call an ambulance, I'll tell them what I did. No one will blame you.'

'You'll be arrested.'

'Yes, but you won't.' He waits for the storm in his skull to settle. 'If I stay here, there's a good chance I'll die and you'll have to live with that, with having killed someone. Could you do it? Because I couldn't.'

'What does that mean?' she asks sharply.

'It means I'd rather not die,' Dan says, 'if it's all the same to you.'

'You should have thought of that before you put me in your cellar.'

'It was a *mistake*. I've admitted that. I unlocked the doors to let you go. You could've gone. Instead you stuck a knife in me. Why?'

'You were going for my shoebox.' Her tone is flat and accusing.

'I was going to take it to the car, that's all. I knew you'd follow that box anywhere.'

'Well then, perhaps I panicked.'

'You?' He rolls his neck to look at her. 'I doubt you've ever panicked in your life.'

'I've never been locked in a cellar in my life . . . In an attic, yes. But not a cellar. We'll wait and see what happens with that wound.' She moves the tray from the bedside cabinet. 'I think if you were dying, you'd be worse.'

'Are you a doctor?'

'No.' She covers him with a sheet. 'But you are. A surgeon, an ophthalmologist.'

He stares at her. His head churns, throwing up random debris –
*torchlight across water, windows lit like eyes, darkness in the shape of
a man* – the same images he's been seeing for days. His memory is
an endless car journey through bad weather and blackness, with
only an occasional glimpse of road signs, wreckage. But she's right.
He is an ophthalmologist. He trained for years. He can't remember
how many. Seven?

'Your name is Daniel Roake. It's on your driving licence.'

Daniel Roake. Dan. Danny. Danny boy.

It's raining, he realizes, a dry sound against the window. He
feels very far away from it, from everything. As if the bed isn't here
in this room in this house, as if he is not on the bed but out on
the water, a long way away, years ago. His teeth ache. He can taste
blood.

The rain plays like a soundtrack, on and on. He wonders how
bad it will get. Whether it will be like the rain when she died,
turning the lane into a mudslide, or like the rain hitting the roof of
Clark's pickup as the four of them sat inside, waiting and watching.
The memories fracture, falling away before he can get hold of them.
He feels dizzy, disorientated.

'Why?' he asks her. 'Why stab me and then stay? Why not run?
Why not leave me to die? Why are you still here?'

'Because you're hurt.' She looks down at him on the bed. 'And
because I need to know who Grace really is. What she did to make
you angry, why you hate her so much. You owe me an explanation,
don't you think?'

He shuts his eyes but she stays there, a ghost against the insides
of his eyelids. Small and narrow but strong enough to lift him. Not
scared. Silent. He remembers her silence, how it filled the cellar,

the house. She can wait. Hours, days, weeks. His wound might heal or fester. He will never outlast her.

The rain hits the window, sliding down the glass. The sound of it unlocks something inside him. The rain and the fact of her standing so still beside him, waiting.

'It was raining.' The words are like stones falling away, leaving him light-headed. 'That night.' The pickup's windows blacked out by their breath. 'It wouldn't stop raining.' Grit pricking the sole of his foot. 'There was a girl. She was killed. Her dad . . . was my best friend.'

'Luke?' She stands with her back to the window.

'No, but he's part of it.' His breath catches in his chest. 'We all are.'

The room changes shape as she moves to sit at the side of the bed, her alloy gaze on his face. 'Tell me.'

PART THREE

1

It was dark by the time Dan reached the top of the road, street light lying in puddles along the pavement. Rain had been coming down all week. The lids of the coffee cups were sloppy with water, and under his suit his skin was damp. Up ahead, the pickup looked like an animal crouched at the neck of the lane. Dan knew Luke was watching the wing mirror, eyes slitted at the street. Owen, too. Clark would be asleep at the wheel, knowing the other two were keeping watch. It was the only time he ever slept, Clark said.

'You're late,' Luke told Dan.

'I know.' He slid into the back seat next to Owen, passing one of the cups to Clark who was blinking himself awake. 'Coffee.'

Luke and Owen had cans of lager. Luke dug out a hip flask, telling Clark to add a splash of whisky to the coffee: 'It'll warm you up.'

'I'm good, thanks.' Clark put his hand across the cup and Luke pushed the flask back into his pocket.

Dan met Luke's eyes in the rear-view mirror, glancing away before Luke did. Owen rubbed the elbow of his parka at the window. The inside of the pickup was soupy, blind with condensation. Owen's parka steamed like Dan's suit. He freed the lid from his coffee, drinking a mouthful. For preference he'd be home right now, pouring a glass of wine, heating spaghetti. But Fridays were pickup days. He knew the rules. He didn't, in any case, want Clark on his own out here, or Owen.

'Do we think anyone will be out in this?' His socks were wet inside his shoes. He should have changed into trainers before leaving work. 'The roads are already flooding.'

'There's always someone.' Luke's jaw bunched as he bent to look in the wing mirror. 'You know that.' He narrowed his stare at the lane. 'We always see someone.'

Box Lane was a shortcut used by nearly everyone in this dead end of town: a long dog-leg littered with cans, drug bags. Dozens of places from one unlit end to the other where you could trip and fall. Trees crowded so close you felt their branches scratching as you walked. In the wet, the trees made a cave mouth curtained by rain. If you wanted the shops on the other side of the estate, you could drive for five minutes (longer when the traffic was bad), walk for half an hour or take this shortcut. Two years ago, few had bothered with the shortcut. But then the new precinct opened with its coffee shop and chemist, and Box Lane got busy. For a public right of way, the council did not seem to care how badly lit or littered it was. Nothing was out here, past the old silk mill with its chimney like a blackened finger to the sky, only the last cough of the council estate before the road that climbed out of town, black and pitted, towards the Peaks. Dan grew up here, they all did. At thirteen, he had climbed the Peaks to stand staring back at the town, promising himself he'd escape. He had escaped. But then he came back.

Clark and Luke never left. Owen, at sixteen, ought to have

been in Manchester. Anywhere but here where jobs were scarce, recession constant. Clark's first job had been with a local lighting company. He'd left school at fifteen, a trainee salesman out on the road. The lighting company was long gone but when Dan looked back on those days he saw his friend lit by a blaze of white, wielding a fluorescent tube like a lightsaber. Clark had laughed at Dan for going away to university when look where it got him – right back here where he started, where they all started.

Dan sipped at his coffee. When did he last see Clark laugh? Or do anything other than sit like this, half asleep, his face a mask of grief, eyes bruised shut?

The flint of heels on the road brought their heads around.

Owen rubbed at the window, making a bigger hole in the condensation so they could see who was coming. A woman, her head down under a cheap umbrella, one of its prongs broken, wet nylon flapping at her face. High heels, short red coat, skinny jeans blackened by the rain.

'State of that,' Luke hissed. 'She'll never be able to run in those ... If she doesn't fall flat on her arse first.'

Dan felt the hairs lift on his forearms. He looked for a safe place to put his coffee cup, watching Clark who was wide awake now, his stare fixed on the rear-view mirror. The woman was coming closer. Rain pushed against her, the ripped umbrella tipping lower, hiding her body.

Owen made a hissing sound through his teeth. 'She needs telling ...'

She was alongside the pickup, less than a foot from where Luke's fist was bunched against the door. He'd punch it open, the way he had countless times before. Punch open the door to bring her to a standstill, shock her into seeing how easily she could be knocked off balance. Snap at her in her high heels, demand to see her run, 'Go on! Just try it!' Then, before she got the chance to recover . . .

At the entrance to the lane, she lowered her umbrella, struggling for a second before collapsing it, fingers wrapping round the soaked nylon. Dyed blonde hair, a smoker's mouth set in a tough, puckered line. In her fifties. Not their type; not what they were here for. She turned up Box Lane, her heels silenced by mud and leaves, no more than a faint ticking now. The sound died, leaving the fast patter of the rain.

Luke took his hand away from the door. Dan let his breath out, hearing it stagger in his chest. The windows misted over, everything in soft focus again. They sat in the silence that always came at these moments, so familiar it was a comfort. Dan's mouth was dry. He sipped at the coffee but it was cold, tasting of iron. Owen's jaw was slack, his bottom lip bubbled by spit.

Rain ran down the windscreen, spat at the gutter.

In the rear-view mirror, Clark's eyes were hot and black with tears. Luke's anger bumped about the pickup like a dog that'd expected to be let out.

After a long moment, Owen crooked his elbow and rubbed at the window again, making a new hole for them to watch through.

2

'How's Tess?' Dan asked when the silence grew too thick.

'Busy with the house.' Clark played with the lid from his coffee. 'You know how she gets.'

Tess had to keep busy. She was getting worse lately, Clark said, so frantic he was afraid she'd have a heart attack or stroke. She was only thirty-one but grief had made her ill. She thought Clark was working, didn't know he'd lost his job because the only time he could keep vigil in the pickup was during office hours. Dan had said Clark didn't need to be part of the vigil, they had it covered, but Clark said he needed to be here: 'Where else would I go?'

The silence in the car nagged. The air was stale. Dan longed to open a window to relieve the pressure, like lancing a wound. He didn't know how much longer he could sit in the stew of damp clothes and body odour. Owen burped, wiping wetness from his mouth. He was so young with his scruff of fair hair sticking up at the fringe. He should be hanging out with mates in a pub or sprawled on a sofa at home, not watching an unlit lane for strangers, waiting for his brother to say the word that would get them out of the pickup and into serious trouble. Sooner or later, someone was going to report what they were doing. Then Luke would be sitting in a police station, they all would. Of the four, Dan had most to lose. This was understood but never discussed. Clark had already lost his job. Luke and Owen were on benefits. Only Dan had a wage coming in, people who depended on him. None of which mattered. Not to Luke, and Owen followed his brother's lead. Clark said nothing. So here Dan was every Friday afternoon for five months now, no end in sight. Sitting in the pickup, watching the wing mirrors with Luke's fist bunched against the door. He had no excuse for it, other than not wanting Clark or Owen alone out here.

Up ahead, the Peaks climbed to the rain-sodden sky. Dan had driven that road countless times. It climbed and dipped, switchbacking between fields, the occasional farmhouse tucked into the folds. He could point out the place where a man murdered his own family decades ago, knew when a dip in the road brought you level with a field of black mud where cattle sat. He hated that field, the bulls like statues waiting for something unspeakable to happen. That was how it felt to keep this vigil, the four of them in the pickup like the bulls in the black field, waiting.

'I should be heading home. I'm in theatre first thing tomorrow.'

'Surgery?' Clark twisted to look at him, dredging interest onto his face. It hurt to see how hard he was fighting to keep one foot in the real world.

'Just routine.' A detached retina. Complicated, if at all, by the patient's age. The anaesthetist would have a harder time of it than Dan. 'Still, I should get some sleep.'

'Yeah.' Luke drained the can of lager. 'We could all use some of that.'

Guilt tugged its short leash, keeping Dan in the pickup. Grit had found its way inside his sock, pricking at the sole of his foot. Owen was humming a song, his thumb tap-tapping at the side of the lager can. He'd been doing it for a while. Dan hadn't been conscious of it until now but the sound was suddenly intolerable, as if he'd reached breaking point without warning.

'Oh, here we go . . .' Luke sat to attention, nodding at the wing mirror.

A girl was coming up the road. Green sweatshirt with a pocket at the front, black leggings, white trainers. No coat. No umbrella to hide her face, which was shiny with rain, long hair plastered to her cheeks, scowling. It made her look younger but even without the scowl she couldn't have been more than fourteen. The pocket held the shape of her hands and a mobile phone.

Luke propped his fist to the door. 'Stupid little cow.' The words seethed against his teeth. 'Come on!'

When she drew level, he shoved the door open and stepped out. Rain ricocheted from the pickup, hitting the pavement. The girl stopped so fast her trainers squeaked. Dan saw her mouth open then close at Luke who was built like a rugby player, all shoulders and torso, his flak jacket black with rain.

Owen slid across the back seat, popping the door. Dan reached a hand for his elbow, shaking his head.

'They need telling!' Owen insisted. 'They need to know!'

Clark was frozen in the front seat, his eyes on the girl.

Luke was in her face, hissing, 'See that?' Jabbing his hand across her shoulder at Box Lane. 'What is it? D'you even know?'

'It's a shortcut.' She stood up to him, thin neck angled in defiance, the kind of girl who talked back to her mum and dad.

'It's a death trap!' There was no talking back to Luke. 'What, don't you read the news? On your little phone there? How old're you? Thirteen?'

'Fourteen!' Two feet shorter than Luke, her eyes wet with the rain splashing up from the shoulders of his jacket. 'If it's any of your business!'

At the wheel, Clark swallowed audibly. Luke had left the passenger door open. They could hear the girl, the quaver in her voice as she squared up to him. Dan's throat clenched, shame souring the inside of his mouth. Owen's elbow was vibrating in his grip. Dan didn't let go, knowing Owen wanted to stand at his brother's side; his empty hand was mimicking Luke's, its fingers thrusting stiffly as Luke pointed towards the lane a second time.

'It's a *death trap*. She was a year younger than you. *Thirteen*. Thought this'd be a quick way to get to Subway and Starbucks, meet up with her mates. Only they never saw her again, did they? No one did. Not alive.'

'He's scaring her.' Dan met Clark's eyes in the mirror.

Clark nodded, blinking. His palms were pressed to the wheel, the rain's reflection running over the backs of his hands. Rain drummed at the metal roof of the pickup, a tribal beat.

Owen hissed, 'She needs telling! They all do.'

It was his brother's mantra, day and night. They had to warn the girls who used Box Lane as a shortcut, remind them of what happened here a year ago. Some of the girls had never even heard about it.

'That's her dad in there.' Luke jerked his head at the pickup. 'He had to identify her body. You want your dad doing that?'

'You're sick.' The girl curled her arms around her torso, making herself smaller. 'Freak!'

Luke batted the word away. 'No, but there's a *freak* out there. One who likes stupid little cows who think it's cool to take a short-cut up an unlit alley when there's no one in screaming distance.' He raked her with his stare. 'Unless you're a sprinter or a kickboxer, you're dead meat.'

She backed away, glaring at him. 'Piss off, perve!' She was shaking and so was Owen, the teeth chattering in his head.

Dan let go of Owen's elbow and opened the door, climbing down from the pickup to the pavement. When Clark followed suit, the girl shrieked in alarm. She tried to swerve into Box Lane but Luke snatched a handful of her sweatshirt, twisting his fist until she stood still.

'Let her go,' Dan said. '*Luke*. Let her go. You're scaring her.'

'Good.' Luke gave her a shake. 'She *should* be scared. Unless you've forgotten, he's still out there. That *shit* is still out there.'

Dan saw the girl gather a breath. When she screamed it was loud enough to make Luke drop her. She didn't stop, backing away from the three of them, her face blurred by rain, eyes wide open, every tooth on show.

'That's good. Like that. Louder.' Clark's voice was low, on the edge of tears. 'She never got the chance to scream. My girl. Or no one heard. No one came . . . Keep screaming. And run.' He pointed a finger at the houses down the hill. 'Wherever there's a light on. A house or a car, whichever comes first. Don't stop until you're safe.' He fixed his eyes on her face. 'Promise me.'

She cut off the scream with her hand across her mouth, her stare wild above it. She hadn't looked at Dan. All her attention was on Luke and Clark.

The rain beat at their feet, making gutters gulp and stutter.

109

Owen was out in it now, standing the other side of the pickup, gripping its bull bar with both hands. The girl didn't look at him. She couldn't take her eyes off Clark.

'Promise me,' he said again. 'You'll stay safe. Remember my little girl. Her name was Elise. *Elise*. She was only thirteen. Remember her, please.'

The rain was still coming down when Dan reached home, the road throwing echoes like punches. The whole street had the shut-up look that was never far away in this town with its soot-stained brickwork, a sense of having been hewn from the foothills only last week. Rain made it all worse, lowering over roofs, blanking out windows. It had been raining when he'd left for work at 6 a.m., before any of the houses in his street were lit.

'Penetrating eye injury,' the admissions officer had called ahead to warn him. 'You'll be in surgery a while.'

Surgery was what Dan did best. He'd welcomed the call, aware the vigil in the pickup was waiting at the other end of his day. Six inches of steel knocked through a man's eye socket kept him sane for the morning. He wondered what that said about his sanity.

This evening, his parents' house was in darkness, its drainpipes seething. He unlocked the front door and went inside, dropping his keys onto the hall table. Luke and Owen would be down the pub now. Clark with Tess, eating supper. The girl from Box Lane would be telling her friends about the freaks in the pickup, how she'd stood up to them. Everyone remaking their day into something tolerable. Dan would call the hospital to see how his patient was doing, pretend his day had been about the surgery that saved a man's sight and not his failure to step out of the pickup sooner, to stand up to Luke.

The silence in the house irked him. He switched on the hall light, seeing shadows jump for the stairs. He hated the house, had done for years.

In the kitchen, he took a bottle of wine from the fridge, filling a glass. His phone rang as he was taking a first mouthful. 'Hey.'

'Just checking you got home okay,' Clark said. 'This rain . . .'

'I'm here. Are you all right?'

'Yep.' The false note of cheer was for Tess. 'See you soon, I hope.'

'I hope so, too.'

Dan waited, wanting to say more. That they should stop it – the vigil, the pickup – it was no way to remember Elise. Luke was out of control, only making matters worse when what Clark needed was to grieve, with Tess. Nothing he hadn't said before, in as many words. Clark wasn't ready to hear it. Dan didn't know how else to be a friend other than by staying close, trying to be a safety valve on the worst of Luke's temper. He despised his inability to take decisive action. It had been the same when his mother was alive. Nothing ever changed because he was too much of a coward to make it change.

'Tess says you should come to supper soon. Now we're settled in the new place.'

The new house was just a short distance from their old one where the loss of Elise felt unbearable. In the new house, they'd replicated her bedroom, Tess hiring a professional packer to make certain of it.

'Thank Tess for me,' Dan said. 'Tell her I'd love to see her.'

Back when they were kids, Clark could make him laugh when

nothing else could. Real laughter, the kind that rolled tears down his face. It was gone now, all that uncomplicated happiness. Now, you could drop a stone in Clark and never hear it splash.

'Okay, well, see you then.'

After Clark ended the call, Dan went to the sink and washed his hands, shaking the wet away, thinking of the girl in Box Lane who'd stood up to Luke, only screaming when she saw the three of them pile out of the pickup.

Luke was right about one thing: the shortcut had been a death trap a year ago and no one had done anything to make it safer. Elise walked into Box Lane in her new jeans and yellow T-shirt, blue lace-ups on her bare feet because Tess couldn't get her to wear socks no matter how many pairs she bought. Was she looking at her phone, like most thirteen-year-olds? Did she hear him coming? Or was there no warning, just a second when the air thickened before her world turned black?

Something pricked at Dan's left foot.

He leant into the counter and peeled off his sock, scratching at the damp sole of his foot, finding a tiny speck of grey-pink gravel, its edges sticking to the pads of his fingers, reluctant to let go.

3

Next morning, the hospital smelt of cold lino and lukewarm break-fasts. Owen was in the waiting area, his fair head bent over his games console.

'Hey, kiddo. You okay?'

Owen squinted up, struggling to place him. He didn't think of Dan as a surgeon, only as one quarter of the vigil, a seat in the pickup.

'Taylor fell,' he said at last. 'She's getting an X-ray.'

Taylor was Luke's youngest daughter with his ex-girlfriend, Shannon.

'Who's with her?'

'Shannon.' Owen pulled a face, mimicking Luke's distaste for Taylor's mum. 'She told Luke to piss off.' He bent back over the console. 'He's gone for a smoke. I said I'd wait for news.'

The console, battered plastic covered in stickers, was one of Elise's old ones, a gift from Clark. They all loved Owen and tried to look out for him. He was just a kid really, trapped like the rest of them in the tragedy of a year ago, his parents absent a lot of the time, his days spent with Luke. Tess cooked Owen supper once or twice a week, knowing he didn't eat properly at home. At sixteen, he was gangly, inclined to trip over his own feet, constantly on the verge of a new growth spurt.

'Did you have breakfast?' Dan asked. Owen shook his head, thumbs busy on the console. 'They're serving fry-ups in the canteen.' He fished for his wallet. 'Get yourself one, yes?'

Owen reached to take the fiver. 'Thanks . . . Dan.'

Ten pounds he'd have spent in the corner shop, on lager probably. A fiver wasn't enough for that so with luck he'd go to the canteen for a sausage sandwich and a hot drink. Dan said, 'Look after yourself, okay?'

'Luke's getting me a Switch. And a new phone.' He bent over the console, thumbs busy. 'Soon's he's got a job. Spar's hiring.'

'That's good. Say hi to Taylor from me.'

Owen nodded, scuffing the heels of his split trainers at the floor. Had Luke promised him new clothes as well as a Switch? Owen wore hand-me-downs, the clothes always too big or too small. It was tough for Luke, who was paying child maintenance, taking whatever work he could find, manual labour, washing floors, he wasn't proud. Except he was. Pride was a big part of the problem with Luke. Pride and anger.

Dan found him under the awning at the side of the hospital, a gulag-styled strip of shelter designated for smokers. Luke was in his old army jacket, rain-stained camouflage, rolling a cigarette. Dan couldn't remember ever seeing him without the jacket. Strangers mistook him for a soldier. Big, broad and blond, even his eyelashes. Lean hands with long fingers, a smoky-green stare that turned to cut-glass if you crossed him or whenever he was watching in the pickup's wing mirrors. Dan thought of the girl last night who'd stood up to Luke. He wished for a fraction of her courage.

'I heard about Taylor. Is she all right?'

Luke pocketed the tobacco. 'No idea.' Pinching the cigarette between his lips. 'None of my business, apparently.'

'You're her dad.'

'Right.' He fished a disposable lighter from the torn breast pocket of the jacket. 'Like that means shit.'

Everything Luke did was flavoured by anger, even the lighting of a cigarette. He held it between his teeth as he snapped the flame, sucking smoke with a hiss. Dan should walk away. He had the perfect excuse: patient rounds. He didn't know why it mattered to him that the vigil wasn't the only time he spoke with Luke. Because it felt less clandestine? As if this casual conversation were proof their relationship was founded on more than the mutual need to avenge what was done to their friend's daughter?

'Well, I hope she's okay. I could try to find out, if it helps?'

He hated himself for offering. But at the same time he was thinking, *This is normal, this is what friends do for one another. Not the pickup or the vigil but this.*

Luke smoked, eyes narrowed against the sting. He'd smoke to the last shred, flick away the scrap of ash. In spite of himself, Dan admired his economy and his focus. When Luke set his mind to a task, it got done. He'd been that way in school and he hadn't changed; if he wanted something, he ran at it. The trouble was, the rest of the world rarely fell in with his plans and there were only so many walls you could run into before it started to sting.

'Forget it.' Luke rubbed ash from his fingers onto the thigh of his jeans. 'Thanks anyway.'

Dan nodded. 'What're friends for?' He knew Luke was watching him as he walked away, his stare red-tipped like a sniper's.

At school, Clark and Dan had been thick as thieves. Then Dan went away to university and medical school before taking up his residency. He was gone five years. By the time he returned, it was Luke and Clark as if it had always been the two of them against the world, Dan on the fringes of the friendship. But Clark was Dan's best friend, in his mind at least. Why else did he sit in that pickup every Friday afternoon?

'He's still out there. That shit is still out there.'

Luke didn't trust the police to do their job: find Elise's killer. They'd tried and failed. Even if they managed it, Luke didn't trust them to make an arrest stick. Dan had tried arguing that the vigil was more likely to harm than help when it came to a prosecution but Luke didn't want to hear it. Luke didn't want to hear much from Dan.

As if to prove him wrong, Luke caught up with him in the corridor as Dan was headed for the ward. 'You seen anyone lately? Who fits the profile?'

Patients, he meant. Luke had a theory the killer had been treated at the hospital. He had many theories but this one required Dan to do some snooping during his day job. He half suspected Luke invented the theory for this precise purpose, as a way of testing Dan's allegiance.

'Just the usual poor sods in the wrong place at the wrong time.'

'That's what they said about Elise,' Luke reminded him. 'But she used that shortcut all the time. It was the right place as far as she was concerned. *He* was the one in the wrong place.'

Dan nodded. Always easier to agree with Luke than argue with him.

'What about victims? Anyone who's been assaulted lately?'

He stood with Luke in the stairwell, waiting until they were alone before he answered. 'Not in the way she was.' He wanted to shut his eyes against the images of Elise, dead.

'She used that shortcut all the time,' Luke repeated. '*He* was the one in the wrong place.'

Back at the start of the vigil, Dan had made a promise to himself to pick his battles when it came to Luke who was going to end up in jail or insane, that much had been clear for months. Dan was damned if he was seeing Clark dragged down the same road, and Owen deserved better. Maybe he was kidding himself, believing he might make a difference. Maybe it was egotism, or envy. Clark didn't trust Dan, not really, not now. Luke was the one he trusted to bring Elise's killer to justice. Dan was good for fetching coffee and checking hospital records but that was about it.

'Keep looking. Everyone needs hospitals. He'll end up here sooner or later.'

Luke bunched his fists as he said it, as if he hoped to be the one to put the killer in hospital. He wanted the man dead, Dan knew. Lying in the mud of Box Lane, bleeding out. A slow, painful death. That was what Luke had planned for Elise's killer. The vigil was only the start. When they found the killer, Luke would demand a second vigil to make certain no one stumbled into Box Lane to stop him doing what he pleased – a vigil to keep Luke safe while he was killing the killer, slowly. Preferably, he said, with Clark's help.

'Closure' was the word he used to describe Clark's part in this plan.

Sometimes, Dan let himself imagine how it might go, how hard the man would fight to stay alive, what the weather would be like, if they'd all be covered in mud by the end of it, like the mud on the day Elise died.

The floods were bad now but they'd been worse a year ago. For weeks, the weather had switched from autumn to winter and back again within the space of the same three days. Gutters ran, and roofs. Pipes froze, thawed and burst. Roads were closed. Cars swooped through waves of water as they came down from the Peaks to find themselves stranded, circling in the floods until their headlights pointed back the way they'd come. Box Lane became a slick mudslide, floating fag ends, beer cans. When the sun broke through to wage war on the rain, the stench rising from the mud was rotten and primordial.

Tess had wanted to keep Elise's shoes but the smell was so bad they'd ended up in the chest freezer, a greying block in a plastic bag. No trace was found of the pendant Elise had worn every day since her eighth birthday and would never, Tess said, have taken off or left behind. Mud and rain destroyed any useful evidence. The police sifted through it for hours, searching for the pendant or anything dropped by the killer. For weeks after the murder, Dan dreamt of that mud and of the frozen shoes in Clark's chest freezer.

Owen wasn't in the waiting area when he walked back through the hospital after his rounds. Dan looked but couldn't find him. He hoped the kid was in the canteen, getting a hot breakfast inside him. He'd call Clark later because it was the pattern they'd fallen into, taking turns to call one another even when there was nothing new to say. It would feel unlucky to break the pattern now. Clark's days were empty enough, or rather they were filled with his pretence of a job taking him out of the house.

Tess was too smart, Dan thought, to have fallen for that lie. But perhaps she needed the illusion of stability, structure. It was possible she knew it was a lie but went along with it for her own sake as much as Clark's.

After Elise died, Tess had said, 'It's like a light going out. At first, you're . . . blind. Then you start to see again but it's very dim, all the colours faded or gone. Nothing is the same. Your whole world looks different.'

4

'Your whole world looks different.'

Dan stops, waiting for Gwen to speak. She is seated at the side of the bed, listening in silence to his account of the vigil and what sparked it. Elise's death. Clark's grief. Luke's lust for vengeance. None of it explains why he knocked her unconscious and locked her in a cellar. If she's impatient for him to reach that part of the story, she doesn't show it. Details are important to her. He knew that as soon as he found the shoebox. He is exhausted from talking, the memories like pulling teeth.

'Is that why you did what you did? For Elise?'

The way she says *Elise* puts Dan on edge. It's private, this pain. And not only to him. It belongs to Clark and Tess. He owes this woman an apology for the mistake he made. But she is after more than just an apology. He wishes he knew what.

'Why are you friends with men like that? You're a surgeon, a professional. But you're sitting in a pickup drinking lager on a Friday night?'

'I was drinking coffee. Luke and Owen drank lager.'

'How long ago was this?'

'The vigil? It started five months ago. But that particular night' –
he concentrates, trying to pinpoint the memory – 'must have been
about three weeks ago.'

'You're a surgeon. Luke is on benefits . . . Clark left school at fifteen, you said. How are these people your friends?'

A good question. 'We were at school together.'

'You went away to university. Why did you come back?'

'Does it matter? In the scheme of things.' He shifts, catching his
breath. She stands, her nearness making it all much worse.

'I'll bring painkillers.' She looks down at him on the bed. 'Luke
doesn't sound like much of a friend. Not to you, or to Clark.'

'He was never my friend.'

Dan thinks of Never Events: serious preventable mistakes, the
reporting of which is a legal requirement in his profession. Or what
was his profession. His mistakes are far larger now.

Kidnap, assault, false imprisonment.

Somewhere in the very back of his mind, Luke laughs at that.
At him. Dan suppresses a shudder, memory like a broad shoulder
shoving at the doors in his head, those he's worked hard to keep
shut. She is the same, he suspects, boxing up the parts of her life
that unsettle or disturb her. He could take lessons from her, in all
likelihood. He remembers the person she became when he took
her shoebox down into the cellar. Screaming, slashing at him. The
knife in his hip was inevitable after that. He should have been on
his guard against it – *a Never Event* – and might've been but for his
need for this to be over. Well, that and the fact the inside of his head
is so much like Swiss cheese.

She waits to see what else he might say but the pain has him biting his lips together. When the fingers of her right hand brush his knuckles, he has to suppress a snarl. 'You're a surgeon,' she says.

'*Was* . . . I *was* a surgeon.'

'What was that like?'

Another good question. 'Complicated.'

'Like your memory,' she says. 'We need to get it back.'

He doesn't argue. He wants his memory back, of course he does. Even if it feels as if something deadly is hiding in his head, crouched with teeth and claws. He wants it back. Why she wants it is a mystery.

She settles at his side, the promise of painkillers forgotten. 'Give me an example,' she says. 'Of your complicated work.'

5

'I have a headache in my stomach.'

'In your . . . ?'

'Stomach.' Jude fingered the silver stud in her eyebrow. 'Do I have to take this out?'

'We can work around it,' Dan said.

The stud was new since her last appointment.

'You look knackered,' Jude told him. 'Late night?'

'Late night nothing. It's these early mornings.'

She grinned then reconstructed her scowl like someone twice her age applying a fresh coat of lipstick.

Dan set her notes aside. 'Time for the big chair.'

She followed him across the room, waiting while he made the necessary adjustments to the chair's height; the last patient had been far taller. Far older, too. Jude sat in the chair, plucking at the front of her T-shirt, which was dirty-orange with a purple cartoon cat's face. Dan wondered if she'd painted her toes to match her fingers: a different shade for each short nail.

'Rainbow hands.'

'You like?' Jude held them up for his inspection. 'Mum says it's better than black.' She wriggled in the chair then sat still. 'I think she thinks Goth's still a thing.'

Dan wondered what lie she'd told her mum to be allowed to wear the orange shirt in public, whether Mrs Horning realized the cartoon cat was the logo for a street drug.

'Goth . . . Living in the past, you think?'

'Years in the past. Before my eyes got fucked. Sorry, Dr Dan.'

'It's just Dan . . . Look straight at me?'

Six weeks since he'd last seen her.

New spots had formed in both eyes.

'Do I need the dilation drops? I love the drops.'

She'd become very good at sitting still. Dan could have progressed to the drops but he'd seen what he needed to see – what he'd hoped not to see – in the first few seconds. He took a seat at her side.

'Tell me about the pain in your stomach.'

'It's like a headache.' She put a fist there. 'My back hurts and my shoulders. From trying to read, I guess.'

'Swimming should help. It'll loosen you up. Is there a friend you can go with?'

'Frankie, I guess.' Jude twisted the stud in her eyebrow. 'I feel a bit sick at the pool. It's like . . . I'm falling. You know?'

'Motion sickness. Your brain's adjusting to the different way you're seeing things now.'

'You mean the way I'm *not* seeing things.' As she slid down from the chair, he put out a hand to help her. 'That bad, huh?'

'It's getting worse faster than we thought it would.'

'Than *you* thought. I didn't think anything, other than what the fuck'm I going to tell my friends?'

'Faster than *I* thought. I'm sorry, Jude.'

She huffed a smile through small teeth. 'I know.'

Clark's grief, Luke's rage, Owen's vulnerability – none of these moved Dan the way Jude's smile did. He washed his hands as she reapplied the scowl, scuffing a hand at her hair, which was brambly and purple-black and gave her a wild look she offset with a flat stare, daring you to pity her. Juvenile macular degeneration. Jude was going blind. She was twelve.

When he'd broken the news, she'd said, 'Well, shit,' and balled her fists in her lap. It hurt him, the way she summoned a smile today. What would she say if she knew how he spent his Friday afternoons? Standing with Owen and Luke while a girl not much older than her screamed in anger and alarm. If the textbooks told the truth, Jude's impaired central vision would have spared her the full picture, the heart of the scene eviscerated. She might not have seen the four of them trying to scare a sense of caution into a schoolgirl. But she'd have heard the screams; nothing wrong with her hearing. Knowing Jude, she'd have run towards the sound, wanting to help. Had Luke given her the warning speech, she'd have fixed her gaze to the left of his face to be certain she didn't miss when she punched him.

Dan could see her throwing the punch, the one he should have given Luke years ago. Before Tess became pregnant with Elise, before Clark was ever a dad. Back when Dan first found out the kind of man Luke was.

Dangerous, conscienceless, unstoppable.

6

I take my time fetching the painkillers. I have the idea he's upset. Part of it is the knife wound I gave him but the greater part is guilt. Grief, too. He knew Elise. Her dad, Clark, is his best friend.

I picture him – Daniel Roake – in the semi where the Franklins lived, enjoying a meal with the family of my murdered girl. Clark's best friend, an eye surgeon, clever with his hands. A good man, once. He hasn't told me what happened to change that but it is connected to Elise's death. It must be.

While the kettle comes to the boil, I open the back door and stand on the step. I do this several times a day; I'm still not used to breathing fresh air or feeling it on my face. At first I had to take sips, afraid of getting drunk.

I've locked the cellar door. Hidden the key in a coffee jar, poking it under the granules with a teaspoon. I do not want to think about the cellar. I made plans – *his turn in prison* – but I cannot bear to be down there. I need to be in the light, breathing fresh air. In the cellar, I was going mad, falling further and further from myself, into my past. Now it is his turn to spend time doing battle with memories he has been trying to outrun. Let's see how he likes it. Not much, is my guess.

'I'm Grace Maddox.'

I whisper it into the garden, my secret still. I don't know why I haven't told him, other than it's too soon. I don't trust him, don't know who he is. He is so many people all at once. It's hard to keep hold of him.

The garden is not at all like the one I conjured in my mind's eye, overgrown by weeds. The weather has been stormy for hours, wind whipping the tops of the trees into a frenzy that sends the crows scattering, crying.

The room where I put him looks out onto the back garden. The shed is a wreck, half gone. My car is parked there, next to his, out of sight of anyone who comes up the potholed lane I took thirteen days ago. I know the date now; I have his phone. He told the truth about the number of days he left me without food and water. Three, not four. And even those were a mistake. He never meant for me to starve. He forgot I was in the cellar.

He's forgotten a lot, too much. It makes me wonder if I have set myself an impossible task. But he's not going anywhere. And he wants to recover what's been lost, to get at the truth no matter how much it hurts. We are alike in that regard. Perhaps in others, also. It is too soon to say for certain.

One thing I know: he boxes things up. How else can he talk about being friends with a man like Luke, 'dangerous, conscience-less, unstoppable,' and in the same breath speak so gently of Jude, a twelve-year-old girl going blind? He's put it all into boxes: his work, Clark and Tess, Elise's murder, the vigil, his reason for luring me here . . . The boxes will be why he's forgotten. His memories are packed and put away, out of reach even before this crisis or breakdown – whatever happened to scatter his mind in a dozen directions.

When the kettle boils, I make two cups of tea, wanting to hear the next part of his story. More than anything, I want to hear about Elise, his memories of her. And about this vigil he is describing: Luke and his brother Owen. Clark. And Daniel himself, of course.

Most murders are committed by someone the victim knows. He must be aware of that fact, but even if he isn't, I am.

I have always known exactly what I am looking for. And I'm in no hurry. I want the whole of his story, even the bits that seem unconnected to Elise. *The devil's in the detail*, as my old dad would have said.

Daniel Roake has scars on his right forearm. They form the rough shape of a Z: a ragged diagonal between two horizontals. I saw his forearms when I was tying him to the bed. The scars look old. Too old to have been made a year ago, when Elise was murdered. Of course, I'm no expert. I don't know how long scars take to heal. But I know about damage. How deep it can go and how it can drive you day after day further and further from who you once were, until one morning you wake to see a stranger in the mirror.

7

Friday again. Dan wanted to call Clark, make an excuse to skip the vigil. Emergency surgery, anything to get out of sitting in the pickup seeing the back of Luke's neck clench as his temper took hold, watching Owen's foot bounce with barely contained adrenaline. What difference would it make if Dan wasn't there? Luke would issue his threat disguised as a warning. Clark would plead with whichever young woman or girl they'd terrorized, conjuring Elise's ghost from the ashes of his grief. It was Elise who held the girls back from reporting them to the police; they felt sorry for Clark. Not for Luke, who got a kick out of scaring them, from the power rush, the threat of violence. Dan didn't want that fate for Owen but if Dan had any sense, he'd stay away. Leave them to it, stick to doing what made an actual difference – his job.

'It's a sterile environment, doc. People've got this idea tattoo parlours are dirty but I've never been any place cleaner. Beats hospital hollow.' Ray Kahn offered his arm for Dan's inspection: the tattoo of a red snake wrapped from wrist to elbow. 'Wouldn't let your kid get one, right?'

'I wouldn't have messed with you before but now . . . ?' Dan held up his hands as if Ray were aiming a weapon at him.

Sitting with Ray Kahn, early last Friday morning, explaining the surgery he would perform, Dan had been stupidly grateful for the chance to feel in control, of use to the world. This follow-up appointment didn't have the same urgency but it beat playing vigilante, under Luke's thumb.

'It's a symbol.' Ray touched the snake's head. 'Life and death.'

'It's great. You're doing fine. Keep up with the exercises, yes?'

Ray flexed his forearm, making the snake's jaw open wide. 'You bet.'

'The eye exercises,' Dan specified. 'What you do in the gym is someone else's business, although if you get any bigger, I'll need a new chair.'

He took a step back reflexively as Ray grinned and stood, filling the exam room. 'See you next time, yeah? I'm thinking monkey.' Patting his right shoulder. 'Up here, tail curling round.' He traced a path for the tattoo, circling his throat with his fist. 'Just a little one, a baby monkey.'

What would Ray Kahn make of the vigil in the pickup? If he knew Dan had gone from the surgery that saved his eye to bullying that girl in Box Lane?

Given the choice, Dan avoided surgery on Fridays. The prospect of the vigil made him over-conscious of his motor skills, particularly the finer ones. He'd been plagued by bouts of vertigo since the vigils first began, five months ago now, taking care to study his hands for tremors, reading the fine print in the Snellen chart to be certain his focus wasn't affected. Needing to know he wouldn't make mistakes his patients would have to live with. He ran these self-diagnostics before performing the surgery that saved Ray Kahn's sight. His hands hadn't shaken once. The vertigo never materialized at work. Like Clark when he was behind the wheel of the pickup, a kind of peace came over Dan when he was in surgery.

Was that why Clark kept going back to Box Lane? For the peace of knowing Elise was there? Because it was where he could be her dad again without having to hide the chaos of emotions he was feeling. Love, loss, rage. Different if they'd caught her killer but they hadn't. He was still out there. Maybe Luke had the right idea, warning girls away from the unlit shortcut. How would Clark feel if another girl was murdered? How would Dan?

8

'Why are you telling me this?' Gwen demands.

Dan shifts tiredly on the bed. 'I thought you wanted to hear about my work. You told me to talk about it.'

'From the sound of it you shouldn't have been leaving the house, let alone performing complicated surgeries. When did this vertigo start?'

'I told you: five months ago. The same time as the vigils.'

'But you kept going into work.' She looks down at him with those chilly grey eyes of hers. 'You're dangerous. A risk-taker.'

'Every surgeon's a risk-taker. I explained the steps I took to make certain my patients were safe.'

'Patients like Jude. What will happen to her?'

'What do you mean?'

'Will you keep seeing her even after she's blind?'

'I won't be allowed to. The hospital asked me to refer her for counselling. She's working with a therapist, Amanda Bowen.' He has to grit his teeth when he says the woman's name.

'What does Jude think about that?' Gwen asks.

I don't need shrinking. My world's small enough already.

'She's angry.'

He remembers another of Jude's T-shirts: *Nella notte buia* in yellow on a navy background. *In the darkness of the night.*

'What's it like for her, going blind?'

'Like . . . grieving, I imagine. The slow loss of focus, of colour, everything that used to be sharp and bright . . .' He blinks at the ceiling. 'She asked me once if she was dying.'

'Is she?' Gwen demands.

'No. But I had to promise her I wouldn't pity her or talk down to her. That's a tougher set of rules than any I'm used to.'

'What caused it? Her blindness. And don't talk down to me.'

'Macular degeneration, inherited probably. The cells of her retinas are worn in places to the choroid. Severe pigment clumping, deformed blood vessels around the nerve heads . . . The damage impairs her ability to perceive detail, to read or write for any length of time without the help of magnifying lenses. Even if she retains decent peripheral vision, she'll be registered blind within the next six months.' Dan is dimly aware of the pain in his own body but it is nothing compared to Jude's pain. 'Until then, she'll have the motion sickness she described, a feeling like falling, of being in a constant state of collapse.'

Gwen is silent for a time. Then she asks, 'Isn't she terrified?'

'Probably, but you wouldn't know it. She asks a lot of questions. Wants to know the names of medical instruments or how the Snellen chart got its name. Likes to be tested on what she's learnt . . .'

'How did the Snellen chart get its name?'

'From Herman Snellen, a Dutch ophthalmologist. He developed the chart in 1862. It's called twenty-twenty vision because twenty feet was the length of the average classroom back then.'

133

'Why did you put me in the cellar, Daniel?'

'I . . . don't know.' Her question came from left field but he understands why she asks it: he is recalling precise details from his training; she's hoping that might kickstart his short-term memory, or else she's testing him, suspects him of lying about what he can and can't remember. 'I'd tell you if I knew. That knife's a fairly sharp incentive.'

'I'd have thought so . . . Do you have twenty-twenty vision?'

'No. Only about thirty-five per cent of people have twenty-twenty vision without glasses.'

'But you have great eyesight. They wouldn't let you do that job if you didn't.'

'It's good enough . . . I had this same conversation with Jude. I was her age, more or less, when I decided I wanted to be an ophthalmologist.'

'You were twelve?'

'Fourteen, actually. But, yes. That's when I decided I wanted to be an ophthalmologist.'

He doesn't tell her why. He has never told anyone that. He's sick to his stomach suddenly, at the thought of the vigil, his role as accomplice to Luke's plans for ending Clark's pain, as if that could be ended by inflicting suffering on someone else. 'If I'd had any guts, I'd have put a stop to it.'

'Put a stop to what?'

'The vigil.' He clenches his teeth against the pain in his hip. 'Insane . . . I was out of my mind, should've stood up to Luke, taken decisive action—'

'You took decisive action two weeks ago,' Gwen says. 'Out there, in the dark.' She nods towards the front of the house where he struck her unconscious as she stepped from her car.

He's hyper-aware of the blood pulsing in his hip. *She is made of knives.* He can't believe she doesn't want revenge. He is tied to the bed, unable to sleep or move to any meaningful extent, but she hasn't hurt him or humiliated him. He is waiting, he realizes, for her to do exactly that.

'Do you remember why you did it?' she asks again.

'No . . .'

It's the truth. She believes him. It is why he's here rather than down in the cellar, or in the ground. He's alive because he hasn't remembered, yet.

'Then you're still out of your mind. Present tense, not past.'

'I am out of my mind. Yes.'

She sizes him up with her stare. 'That's why you like talking about your patients. Ray and Jude. Because there was a time when you weren't out of your mind, when you were good at what you did. A time when you made a difference, when you were a decent person.'

Hurting and humiliating him. He's a fool. She's all over that.

'I expect so.' He turns his head on the pillow. The bed smells of sickness and sweat. He is running a fever, has been for hours.

She reaches for his wrist. 'I'll change the bedding.'

She waits for him to stop cringing before unbuckling the belt. He is wide open to her. As if she's reached inside his head to steal his fears, sneaking them into that shoebox where she keeps whatever catches her eye in the houses she packs. He has to remind himself he took the wrong woman. She isn't Grace Maddox. Not that it matters now.

'I want you to tell me about Elise. And these.'

He's confused, can't feel her fingers around his right wrist until he forces his head from the pillow to look. She is touching his scars. He swallows a sound of distress. She's going to empty him out. Well, he always knew that. Whatever else he has forgotten, whatever form the tiger took when it laid hold of him – he knew it was the end. He chose this path and it is true what they say: you should dig two graves when you go after revenge. She is going to bury him.

Never Events

Never Event (noun): a serious incident or error that should not occur if proper safety procedures are followed

- He should never have lured her here, or knocked her out, or held her prisoner.
- He should never have taken part in the vigils. Five months of vigils. Never have let Luke take charge of anything, everything. Clark, Owen, him.
- Elise should not have died a year ago. That should have been preventable.
- Her killer should never have got away.
- Dan should have been able to comfort his friends, Tess and Clark. He should not have let Clark fall into the trap set by Luke to seek vengeance at all costs. It's already cost Clark his job, might yet cost him his marriage.
- Dan should be able to remember the steps that brought him here. Thirteen days ago now.
- He should never have let the vertigo and panic and the memory loss get this bad. Preventable, all of it.
- What he cannot prevent is what happens next. That's in her hands. Like the knife she used to stop him, the knife she keeps close. She is biding her time, wants to extract his secrets before she exacts her revenge. He doubts she believes in Never Events or if she does, there is only this:
- She will never let him get away with what he did to her.
- Never let him go.
- Never stop.

9

Clark and Tess were seventeen when Elise was conceived, marrying a month before she was born. Dan was fourteen, taking his A levels early, hoping to get the results he needed for medical school. They were all just children really, except Luke who grew up fast and hard while they were in primary school. Owen was two when Elise was born. At her christening, Dan was put in charge of keeping him out of trouble, an easy task since Owen was a placid little boy, proud of the tiny suit and tie his mum insisted he wear. Dan helped him clip the tie in place, sponging ketchup from it when the buffet got in the way of Owen's best efforts to stay tidy. Not long after that, Dan left for university, returning after five years to find everyone changed. New lives, new friends, new priorities.

That year, Luke was twenty-three but he looked older, muscle-bound from manual labour. He made Dan feel weak, pale and pretentious. At school, Dan had been fast-tracked, 'gifted and talented', which sounded impressive but in reality meant he attracted the attention of bullies and spent his time hiding in the library. He was the youngest of the friendship group that formed around Clark's sunny temperament, three years younger than the others, feeling their age difference more acutely when he returned from medical school to find Clark and Luke holding down jobs, Clark with a mortgage and a five-year-old. Elise was a sunny little girl with a gap-toothed smile, wrapping herself around Clark's legs when he introduced her: 'This's my friend, Danny.'

Only Luke had ever called him Danny.

Owen, at seven, was a miniature replica of Luke with a swagger that would've kept the other kids at bay if he hadn't also had a sweet nature. He no longer needed Dan's help staying neat and tidy, favouring his brother's style: tracksuit bottoms and a camouflage jacket, grubby at the elbows. Despite this tough disguise, he was a kind kid, careful and patient with Elise, who loved him in return. She loved everyone, even Dan who'd been a stranger for the first five years of her life. After medical school, he worked placements, not always living at home. Then he was in specialist training: a seven-year slog he'd not long completed when the call came through from Clark about Elise's murder.

'Dan?' Clark's voice was grey. 'She's gone. I can't . . . She's gone.'

By the time Dan reached the house, the police were there. They would be there a lot over the coming days and weeks. Asking endless questions about Elise's friends, possible boyfriends, anyone she'd been scared of or interested in. Clark switched between grief and rage. In the grip of the latter, he turned to Luke, whose anger was never far from the surface.

'We'll find him,' Luke promised, 'and string him up.'

That seemed to help, some of the time. When Clark crashed, he turned to Dan: 'She was special, wasn't she? Even as a teenager. She wasn't like the others with their nails and hair. She was just a little kid, my little girl.'

Clark could talk to him like this because, unlike Luke and Owen, Dan had no real memories of Elise. His grief was for Clark and Tess, that's what Clark believed. But Dan was grieving for Elise, too. He saw her whenever he shut his eyes. Even now, a year after her murder, he saw her.

In those first months while the police were hunting her killer, before Luke decided it was up to them to find him, Dan was haunted by her short life and violent death in the place where he grew up.

Seven months after her murder, Clark was saying, 'She was special, wasn't she?'

Dan had reached out his hand but Clark's phone was ringing and when he answered, Luke was saying, 'We're going to get him. I've got a plan.'

10

'You saw her whenever you shut your eyes?' Gwen studies him from her seat at the side of the bed.

Dan tries to interpret her expression but his expensive training has deserted him. He ought to be able to read clues from her face, or her body language. All he can see is stillness and even that's confused by the distress signals from his own body. She always sits at his left side, within easy striking distance of the knife wound.

'Her face was on the news, that was part of it. But she was in the house, too. Tess and Clark's house. They had photos of her everywhere.'

'You went there?'

'Whenever Clark wanted me to. And Tess asked me, sometimes. It was hard for them, living there after she'd gone.'

'Maybe they should have moved.' Gwen's voice is chilly.

She is losing patience with him, that's how it feels. He tries not to fidget but every part of him hurts, to one extent or another. His left side rings with alarm at the nearness of her knife. She hasn't forgiven him for the cellar. Why would she?

'They did move. Not far. Luke talked them out of that, said they should stay close to where it happened.'

'That was Luke, who talked them into staying close?'

'Yes . . .'

She looks down at him. 'You're tired.'

'It doesn't matter.' He blinks to clear the confusion in his vision. 'Aren't you going to ask me about Grace? Why I did it?'

'When you reach that part of the story. It won't make sense out of context. Easier this way.'

Harder for him to lie, she means. Harder to excuse what he did once she has all the facts at her fingertips. Like the knife. He looks across her shoulder to where the sky lurches against the window. He wishes it was over. Her and him. All of it. It *was* over, until she stabbed him.

'One thing you can tell me.' She folds back the sheet to examine the wound. She does this multiple times a day, a way of marking her place and reminding him who's in charge. 'Who was the person you buried?'

He blinks, retracting his focus from the window. 'What?'

'You said, "I buried the last person who lied to me." Who was it?'

Her stare is like the blade all over again, sharp and jarring. He misses the cellar's darkness, its shadows at his beck and call. She's stripping every one of his defences. He'd thought if he answered her questions, it would be easier. Damage limitation. What a joke. There's no limit in sight.

'My father. He died a year ago. It was his funeral, that's what I meant by buried. I didn't . . . It wasn't a threat, not really.'

She seems to accept this. 'What lies did he tell?'

He moves his eyes away from her face.

142

'What lies, Daniel?'

'It isn't any of your business, is it?'

She absorbs his anger, drinks it up and stands taller. He won't win this battle by being hostile. Apart from anything else, it's exhausting him. He needs all his strength just to stay alive, fight infection, heal the wound in his hip.

'He lied about my mother.'

Gwen waits. Something in her silence warns him to tread carefully. It is easier to read her when his eyes are averted. That makes him think of Jude, the blind spot at the centre of her vision; he can see Gwen more clearly when he looks to one side of her. She is waiting. She can wait a long time.

'About her death,' he says finally. 'How she died.'

'How did she die?'

'She took her own life when I was fourteen. Dad said it was an accidental overdose but it wasn't. She'd been trying to kill herself for years.'

The silence in the room is underscored with static, the buzzing of his blood. He remembers his delusion from days ago, that his parents were alive in this house, Dad wanting his help emptying the bath, Mum in bed upstairs. The past rushing in from all directions to fill the holes in his head.

'Did he help her?' Gwen asks. 'To kill herself.'

'What? *No.* I don't think so . . . No.'

'Did he help you?'

Dan blinks at her in confusion. 'Did he . . . ?'

'Afterwards. If he lied about what happened, how she died, who helped you come to terms with it?'

'No one. But it isn't connected to this, to what I did to you.'

'You were fourteen. Not much older than Elise. A child.'

'I was studying, taking exams. A levels. That helped.'

'Gifted and talented.'

It surprises a laugh from him, unguarded and unhappy.

'Grieving, too,' she says softly.

'Please don't.' He does not want her pity, thinks it might actually kill him. 'It was a long time ago.'

'Fifteen years.'

Is there anything she doesn't know about him, his life?

Your own fault, he thinks savagely, *for taking the wrong woman.* Who did he imagine Grace Maddox was – a killer? Or a killer's confidante? That would have been preferable, to this.

'You lost your mum when you were fourteen. And then your dad died, a year ago. The same year Elise was murdered.'

'I'm not looking for excuses for what I did . . .'

'I realize that.' Her voice is flat, devoid of sympathy. 'You think you should be punished. You're hoping I'll punish you. Then it'll be over.'

He has no answer to that.

'Tell me more about Jude.'

As if she is giving him a gift, a respite from the real questions. She can't know how much it hurts him to think about Jude, who must be imagining he's given up on her, cut his losses and run, leaving her to the dubious care of Amanda Bowen who doesn't understand Jude and is probably writing a paper on her, or perhaps it's simply professional distance, a thing Dan was still learning, something he'll never learn now. It's too late. All that's left is this room and this woman and her vengeance, which he thinks he understands, the only thing he does. But perhaps he is wrong about that, too.

144

11

Amanda Bowen, therapist, made it a rule to determine the extent of any hope she could hold out for her clients, most of whom were children or young people like Jude, who was born sighted but would be blind before her thirteenth birthday. Dr Bowen had called Dan to say, 'I'd like to meet to discuss your prognosis. Jude has started asking questions I can't easily answer, even with your excellent notes to hand.'

Dan knew the questions she meant. Jude had asked him once, 'So if I'm kissing a girl and I can't see her mouth, where'd I aim? For her forehead?'

He did as Dr Bowen requested, submitting to an interview at her clinic on Friday afternoon. He was conscious of the time, didn't want to be late for the vigil. Clark had been on his mind all day.

'You've seen the eyebrow stud, I take it. I'm a little worried what she might do next to demonstrate her independence. Or simply to rebel.'

'Jude isn't independent. Even without the vision loss. She's twelve.'

Amanda Bowen had an emphatic profile, her dark hair lightened in places to mink-brown to match her eyes. Dan was certain she was writing a paper on Jude: *A young girl's journey into darkness* . . . Everything about her was slick, ambitious.

'Jude's very resistant,' she said.

'Yes, she is.' Her raised eyebrows told him he had said the wrong thing. 'I'm sorry, you said resilient?'

'Resistant. I'm finding our sessions a challenge.'

Dan wasn't surprised. He could picture Jude in here, wearing her blackest scowl, a T-shirt with an obscure obscenity. His heart ached for her.

'The way Jude speaks of you . . . I might wish for the same confidence in my ability to help her.'

Dan drank the water he'd been offered, considering the ways in which he might cut this session short. He was in no rush to get to the pickup and sit under Luke's thumb but this was a waste of time. Dr Bowen had no real interest in Jude and therefore no hope of helping her. He wanted to tell her to go to hell. Deeply unprofessional of him, no doubt, but it'd been a long day.

'You're not concerned she might be developing a crush on you? She's at a sensitive age and you're a very good-looking man . . . Oh, I'm sorry. I didn't mean to make you angry.'

'You didn't.'

That was a lie. The water, when Dan drank another mouthful, tasted foul. What she was inferring unsettled him. For five months he had avoided thinking about it but the hormonal fug in the pickup had a flavour beyond rage and grief. Animalistic. Arousal . . . ?

'It's a difficult adjustment for Jude and her mother,' Dr Bowen was saying. 'Her mother tells me she's started to withdraw, spending time in her room sleeping. She didn't notice at first as Jude leaves the curtains open.'

Jude didn't close the curtains because she didn't need to. Surely Dr Bowen realized that much?

'Isn't it usual for teenagers to need a lot of sleep?'

'The pattern seems excessive to her mother. She asked me to make certain there's no underlying condition to account for it.'

'The records are up to date. All Jude's symptoms, the full implications of the diagnosis and prognosis, are in the report you requested.'

Did he sound defensive? Resistant, like Jude? Too bad.

'She's twelve,' Dr Bowen said. 'Under her mother's care . . .'

A fly snarled at the inside of the window. Dan wanted to smoke, a thing he hadn't done in years. He tried to remember how he'd felt when he was twelve and found himself thinking of Elise at that age.

Clark had said, 'She's not like the others with their hair and nails. She was just a little kid, my little girl.'

How had they gone from that to the vigil?

From Amanda Bowen's clinic it took twenty minutes to reach Box Lane. Sitting in a knot of traffic, Dan wondered whether Jude was more tired than usual because of the mobility exercises. She'd just been measured for a cane.

'They come in different sizes?'

'Absolutely. Yours will be exactly right for you, no one else.'

'And colours? Can I get a purple one with flames up it?'

Dan shook his head. 'Has to be white, I'm afraid. It's a signal to other people, especially traffic.'

147

'Run screaming, it's the blind girl?'

'It reminds drivers to slow down. More cars should do that.'

Dan was turning down a side street when a blue Prius cut him off, the two cars coming close to collision. He hauled on the hand-brake, his palms freckled with sweat. The other driver was already out of his car. Knuckles rapped the window by his head. Dan opened it an inch.

'See this?' The man nudged at the wing mirror on Dan's car. 'Mirror-signal-manoeuvre. Fucking-*mirror*-signal-manoeuvre!'

'I checked the mirror. You were coming rather fast, weren't you?'

'I was doing twenty-eight.' He leant in, face knotted with anti-pathy. 'Tops. This is a thirty zone.'

'All right. Well, no harm done.'

The man was spoiling for a fight. Hostility – road rage or what-ever it was, a bad day at the office – squirmed under the surface of his skin. The near-collision was an excuse to lose it, give vent to his frustrations. A car sounded its horn behind them.

'You'll want to move,' Dan said mildly. 'You're right across the road.'

'Thanks to your piss-poor roadmanship.'

Roadmanship. Dan hadn't heard that expression since his dad taught him to drive, years ago. Had this man learnt it from his own father? Was he channelling aggression a generation out of date, kept in cold storage all this time? Anger could do that. Lie in wait for a throw-switch, a random connection bringing an age-old griev-ance explosively up to date.

'Would you take your head out of my window? I'd like to close it.'

'Next time, watch where the fuck you're going!'

'Next time,' Dan promised.

He drove to the junction at the end of the road, glancing back to see the man at the side of the Prius with his head down, feet stamping to get shot of the frustration. The town was full of men like him, barely containing their rage. Luke was the same; perhaps they all were. Clark, Owen, even Dan.

Box Lane was shrouded in rain. It was always raining here. The official explanation was a weather line but to Dan it felt as if Box Lane was trapped in time, forced to re-enact the day a year ago when Elise fought for her life in the mud and litter. The police said she fought. It was one of the reasons Luke was convinced the killer was on the hospital's records: 'He'll have scratches at least. Defensive wounds,' but what sort of fight could a thirteen-year-old put up against violence of that kind?

Dan parked at a distance, walking uphill to where the pickup was waiting. He didn't want to be here but nor could he stay away. It wasn't solely concern for Clark, who was in any case too shut off to be affected by anything Dan did or didn't do. Fear of Luke kept him coming back. Irrational, really. But then nothing about this vigil was rational.

'No coffee?' Luke said when Dan climbed into the back of the pickup.

'The place was shut, short-staffed.' He touched a hand to Clark's shoulder. 'Sorry.'

Luke threw him a can of lager. 'You can thank me later.'

Dan put the lager in the footwell. Next to him, Owen's heel was bouncing. He was on the games console, volume turned low, a

149

whisper of gunfire and explosions. His hoodie was soaked through at the shoulders.

Dan said, 'You okay, kiddo?'

It was Luke who answered: 'He's good.' His voice was a full stop and a threat, warning Dan to back off, mind his own business. Owen bent closer to the console, shutting Dan out.

The rear-view mirror showed a slice of Clark's profile: face slack with the peace that came from sitting here. There was a crumb of comfort in seeing his friend free of the pain that usually tightened his face; Dan tried telling himself that was why he kept coming back. But it was about being part of this, included. And the pickup was a place to bring his day's frustrations – at Dr Bowen for failing to recognize Jude's uniqueness and her courage, at the prick in the Prius – the only place he could put those things down. His parents' house was too full of memories; he should pack up and sell, move away. At the vigil he could shrug off the week's tyranny. He scooped the can of lager from the footwell, opened it and drank a mouthful. Luke threw him a look, part approval, part contempt, the usual thing. Dan was sick of Luke and of this vigil but mostly he was sick of himself.

'We're staying later,' Luke said. 'Today.'

No one asked why.

The rain got darker, thicker. Box Lane began to tick, like a clock, like a bomb. Clark slept, Owen played his war game, Luke watched the mirrors. Dan finished the can of lager, accepting a second one to keep his hands busy. He watched Owen squinting at the console in the half-light and thought of the dilation drops Jude loved so much, her eyes streaming, cheeks flushed and damp. 'It's the colours.' She gave a deep, shattering sigh. 'Best test ever . . . You'll keep doing it, right? Even when I'm totally blind?'

'You won't ever be totally blind. The signs are your peripheral vision will remain intact—'

'Yes, you said. But that doesn't mean you'll stop testing?'

'Unlikely. Your eyes are too interesting. There'll always be someone wanting to look at them.'

Dan had rolled up his sleeves to wash his hands at the sink. When he came back, Jude was leaning sideways in the chair as if she'd lost her balance. He reached to help and her hand found his right forearm. He had to stop himself shaking her off, standing instead very still. She looked at his shoulder but he knew she was seeing his forearm. His scars. Her fingers traced the silver hatchmarks at the inside of his forearm, between his elbow and wrist.

'What happened?' She sounded shocked.

'An accident a long time ago, when I was at school.' He eased his arm from her touch, rolling his sleeve down over the damage. 'Not as serious as it looks. They made a hash of the stitches, that's all. It was a climbing accident on a school trip. Now sit back. Tell me what's so good about the drops.'

She relaxed in the chair. 'Like seeing rainbows. There're fewer than ten rainbows a year, you know. Usually what we see are halos from ice crystals. *Love* rainbows . . . Coronae. Supernumeraries. Moon bows . . .' She wet her lips as if tasting the sound of the words. 'Where was the school trip?'

'Scotland.' The second lie was easier. 'How're things otherwise?'

'Okay, I guess. Did your mum and dad sue the school after you fell?'

'No. Have you had any new headaches?'

'My dad would've sued . . . He wishes there was someone he could sue over my eyes . . . I only get headaches if I read too much.'

'And you're sleeping okay?'

She stretched in the chair. 'All the time.'

'Dr Bowen's worried you're sleeping too much.'

'Only because I won't tell her my dreams. I have the best dreams. I can *see*. Everything. Colours. Details.' She looked up at Dan. 'Do you ever have cool dreams like that?'

'Sometimes.'

Not lately. Not this last year.

Box Lane ran with rain, bringing cigarette ends and empty bottles to the tyres of the pickup. Dan had to stop seeing Jude. He couldn't justify it when there was so little he could do for her. He needed to let go. He set the lager can down in the footwell, pushing the fingers of his left hand into the right sleeve of his sweatshirt. He knew what Amanda Bowen would make of scars of that kind in that place. He wished Jude hadn't seen them. She had a right to be angry, to hate the necessity of counselling, to grieve in whichever way she chose. Let her set fire to the white cane if that was where her anger took her. He'd confirm the absence of headaches, no underlying cause for the excessive sleep patterns. Dr Bowen could figure out the rest of it for herself.

'Shut the fuck up.' Luke twisted in the passenger seat.

Owen was making popping noises in time to the joggling of his foot. He shut up when Luke told him to, pushing the console into the front pocket of his hoodie. Dan tried to catch his eye and smile but Owen was facing away from him, towards the window.

'You know what really sucks?' Jude had told Dan. 'They don't print *Hellblazer* in braille. Eleven thousand braille books but no

Hellblazer. Even if I learn it, I still can't read my favourite stuff. Dr Bowen says, "Maybe this's a chance to discover a world of new favourites!" She doesn't get it. It's *my* life, my whole *life* that's screwed. Not just my eyes. I can't even have laces on my boots. It's all *ruined*. Over.'

'No laces?' Dan repeated. 'That's nonsense. You're not losing the use of your hands. You can fasten laces with your eyes shut.'

'That's not what Mum thinks. She bought me a pair of boots with Velcro, said they were a present but I know what she's doing, she can't help herself. Dumbing down my whole life.' Jude freed her hands from her lap, held them in front of her. 'No more nail varnish, no make-up. Bloody Jane bloody Austen in bloody braille . . .' She was shaking with rage and grief.

Dan put out his hands and took hers, smoothing the skin of her palms with his thumbs, not speaking because there were no words to fix her pain. All those years of specialist medical training and he was no use to her.

'I was just getting started,' she whispered. 'Why doesn't anyone get that? I was just getting started and now it's all over.'

Box Lane hissed with rain, dark.

Dan had the sense of missed time – hours stolen by the vigil. He rubbed a hole in the condensation, peering out at the unlit mouth of the lane. Had there been no one in all this time using the shortcut to the shops? He checked his watch: past seven o'clock, much later than he'd thought. He slid his hand free from his sleeve, away from the glassy feel of his scars. When he looked up, Luke was watching him, mouth carved into a grim smile.

'What?'

'Those fuckers.' Luke was looking across Dan's shoulder.

Dan turned in his seat to see a trio of men coming up the street. Two wore black bomber jackets over jeans, the third a camel-coloured coat with tracksuit bottoms. All three were thickset with crew cuts, late thirties. The man in the camel coat was vaping. When he passed under the street light, his knuckles grinned with sovereign rings.

Luke said, 'Right, we're on.'

As Owen fumbled for the door handle, Dan reached to stop him. 'Don't be stupid—' and Luke turned in the passenger seat to punch Dan's hand from his brother's shoulder.

'We're on!' He slapped at Clark's arm on the backswing. 'This's it, c'mon.'

He was out of the pickup, Owen following as if tied to Luke by a lead. Clark blinked awake at the wheel, meeting Dan's eyes in the mirror.

'Don't,' Dan said. 'Luke's after a fight. He's going to get Owen hurt.'

'Then we'd better help.' Clark scrubbed a hand at his face, opening the driver's door into a squall of rain.

Dan was the last to leave the vehicle, only a beat behind Clark, but the situation was already incendiary. The three men, faces and fists bunched, came at them fast, street light pulling shadows from their cropped heads.

Luke met it dead on, swinging a fist to land a first blow then a second in quick succession, knocking the camel-coated man to the ground as the two in bomber jackets lunged in.

Dan pushed the passenger door open into the path of the nearest man, cutting him off at chest height as he went for Clark, who closed in to kick the man's feet from under him. On the other side of the pickup, Owen was trading blows with the third man, managing to land one but tripping forwards with the force of it, more or less into the man's arms.

Dan swerved around the rear of the vehicle, grabbing the man's arm to shorten a punch to Owen's nose, putting himself between Owen and the assailant. His feet skidded on the wet road but he stayed upright long enough to put his elbow back into the man's chin in a savage rattle of teeth. He went down with the momentum, catching sight of Luke kneeling on the first man's thighs, his fist hitting the man's face, on repeat. Owen ducked past to join him, kicking at the prone man's legs. From the other side of the pickup: the sound of Clark and the third man slugging it out.

Dan rolled away from the second man's foot as it swung for his head, snatching his hand out of the road seconds before the foot stamped down.

Above him: the snap of the knife coming open.

Owen and Luke were panting, the thump of fists and feet coming from either end of the pickup. Dan was pushing upright when the second man's foot connected with the small of his back, pain slamming his kidneys. He rolled with it, came up against the rear tyre, tasting blood and rubber.

Behind him, the attacker's weight was removed abruptly, Luke hauling the man off Dan, punching him to the ground. Grunting, the slam of fists on skin. Owen in the middle of it, kicking viciously, a whooping sound coming up from his chest.

Dan forced his body from the road, out of the way of the booted feet. He scanned the ground for the knife. *There.* Under the offside front tyre. He reached for it, rain making everything a mad blur. Clark was dodging blows from the third man. Dan had no idea who'd pulled the knife. He put his foot on the short blade and bent the weapon at the handle, snapping it, making it safe.

Owen and Luke had finished with the second man. The first was face down in the road, breath clattering in his throat. The third was on his feet, heading into Box Lane.

Luke jerked his head. 'Danny!' pointing after the man.

Clark got there first, disappearing into the shortcut on the heels of the escaping man. Luke and Owen raced after him, abandoning the other two to the road and the rain.

Dan followed, doubling back almost immediately to roll the first man into the recovery position, clearing his airway with two fingers, dropping a broken tooth next to the man's head. He was out of breath by the time he joined the others.

Box Lane was slick with mud that slid under his feet as he reached what looked like a knot of trees in the centre of the shortcut. Not trees. His friends – Clark, Owen and Luke – kicking the shit out of the man who'd tried to escape up here.

'Stop it!' Dan reached for Clark's arm.

'Get in here!' Luke grabbed Dan's wrist, hauling him into the fight, clearing a space for Dan to join them for his fair share of the violence they were meting out.

The man twisted, panting at their feet, trying to protect his head and crotch. He looked like a big fish flopping in the slop of wet mud.

Dan freed his wrist from Luke's grip, reaching for Clark again. 'It's enough! You've done enough. Let him . . . *Stop.*'

Luke spun Dan at the hip, shoving him to arm's length. In the dark gully of the lane it was impossible to see anything clearly but the whites of Luke's eyes blazed as his balled fist struck Dan in the ribs, punching the air out of him, landing him flat on his arse in the stream of water that ran down the centre of the lane and out into the road where the pickup was parked. Owen and Clark didn't notice or didn't care, just carried on kicking until everyone's breath was as ragged as Dan's and the man on the ground wasn't moving.

'Yeah!' Owen was saying. 'Yeah!'

When even he fell silent, Luke said, 'C'mon.' He scooped Dan up, shoving him in the direction of the road.

The other two men were long gone.

Clark headed for the driver's side of the pickup, Owen for the nearside back. Their usual seats. The street light turned the road silver. All four of them were stained with mud and blood.

Luke dropped an arm across Dan's shoulder, laughing low in his chest. 'That arsehole! He's going to need fucking crutches just to get back up!'

The nearness of him – musk, skin, cigarettes – was a worse punch than the one he'd landed in Dan's ribs. He turned away, sliding free from Luke's grip, reaching for the chrome bar at the rear of the pickup, leaning his weight into it. The truck's logo glinted at him: *Animal*. Heat shimmered behind his eyes. He wanted to vomit, to fall to his knees and howl. Instead, he did exactly what the others did. Climbed into the pickup and let Clark drive away.

Clark was halfway to Luke's house before he said, 'Shit, your car.' He met Dan's eyes in the mirror.

'It doesn't matter,' Dan said. 'I'll get it in the morning.'

'I'll drop you home in that case.'

'They started it.' Luke was rolling a cigarette. 'If we get asked.'

'Right,' Clark said.

'They started it,' Owen agreed.

Only Dan didn't speak. Until Luke twisted in his seat to stare at him. Then he nodded, despising himself, despising all four of them.

After Clark had dropped Luke and Owen at home, he turned the car in the direction of Dan's house. Neither of them spoke until Dan climbed from the pickup. 'Call me when you get home?'

Clark said, 'It's late and I need a shower. See you, mate.'

Dan stood in the street until the pickup was out of sight. The closed look of his parents' house put its own blunt pain under his ribs.

As soon as he was inside, he staggered, vision swimming, sweat lining the palms of his hands. He sat on the bottom step of the stairs, putting his head on his knees until the dizziness subsided. The air in the house was too thin to breathe. He laboured after it a long time, his body burning from his temples to the balls of his feet. He needed to get clean and sleep. If he stayed like this much longer, he was going to lose it. Lose all pretence that he could function as a human being, as someone who didn't want to put his fist through the glass of every window in this house. His tongue found a raw patch on the inside of his cheek. He lined his teeth up and bit there until he tasted blood.

The next morning, his skin itched and his eyes ran until he couldn't see. In the bathroom, he filled a basin with cold water, lowering his face to its surface, afraid of igniting the migraine that was flaring above his right eye.

When he straightened, he avoided his reflection then forced himself to look, needing to quantify the damage. His jaw tightened as he considered his reflection. His skin was grey, the whites of his eyes jaundiced. He stank of lager, its toxins pushing through his pores, stippling the surface of his skin.

Pulling a sweatshirt over his head, he leant into the sink, seeing the silvering of scar tissue on his right forearm, hearing Jude's voice in his head.

I was just getting started and now it's all over.

12

'You lied to her,' Gwen says. 'To Jude. About the scars.'

This is what she picks out of everything he confessed. Skipping over that night of violence, back to Jude. No, back to *him*. His scars. His lies.

'How did you get them, really?'

'I . . . can't. Not yet.'

Not ever, he wants to say. But that's no good, she won't accept that. If his head were a tin can and all she had was a teaspoon, she would find a way to open it. Who is she? Why is she doing this?

'Tell me about Luke,' she says next.

Same answer. Not yet. Not ever.

'Why did he initiate that attack? I thought the point of the vigil was warning girls to stay out of Box Lane.'

'The point was revenge. Not even that. Violence . . . With Luke, it is always about violence.'

'Is that why you did this?' She makes a gesture that includes the pair of them, the house, the cellar. 'Because of Luke?'

'I don't understand . . .'

'Was it his idea? *Grace Maddox*. Or yours?'

160

He can't answer, can't separate the words from the mess in his mind. He can taste the mud and blood from the fight with the three men whose names he never knew. Is that when he lost his mind? Leaving it in the litter of Box Lane with whatever small claim he once had to honesty, decency?

'Luke punched you,' Gwen says. 'Was he violent with the others, too? Clark or Owen?'

'No. Not . . . that I saw.'

Owen followed Luke's lead, never a step out of line, but that was hero worship, not fear; Dan had never smelt fear on Owen.

'Luke cares about them. Owen's his brother, Clark's his friend. He thought the vigil was helping, probably thought the same about the violence.'

Gwen lets this sit for a second. He has a flash of memory from his childhood: a seaside arcade, feeding coins into slots, 'Penny Falls', watching the coins crowd, shoving closer to the edge. She is like that, gathering each piece of information from him until she has enough to pay out, pay back. He keeps feeding her like a fool, unsure where the value lies, not knowing which piece of information is the one she is after, to tip this impasse into open warfare. The knife is right there, like an extension to her hand.

'Was Luke violent with women? You've implied it. Shannon, his girlfriend. Maybe his daughter, Taylor. From what you've said, he doesn't think much of women. Was he ever violent with Tess, or Elise?'

'No.' Dan goes with his gut reaction then tempers it, wanting to tell the truth: 'Not that I saw. He loved Elise, everyone did.'

'Not everyone. Unless you think her killer loved her. Some people do kill for love. Is that what happened to Elise?'

161

Her voice is light, as if her question is inconsequential. But he senses it is not. She has hit the heart of why they are here. What she wants to know, what she thinks *he* knows. *Elise.* Is this about Elise?

Light snaps from the knife. 'Answer my question, Daniel.'

'I never saw Luke hurt her. He and Owen were always over at Clark's place. Tess trusts them, she cooks for them, for Owen. And Luke fixed up the boat for Elise; she liked to hang out there at weekends and holidays.'

'The boat?'

'A narrowboat, on the canal.' Pictures burst like flashbulbs in his head. 'An hour or so from here, out of town. Clark's dad's boat. No one lives there now. They can't sell it, no one wants to buy a boat around here; we're all too sick of the rain to want water. Luke looks after it. Elise loved it there.'

'Daniel, why are you crying?'

'I'm not . . .'

'Yes,' she says softly. 'You are.'

His face is wet, it's true. The tears are reflexive, the kind that come when you stub your toe, or after dilation drops. The tears aren't for Elise, or not just for her. They're for Jude and Clark and Tess and Owen. For his patients and his parents, even for Gwen. And Dan – the boy he was back then, the summer he turned fourteen. The summer spent on the narrowboat.

The Facts As I Know Them

- Elise was killed a year ago. She was sunny, happy. Everyone loved her, maybe even her murderer.
- She was strangled in Box Lane.
- The killer took her pendant.
- The killer has never been found.
- The narrowboat belonged to her grandfather, Clark's father.
- Luke fixed it up for Elise. She used it in the holidays.
- Daniel does not want to think about the narrowboat. He disappears when I ask about it. Pain puts a shadow so dark it is like a fracture running down his face.
- He's clever. Gifted and talented. If his head was working properly, he'd have worked it out by now. Who I am. Why I am asking all these questions about Elise and the others.
- Both his parents are dead. His mum took her own life when he was fourteen. His dad died the same year Elise was murdered.
- Luke lives for violence. Daniel is afraid of him. He disappears when he says Luke's name, or when he hears it.
- Jude brings him back, the thought of her courage. He was helping her even when he felt helpless. He was a good man. Maybe he still is.
- He still does not know who I am.
- He has a hole in his memory, can't remember that night – or won't.
- But I remember. Like the glass caterpillar with the chipped nose, I have his memory safe.

13

A new morning, another day. How many now? Fourteen? Fifteen? He's lost count. The pain is deep in his hip, as if something small and sharp-toothed is trying to claw its way out. It shocks him; it's been hours since he felt the knife wound so keenly. He blinks at the window, wishing he could turn onto his side, the way he usually sleeps. But he should be grateful to her, all the same. In spite of the belts and the hardness of the bed, the bottles he fills and she empties; these humiliations are nothing compared to the shame he felt before. He hadn't known how to end it, this madness he started. It needed her to do it, someone with an unwavering hand and a clear aim.

As soon as she opened her eyes at him, he knew she wasn't Grace – was not the woman he'd expected. She is small and strong, her wrists roped with muscle. Her head is neat, hair clipped close to her skull. With her heart-shaped face, the waxy perfection of her eyelids, she's a modern-day Joan of Arc in a flannel shirt and dirty jeans. When he carried her down into the cellar she seemed to grow lighter, bird-like by the time he laid her on the mattress. Unconscious, she looked forgiving, her head wound bloodless, not even a bump for his fingers to find as he checked for the edges of the harm he'd done. He had never hit anyone over the head before, let alone a woman. He knew what his dad would say, his mum, too. Luke would have laughed and thumped his arm, told him to get on with it, this thing he'd started. Day One and he was already wavering, regretting the harm he'd done. 'Get on with it, stud.'

He wishes he could remember what he thought he was doing bringing her here, holding her prisoner. He planned it, he must have done. Bought blankets and a camping toilet, insulated food bags, unreeling an extension cable for a dehumidifier to rid the cellar of damp. He has this idea Luke was with him the whole time, standing at his shoulder, 'She doesn't deserve any of this,' but Luke didn't mean the prison Dan was making. He meant the towels and pillow, the effort Dan was putting into making the prison less awful.

Dan was not a monster. He told himself that every day. Standing in the kitchen pouring hot soup into a Thermos for her lunch, 'I am not a monster,' and again at the end of the day, looking out across black fields to a dying sky, 'I am not a monster.' It was hardest first thing in the morning, waking in the sleeping bag in the cold room (he wasn't getting comfortable here any more than she was), trying to remember what he was doing, to reinforce his resolve, 'I am not a monster,' with Luke dropping an arm across his shoulders, no less heavy for being an illusion, 'Sure, mate, whatever. But today, yeah? You need to make her talk today. Make her tell you what she did.'

Because Grace Maddox knew something, Dan was sure of it. She knew whatever it was he'd forgotten. And she was dangerous. Deadly. For nearly two weeks, he convinced himself the real monster was in the cellar. He fed her, kept her safe, waiting until she gave up her secrets. The woman who made this bed, dressed the wound in his hip – *her* wound in his hip – was a stranger. But Grace Maddox? He had been certain she was the monster he was seeking. If he could only remember how, or why.

'I am not a monster,' as he opened the door into her darkness.

'I am not the monster,' with her bright eyes staring up at him. Sitting so still on the mattress, making herself small, arms around her knees, the pale heart of her face betraying no quiver of fear.

She was strong, he'd known that. Somehow. Before she carried him to this bed, made him comfortable in a way he hadn't wanted, would never have allowed himself to be. He doesn't deserve comfort, or care. He deserves to suffer for what he did, even if he cannot remember what that is. Even if he isn't a monster, he is a long way from a good man. Too far to turn back.

Luke would have laughed, slung an arm across his shoulders, knuckled the crown of his head. He had always been taller, bigger, stronger than Dan. Older, too. Ever since school Dan had felt that age gap between him and the others ('gifted and talented', what a joke). In the house with her now he feels ancient. Used up, worn out. There isn't any way out of this.

So yes, he is grateful for the knife that ended their deadlock. He was afraid he'd try to run from what he'd started, leaving her to rot in the cellar. Let God punish her, he thought wildly, a week into the nightmare.

There is no running now.

No escape, for either of them.

He is sleeping when she brings the tray of food. She sets it down, draws the curtains, lets daylight crowd the room. Dan turns his head away. Her stab wound grinds in his hip but he's glad of it, holding him in the here and now. She wants him back in the past. She doesn't understand digging under that rubble will bury the pair of them.

'This looks bad.' She is changing the dressing, frowning. 'I need your help. You need to tell me if it's infected and, if so, what I have to do.' She takes the belt from his right wrist. Waits for him to lever himself onto his elbow, enough to see the mess under the dressing.

It looks about as bad as he expected but no worse. 'It's fine. If it was infected, you'd smell it.' The only thing he can smell is the rest of his body, sour and unwashed. He thinks with brief longing of a warm bath.

'I'll bring hot water and towels.' She is smearing antiseptic cream onto a fresh dressing. 'You can wash yourself, or I can.'

Dan lowers himself onto the pillow, returning his wrist to the bed frame for her to belt it. When she doesn't, he feels a rush of panic, turning his head to look at her.

'I trust you.' She finishes with the fresh dressing, moves to free his left wrist. She fastens the empty belts to the bed frame to prevent them falling to the floor. He is very conscious of her eyes on his scars. 'There's toast, on the tray.' She clears away the soiled dressing and goes, leaving him alone in the room with his hands free for the first time since she stabbed him.

He lies blinking at the ceiling, aware of gripping the bed frame, fingers fretting with the loose fastening of the belts. He lifts his right hand to block out the light, sees the scars she wants him to explain. He shuts his eyes in a bid to blank out the damage, wanting to blank out everything. The past fifteen years of his life. He wants it gone. Enough of it is missing – the days before he lured her here, and the ones before she stabbed him. But it is still too much. Mum's suicide. Dad's death. Elise's murder. Lies he's told. Truths he's kept hidden. *The smooth decking on the narrowboat, sun splashing through the windows, fast breathing, a jolting in his chest.* There is more of him on that boat than here in this room but it is still too much. He wants to be less. If he cannot be whole . . . he wants to be less.

She brings the promised hot water and towels. Helps him remove the T-shirt, wets and wrings two hand towels but makes no attempt to assist with the rest of the task. He's grateful, again. She is very good at making him grateful. He washes his face and neck, scrubbing his armpits and groin as far as he is able to reach without compromising the knife wound. After that, he washes his hands with the second towel, the knuckle of each finger, his wrists and forearms, wetting a corner of the towel to soak away the dirt lodged under his fingernails. He wonders what he's washing himself for exactly. But it feels good to get clean. When he's finished, she clears it all away, coming back to sit with him as he eats toast, drinks a cup of tea. He owes her something for the fact his hands are free and he can no longer smell his own sweat.

'My mother,' he offers.

'Luke,' she says.

As he hands back the empty plate and cup, she dips her head a fraction as if she can hear something in his silence, some strain of music or madness that he cannot hear. 'Your mother, then.'

14

She hadn't locked the bathroom door, that's what Dan remembers chiefly of his mum's first attempt at suicide, the first he witnessed. The unlocked door suggested an invitation. He'd thought she left it like that so she could be saved, wanting him to play the hero, burst in and rescue her. It wasn't until years later that he understood all she'd wanted was a witness. Someone to see the black pit she'd fallen into and couldn't climb free from.

He was twelve. It was a Sunday. Sundays had a different shape to the rest of the week. You got up when you felt like it, fended for yourself. From the age he could open the fridge, he was left alone on Sundays, could spend the day in his pyjamas, watch TV, go into the garden and get as dirty as he liked, which was never very dirty because he didn't trust the freedom, suspecting a test or consequence he couldn't see. From the age of eight, he was expected to take his turn tidying, cooking meals, washing clothes. It was a commune on Sundays, a valve on the week's stress, a day when breakages didn't have to be paid for. *Hypocrite's charter*. Dan hated Sundays.

That Sunday, he was supervising the boiling of rice in the

kitchen. It was 5 p.m., Dad in the garden, Mum running a bath. She had a collection of bath oils in glass jars on a mirrored shelf. When he heard the noise, Dan knew straightaway it was the bottles being smashed. He didn't like to leave the rice. If she'd broken a bottle, she'd want to clear it up herself, she hated fuss. When the crashing didn't stop, he switched off the gas under the rice and went to the foot of the stairs. 'Mum?'

More crashing. A noise like wind through a nylon kite. He ran up the stairs, knocked on the bathroom door.

'Mum?'

Water thrashing, slopping onto the floor. He tried the handle and the door opened. He hadn't thought it would. She was in the bath, underwater, her hair clotting the surface. The mirrored shelf was smashed. The bathwater was brown. He understood straight-away that she'd cut her wrists.

He pulled the plug, grabbing a handful of her hair to bring her head above the surface of the water. She was wide awake, her eyes open. She reached for his face, bringing it close to hers. 'I love you' – water leaked from her mouth and nose – 'more than anyone. You're the one I love the most . . .'

The water made her heavy, too much for him to hold. The bath was draining too slowly. She'd drown in a foot of water. People did that.

'Mum! Get out!'

He pulled at her but the water pulled back. Holding her under would've been easier. That wasn't right – easier to drown her than save her – gravity should be on your side when you're trying to do the right thing. He heaved. Water slapped over the side of the bath, drenching his legs. A rainbow slick of oil sat on its surface, peeling like a transfer onto her skin whenever he got her high enough. He'd never have been able to get her out if Dad hadn't come.

'Get her legs.' He put his hands in Mum's armpits. 'Dan, get her feet.'

They heaved her free from the bath, Dad kicking at pieces of broken glass, knocking them out of the way. 'Towels.'

Dan pulled two bath towels from the door. Dad pressed one to the cuts on her wrists. Not deep cuts, too near her hands. Even at twelve, Dan knew that. She was babbling, wet running down her face so he couldn't tell if she was crying, her mouth made strange shapes – *smiling*. She was smiling. She smelt funny, feverish. He discovered later it was gin. A lot of neat gin, helping her make this mess. He stayed with her while Dad called an ambulance. When he came back, Dad said, 'Get her a pair of pants,' but it was impossible to work the underwear up her wet legs. The cotton kept rolling back on itself, making a twisted band that was hard to unravel. 'I can't manage this.' Dan felt desperate. The knickers were just above her knees. She'd looked less naked without them. Dad swapped places, putting him in charge of the towels around her wrists. He pulled up the pants, his sweat adding to the perfume of the bathroom. Dan was frantic with worry for him. 'It doesn't matter, does it? The ambulance won't care if she's dressed or not.' He ducked from her reaching hands, awful smile. '*She'll* care,' Dad said, hitching at the wet cotton.

The hospital had a sweet smell, intimidating. The police were there. 'Standard procedure,' a nurse told Dan. They gave Mum fluids. Straightaway she became coherent, apologetic: 'I had this feeling of time moving at the wrong pace, too slowly, nothing ever getting better, getting done . . .' She'd broken the mirrored shelf with her elbow; the skin over the bone had to be glued back together. The nurse gave Dan a sandwich from a vending machine, 'To keep your strength up.' He ate it then threw it up in the hospital toilet.

They referred Mum to a psychologist and discharged her. Back home, Dad put her to bed. 'I'll clean the bathroom,' Dan offered.

He wrapped the broken bottles in newspaper before putting them into a bin bag. The worst part was trying to get the oil out of the bath; he used nearly a bottle of bathroom cleaner, the chemicals burning his eyes. With a spoon handle, he removed what was left of the mirrored shelf, making it safe. When all the fragments were on the floor, he sat and looked at them, trying to see what she'd seen. He shivered. She'd broken her own rule: no fuss. He checked the lock on the bathroom door: it worked. She'd chosen not to lock the door before she did this. When the bathroom was tidy, he emptied the ruined rice into the bin and scrubbed the saucepan clean.

'She's sleeping.' Dad came downstairs. 'She's okay now.'

'She didn't lock the bathroom door.'

'What did you do with the broken glass?'

'It's in the bin. I wrapped it up first.'

'Good. That's good.'

Dan wanted to ask why she did it but the look on Dad's face shut him up. *You're the one I love . . .* He didn't feel loved. He felt punished.

For years, he failed to make sense of the unlocked door, the shallow cuts near her hands. He repeated the cliché he knew about suicide: 'A cry for attention.' It was years before he realized she'd wanted a witness. Not just to her unhappiness or her struggle but to her love and her life. Everything.

He got away by going to university, studying to become an eye surgeon, the longest and most complicated degree he could find. Studying every day except Sundays when he stayed in bed staring at the desk where his books were piled, struggling to breathe, waiting for Monday to come and rescue him. During holidays, he stayed away from home. Dad didn't seem to mind. No matter how they couched it, their past was pushy, pitiless; Dan had taken care not to let it bully its way into his present. Now he wondered if the past had made a coward out of him.

Living in that house as an adult, he found it hard to get up on Sundays, showering on Saturday night so he could avoid the bathroom the next day. He went running, up into the hills or along the towpath that took the canal out of town. Hating Sunday had become a habit; a day of freefall when you fended for yourself and breakages didn't need to be paid for.

15

'I'm sorry,' Gwen says.

'It was a long time ago.' Dan is exhausted, wants to sleep. 'And it's still not an excuse for what I did to you.'

'Tell me something she liked. Your mum. What did she like?'

'She liked all shades of blue.' Paul Klee's paintings, cursives like words. And black, except black isn't a colour.

'What was it like when she died?' Her questions are pitched low and gentle but each one drives into him, precise as a scalpel.

'It was a relief.' The exhaustion is like a fever. He can't imagine ever getting clean or cool again. He wants to be clean. Then he remembers: she let him wash. He is clean. 'She'd been failing at it for years.' He tries to be accurate, stick to the facts. 'At least two that I know of. Two years of trying, I can't remember how many times. She bounced back, always. It's how it is with manic depression: the highs are as scary as the lows. You can't trust any of it because none of it lasts. I suppose you'd say she was happy, between attempts. But I never got over that first time.' He draws a shallow breath. 'What no one tells you about suicide is the failed attempts feel the same as the real thing. The terror's the same and the distress. The fear they'll do it again. *Knowing* they'll do it again. That never goes away. That's what I meant by relief, not that I was glad.'

'Tell me something good you remember about her.'

He's too tired to protest about his privacy. This pain is old in any case, safer than the pain he feels for Elise. 'She loved art. The places she took me . . . Underground art shows, exhibitions by ex-convicts. All art is struggle . . . Every painting should contain a little poison, that's what she believed.'

All art is struggle. Trying to connect to her – to make sense of who she was and what she wanted from him – had been Dan's struggle for as long as he could remember. Dad had protected him from a lot of it but he'd worked night shifts, even after Dan told him how much he hated being left alone with her, dragged to look at art he didn't want to see. It was where he chose to go, he remembers with a shock, after she died. Underground. Car parks, underpass tunnels – it was where he felt safest. He can guess what a psychiatrist would make of that, what Amanda Bowen would say.

'Didn't she try to get help?' Gwen asks.

'Yes, but she hated pills, didn't believe she was sick. Most of the time she was functioning well enough for other people to believe that. No one but us saw what she was like when she wasn't functioning.'

'What did she have against pills?'

'She said she couldn't swallow them.'

But she'd managed thirty-eight anti-depressants when Dan was thirteen. He took a physics textbook with him in the ambulance, trying to revise with her stomach being pumped noisily next to him. He feels a jolt of love for her, a sudden rush of uncomplicated grief. It scares him. He tries to claw back neutral ground . . .

'She didn't believe she had a problem, just that she was wired differently to the rest of us. She could be very rational; it was hard to win an argument with her. And she believed she was doing a great job of raising me, giving me more freedom than the average kid. Lack of control was her way of controlling me, maybe.'

Gwen sits with this idea in her hallmark silence. Then: 'So you became a surgeon. An ophthalmologist, specializing in how we see the world.'

'I get it.' Dan shuts his eyes. 'You're a great therapist and I need one, clearly, to have done what I did. But can I sleep now? I'm knackered.'

He doesn't tell her the real problem. The real problem is slouched at the foot of the bed rolling a cigarette, asking where his fucking guts are, why he's lying here like a little bitch when his wrists are free and she's *right there*, within striking distance. *Are you going to be a little bitch about this?*

'You don't think it's more than a coincidence, the career you chose? After everything you'd lived through, all you'd seen?'

'All seeing's painful. Light entering the eye . . . It's an intrusion.'

Luke leans his pelvis into the foot of the bed and laughs.

Never Events

- He should never have come home after university.
- Never have been here a year ago when Elise walked into Box Lane in the rain.
- Never have joined the vigil, the violence. Five months of violence, leading him here.
- He should certainly never have let the vertigo get so bad it affected his memory like this.
- Never have taken her, or held her prisoner.
- Never survived her knife attack.
- Never lived to let her take her revenge like this. Day after day drilling him with her questions while he hallucinates a man who was never his friend or Clark's and who is to blame for at least some of this if only Dan could get his memory back. Remember. Before it's too late.

The Facts As I Know Them

- Elise was murdered in Box Lane. The killer took her pendant.
- She spent time on the narrowboat. Luke fixed it up for her.
- Daniel won't talk about Luke. He sees him sometimes, I think, here in the house. He's terrified of Luke. I don't know why. Preferred to give me his mum's story despite what it revealed of the damage that runs through him.
- His mum was secretive, silent, complicated. I expect it's why he thought he needed to put me in the cellar to make me talk; he thinks women are stitched shut.
- But he is the one whose secrets are hidden, out of sight.
- He cannot remember that night.
- He needs to remember that night.
- I have his memories safe, the night on the narrowboat. A skid of feet on the towpath, shadow at the window, all torso and shoulders. The hems of my jeans, afterwards, heavy with dirty water.

16

'My life sucks.'

'Jude . . . Let's talk about why you feel that way. What's troubling you?'

'Being here's *troubling* me. At least in school I'm learning something.'

'You're learning about the cane. Daniel has shown you how to use it.'

'Yeah, you know what? It's *my* life. I get to say whether it sucks.'

'Let's talk about the cane.' Amanda Bowen smiled. 'It's the right height, Daniel says it's exactly right.'

Jude drew her face into a scowl, curling her feet under her, so angry it hurt Dan's chest to look at her.

'Jude, these sessions are for you. It's your time, to say what you want.'

'I want my life back. To not be blind.' Jude shoved a hand out, knocking the cane to the carpet. 'To be left alone's what I want. No one'll ever just *leave me alone.*'

Mrs Horning moved to pick up the cane but Dr Bowen stopped her. 'Let Jude do it. She wants to feel less dependent. Isn't that what you want, Jude? Please pick up the cane, in case it trips someone.'

Dan felt a surge of revulsion for Bowen's bullying tactics. Jude located the white stick, propping it at the side of her chair. The attempt had subdued her, anger elbowed out of her face by a numb look of acceptance: this was the limit of her independence. Her mum said, 'Well done, love.'

'Yes, well done.'

Dr Bowen's smile was fronted by expensive teeth. Dan entertained a fantasy of breaking one of the teeth, recoiling in the same breath; the vigil was a slippery slope, its violence like an infection in his blood. He had thought he could split his life in two – his work on one side, the vigil on the other – but he should have stayed away. After Friday, he belonged on Luke's side of the line. Far away from Jude and his other patients, from everyone who mattered.

The day after the vigil turned violent, Luke had summoned them to his favourite pub, not far from Box Lane. Dan was collecting his car when the call came through. Seeing Luke's name on the screen made his vision blur. He considered ignoring the call but what was the point? Luke knew where he lived, where he worked, where he went. He picked up. 'Yes?'

'Puddle Duck. Soon's you can make it.'

'I'm working.'

'You're lying. Puddle Duck. First round's on me.'

Dan threw the phone onto the passenger seat, starting the engine. By the time he reached the pub, last night's fear had given ground to anger, blood pricking at his wrists. Luke had brought the whole thing down, thrown away any pretence the vigil was helping, and for what? Because he had itchy fists?

In the Puddle Duck, he headed for a poorly lit corner, its walls knuckled with horse brasses. Luke was sprawling in a chair facing the bar, laughing. Owen was a mirror image, his legs kicked out under the table. Clark glanced up, a shadow crossing his face when he saw Dan. It was the clothes; Dan had made himself put on a suit, some idea about looking respectable, calling into the hospital later to mark his place for next week's work. The others were dressed in tracksuit bottoms and hoodies. Luke wore the old army jacket, Owen the split trainers. All three had grazed jaws, puffy knuckles. Dan had bruises on his ribs (Luke's bruises), in the small of his back and on the elbow he'd used to fight off one of the men but his face wasn't marked and his hands were clean. He was the only one reminding Clark life wasn't about bare-knuckle fights and pints of beer in the middle of the morning.

'Took your time,' Luke said. 'It's your round.'

Dan nodded, looking at Clark. 'What'll you have?'

'Get me a coffee?' Clark scrubbed at his hair. 'And some tap water.'

'Kiddo?' Dan put his hands on the back of the empty chair. 'Get you a Tango?' It'd been Owen's favourite drink for years. Elise's favourite, too.

'Piss off.' Luke pushed his hands into his pockets, his eyes on Dan. 'He's drinking Carling, same as the rest of us.'

Owen punched at his console, head down. 'Carling.'

'Same here.' Clark slid his eyes from Dan, back to Luke.

Luke gave a laugh, kicking a foot at the chair Dan was holding. 'Manage that, can you? You uptight prick.'

Dan measured out a smile. 'I can manage, thanks.'

You out-of-control arsehole.

'Wouldn't want you running to the police because things got a bit handy last night.'

'I don't suppose you would want that, no.'

'Any one of those fuckers could've been the one who did her.'

Clark made a movement that was pure pain, shoulders and mouth flinching. Of the six empty glasses on the table, Dan wanted to bury at least one in Luke's face.

'That wasn't why you started it, though, was it?' He looked Luke in the eye. 'You started it because you were bored, wanted to punch someone. And that's fine if you want to go to prison, good. Go ahead. Just don't drag him there,' nodding at Owen, 'or him,' nodding at Clark.

'Piss off and get the drinks.' Luke shoved up from the table. 'I'm going for a slash.' He dropped a hand to Clark's shoulder. 'Any one of them, mate, could've been. I've got your back.'

A glass was no good, wouldn't even scratch the surface of Luke's lies. What Dan needed was a chair, or a window. He paid for the drinks, carrying them to the table. Went back for glasses of tap water, bags of crisps, peanuts.

Owen opened the nuts, tipping them into his hand. Clark reached for a glass of water. 'Thanks . . .'

Luke hadn't returned. Dan cleared the empty glasses out of his way, sitting down as his phone buzzed with a text message.

'Outside, important,' from Luke.

Dan ignored it, splitting open a packet of crisps and pushing it towards Owen. 'You okay, kiddo?' Owen grunted.

Luke's second text said simply, 'Clark.'

Clark was on his phone, looking as bleak as Dan had seen him in the twelve months since Elise's murder. Perhaps even Luke had noticed the danger signs. He climbed to his feet. 'Back in a bit.'

The sting of brick was what he remembered most clearly, afterwards. Cold and unyielding against his cheek, a sensation like the pressure from a thousand needles. Brown brick, chipped with age, ugly with graffiti – a wall around the back of the pub, away from the doors and street, the sound of the bar a distant yammer as his body heat bled into the bricks, leaving him chilled.

Luke had grabbed him as he turned the corner, hauling his arm by the wrist until his hand was between his shoulder blades, fastening fingers at the back of Dan's neck, the pressure threatening and frighteningly familiar. Blood thumped in his temples, the wall swimming, everything fracturing until he wondered who the hell he was and where and why. *Vertigo.* He'd been suffering it since the vigil started. It never went away, just hid behind whatever cloud cover he managed to muster to get through a day's work, sliding out under fear's fierce searchlight.

Luke put his teeth against the side of Dan's neck, close to his ear and hissed, 'Are you going to be a little bitch about this?'

'Luke . . .'

'Are you?' He ground his crotch against Dan's arse. 'Because every hole's a goal, Danny boy. You remember that.' He punched his fist into Dan's shoulder then stepped away.

Dan felt the thin skin over his cheekbone tear as his feet slipped. He had to grip the wall to stay upright. When he turned, Luke was gone. Back inside the pub, to Owen and Clark.

17

'He threatened you. And he punched you.'

Dan needs to sleep, to be unconscious. Why won't she let him sleep? His head is too heavy, his jaw like glass. His body feels alien, untrustworthy. He is repelled by his weakness, the way his bones stand out. He cannot control the trembling in his fingers. Reluctantly, he identifies the ache in his throat as the effort of holding in tears: a dumb, macho reflex.

'Why do you care? About any of this? I don't mean what I did to you – of course you care about that. But Luke and Elise. Why does it matter to you?'

She looks down at him. 'You really don't know, do you?'

'I don't, I really don't.'

'If you had to hazard a guess then.' The light is behind her, setting a steely halo around her head. 'You must have thought about it.'

'I made a mistake, taking you. I'm paying for it now, though. I know you want revenge, I understand that. It's the rest of it I don't understand.'

'Talk to me about the narrowboat.'

'What?'

She's vertigo in human form, making his head spin with her questions, the way she pivots, picking off the parts of his past he has worked hardest to forget. She is a never-ending Never Event.

'You said Luke made the boat safe for Elise. Did you spend much time on it? The summer you were fourteen, you said.'

Did he say that? He can't remember, half suspects her of drugging him: pills in the endless cups of tea, bottles of water she brings. He is thirsty all the time. He thought it was fever but it's too constant for that and anyway, the wound isn't infected. His body heals quickly, always has. The scars on his forearm healed in under a week. Easy to keep them hidden, at home and at school. He bunked off PE, got detention, spent it studying. The downside to detention was Luke was invariably there. Clark too, sometimes. Dan hardly ever got detention on account of being an uptight prick or in the school's parlance 'gifted and talented'. If he'd been less of a prick, he'd have failed the tests to avoid being in a class with big bastards three years older than him.

'You're angry,' Gwen says.

'I'm tired.' He's ready to weep. 'And I don't understand what it is you want from me.'

'What did you want from Grace Maddox?'

'I can't remember. I thought I knew . . . In my head it was clear. But now it's just pictures.' Why can't he make her understand? But then he doesn't understand. Why he did this thing, where it came from – the furious conviction that Grace held the answers to his questions. 'I can't tell if the pictures are real, something I saw, or dreamt.'

'Tell me what you saw then. Or what you dreamt.'

'To what purpose?' He shifts on the bed, not much because she's

185

belted his wrists again. When? He doesn't remember and it scares him. 'This . . . free therapy, whatever it is, is pointless. You punishing me makes sense. The knife made sense. But not this.'

'You're angry. You should be. Everything that's happened to you since you were a child? I'd be angry. And I'm not as clever as you are.'

'You call this clever?' He rattles his wrists. 'I'm tied to a bed being made to tell my life story to a stranger I mistakenly kidnapped and held hostage in a cellar.'

'You started it.'

She's goading him, wanting him to let go of the anger when it is the only thing holding him together. He won't let it go, he can't.

'So finish it. Go on. What're you waiting for?'

Her face is stony. 'I'm waiting for you to get to the point.'

'And then what?'

'And then we'll see. What you deserve.'

They're talking in circles. He sees himself as an old man, bearded and incontinent, flayed to this bed, parsing out his memories in a bid to satisfy her desire to see him punished. He has to make this stop. He has to. It needs to be over. He thought she'd stopped it when she stabbed him but this is worse than before. What can he give her to make it stop?

Talk to me about the narrowboat. All right. *All right.*

'After that night we fought with those men . . . everything changed.'

This is all it takes to summon the panic, his chest tightening, vision sliding sideways into red.

'Everything? Or just you? Did Luke change?'

The fear narrows to a point, blade-like. There is something

terrible in the thought of Luke and the narrowboat, something closer than fifteen years ago. Here in the room, squatting on his chest.

'Daniel . . . Did Luke change?'

He wants to reach for her, the only steady point in the room. His chest heaves, squeezing his breath to a rattle at the back of his throat. His head is packing with thunder. He's aware of her hands on him, tries to suck air into starving lungs through teeth that won't unclench, heart jumping in his chest, throat convulsing. The room swarms. He's suffocating . . .

'Just . . . breathe. *Daniel*. Breathe.'

He must have blacked out. Comes round as his body kickstarts, taking in air, letting it out. Normal again for whatever that's worth, for the time being. He lies on the bed, her hand at his shoulder until the room stops shuddering. Even then an undertow of panic catches him, dragging like a claw. He wonders if she understands what is happening, how little of it is under his control. Then he wonders if she was waiting for this, for her chance to finish him.

18

The sky's still scratched by light but it will be dark soon. He's sleeping. The panic attack nearly finished him off. I'll have to keep a brown paper bag handy in case it happens again. There is so much to think about, to do. Some days I feel I'd be better off back in the cellar.

I sit on the terrace, waiting for the stab of stars in the sky. I can't leave. I've tried, got as far as turning on the car's engine, fastening my seat belt. It's the thought of him lying with my wound in his side that stops me. But this is no good either. All I've done is switch our roles: prisoner and captor.

He says the wound isn't infected, that it's healing. I'm not sure if he really believes this or if he wants me to believe it. He went to medical school; he knows best. On the other hand, I'm not convinced he cares very much whether he lives or dies.

He still doesn't know who I am. I still don't know why he lured me here, what he was capable of before I put a hole in him, stopped him in his tracks. From what he has said, I can see where it came from, the idea to trap me. His mother's illness taught him to suspect women of keeping secrets. And Luke is in the picture, somewhere. There is more he hasn't told me. He expects the worst from people, that much is clear. We talked about trust – when I had the knife in my hand – but that part of him is broken.

It's possible he thought he was keeping me safe here until I could tell him what he needs to know. He was so certain I had the answers. As if he trusted a secret to me that he has since forgotten. I hold the key, that's what he believed when he brought me here. His life crashed and burnt and Grace is the black box. I am the black box.

He still hasn't explained the scars on his arm. And there is another thing, a secret I haven't shared with him.

His phone keeps pinging messages. From Clark, Elise's dad. From her mum, Tess. From the hospital where he works. Luke's brother Owen. Jude's counsellor Dr Bowen. They're all worried about him, want to know where he is, why he hasn't been in work or in touch.

Clark's messages are getting frantic. He asks if Dan has seen Luke. Owen wants a lift home from 'HB' at the end of the month. From the dates, no one has seen Luke in over two weeks. Dan kept in touch with them during the first few days of my captivity. He messaged Clark and Owen saying he hadn't heard from Luke. He told the hospital he had a virus, telling Dr Bowen the same lie, asking her to please pass his apologies to Jude.

To Tess, he wrote: *I'm sorry. I didn't think it'd go this far.*

Dear Dan, Tess typed back, *I know you did your best. You're a good friend.*

That's the message I keep coming back to. *I know you did your best.* But she doesn't know. No one does, except me.

Now her messages are all: *Please get in touch, Clark's going spare* and *Dear Dan, I'm worried about you.*

I want to type back: *Hi Tess, I'm fine. At last I'm getting the help I need to get well.*

The only reason I don't type this is because sooner or later one of them will contact the police and I don't want to incriminate myself. Or Daniel. But time is running out. He needs to remember whatever it is he's forgotten.

When he wakes, I will make him tell me about Luke and the narrowboat. He'll want to tell me, I think; the panic attack scared him. He knows he can trust me but even if he doesn't, what choice does he have?

I'll make him tell me. I can make him do anything I want. That's the real difference between the cellar and the bedroom.

Before, I belonged to him.

Now, he's mine.

19

The road out of town was waterlogged but climbed steeply, leaving the flooding behind with the shops and offices as it thinned to terraced streets whose gutters gurgled with the rain that hadn't stopped in days, beating down blackly from a grey sky. Dan had accelerated when he hit the incline but he slowed now, taking the corners with care, blasting AC at the windscreen. He'd changed at the hospital into his running gear. The tread on his shoes squealed on the accelerator and again on the brakes. He'd zipped a thin thermal jersey over his T-shirt, packed a beanie to keep his wet hair from his eyes. The idea of running in these conditions was borderline irresponsible; if he slipped and fractured his wrist, who would take his surgeries? But he needed to run. Driving out here after his clinic appointments had become another habit like the Friday night vigils, only on his terms. Alone.

A bend in the road brought a truck roaring at him. He hugged the kerb, aware of the road falling away to his left, a sharp drop to a dry-stone wall. His tyres sizzled through the slick, the car gliding for a second, wheels suspended on the margin of wet. He knew this road like the back of his hand; it took more than a speeding truck to unsettle the smooth pattern of his driving.

Another corner then a straight stretch, the road running adjacent to the field of cattle, their backs bronzed by rain. He suppressed a shudder, which was another habit like the drive, the run, the vigil. The bulls no longer scared him but he needed to acknowledge they once had. It was Owen, aged seven, who'd first pointed out how creepy they looked: black bulls in a black field, so much a part of the mud they could have been carved from it. Dan had told him the story of the minotaur to keep him calm in the car. Owen leant into him as he listened, his small sticky hand in Dan's, trusting him to make the story scary enough to satisfy his seven-year-old bravado while reassuring him the field of bulls had been left far behind them. 'Labyrinth,' Owen whispered. 'Labyrinth.'

At the next bend in the road, Dan veered right, turning into the car park to the pub where they would stop sometimes if Owen was feeling carsick or if Elise was. Dan cut the engine and sat watching the rain sweep down, the windscreen growing misty. Then he reached for the beanie and pulled it on before opening the door and stepping out into the weather.

Rain soaked through his clothes in a matter of minutes.

He ran on the pavement in the direction of oncoming cars. His gear had hi-vis stripes but how visible they were in these conditions, he'd no idea. The rain made everything monochrome. Headlights dazzled, tyres throwing arcs of water. He tuned it all out, everything but the thumping of his feet. It felt good to run in the cold and wet, his chest labouring as the road climbed, everything aching by the time he reached the turning down to the canal, the bruise in his kidneys and the one in his ribs legacy of the last vigil. It felt good to feel bad, the physical punishment simple and straightforward.

By the time he stopped, he'd covered three miles. He leant into a stone stretch of wall, flexing the cold from his joints. From here he could see the roll of fields in all directions, heaped lines of dry stone, the farmhouse where a family of four was murdered. Down in the valley, the River Dean boiled, its banks a distant memory. The rising floodwaters were a series of long white scars. Houses in the valley had been evacuated weeks ago, unlikely to be habitable when – if – the water receded. He began running again, headed down, down, down to the towpath. An abandoned allotment straggled by the side of the road, its trenches filled with water where bamboo canes floated, its sheds dilapidated, roofs black with rot. He made his way across a slippery stretch of duckboards onto the relative safety of the towpath.

The narrowboat was moored at a bend in the canal, its wet brasswork gleaming gold. He climbed into the well deck, using the key dug from his pocket to unfasten the padlock, latching the cabin door once he was inside.

The boat was miraculously dry. Well, not quite miraculously; he and Luke had weatherproofed it fifteen years ago. Before Elise was born, when Clark and Tess were first dating.

Elise started coming here when she was ten. Her safe place, she called it. Her seedlings were spaced out on a trestle table, dried curls in greying soil, some green shoots from the bottled water Dan fed them on his last visit. Prints hung on the red walls. The boat had a wood-burning stove, a galley kitchen, a truckle bed with red blankets, blue cushions.

He squeezed rain from the beanie, tossing it into the sink.

Taking a towel from a peg, he sat on the bed, rubbing the wet from his hands and head. The bed was hard despite the blankets. Underneath, he could feel the canal roiled by the rain. Vertigo tugged at him until he sat forward, surrendering to it for a second, the cabin floor opening like a long wound under his feet. He breathed through the vertigo until everything settled into place.

For a long time after that he sat with the towel around his shoulders, hands linked, head bowed. A matting rug covered the floor, rubbed away in places by footfall over the years. Rain drummed on the roof but none of it found its way inside. The boat was better insulated than his parents' house where water crept through window frames, gutters leaking. The boat's windows were coated on the inside by opaque sheets of plastic that let the light through but nothing else. From the outside, you couldn't see the galley, the truckle bed or the table with Elise's seedlings. Luke had put up the plastic, cutting each piece with a Stanley knife, smoothing air bubbles with the ball of his thumb, making the windows blind. While he did this, Dan kept the stove hot, feeding it the fat round pegs of wood it liked.

Clark didn't care about the boat that summer, too busy with the girl he'd fallen for. They were nearly seventeen, he and Tess. Luke was eighteen, Dan just fourteen. The narrowboat belonged to Clark's dad but he didn't use it and couldn't sell it, happy for Clark and his friends to take it on. Dan knew Luke would rather it was Clark helping him on the boat. Luke had been pleased with himself for finding an allotment just up the towpath; Dan hadn't seen him so excited about anything before. Working on the boat, he saw a side of Luke he hadn't known existed: energetic, meticulous, tireless.

Half the summer they worked on the boat, each day catching a lift out here with whatever tools and materials they'd begged or bought. Operating the bilge pumps, blacking the hull, fixing up the stove. Luke was determined to make the boat habitable, as if he intended living here. Dan could see the sense in that, given what he knew of Luke's home life.

'Hand us that wrench . . .'

Luke took care over every detail on the boat, large or small. He'd have preferred Clark's help but he accepted Dan's, even thanked him for it. It was the closest they came to being friends, until the afternoon of the thunderstorm.

They'd known a storm was coming. Living where they did, the weather was never far away. People talked of smelling storms and it was true, at least in their town. Even truer out on the water, surrounded by fields and sky.

Luke had finished putting up the window liners when the first clap of thunder sounded. Dan had the stove going and they'd brought a carrier bag from the Spar with cans of lager, packets of crisps. The lager was for Luke but Dan was drinking too because it was easier than arguing about his age; Luke didn't like to be reminded that Dan was four years younger, just a kid really.

When the lightning came, it lit the windows a weird acid yellow.

'Here we go,' Luke said, as if the storm was part of the reason they'd come all this way. He opened another two cans, passing one to Dan.

They sat side by side on the truckle bed watching the lightning and listening for the spit of rain down the stove's piped chimney. They wore their oldest jeans, Luke's with a faded green T-shirt. Dan's T-shirt had been red once, stained with paint and smelling of creosote. Luke sprawled next to him, the lager can resting on his chest, his eyes on the roof. 'It'll hold,' he said. He kept saying it, on and off, as if there was some doubt in the matter.

Dan was tired from the long trek up here. The boat was warm, like the lager. He was drunk, sleepy. They'd walked a long way, worked a long time. Luke worked like a maniac when he was here, expecting the same from Dan. To begin with, it had felt like a condition of their new friendship but then he realized Luke just liked to go at things full-pelt. Whatever he was doing, he had to be doing it 100 per cent. Working on the boat had made them fit and tanned. Luke's hair had gold highlights, his shoulders brown. Dan had muscles where he'd never had them before. The days were hot, stacked with sunshine. This storm was the first of the summer, a good test for the boat now it was nearly finished.

We did this, Dan was thinking. Fixed up the boat, made it weatherproof and watertight. *We did this.*

The work served another purpose, helping him to avoid thinking about his mum's death. He wasn't allowed to call it suicide, not at home or at school, found himself whispering the word like an obscenity, 'Suicide,' as he sanded the narrowboat's cabin door or polished the brass mushroom vents.

Clark knew about his mum, and so did Luke. Dan had told the pair of them not long after the funeral because the school was making a fuss and he was embarrassed but also ashamed to have told Clark and Luke as if it were currency of some kind, a way to get them to take him seriously, closing the age gap between them.

Clark had said, 'Shit, mate, I'm sorry.'

Luke had looked at Dan, not speaking. But he seemed to take more notice of him after that, as if it made Dan more interesting or at least less uninteresting. Working on the boat, he'd say stuff like, 'Where'd she get the pills?' Or, 'You ever think about doing it?' There was rope on the boat, knives in the toolkit Luke carried. He'd knot the rope, play with the knives, spinning them on the deck or between his fingers. 'How'd you do it, if it was you?'

Dan went along with it, the way he went along with everything, trying to fit in, to find *normal*. In bed at night he'd blink back tears, sick of himself. But during the day he played by Luke's rules, always.

Looking back, it was hard to see how it started.

The storm was shaking the trees outside, water slapping at the hull, wind rattling in the stove's chimney. Dan turned his head to check the fire he was feeding and Luke's hand was on his waist, the bed creaking as he leant over, his tongue sliding into Dan's mouth.

He froze in panic, pinned by the hardness of Luke's hip against his. All he could think was how Luke hated him; it was *Clark* he liked, not Dan, Clark he'd wanted to work with on the boat.

Dan jerked his head and their teeth clashed, tasting of blood. Luke drew back but not enough to let him off the bed. Dan was too close to see him properly, just a green band for his eyes, wet line for his mouth. Panic warped into fear. This was a test; he could hear the playground taunts, feel himself shoved into walls where nerds were shoved or little kids with red hair and freckles. Luke had been one of those bullies not so long ago. And he hated Dan. Dan was suddenly more certain of that than anything else.

Luke nudged a knee at his thigh. 'Take these off then.'

He struggled upright but Luke pushed him back down, holding him to the bed with a hand at Dan's shoulder, his other inside Dan's T-shirt, feeling up the muscles the boat had given him. 'Take them off and I'll blow you.'

Dan felt sick, as if he'd stepped off a fairground ride too fast. He mumbled something like, 'No thanks,' and Luke said, 'Piss off, you turning down a blowjob?' and Dan tried again to get up off the bed and this time Luke punched him to put him back down, leaning in, lips moving against Dan's mouth. 'You fucking love it.'

Dan didn't love it. He didn't even understand it. When had he ever given the impression this was what he wanted? If anything, he'd given the opposite impression – putting physical distance between them because he was ashamed of how scared he was of Luke, more scared than ever now Luke was pinning him to the bed, pushing his tongue into his mouth. He fought until a thumb in his armpit stopped him, drilling into a tendon or nerve, sending a shock of cramp up the side of his neck, down the length of his body.

'Yeah?' Luke kept kissing him, pushing his tongue against the clench of Dan's teeth. 'Yeah?'

He moved his hand over Dan's stomach, gripping his waist then his hip, hauling at him. He was strong and angry in a way Dan didn't understand and then suddenly he did – Luke's hand was rubbing at his chest, pinching fingers making him flinch. This was how Luke kissed girls, feeling them up. He'd never done it to a boy before. The knowledge slotted into Dan's head but it didn't help him, nothing did. He fought but Luke was stronger and he knew what he was doing even if he'd never done it to a boy before. Where to put his hands and how to kiss in a way that shut you up even if you didn't want it, even if you wanted to scream. Better to lie still, not to fight.

The worst part was how his body responded to what Luke was doing. Not to the kissing, which was sloppy and horrible, but when Luke moved his mouth *there*, propping an elbow in Dan's chest to keep him still. Dan hated the sound it made, hated himself for not being able to fight and for how quickly he came. *Hated it.* When Luke lifted his head, he cringed, terrified of being kissed, of tasting himself in Luke's mouth.

'Knew it,' Luke said. 'My turn.'

He grabbed the back of Dan's neck, dragging his head up from the bed. His horror must have been obvious because Luke made a disgusted sound and said, 'Just bring me off then.'

He let go of Dan's neck and grabbed his wrist, pushing his hand down, 'Do it, bitch,' and Dan didn't want to but he didn't know how else to make this stop so he did as he was told, Luke's hand over his to make sure he got it right, his mouth damp at Dan's neck. He kept calling him a bitch, saying he was doing good, 'Yeah, like that, you love it, you dirty bitch, you'll learn,' and Dan wasn't sure when he started sobbing but he did, not stopping for a long time, not even after Luke had finished and it was over.

The rain drummed steadily on the narrowboat's roof, Elise's seedlings shivering to the percussion.

Dan took the towel from his shoulders, using it to wipe the last of the wet from his face. He should be heading home, at least back to the car to check his phone. He wasn't on call but emergencies happened, more and more during this spell of bad weather. He might be needed. He sat looking at his feet, thinking of Luke and the thunderstorm fifteen years ago. Neither of them spoke of it, certainly not to one another. Dan had lived in dread of Luke starting a rumour at school, the sort to get the shit kicked out of him, but Luke must have kept quiet because nothing happened for weeks, months. Dan put it away, the way he'd put away his mother's suicide, hiding himself in his studies. His father's grief insulated him from questions at home. For three months, it was over. Then it was Clark's birthday and Tess wanted to hold a party on the boat. Luke told her they'd tart it up, 'Balloons and shit,' nodding at Dan, 'Right, stud?' and there was a moment when Dan thought he'd puke but instead he said, 'Sure.'

Tess was so happy, Dan almost forgot why he was afraid to be back on the boat. She had a foil banner and party plates, a CD player, the cake she'd baked. Luke brought cans and an ancient-looking helium tank – corroded, its aluminium handles brittle – to blow up the balloons Dan had bought.

The narrowboat stank from being locked up. They opened windows, Tess lighting scented candles, giddy with the surprise she had planned for Clark, her excitement infectious. When she put on a Beyoncé CD, she had Dan dancing with her to *Single Ladies* while Luke rolled a cigarette (and his eyes). Then a text from her mum reminded Tess of the time and she was gone so suddenly there was no chance for Dan to make an excuse to go with her. He was alone on the boat, with Luke.

The CD was still playing, the music sounding mindless until Luke punched it off with his thumb. He was smoking as he crouched to attach a balloon to the helium tank's nozzle. He gripped the cigarette with his lips as he pinched the neck of the balloon. 'Give's a hand with this?'

Dan had helped with the rest of the balloons, tying them off as Luke filled them, but he hesitated now, hyper-aware of the distance between them, of Luke's shoulder span, the smoke from his cigarette blurring his face.

Luke squinted up at him. 'Danny?'

Dan toed balloons out of his way until he was at Luke's side, squatting on his heels to help.

Luke caught his wrist and dragged, trapping his arm across the brittle handle of the helium tank where the corroded metal was sharp enough to cut and did, drawing blood.

'*Don't*—' Instinctively, he pulled back, which was the worst thing he could have done as now the metal was slicing into him, pain bolting up his arm to stuff his mouth with a scream.

Luke dragged at his wrist, still smoking, as if the fact of Dan's blood running down the tank was nothing, as if the handle wasn't a knife and Dan's arm wasn't full of arteries and tendons and bones that felt like sticks in danger of snapping. 'Saw you looking sick earlier.' He dug his thumb into the gap between Dan's ulna and radius, grinding there. 'You'd better not be about to puke your guts about what happened the last time we were here.'

He underlined the threat by sawing Dan's forearm across the cutting-edge of the handle, making more blood run down the side of the tank.

Anatomy crowded Dan's skull: *transverse carpal ligament; abductor pollicis longus; flexor digitorum profundus* – the muscle in his forearm responsible for flexing the joints in his fingers – that's where Luke was cutting him. If he cut deep enough, Dan would lose the use of his hand.

'I won't – Luke, *don't –*'

'*All the single ladies . . .* You little queer.'

'Stop it . . .' Panic overrode the pain, overrode everything. He'd lose the use of his hand, wouldn't be able to write or work. 'I'll need stitches . . .' Dad would think he'd slashed his own wrist, months after Mum. '*Please!*'

Luke let him go as suddenly as he'd stopped the last time. Dan fell back, clutching his injured arm to his chest, staggered by relief.

'Better put something on that . . .' Luke straightened and stepped away, rummaging in his toolkit.

He threw something at Dan, who ducked in terror before realizing it was a wound dressing, the kind you'd put on your knee if you came off a skateboard. He reached for it, seeing blood wetting his fingers. He needed to clean the cuts – the helium tank was filthy – but he was shaking too much to get to his feet. Luke was between him and the door, a thin glaze of smoke trapped in the light from the windows, adding to the illusion this wasn't happening, wasn't real.

No one'll believe me if I tell them about this.

That was the only thought in his head.

'Better let me look at that, mate.' Luke reached down and scooped Dan to his feet, steering him by the elbow to the sink gently, as a friend might. He ran the tap, splashed water over the damage he'd done, helping Dan to stay upright by propping him at the hip and shoulder.

Under the blood, the cuts were ugly, zigzagging the inside of Dan's forearm between his elbow and wrist. Blood kept coming but not enough to scare Dan as much as Luke's nearness scared him or the performance Luke was putting into washing out every stray scrap of aluminium and dirt (*peritonitis, cellulitis, tetanus*), using one of Tess's party napkins to blot the water and blood before fixing the wound dressing in place.

When it was done, he stepped back, waiting to see if Dan would find his centre of gravity. 'All right? You'll want to put antiseptic on it when you get home.' He shook his head sadly. 'You clumsy bugger . . . Better not tell Tess, might kill the party mood.' He turned his back, began cleaning the helium tank with a cloth, wiping away Dan's blood.

All of it was unreal, as if Luke was miles away from where Dan was standing with his arm throbbing, head pounding.

It wasn't until he was at medical school that he looked back and realized he remembered nothing at all of Clark's birthday party, other than it took place at night on the narrowboat. He knew he was there with Tess and Luke and people from school because there were photos. He wore jeans and a navy sweatshirt and he danced and drank vodka shots, stood with Clark's arm around his neck, grinning for the camera. If the photos hadn't existed, Dan would not have believed any of those things happened.

Soon afterwards, Luke started going with girls, getting them pregnant. Clark married Tess. Years went by. When Dan returned from medical school, Luke was Clark's best friend, the pair of them inseparable.

Elise turned ten and took an interest in the boat. Luke gave her a set of keys so she could come and go. As far as Dan knew, Luke hadn't been inside the place in years. He climbed to his feet, returning the damp towel to its peg.

Outside, the rain had stopped, the canal no longer thrumming under it. He stood looking blindly at the truckle bed, the sink, the seedlings. Had he handled things better, been less shocked or scared when Luke kissed him, might Luke be a different man now? For fifteen years, he'd been angrier than anyone Dan had ever known. Elise's murder made it much worse, the vigils enforced with threats if anyone flagged. Fifteen years of trying to prove . . . something. Could Dan have changed that? If he'd reacted differently, talked to Luke or let Luke talk to him? Had he singled Dan out because he was the quiet one? Boring, bookish. Sensitive, although Luke would never have used that word, would have bitten off his own tongue first. *Luke fucking Hooley. If you look at him funny, he'll fuck you up.* One summer he'd worked in the bargain booze shop and always after that he was known as Thresher. You didn't mess with Luke Hooley. Dan had the scars to prove it.

Trying to talk to Luke about his feelings would have made it worse; Dan didn't believe Luke was gay, or bisexual. What he'd done had nothing to do with sexual preference and everything to do with power, violence. A predator's urges, unstoppable. He knew the word he was supposed to use. *Assault*. Luke had assaulted him. Except that was insulting to women and girls like Elise who had been dragged into dark alleys and beaten, left bloodied or dead. Luke hadn't hurt him, not during the assault. A bruise in Dan's armpit, another on his thigh, ugly bite marks on his neck, but that was the extent of it. Luke hadn't threatened him, just insisted Dan loved it, as if he were proving a point rather than performing a sex act.

The helium tank was different. After that, it took Dan weeks to stop feeling terrorized whenever Luke came close. Months before he was able to do what other teenage boys did without thinking, his hand inside his jeans, watching porn on his phone, afraid of the pictures in his head. Years before he could kiss anyone, before he trusted himself to be alone with anyone. Even now, his first instinct was to avoid other people.

Elise's killer was a violent predator. He'd strangled her, torn at her clothes. The newspapers speculated about the sort of monster he might be. A victim of abuse himself perhaps, or a repeat offender.

And still Dan said nothing.

For fifteen years, he said nothing about what happened on the boat, what he knew. That Luke Hooley assaulted a fourteen-year-old. That he used violence to get what he wanted, and what he wanted was Dan's shame, humiliation. He laughed when he saw Dan's tears. Laughed and punched him. And Dan, scared out of his mind, said nothing.

20

'Was it Luke who killed Elise?'

Dan moves vigilantly on the bed. The whole of his left side feels raw, each rib scored with a separate, distinct pain. His temples burn. He has just told her what he has never told anyone, a thing that has eaten him alive for fifteen years, but Gwen isn't interested in his shame, only in Luke.

'Did he?'

'I don't know . . .'

'This is important.' She crowds him, her face carved with concentration. 'Did Luke kill Elise? Is that what happened?'

'*I don't know.*'

Why won't she believe him? Can't she see he's lost his mind, that he is made of fear and confusion and nothing else – no specialist training, no gifts or talents, *nothing*? He's nothing.

'Your memories of Jude' – she changes tack – 'you do know there's a reason for those, why you're thinking about her so much with everything else that's going on? You implied her blindness is like a vanishing centre, "the heart of the scene eviscerated". You have a vanishing centre too, Daniel. Don't you? Something you can't bring yourself to look at, can't remember. Something you *need* to remember.'

'I'm telling you everything I know. Things I've told no one—'

'About Luke.' She stares down at him. 'That he's a rapist. You were Elise's age when she was attacked, more or less. He's violent, out of control, cunning. You told me all this and you still don't know if he killed her?'

She is furious, out of all patience with him. He's forgotten she can look like this – the way she did when she surged up the cellar steps, or swung at him with the knife. He's forgotten who she is.

'Please . . .' Why is that word so hard to say, even now? Like pulling a rusty nail from his throat. 'If I knew, I'd tell you—'

'Are you protecting *him*?' she demands. 'Or *yourself*?'

He stares at her, shocked into silence.

'You're impossible.' Her mouth curls in disgust. 'You've boxed it all up, every part of your life before she died. You made all these insane choices, like being friends with men like Luke, staying in that dead end of a town when you could have got away. You can't remember because you have spent so much of your life *hiding*. Who you are and what you feel. You lie about it, to everyone. It is all hidden, inside your head. You're a coward—'

'At least I never stabbed anyone.'

'There's a reason I stabbed you.'

'No,' Dan says angrily, 'there's not. I opened the doors, asked you to leave. You could have left. I wasn't stopping you. You didn't need to stab me. If there is dirt in this wound, I will die from it, you do know that?'

'If you starve someone for three days, Daniel, it diminishes their critical faculties. You do know that?'

'I made a mistake, thought you were someone else.'

'Grace Maddox.'

'*Yes.*'

She rolls her eyes then reverts to her stoniest face. 'For a clever man, you're outstandingly stupid.'

'Meaning what?'

'I'm Grace Maddox,' she snaps the words. 'I was always Grace Maddox. I was Grace when you knocked me out and put me in that cellar. Grace when I belted you to that bed. And I'm her *right now*, the only person who can keep you alive. If I decide that is what I want to do.'

He stares at her and she stares straight back.

Abyss, he thinks, *abyss.*

His mind has never felt more broken.

She has never looked more deadly.

'So you'd better think about how little you'd like to die. Because the only way you're getting up from that bed is if I let you and I'll only do that when you start telling me the truth. When you start *remembering.*'

She turns, takes the tray and goes, shutting the door behind her.

When he is capable of thinking anything he thinks, *She isn't coming back, that's it. She's gone and I'll never see her or anyone else ever again.*

Later, he turns his head to wipe the tears from his face. He wept for a long time, unable to stop. Now he feels like storm wreckage, empty and aimless. Her anger stayed in the room after she left, the air static with it.

'I'm Grace Maddox.'

Of course she is. *Of course.*

The house is silent, eery. He thinks of his parents bringing him here as a child. Usually his mind swerves from these memories like a well-trained dog. How will it help Jude, or Ray Kahn, if he is distracted by memories – good or bad – of the boy he once was? Well, he is reduced to that boy now, for better or worse. What he feels is pity but also relief. It can't be that easy, can it? Her interrogation – declaration – delivering him to this place of tears and pathos? No. For one thing, he is tied to a bed. For another, there is a hole in his head where days have been lost. The vigil, the fist fight, Luke grinding him against the wall outside the pub then . . .

Here, the house. The cellar. Grace. The fury in her face: 'Are you protecting *him*? Or *yourself*?'

Of course she's Grace. She's right, he's been an idiot. What did he think was happening here? And she's right to say he's been hiding, who he is, what he feels. His whole life is like that shoebox of hers: compartmentalized, nothing touching anything else. No wonder he's finding it so hard to piece it all together now. He tries, again, to retrieve the time he's lost. Remembers thinking his phone was faulty, that an upgrade must have caused the date to skip forward by a week. He kept pressing the 'today' button in its calendar, expecting the date to scroll back to the one he knew was today. But the phone insisted it was six days later. When he saw the missed appointments, messages from the hospital and his friends, he knew things had gone seriously wrong, not with the phone but in his head. He had this idea – the only one he could hold on to with any certainty – that *she* knew. Grace Maddox. She stole six days of his life and he needed them back. It was life and death and it was Luke hissing instructions at him, telling him to stop pussyfooting around the task he'd set himself and make her talk, give up the answers he needed.

Was that real, or in his head?

Luke's been in his head for months. In this house, laughing at the foot of the bed as Grace quizzed him about his career choice – that wasn't real. And if that wasn't real, how can he trust any of it?

He hears Dad's voice, 'I'll get the kettle on,' from years ago when they were on holiday, arriving to find the house cold even in the height of summer. He taught Dan the art of laying a fire, coaxing it, establishing each layer of heat before adding more fuel. The heavy feel of Dad's cigarette lighter sparking under his thumb: 'Build it slowly, start with the small twigs.'

The light is fading, the window filling with shadows. *This is how I'll die. Under a sky I can't see, with my father's voice in my head . . .*

All right, enough.

He's thirsty, needs to relieve himself, needs *her*. He drives his mind away from the despair, back to when he still had a mind and knew what he was doing, no matter how badly he was doing it. Back to Jude.

21

'Hey, Dr Dan.' Jude was with her mother in the hospital car park, a wound dressing at her jaw, fresh scratches on her cheek and the bridge of her nose.

'What happened?' Dan crossed to where they stood. For a second, he was in the grip of the vertigo but it settled as he reached her side.

'Told you I saw him.' Despite the damage, Jude looked happier than she'd been at Dr Bowen's. 'Peripheral vision. See?'

'A skateboard.' Her mum sounded under siege. 'She fell off a skateboard in a graveyard.'

'Ouch,' Dan said. 'Must've hurt.'

Jude grinned at him. 'Like a bitch.'

'Jude, that's not nice for Mr Roake to hear.'

'He doesn't mind. Do you, Dr Dan?'

Jude was wearing a purple T-shirt and denim shorts over thick tights laddered at both knees, more wound dressings taped over the worst of it.

'Who patched you up in there?'

'A nurse. She said it was superficial. Didn't hit my head, just sort

210

of skidded.' Jude mimed the movement with her hand. 'It was cool. The rest of them wanted to go home when it got dark but I can skate with my eyes shut.' She bounced on the heels of her boots. 'The graveyard's really cool.'

'Were you wearing a helmet?' Dan asked.

'Won't fit over my hair.' She patted the brambly curls.

Mrs Horning looked at Dan. 'Do her eyes need checking? I didn't know you were on duty tonight or I'd have asked the nurse . . .'

'If Jude says she didn't hit her head, I'm sure it's fine.'

'You can check me out if you want.'

Jude put her hands into her pockets. Giddy with adrenaline, she'd crash in a short while, feel unwell.

'Come back inside and let's look you over.'

He found an exam room, sat Jude in the chair. 'Wait here a minute.'

She swung her feet. 'Okay.'

In the corridor, Dan spoke with her mum: 'She's fine but it might be a good idea to keep her here until the adrenaline levels out. She's going to be a bit wobbly when that happens. Can I get you a coffee?'

'I can get one, thanks. I'm sorry, I don't know what she was thinking.'

'She was thinking like a teenager. There's no harm done. She seems a lot brighter than she did at Dr Bowen's.'

'She doesn't want to go again, that's what this was about, says she doesn't want protecting. I've tried telling her we'd be like this whether or not she was blind. It's what parents do, we look out for our kids. We can't help it. It's human nature.'

Dan thought of Clark and Tess and Elise. 'Yes, it is.'

In the exam room, he checked Jude's eyes, taking his time over the tests to let her come down from the evening's high. The accident hadn't affected her vision but he was troubled by what he saw in her right eye.

'Your right eye's very bloodshot. Have you been rubbing it?'

She hesitated. 'I guess.'

'With alcohol?' Dan stood where he knew she could see his face. 'Jude? I can smell vodka but it's not on your breath.'

'It got spilt.' She mumbled the words, her cheeks flaming.

'Vodka was spilt in your eye.'

'Yes . . .'

'It's called eyeballing,' Dan said inflexibly. 'I've treated students who've tried it. Some have permanent corneal scars.'

'So? My eyes are fucked anyway.'

'Did you think you were drunk?'

'That's the point.' She glanced in the direction of his face, biting her lips together. 'It gets into your bloodstream really fast.'

'Not true. A tiny percentage might but your eye doesn't have any kind of lining to help it absorb alcohol, or to protect it for that matter. Vodka's forty per cent pure ethanol. In an emergency I'd use it to sterilize surgical equipment.' She gave a nod, holding herself in a protective curl inside the chair. Dan kept his native sympathy at bay; this was more important. 'If you put ethanol in your eye, it causes inflammation and possibly thrombosis – that's the clotting of blood vessels. The whites of your eyes discolour and your eyes weep, like you're crying even if you're not. Of course you might *be* crying, because the other thing it does is make your eyes really sore.'

212

'Are you going to tell Mum?' Jude whispered.

'I really should.'

'Don't. *Please*. She'll go mental, stop me seeing Frankie . . . I won't do it again, I *swear*. It wasn't any fun. You're right, I didn't get drunk and it really stung. I already promised Frankie I won't do it again.' She hiccupped in distress. 'It was my idea. She didn't want to drink vodka, let alone do *that*.'

'Who sold you the vodka?'

'No one. It was in Frankie's house. We nicked a capful, that's all. Most of it went down my neck. I thought I'd washed it all off.' She squirmed to the edge of the chair. '*Please*, Dr Dan. I won't ever do it again. Frankie hated it, said she won't let me come round if I try it again. She's much more sensible than me. I love her and she's my best friend, I can't stop seeing her. It was a tiny, *tiny* amount. I stopped as soon as I felt it sting.'

Dan knew she was telling the truth; very little vodka had gone into her eye, which was bloodshot but not damaged, not by the ethanol. Still, keeping the secrets of a twelve-year-old girl was not a good idea. He ought to be on her mum's side, with the rest of the adults.

'*Please.*' Jude made a prayer shape with her hands. 'She'll tell Dr Bowen and then the therapy'll be ten times worse . . .'

'The therapy needn't be bad. You should have someone to talk to.'

'I can't stand her,' Jude said ferociously. 'That stupid shiny hair. I bet she's writing a paper on me for a medical journal. I'm her pet project.'

'If I can find you someone else then, another therapist who specializes in what you're going through. Will you think about it?'

'Is that the deal? You won't tell Mum as long as I talk to a shrink?'

'Counselling should help. It helps lots of people. I wouldn't recommend it otherwise.'

'Okay.' She pushed her hair off her face. 'Deal.'

Dan spent a while longer rinsing the sore eye then told her she was good to go. She slid from the chair, letting Dan steady her with a hand to her elbow. 'Skate safe, okay?'

She lifted her face to his and grinned. 'Promise.'

22

He's weeping again. For Jude, her faith in him, his broken promise to find her a new therapist, a replacement for Dr Bowen whom he hates for being sleek and professional but who has at least not gone off the rails and dropped off the map, leaving everyone in the lurch. *Enough.* He forces his body to move, marshalling pain to put things in perspective, raising the brutal spectre of the knife in his abdomen. *Better.* He sucks down the last of the sobs and says out loud, 'How are you going to make this stop?'

Raising his head, he squints down the length of his body to where his wrists are shackled. He tests the strength of the belts, the degree to which he can move his fingers, what leverage he has to free himself. The answer is none as far as the belts go. He moves his legs, attempting to twist sideways, rocking the bed under him. If he can get close enough to the wall, he can use it to work the belts free maybe. This isn't a great idea according to his left hip, which starts its usual plaintive grinding, but it is the only one he's got. He tells his hip to shut up, wrenching his shoulders from side to side in a bid to make the bed move. Keeps it up until the pillow is soaked with his sweat and he's shouting in frustration, pain as an afterthought. The bed is no nearer the wall than it was before. He goes limp to catch his breath, turning his neck to rid it of the ache lodged there. That's when he sees it on the bedside table, glinting green in the sunlight.

The glass caterpillar he gave Elise on her seventh birthday. He stares, afraid he's seeing things, a new layer to his madness.

Tess said Elise was obsessed with caterpillars so he bought half a dozen different ones, from a big plushie to this tiny knuckle of coloured glass. He packed each caterpillar inside the next – in boxes of ascending size – a party game for Elise to unwrap. He knows it is the same caterpillar because of the chip on its nose; it fell from its box to the flagstones in the garden where Elise's party was held. He remembers the party – fairy lights in the trees, balloons everywhere – another of Tess's triumphs.

Light from the window winks on the caterpillar's chipped nose, teasing him with the idea he has lost what little was left of his mind. The answer slots into his skull a second later. *The shoebox.* Her shoebox. All those treasures wrapped up tight and the rain spotting down; he stopped looking through the shoebox, conscious of invading her privacy, although why that matters after everything else he did to her, he doesn't know.

She put the caterpillar here on the bedside table, before she took the tray and left. *Grace Maddox.* He stopped thinking about Grace when she convinced him he'd made a mistake, taken the wrong woman. But it's her, she's Grace Maddox. That changes everything.

Never Events

- He should never have doubted his instinct, never have listened to her lies.
- She's Grace Maddox. She packed Elise's room. She stole her glass caterpillar.
- He didn't lure the wrong woman, or trap the wrong woman.
- She came here, willingly. Knowingly. Why?
- He should never have told her about Elise, or the vigil, or Luke, or his mum. He's given up so much to her.
- He unlocked the doors, let her out.
- Left a knife in plain sight.
- Let her stab him, strap him to this bed.
- Blamed himself, apologized, tried to make amends by answering her endless questions when all the time she knew who he was, knew about Elise and Clark and Tess.
- The cellar wasn't the start of it. The cellar just made it worse. The cellar was his idea.
- He said it was a mistake but it wasn't. He lured her here for a reason, even if he can't remember it.
- She came for a reason. She can remember it.
- This was her plan, right from the start. That's why she stayed so calm in the cellar, why she looked so unafraid.
- She knew what she was doing. She doesn't make mistakes.
- None of this was a mistake.

23

A fortnight ago, Dan remembers, he couldn't sleep. The woman in the cellar had been silent for hours. He'd expected screams, pleas, violence even. He must have had a plan for that, a way to block out the noise she'd make without resorting to threats or violence of his own. Maybe he thought the stone walls would muffle it. And he could always step out of the house, walk to the foot of the garden where the air was easier to breathe.

Day Three but already he was struggling to remember what he'd done or why he'd done it. He'd had the thread of it two days ago when he locked her in the cellar but that was unravelling, fast. He'd thought she'd help by asking questions or making accusations – information to line the empty inside of his skull. He hadn't anticipated silence. It nagged at him, at his conscience and his skin, at the holes in his head. In a few hours it would be dawn, time to start all over again. She said she wasn't Grace Maddox. 'I'm Gwen Leonard!' He was beginning to believe her.

The air was like feathers against his face. He stood in it, listening for sounds from the house. The trees were quiet, an ironwork of black branches. Pigeons rattled in the woods, rooks, jackdaws. He could smell the fetid water of a canal but the house was landlocked, miles from anywhere. This was the holiday home where he'd spent his summers, reading and walking, building a den in the woods, fixing felt to the roof of the shed with Dad while Mum rested in the room upstairs, curtains closed at the small, square window.

Nights ago, he'd watched from that window for the wavering of car headlights, bringing her here to the trap he'd laid. If she wasn't Grace – if that was a mistake like everything else – what would he do? Let her go, obviously. He'd always intended to let her go once she'd told him what she knew of the night on the narrowboat.

Tess, he remembers, *Tess* gave him the name of the woman who packed their house. The woman she'd trusted to recreate Elise's bedroom in their new place.

'Grace Maddox. She's a professional packer. She took such care . . .' Tess was crying, not loudly, just the same steady leaking from her eyes whenever she spoke about Elise. 'Everything was exactly as we'd asked.'

'But the keys were missing, you said. From Elise's room. Her keys to the narrowboat?'

Tess wiped at her face with the cuff of her shirt. 'I looked but I couldn't find them . . . Does it matter? The police were all over the boat last year, in case there was someone she'd met that we never knew about. There wasn't anything, they said, just those plants she was growing.' Fresh tears crept from her eyes. 'Some books, a scarf. No sign anyone else was with her. Only Luke's things and stuff from Clark's birthday – the banner and that old helium tank, party plates . . . God, it was all so long ago.'

Dan was dreaming of the boat. Of fire, flood, explosion. He hadn't been able to get it out of his head since the night the vigil turned to violence. His days were spent battling vertigo but his nights were worse, lurching on the dark water of the canal, its lock like a hungry mouth. He'd asked Tess about the keys because he couldn't shake the nightmares about the narrowboat.

'Luke's looking after it. His bolthole whenever Shannon and the girls get too much . . . Clark says he's not heard from him in days.' Tess wiped at the tears. 'You know what Luke's like.'

'How's Clark, really?'

'Since the fight, you mean?' She pulled a smile onto her face when Dan looked guarded. 'He made an excuse but his knuckles were a giveaway. Pretended it was his idea but I bet Luke was behind it.' She waited for Dan to confirm or deny this. When he didn't, she said, 'Clark's been weird about him ever since. Said you and Owen were caught up in it, too.' She turned Dan's hand in hers, inspecting his knuckles.

'I'd have stopped it,' Dan said. 'If I could.'

'I know.' She lifted his hand and kissed it, a sisterly kiss. 'I do know.'

How long ago was that? Tess telling him about Grace, about Clark, kissing his hand? Not long, he thought. Three weeks? Four? No more than four. What happened between Tess taking him to the narrowboat – telling him about Grace – and the key turning in the cellar door, locking Grace inside? He can't remember. He was in shock that day – doing as Tess told him, not taking much in. He'd been in shock for a while by that point, since the Puddle Duck.

The narrowboat looked the same when he stood there with Tess. It looked the same but it wasn't. It was cold on the towpath; he was wearing his running clothes. He waited for his body to shiver but it didn't. The cold was like a forecast – *fire, flood, explosion* – rather than a reality. Everything was remote, out of his reach. He was desperate to put that right, get a handle on what was happening, what had gone wrong.

'Do you have a phone number for Grace Maddox, or an email?'

'Yes, somewhere.' Tess reached for her phone. 'Hang on.'

As she was scrolling through her contacts, Dan looked down at the hand she'd kissed. He couldn't feel it. He hadn't been able to feel any part of his body in days. Since the brick wall at the back of the Puddle Duck, Luke grinding against him, breathing threats. Everything was numb, lost.

'Here you go. Grace Maddox. I'll text you the details.' Tess pinched out a frown. 'You're not going to accuse her of stealing the keys? Only I've no evidence and the last thing we want is the police back round . . .'

'I'm not going to accuse her,' Dan promised.

Then . . .

Nothing. A blackhole in his head. Until the house, the cellar, the long wait for her to start speaking. He remembers . . .

Jackdaws clattered from the trees. Shivering outside the house where he spent his summers as a child, thinking of the woman he'd put in the cellar.

'I'm not Grace Maddox!'

What had he done?

The Facts As I Know Them

- Elise Franklin was murdered a year ago, her killer never found.
- Luke Hooley started a vigil five months ago, to warn other girls there was a killer out there.
- Fifteen years ago, Luke Hooley assaulted a fourteen-year-old boy. That boy was Daniel Roake.
- Fifteen days ago, Daniel Roake put me in his cellar.
- To begin with, I told him he'd taken the wrong woman, that I was not Grace but Gwen.
- Three days ago, he let me out of his cellar. That's when I stabbed him.
- Today, I told him I'm Grace. But I wasn't lying fifteen days ago when I told him I was Gwen. It's complicated, like his job. Like the inside of his head.
- He boxes things up, from habit. I do that, for a living.
- The pair of us are complicated. We're either the worst people to try to solve this murder, or we're the best.
- Time to find out.

—

24

To understand why I wasn't lying when I told Daniel I was Gwen, you need to understand the matryoshka, my Russian nesting dolls. A gift from Mum, look-but-don't-touch like all the others but allowed to live in my room, on a high shelf put up by Dad.

My matryoshka dolls were Genevieve, Gertrude, Gwendoline, Gypsy, Gillian and Grace.

Genevieve was the biggest, a benignly fatuous matriarch in whose body the others lived.

Gertrude was next, a smaller version of Genevieve but otherwise identical, with the same smile spread from cheek to rosy cheek.

With Gwen, the difference became more marked, no blushing cheeks, no painted spokes around her eyes. A pleasing smoothness to Gwen, a nothingness that suited me sometimes, like glass under my fingertips.

Gypsy was slender, her expression slyly serene. She wore a red-green dress like a poke in the eye and was hard to take apart.

When you did, there was Gillian with her look of utter, intractable indifference.

Finally, the solid seed at the heart of all the others, the only one who couldn't be twisted open, split or filled – Grace.

25

When Dan wakes, she is standing at the side of his bed. Relief thuds through him – *she's back* – swiftly followed by confusion; he has the impression he has missed something vitally important. 'What . . . ?' He battles to wake up, scared by the intense look on her face.

'I'm sorry about before. You didn't deserve that.'

He can't make sense of the apology until he recalls her anger at his confession about Luke and the scars, his cowardice in keeping the assault to himself, even after Elise's death. She's not the one who needs to apologize.

'I should have told you I was Grace.' She reaches a finger to touch the glass caterpillar. 'But I didn't know if I could trust you. Because I came here to find a killer, and I found you.'

She moves to block the light, letting him see her face. She looks sad and serious. Dangerous, too. As if she's about to bring down a brick wall with her bare fist. 'I'm Grace Maddox. But I'm still not who you think I am.'

His mouth is dry. His pulse slams in his side, north of his hip. What is left of the night's fever is speeding in his bloodstream. *Where's the knife?*

She brings a cup of water to his lips, cradling the back of his skull as he swallows. His scalp contracts, expecting her fingernails to dig in, draw blood. She lowers his head onto the pillow, tidying the cup away.

'I know about Elise.' She unbelts his right wrist, puts an empty bottle into it, moves the sheet over his hand. 'She won trophies for her gymnastics, collected glass animals and beads. She had a matryoshka, like mine. She wanted to be a gymnastics teacher when she grew up.'

Her shoulders drop. Is she weeping? Dan finishes with the bottle, watching her. The fever makes it hard to focus on what she is saying.

'I know because I packed her family's home.' The fine bones of her face shiver through his fever. 'I've packed a lot of broken homes. Too many. There was a boy before Elise, an ordinary boy. Men found him, turned him to drugs, violence . . . Have you any idea how it feels to be the one who goes into those houses to pack up the pieces? Or do you only care about Luke?'

He shakes his head, his vision sliding, sending her out of focus. He has to fight to stay conscious, alert to what she is telling him. She's more dangerous than ever, far worse than when she was pretending to be Gwen.

'No one messes with Luke Hooley. That's what you said. But someone did. That night on the narrowboat, right before you lured me here. You knew I knew something. You got my name from Elise's mum. From Tess.'

She takes the bottle from him, going to the bathroom. Dan clenches his free hand into a fist repeatedly in a bid to get his blood moving. When she returns, he is still clenching it. She walks to the left side of the bed, unbelts his other wrist. 'Go ahead. You need to get back in shape.'

He has no idea what that means, whether it's a threat or an order, but he flexes his wrists, easing upright in the bed. She leaves, returning with a tray of food. A white bread sandwich on a paper plate, one of the bottles of mineral water he bought in bulk for this interrogation or vigil, whatever it was – the disaster in the cellar. A foil strip of paracetamol. He remembers how grateful she was for painkillers when she was his prisoner. His chest packs with remorse but he swallows an apology; they are beyond that now, into new territory. He doesn't know where, only that it's where she always intended for them to be. She's Grace Maddox. She planned this. She has the answers he needs to make sense of the holes in his head. She knows everything.

She moves a chair to sit at his side. 'Eat.'

He does as he's told. The sandwich is made with cheese spread squeezed from a tube in the fridge. It tastes of nothing; the best thing he has eaten in weeks. He takes two of the pills with a long drink of water.

'Have you figured it out yet?' Grace says.

'Some of it.' His shoulders ache and his neck. He does what he can to stretch. 'I got your name from Tess, that's true. I needed to know who had keys to the narrowboat. Apart from Luke.'

'Why was it so important to know who had keys?'

A fire, a flood, an explosion.

'You said it yourself: "That night on the narrowboat, right before you lured me here." I needed to know who'd been on the boat.'

'What happened on the boat before you lured me here?'

'I don't remember. I tried all night to get it back. But it's gone.'

227

Grace subjects him to her cool grey stare. He looks back at her without flinching. She knows he is telling the truth. She's known from the start. All this time – she was in control. She came here for a purpose. Everything she does is precise, careful, considered. He used to think he was like that. But next to her he's a rank amateur. A rank amateur with dissociative amnesia. Are there four types of dissociative amnesia? *I can't remember*. Jude would enjoy that, he thinks. The joke of that.

'Luke had a key to the narrowboat,' Grace says. 'Elise, too. And you, Daniel, had a key.'

He rubs the heel of his hand at his eyes. He doesn't argue. He wants to tell her the truth, if only he could remember it. But even if he didn't want to tell her, she'd get it out of him. He turns his head to look at Elise's caterpillar.

'You told me about the key,' Grace says. 'That day you went running. You kept a key to the boat all that time. Why?'

'I'm not sure. I suppose . . . I wasn't ready to let it go.'

'You and Luke. That summer.'

'Me and Luke. And Elise. Knowing she loved it there.'

The thirsty sound the soil made when he fed water to her seedlings, the party when he gave her the caterpillars, Elise turning cartwheels on the grass until Tess called her to come and blow out the candles on her cake; Clark showing Owen how to level up in the video game he was playing; Luke lying on the lawn, watching Elise.

'The vigils,' Grace says. 'Must have been traumatic. Shut in the pickup with him, the four of you stewing in all that violence. You must've hated it.'

A door slams in his head, shutting out the sunny memory of

Elise's birthday, pitching him into the rain outside Box Lane. 'I did . . .'

'But you didn't stop. You fought those men, gave in to temptation like the others. Did it feel good? Before you realized what you'd done?'

'Yes.' He can't lie to her and doesn't want to. 'I was frustrated. At work and about Jude, my inability to change anything that mattered. Dr Bowen bullying her about the cane . . .' He draws a breath, knowing she needs more. 'Living in that house, unable to move on. I spent my whole life keeping my head down. What good did it do me? None. So yes, it felt good to fight those men. In the moment. Before I realized what we had done.'

Grace takes custody of this admission, her expression unchanging. 'And afterwards, when Luke threatened you? How did you feel then?'

'Numb. Disconnected.' He chases down the memory. 'I couldn't concentrate on work, had trouble sleeping. I wasn't eating properly, stopped running because of the vertigo. Started dreaming about the boat and Elise.'

'Then what?' Grace leans forward a fraction. 'What did you do about it? The dreams, the numbness. What did you do, Daniel?'

'I don't know. I can't remember . . .'

He looks at the glass caterpillar in its little spot of sunlight. 'But you do. You were *there*. You remember. Don't you?'

26

To understand the glass caterpillar, you need to understand the doll's house. It lived on the first-floor landing in my parents' home. A four-storey doll's house with a hinged door that swung open to reveal twelve rooms fully furnished, curtains at the windows, working lights and lamps, red tiles on a sloping roof. The doll family sat on upholstered sofas or stood by the side of the range in the kitchen, watching a tiny copper kettle. I was not allowed to touch the doll's house. It was out of bounds.

'Don't give me that face, madam.'

The one time I played with the doll's house, I ended up with my fingers trapped in a door (not a doll-sized door, an adult-sized door), the backs of my legs slapped silly. That might have been enough to put another child off wanting to play with the doll's house but I coveted it all the more. Longed to touch the miniature flower arrangements, the glazed ham no bigger than the tip of my little finger. Whispered to the dolls – the little boy with his scrap of yellow hair, grandma with her wire spectacles and knitting – made up stories about them, even wrote miniature books for the family to read, including a risqué volume for the father who had a rouged mouth and a raunchy angle to his jointed hips. My greatest wish was to shrink myself to the size of a doll and creep into the house to live with the family there. No one would think to look for me in the place I was forbidden from touching. From this, you might reasonably deduce I was a lonely, fanciful child, a cliché in many ways, although like every other child I'd no way of knowing my parents' rules were brutish, or different to those of other families. I imagined everyone had toys they weren't allowed to touch, rules they weren't allowed to break, legs that stung, fingers that throbbed.

When, having become a packer, I discovered how other families treated their children it would have been easy to become jealous or resentful. I'll confess to wishing I might return to the too-big house to confront my tormentors with their many casual cruelties, and I even fantasized about burning it down (after first rescuing the doll's house). Ultimately, if perhaps now ironically, becoming a packer was what saved me from sinking into the iron grip of my past. Instead, I became obsessed with other people's families, in particular children. Young children, like Elise Franklin. Old children, like me.

My favourite room to pack is a child's room. All those treasures that mean so much, cheap trinkets and toys with their faces worn smooth. I longed to pack a doll's house but nowadays most are made of smooth sturdy wood, nothing like my forbidden house with its many and varied choking hazards. Just sometimes there is a box of childish pieces tucked away, sharp-edged toys from another era. Over these I will pore, stirring my fingers to see what will prick and nick. Tin soldiers with pin-sharp bayonets, jointed wooden dolls with splintery hands and feet, sick-glass eyes. Toy milk bottles chipped and deadly at their lips; it only takes a little damage to turn glass into a weapon.

Mirrors are my other passion. Every house has mirrors, even in the children's rooms. Elise had one on her dressing table next to the pin boxes where she kept the grips and spidery nets used to control her hair for her gymnastics. Every day when I was packing her room I set time aside to sit looking into that mirror, conjuring Elise. There wasn't anything morbid or gruesome in my curiosity. It was simply that I missed her. What people don't understand is that it is perfectly possible to miss someone you have never met, whom you will never meet. I'd never heard of Elise Franklin before I was hired to pack her room after her sudden, unnatural death. But after only one morning amongst her treasures, I felt I knew her. I know I loved her. In one sense, she was like all murdered girls – full of shine and promise. Beautiful, a for-ever angel. In another sense, she was unique because she was mine. My first murdered girl. And my first real mystery.

I want very much to solve the puzzle of who killed her. Because it is wrong that she is dead and her killer still alive but also because my job – the relocating of her bedroom – feels incomplete without this resolution.

The glass caterpillar is a token of my faith, the promise I made to Elise to find her killer if I can. Of course, a thief will always find an excuse for stealing, just as a bully will find one for trapping your fingers in a door. I'm under no illusions about that.

The key to the narrowboat was different. I feel guilty about taking the key in a way I don't about the caterpillar. Stealing keys goes against all I hold sacred. But I spent such a long time in the Franklins' house I felt I had to know where else Elise had been.

Had, at least, to look. My parents would have been horrified to discover their constant lesson 'None of your business' led to this conviction that everything is my business. Well, not every lesson lands.

One thing struck me as odd about the evidence.

Elise was strangled and her clothes torn but there was no definitive proof of a sexual motive. Perhaps the killer was disturbed. Or, as one of the detectives speculated, her clothes were torn to mislead the police into assuming her killer was a sexual predator, most probably a man. For all my faults, I'm not an eavesdropper. But the Franklins' old house was so full of whispers, it would have been harder not to hear what was said.

To anyone else, the narrowboat might seem less promising than, say, the forensic evidence, or lack of it. But to me, the idea of the boat is irresistible, linked as it is with romance, stealthy escape. Elise kept a key to the boat on a chain attached to a little cork buoy so it wouldn't be lost if it landed in water. This made it easy to identify among her other treasures.

I searched for her pendant too, of course. The one Tess said she'd worn every day since her eighth birthday and would never have taken off. From photos in the house, I knew the pendant was a tiny glass gymnast on a slim gold chain. It wasn't found on her body. The police considered this significant, enough for them to refer to the pendant during a courtesy call at the house while I was packing, at which they informed the Franklins no new evidence had come to light. It was clear to me that left to the police this crime would never be solved, her killer never brought to justice. Months of investigating and the police had nothing to show for it. No wonder Tess wept.

I wasn't present in the immediate aftermath of the murder, never saw the wound when it was raw. But I know Tess hasn't healed, that if she makes it through a day without weeping, it is only because she is exhausted, hollowed out by grief.

The police searched their house thoroughly after her murder. By the time I arrived to pack it, months later, it had been cleaned several times by Tess. Even so, I found traces of fingerprint powder, the tackiness left by latex gloves; I could see at a glance everywhere the police had poked and pried. I was glad Tess and Clark had decided to move, and not just for their peace of mind. I was glad because it brought me into their orbit – someone new to love their daughter, a fresh pair of eyes over the evidence. And because we became friends, Tess and I. Or so I believed.

Daniel Roake didn't come to either of the houses while I was packing and unpacking for the Franklins. Just as well or I'd never have been able to pass myself off as Gwen as long as I did. I had, however, heard his name. The first time I heard it, Tess and Clark were talking about Luke, sufficient friction in their exchange to make me pay attention.

'It's fine,' Clark was saying. 'Luke's okay.' His voice was monotone, almost automated. I had the impression he'd been saying this about Luke for a long time, perhaps all his life.

'Dan's worried about you.' Tess used the light voice she used when she was trying not to cry.

'Is he?' Clark's tone was dull.

'He wondered if we might like a few days away, says his parents' holiday house is free. We could be off-grid, a proper break . . .'

'I'd never be able to get time off work, love.'

That shocked me. I put down the box I was packing, listening more keenly. Nothing more was said. Not long after that, Clark left the house.

I was shocked because I'd seen him at 8.26 the morning before, as I was parking up for my day's work. He was leaving in the big black pickup with the chrome bull bars. On a whim, I followed. It was too early for me to knock on the door; I'd intended to sit and read for forty minutes. I was always early for work, keen to get started. I followed because I wanted to see where Clark worked, collect another piece of the puzzle. Only he didn't go to work that morning. Or any of the other mornings when I followed him, trying to understand why he would lie to Tess. It made sense he might have lost his job or resigned, unable to bear the charade of carrying on as if his life wasn't in ruins. But not to tell Tess felt to me like cheating. He kept up the pretence day after day, driving off at 8.26 a.m., in his suit and tie. Most days he parked by the school, watching Elise's classmates going through the gates. Once he drove out of town, up towards the Peaks. I didn't follow as I'd have been late for my day's work and Tess would have worried about me.

Later, when I looked it up on a map, I realized the narrowboat was out in the direction Clark had taken. He'd spent the day there, I decided, sitting with her plant pots; I pictured him pressing seeds into soil, sprinkling water. Now I think he sat in silence, weeping. Or else he walked the towpath looking for trouble, hoping for a fight. There is a lot of anger in Clark, too much for him to sit for any length of time. It is why he keeps going back to Luke who feeds the fire in him, stoking it. From what Tess said, Daniel was trying to pull Clark in the opposite direction but I didn't trust either man, back then. Men find such comfort in anger, a place to put their grief without acknowledging it. Women are different. We have the patience to let pain take shape, ebb and flow. Perhaps it is our bodies, the way we learn to live with inconstancy. Tess carried Elise for nine months. She kept carrying her after the murder, holding the pain close. She wasn't at risk of going mad from it, the way Clark was.

'Dan's worried about you,' I heard Tess say.

'Is he?'

As soon as I found the cork keyring in her dressing table, I knew I had to see the narrowboat, Elise's safe place, searched by the police as her bedroom had been. Clark's dad had tried to sell the boat; this meant it wasn't hard to find. There were pictures online, details of its mooring. An address. I went to see for myself, expecting to be alone, but I wasn't.

The black pickup was parked at the top of the towpath. Clark's car. I'd followed it often enough. I saw it again, six nights before I was lured out here to Daniel's holiday home and locked in his cellar. After dark as the canal froze, on the night that changed everything.

Sometimes you get a feeling, don't you? A sense of being given vital information, like a note slipped into your skull. That night I knew I'd find Elise's killer on the narrowboat. Her killer, her pendant and death.

27

'You were there that night.' Dan sits forward. 'On the boat.'

Grace draws up her knees, resting her narrow feet on the bar beneath the chair's seat. 'I was there.' Her face is smooth and pale, her gaze fixed on his face. 'And so was your best friend. Elise's dad, Clark.'

Torchlight moving across water, windows lit like eyes, darkness in the shape of a man. Was that Clark?

'His pickup was parked on the road near the allotment.' Grace props her chin on her knee. 'It's where you parked too, isn't it?'

'Not always but yes. It's the nearest parking place to the towpath. I told you why I went back . . . What were *you* doing there, really?'

'I was looking for Elise.'

'Looking—'

'For some sign of her. After they moved, I missed her. Packing her room, being with her in that way, was the safest I'd felt in a long time. And the saddest.' She doesn't smile, wholly serious. 'Her room was special. Everything in it' – she reaches a finger to the glass caterpillar – 'was special.'

Dan shivers. Her madness is different to his own yet it feels so familiar. As if they were drinking, miles apart, from the same poisoned river.

Grace studies him. 'Tell me about Elise. When you talk about Jude, I can picture her so vividly. I want to see Elise the same way.'

He looks past her shoulder to where the window is carved with light. Two weeks ago, he'd have refused to answer. Elise is none of her business, she belongs to Clark and Tess. But Grace isn't a stranger, not in the way he thought. There is a strangeness to her obsession with Elise but given the state of his head, he doesn't feel equipped to judge her for that. In her own way, she loves Elise. He tests that thought, the way he'd examine a patient's eyesight after surgery, for evidence of distortion or acuity. *She loves Elise.* It feels authentic. In any case, what choice does he have? This is her plan, not his. Her rules. Her vengeance. Her knife.

'She was loved.' The memory comes easily, as frictionless as one of Elise's gymnastic moves. 'We all loved her. She was smart and kind and she wasn't always happy but she was always very . . . *real*. She had this fire. She was just a thirteen-year-old girl but she was unstoppable—'

He breaks off, aware he has used the wrong word. Because Elise was stopped. Someone stopped her in the most vicious way imaginable. Anger stirs under his sadness, a last thin flame from the fire that's been burning in him for the past year.

'You loved her,' Grace says.

'Everyone loved her.'

He's aware of having spoken these words before, aware she corrected him: *Not everyone. Unless you think her killer loved her. People do kill for love. Is that what happened to Elise?*

'That's how we know it was a stranger who killed her. No one who knew her would've hurt her. Everyone loved her.'

At Elise's funeral, he remembers Tess saying this to comfort Owen: 'No one who knew her would've hurt her,' signalling to Dan for his help. He'd put his arm around Owen, hugging him hard, 'Come here, kiddo,' Owen in his best suit and tie, trying to keep tidy the way he had at her christening.

Grace says, 'When Luke made you watch Box Lane, did you believe you'd find the killer?'

Dan shakes his head. 'It was about warning the other girls who used the shortcut. Too many of them didn't know.'

'So you thought the killer was local, close to home. How close?'

He has no answer to that. He knows where she is going with it, hasn't forgotten what she said about the pickup parked by the towpath that night.

Sure enough: 'Tell me about Clark,' she says next. 'Why did he keep lying to Tess? About the fight with those three men. And about losing his job.'

She was in their house for days. Not just the old house, the new one. Moving Elise's room from one place to the other. When Tess gave him Grace's name, Dan was sick at the thought of a stranger in Elise's room. But the police had already been there, Tess reminded him, and besides, Grace was careful, respectful: 'Honestly, Dan, she's a godsend.'

The godsend sits at the side of his bed, waiting for his answer to her question. The godsend has a knife.

'Clark didn't lose his job,' Dan admits. 'He quit. Because he couldn't get time off for the vigil.'

'On Friday afternoons. What was so special about Fridays?'

'It's when it happened. On a Friday afternoon. She was walking home from school. It was raining. That's why she took the shortcut, we think.'

'*We* think? Who thinks?'

'Tess and Clark and the police.'

'Clark quit his job over the vigils? Is that true?'

'It's what he said . . . I tried to talk with him about it but he wouldn't open up. It's possible he was fired. He said he quit to be part of the vigil.' Dan sees Clark's face smoothed by sleep, the peace that visited him on Friday nights. 'He didn't do it. He couldn't have slept like that, right next to where it happened, if he'd killed her. No one could.'

Grace is silent, as if lost in thought.

Dan shifts his shoulders, getting the measure of his returning strength. 'I could use some fresh air. Can we go outside?'

She moves the chair out of his way, watching as he stands. He has to reach for the wall to steady himself. It is odd to be on his feet. Gravity feels unfriendly. The chinos slouch at his hips. He's lost weight even without the running to keep him in shape. His blood feels like water and his vision is a mudslide until he finds his balance. He misses the vertigo, its unequivocality.

His deck shoes are by the back door where he left them, his coat on a peg. She helps him put it on. It was winter two weeks ago but autumn is clawing back a little of what's left of the year. Outside, the sunshine has enough warmth to surprise him. Grace stays close, with the intention of catching him perhaps if he falls or thinks of running. He wouldn't get far. Not without a car, and he is fairly certain she's put the keys to her Fiat and his Saab somewhere safe. It is good to be outside, though.

He sits on the low stone wall at the foot of the terrace, looking to the mass of trees where jackdaws dip in and out of branches. The air smells bitter, blackening. He takes a deep breath, holds it in his lungs. Crows rasp overhead. As he sits there, they start to settle in dark thorns along the branches of the furthest trees. Creosote adds its scratch to the air. He feels the pull of the past: childhood games in the garden, eating potatoes baked in a fire pit built by Dad, Mum adding butter with a blade. The memories shiver in his skull, fusing with the recent past: Elise's seedlings on the narrowboat; a damp towel hung on a hook to dry; Grace's knife in his hip. She sits beside him on the wall, neatly. He thinks of her shoebox with its clever compartments, wishes his head was like that. It used to be. Everything boxed up and kept separate. Mum's death unconnected to Dad's. Elise's murder detached from Clark's anger. Luke's vigil not touching the summer fifteen years ago. The narrowboat. The pickup. His parents' house. His unhappiness. His work. No danger of cross-contamination. No danger, either, of feeling any of it. Until now.

'You were knocking it down.' Grace nods at the shed. 'Why?'

'Exercise . . . ?' He is unsure of the reason but his shoulders hold the memory of an ache at the end of each day. 'No . . .' Her nearness helps him to retrieve the memory: 'I didn't know I was knocking it down. I thought I was building it. With Luke. I thought it was the narrowboat.'

'It scared me.' She shades her eyes. 'The sound of it, not knowing what you were doing.'

'I'm sorry. It wasn't . . . I should have thought of that.'

'I think you did. I think you meant to scare me. You didn't know how else to get me to tell you what I knew about that night on the boat.'

He believes her, at some level. She knows him better than he knows himself. He can't make sense of his actions or motives but she's had to make sense of them to survive what he put her through. Survival is such a tricky business, primal and complex at the same time. Strapped to that bed, he thought it didn't matter if he lived or died but it does. It matters to her.

'Why did you pretend you weren't Grace?'

'I was scared. You were so strange, not what I'd expected. I realized you didn't know what Grace looked like, that you'd never seen me before. Or else you'd forgotten.' She watches a jackdaw stalking the lawn. 'I wasn't sure, though. You didn't give me many clues.'

'You didn't give me any,' he remembers. 'No bag in your car, no purse or wallet. Nothing to identify you.'

'I left all that at home, thought it best. Not knowing exactly what you wanted, or how far you'd go to get it. That way I could deny being Grace, pretend to be Gwen. There was a protection in that.'

'But you knew about Elise.' The low winter sun is dazzling, hiding the details in her profile. 'And me. You knew it was a trap – whatever I was doing here. Why did you come?'

'For the same reason you did. To find her killer.'

'Is that what I was doing?' Dan wonders.

'It must be. It's the only thing that makes sense.'

'Not the only thing. I could be hiding. On the run.'

She eyes him sideways. 'Running or hiding from what?'

'I don't know. I can't remember.'

They are quiet for a long time, sitting side by side on the wall with the half-demolished shed to the right of them, the house behind. Dan is struck from nowhere by a love for life he thought he'd left behind months ago. He wants to see Jude, keep his promise of finding her a better counsellor. Wants to go home to his parents' house, make his peace with the place before selling up and moving on. It will never happen now but in this moment the feeling itself is enough, spreading warmth across his chest.

'Thank you . . .' His apologies were always sincere but this *thank you* comes from a place of real gratitude, not simply fear or relief.

Grace looks at him closely. 'For what?'

He can't explain so he gestures at the garden. 'Letting me outside.'

'You let me out.'

'You didn't want to go.'

She shrugs. 'Things to do.'

'Right . . .'

'How's your hip?'

It is the strangest conversation they've had, and that is saying something. 'It's good, better. How's your head?'

Where he hit her, he means, but the moment's passed.

She's back to business: 'So Clark and the vigil that was worth giving up his job for. What do you make of that?'

'He's grieving—'

'We're all grieving, Daniel. You, too. You didn't pack up your job just to have the chance of exorcizing your anger once a week.' She narrows her gaze at the trees. 'Clark didn't like the idea of her growing up. He spoke about her like a little girl, *not like those others with their nails and hair . . .*'

'You can't really believe he killed her for growing up.'

'Fathers can be funny about things like that.' Her voice is bland but her fists are balled. 'About their daughters. Little girls.'

He senses a fresh pit opening at their feet, as she threatens to draw him down into whatever darkness is in her past. He doesn't want to go there. Searches for a way to bring her back: 'Tell me about the boy before Elise. Just an ordinary boy, you said. Men found him, turned him to drugs and violence.'

'You remember that, then.'

'I remember everything from after you stabbed me.'

She twitches a smile from her lips. 'You're welcome.'

'Tell me about him?' Dan wraps the coat more tightly around himself. 'The boy. What was his name?'

'Joseph. Joe.' She presses her lips together as if resisting the temptation to talk. Then she says, 'I found drugs in his bedroom when I was packing it for the move. I did nothing about it, told no one. Put the pills back where I found them, packed his things. Posters and CDs, pencil cases, old comics, bits of Lego, cars he'd collected when he was small . . .'

Dan waits, aware of holding his breath. He catches a glimpse of her life when she isn't moving, when the day is over and she is alone with only herself for company. It shakes him.

'Then . . .' She drops her head back, tipping her face to the sky. 'Weeks later, I heard on the news a boy had been found stabbed to death, left by the bins on an estate not far from the house they moved to.' She brings her stare down to the garden, sitting very small on the wall. 'They were well-off, his dad an entrepreneur, mum an anaesthetist. Decent middle-class people. Joseph was their only child. He had all the latest gadgets, smart clothes, money. They weren't neglectful in the way we think of parents being neglectful. They were just . . . busy. At the inquest they said they'd had no idea he was taking drugs, let alone dealing them for a gang of older boys.'

Dan sits in silence with what she's said, thinking of what it means. To her, about her. He is wary of making this worse, doesn't want to offer anything as simple as platitudes or sympathy. 'You blame yourself?'

'That would be neat, wouldn't it? I failed with Joseph, Elise is my chance at redemption?' She shakes her head. 'No, Daniel.'

'What could you have done differently?'

'Nothing.' She turns her hands up. 'This is who I am: I pack and I pry. But I don't tell tales, especially not to busy parents with better things to do.'

It chills him all over again. He is no nearer knowing who she is or what she wants. She's haunted by Joe. He sees the boy's shadow in her eyes, the way he sees Elise's. Does she feel the way Dan does, a stranger in his own skin? He wants to tell her he understands but he's not sure it's true. The pain of self-reproach is unlike any pain he has suffered before. But if she's taught him anything over the past fortnight it is that the past fifteen years are a part of him – *are* him – and shouldn't be unwished. He wants the chance to learn to live with his loss, find a proper place for it. He can't be whole until he's reconciled the pieces, even the ones that hurt, especially the ones that hurt, whose edges are so sharp he didn't notice the sting until the damage was done.

'I'm sorry you went through that.'

'Thank you. Now tell me what you meant when you said Elise wasn't happy all the time.'

Dan hesitates, pressing his palms to the rough stone wall. 'It was the police,' he says finally. 'They found things on the boat, things she'd hidden. I suppose she thought Tess might find them if they were in her room.'

'What sort of things?' Grace is rigid with attention.

'Bits of jewellery mostly. Earrings, bracelets . . . Things she'd stolen.' He blinks, remembering the bleakness in Tess's eyes when she told him. 'From the girls she was in competition with at gymnastics.'

Grace is silent. He shares her unhappiness. It hurt Tess horribly to be told her dead child was a petty thief. 'On that *bloody* boat,' Tess said, as if the narrowboat was the problem.

'How certain were they,' Grace wants to know, 'that it was Elise who took the things? Her pendant's missing, too.'

'It was missing.'

'*Was?*' She looks at him sharply.

He's as surprised as she is by what he's just said. More words crowd behind his teeth, spill out: 'Tess found it.'

The memory lands like a prize from a slot machine fed by her questions. 'The day after the fight at the vigil.'

He stops, out of breath.

'Tess found the pendant?' Grace demands. 'Where? It wasn't in her room. I looked for it. Harder than the police did, I'll bet. It wasn't there.'

Dan draws a breath and holds it until the garden goes out of focus. Summoning the memory, seeing Tess more clearly than he sees Grace now. Slowly he lets the breath go, giving her what she wants: 'The pendant was in the pickup the day after the fight.'

Grace starts to speak then stops. Dan can taste iron, from the fight. He is back in the immediate aftermath of the violence, in the damp heat of the pickup, all four of them panting and sweating, stripping off their coats, wiping their faces. Luke's laughing, Owen's hiccups like an echo of the same sound. Clark's breathing hard, knuckles white under the blood as he grips the steering wheel. Dan is struggling to unclench his own fists, to put the anger back in its box and become human again. *Animal.* They're animals.

On the floor of the pickup, dropped from a pocket as they stripped: a slim shiver of gold, the flare of glass. A tiny leaping girl. Elise's pendant.

'Tess found the pendant,' Grace repeats. 'In the pickup. After the four of you fought those men.' Her words cut through the chaos in his head. 'One of you dropped it, then. One of you had her pendant all that time – for a whole year after her murder – and dropped it that night. Is that what you're saying?'

'Yes. I think . . . Yes.'

'Who was it, Daniel? Which one of you?'

'I don't know . . .' Despair is a stack of stones in his chest, reaching all the way into his throat.

'Who killed her, Daniel?'

'*I don't know. Do you?*'

Grace falls silent beside him on the wall. He is more afraid in that moment than he has ever been in his life. The old fears slip away: *his mother twisting in the bath. Luke grinding his arm into the helium tank. Darkness in the shape of a man moving on the narrowboat.* All gone. There is only this: Elise's pendant in the pickup. Elise's *killer*, in the pickup.

'Grace . . . If you know, please . . . tell me.'

'I know who was on the narrowboat that night.' She turns to face him. 'The night you can't remember.' She holds up her left hand. 'Clark.' She tucks her thumb into her palm. 'Luke.' She folds her index finger.

'And you, Daniel.' Her middle finger: 'You were there.'

247

28

By the time I'd parked up behind Clark's truck, it was late. Close to ten o'clock. The pickup had its lights off, empty inside. I'd half expected to see Clark sitting in a trance like the one that took him out of the house every day, pretending to Tess he was headed to work. I was furious with him. He was grieving for Elise, I understood that. But to leave Tess on her own when he could have been home with her, leading her on this merry dance while she held down the fort, imagining her husband bravely taking himself into work as she struggled to face cooking or shopping? I found that hard to forgive.

I remembered her concern, 'Dan's worried about you,' and the dull way Clark dismissed it, 'Is he?' My hands had been full of Elise's books at that moment, holding them as tenderly as I could. Elise was there in the room with me. Tess trusted me to take her to the new house, not to lose her in transit. No damage, no breakages. Tess and Clark were broken enough already.

The towpath was unlit, pitted with rain damage.

I was swathed in layers enough for the Arctic, two pairs of gloves, woolly ones over a thin thermal pair to keep my prints off the surfaces. Doors, cupboards, boxes. I'd made a promise to Elise that I wouldn't leave until I was a step closer to her killer. Shadows prowled down by the lock, the canal curled and muscular as if something monstrous were surfacing through the water's skin. My breath hung white on the air. The towpath was deserted, no dog walkers or late-night revellers, no muggers or rapists. *Sorry, Mum.* Unless Elise's killer was on the narrowboat, as I half wished they were; the sight of Clark's pickup had lit a flare of fury in me. I was reckless, in search of a fight.

The boat was black, blending with the night but for the glint of its brasswork. I should have put my hand to the bonnet of the pickup, the way detectives do in TV dramas to see how recently the engine was running. Why would Clark park so close to the boat then not go aboard? The towpath was popular with runners. Had he come here to run? His friend Dan was a runner; Tess had said, 'You could go running with Dan like you used to.'

In my pocket, I had the key from Elise's room. The key I'd borrowed, with no plan to return it. It wasn't as if I could knock on Tess's door and say, 'I'm sorry, I seem to have walked off with this when I was packing your daughter's room.' But Tess would thank me if I found a new clue tonight, answers to the terrible questions in her head. She'd thank me.

The well deck was slippery, I was glad of the cleats on my boots. I brushed my knuckles at the cabin door, not wanting to knock, partly for fear of finding someone inside but mostly because I didn't want to be stopped from turning the key and going in there myself. I was so close to her now, closer than I'd been at any point since I finished the unpacking in the new house, a task I'd kept going as long as I could, more reluctant to leave with each passing hour, knowing that when I did I'd be abandoning her with questions unanswered, her death unsolved, her killer at large. You'll say I was mad but grief takes many forms; I was grieving for Elise. If Clark could do that by giving up his job and lying to his wife, I could do it by coming out here to trespass on a boat.

The key turned smoothly in the lock. It was colder inside the cabin than on the towpath, droplets of moisture studding the insides of the windows, turning them to the hobnailed glass of old poison bottles: *Not To Be Taken.* A seating area, double berth, took up one side of the space, together with a table and a foldable bed; I knew the layout from my searches online. A galley kitchen stood beyond with a stove towards which I moved as if tugged: *Light a fire, get warm.* Searching the kitchen cupboards, I found a box of matches that rattled in my hand but the box was damp, reluctant to strike. I put it down and moved deeper into the boat, discovering the small bathroom and bedroom at the rear where a truckle bed was made up. Light switches were set at intervals but I used the torch on my phone, cupping my hand to limit the glare. As I swept the torch around the cabin, I saw a tray of plant pots: Elise's seedlings. In her diary, she'd been recording their progress. Chives, mint, basil, lamb's lettuce. I touched the tips of my gloved fingers to the straggling shoots, wondering who'd been watering them. The plants would surely have died by now if left alone. Most were dead but a few gave out leggy green shoots.

On the towpath, the slight skid of boots.

Don't give me that face.

The voice was a jolt in my head. Through the frosted window I was sure I saw my old dad on the towpath. Warpath. *Not him, not that.*

I was trespassing but that wasn't why I crouched. I knew who was out there. Not a dog walker or a drunk. Not my old dad or my mum.

A killer. Her killer.

Call it instinct, call it what you like, but I *knew*. The skidding came a second time and then he was stopping, taking his hands from his pockets as he reached for the rail to swing himself from the path into the well deck. I'd hooked the latch across the inside of the door but it wouldn't hold if he put his shoulder to it. I cowered on the floor, scared out of my mind. Tess had said, 'He's not helping. He thinks he is but look at you, the state of you,' and Clark had told her, 'It's fine. He's okay,' as he'd been saying all his life.

The boat shuddered under the weight of him in the well deck. I'd known his name for weeks. It was written in Elise's diary, in purple biro, circled with stars. *Luke Hooley.*

29

'She had Luke's name written in her diary?' Dan shivers on the stone wall.

'You're cold,' Grace says. 'We should go back inside.'

'No.' He needs to breathe, can't be shut up in the house when she says whatever she is going to say. 'Finish it, please.'

The crows are going wild in the sky over the trees, massing against what is left of the day. Dan keeps his gaze on them, the shapes they make: separating, converging, the pattern repeated over and over.

'I knew he was no good. Luke. Even before you told me what he did to you that summer. From the way Tess talked about him, I knew.' Like Dan, Grace is watching the crows. 'And when a girl writes a grown man's name in her diary . . . ? I know what that means, too.'

Dan drops his eyes to his hands, resisting the urge to touch the knife wound, which is wet again. He wants her to finish but she won't be rushed. If she senses she is torturing him, she gives no clue, carrying on in her usual voice, her usual way, stretching on the wall next to him as if easing an ache.

'I can't believe Elise liked him. From what I saw, he wasn't charming.'

'He can be. And there's Owen – we all looked out for him, even Elise. Luke looks out for Owen, too. If you saw that side of him, you'd understand.'

'Well,' she says, 'I'm not likely to see it now.'

Dan stares at her. 'What does that mean?'

She shakes her head.

His stomach churns, unease a distant outpost. The crows scratch at the sky, bruising the branches of the trees.

'Tell me,' he says again. 'Finish it. Please.'

30

Elise's seedlings trembled as footfall shook the deck, a long tremor moving down the flank of the boat to where I was crouched, waiting.

Let it come, I thought. *I'm ready.*

Was I mad? Perhaps. So deep in my obsession it hardly mattered who found me or what they thought, or even what they did.

Who are you and what've you done with my daughter?

Elise was on the boat with me, that was how it felt, the pair of us waiting for her killer. *I'll fight,* I told her, *I'll fight for your life.*

He was fighting the lock on the cabin door. I'd failed to fasten it or he had a technique to get around it – a screwdriver slipped in the gap – because the next thing I heard was the door opening, boots scuffing the floor.

In my mind's eye was a schematic of the boat from the well deck where he'd entered all the way back to the place I was hiding near the rear of the vessel where the engine and tiller were housed. My dad's voice provided the proper word: *aft.* Tarpaulin and rope were stored in the aft, an old tyre, a bag of coal for the stove. Fifty

254

feet separated him from where I was crouched, my face swathed in scarves.

He was breathing hard as if he'd been running or fighting. Tess had said, 'He's dragging Dan and Owen into it, too. Don't you care about that?'

Owen was Luke's baby brother; I'd read about him in Elise's diary. There was no mystery about Owen, the way there was about Luke. Elise wrote of Owen as one teenager might about another, a friend. It was only Luke's name she'd surrounded by stars.

New footfall on the towpath. Not boots this time or not steel-toed, a stealthier sound. The door creaked twice, a fresh tremor moving down the boat as the second body came aboard. If they spoke to one another, I didn't hear. Just the half-sound of water tapping at the hull. The newcomer was lighter than Luke, or quieter on his feet. Luke's boots scuffed at the floor again.

The door creaked a fourth time before a small explosion thundered through the boat, sending me scurrying backwards in fright.

Almost instantly a second explosion, louder, rocked the hull under my splayed fingers. Then a third.

Not actual explosions – noise amplified by wood and water – violence erupting ahead of me.

More sounds followed, familiar from my childhood and from fights I'd witnessed in the street, in pubs and houses. A sickening force from fists or feet, an echo to every contact as if a weapon were involved, heavy, metallic. I covered then uncovered my ears, terrified of losing track of the fight, of the attacker working his way back to where I was hiding.

The fight stopped as suddenly as it had started, gutting every inch of the boat: the furniture, the seedlings and their tray, the stove, my heart and stomach and mouth – I was empty until black terror rushed in to fill me.

The harsh sound of breathing. A thud, echoing, ringing like a dropped bell. The smell of burning, of dead water, my own fear.

The boat steadied under me and I realized it must have been shaking with the force of the fight. It kept shifting, as if to remind me I was on water, not dry land. I started to unfold myself but shrank back as something slapped the canal behind me – a light sound like a ball being thrown.

I curled back down, waiting for the creak of the door to tell me they'd gone, but the sound never came. I thought I heard the pickup's engine, I definitely heard tyres. In the end, I gave up waiting and stood.

The boat was in blackness like before. But there was a different shape to it and I knew I wasn't alone. Someone else was with me.

In my mind's eye, the two of us stood at our opposite ends of the boat, staring into the darkness where the other stood, also staring.

Finally, I worked up the courage to move, putting one foot in front of the other until I was within sight of the cabin door.

No one was standing, or watching. I'd been wrong about that. Instead, a dense patch of shadow lay on the floor at the foot of the berth, which, when I shone my torch on it, morphed into the body of a man.

31

'Luke.' Dan thinks he might puke, or pass out. 'Luke's body.'

'That's what it looked like.' Grace sounds as sick as he feels. 'But it was hard to tell what I was looking at.'

He stares at her. His mind turns, empty of thought.

'The metallic sound I kept hearing. Explosions.' She brushes dust from the stone wall. 'Something solid smashed his skull. There wasn't much left. But he was wearing boots and that green army jacket you said he always wore.'

'Something solid?' Fear prickles the length of Dan's spine, across his shoulders, into the palms of both hands. 'What was it?'

'An orange tank, with handles. I think . . . that was the weapon.'

The murder weapon.

'The helium tank.'

Dan pictures it clearly. Orange paint flaking from corroded aluminium, handles sharp enough to cut. What he cannot picture is Luke's skull smashed to blood and bone. 'You're sure it was him?'

Grace nods. 'I'm sorry.'

There is a strange flavour to her apology, like pity. Or caution. He stares at her. 'You think . . . *I* did it . . .'

257

Crows track blackly across the sky.

'Grace? You think I did it. Because of this.' He pushes the sleeve from his right forearm, showing his scars. 'Because of what I told you.'

She is holding her breath. She's afraid of him. Is she?

'You should have left me on the bed.' He drops his arm to his side. 'With the belts on. If you think I'm a killer, capable of that.'

The silence stretches between them. It is Grace who breaks it: 'Luke killed Elise.'

Dan shakes his head. 'Prove it.'

'The pendant in the pickup. The violence.' Her voice is fierce. '*You.*'

She's not afraid of him, she's trying to find excuses for him. For why he might have lost his mind and beaten Luke Hooley to a bloody pulp with the weapon Luke used to scar his arm fifteen years ago.

'He killed Elise so I killed him? That's what you think?'

'*Yes.*'

He shakes his head a second time. 'No.'

'The stars in the diary.' Grace balls her fist on the wall. 'The pendant. He attacked you when you were her age. He lured her to that boat, made it a place she'd want to be, the way he made it for you all that time ago. She trusted him, her mum and dad trusted him—'

'Yes, they did. That is why he did not need to kill her if you're saying he wanted to rape her, if that's what you think he wanted. And anyway, she didn't die on the boat. She died in Box Lane.'

She recoils from whatever expression is on his face. Grief or anger, he can't tell. He knows his eyes hurt and his mouth, too.

'Luke got what he wanted, from everyone. Me, Clark, Owen,

Tess . . . Every one of us jumped when he said jump. He didn't need to use violence. He certainly didn't need to kill anyone.'

Grace grabs his right wrist, dragging his scars into the light. 'He didn't need to do this but he did. He was a monster. *He* was the monster.'

Dan waits for the worst of the rage to leave her face before he frees his wrist from her grip. Her fingers are icy. Shock, he thinks. He can't imagine what it was like listening to the sound of Luke's face being smashed from his skull, finding his body like that. He can't imagine . . . He tries but he can't. All the images bursting like flashbulbs behind his eyes are from *outside* the boat. If he was there, if he's a killer, surely he would have memories from inside the boat? He has a vague idea that is explained by dissociative amnesia but the weight of the helium tank in his hands, the sensation of it slamming into Luke's skull . . . He couldn't have forgotten a thing like that. Could he?

'It wasn't me. I'd remember if it was me.'

'You *can't* remember.' Grace shivers. 'That's the problem. You're suffering from some sort of amnesia.'

'Clearly. But even so, I think I'd remember if I had pulverized his head with a helium tank.'

She squints sideways in response to the dry note in his voice. He gives a slight smile, wanting her to stop looking so sad and accepting. She is not afraid of him, even now. Is it that easy for her to see him as a killer? Of course, he put her in his cellar after knocking her out cold. First impressions count.

'Unless there's something you're not telling me . . . Is there? You said I was there that night.'

'It was a Friday.' Her answer sounds reflexive. 'You'll have been in the pickup, all of you. Clark, Luke, Owen and you.'

Dan acknowledges the likely truth of this, despite the fact he cannot retrieve any memory of leaving work on that particular day, or of seeing Luke and the others, or attending the vigil. The whole day is lost to the amnesia.

'You said you saw Clark.' He holds up his middle finger as she did when counting off the players on the boat that night. 'And you saw me.'

'I thought it would help.' She rests her cheek on her knee, looking at him. 'That something would click in your head.'

'So you *didn't* see me?'

'I didn't see anyone, not clearly. But the pickup was there and it was Friday night. It's a reasonable assumption.' She appears to weigh her next words: 'During a psychotic episode, some people can see themselves from a distance. *Out of body.* I looked it up on your phone when I was trying to figure out what's wrong with you. You could have memories that make you think you were watching someone else kill him when it was really you.'

'You think I'm a killer but you let me up from that bed.' He raises his eyebrows at her.

'What can I say,' she gives back. 'I'm gutsy like that.'

'Or you don't think I did it. Not really.'

'Or that,' she agrees.

Silence again but it's different, companionable. The day is dying around them, shadows reaching from the house.

Dan has the clearest sense of his mother standing at the upstairs window. If he turns, he'll catch her, looking out at him. Rationally he knows this is nonsense, a measure of his madness. But the feeling persists and after a minute he realizes he wants it to be true. He wants Mum to be there, waiting for him to make his peace with her. He shivers at the thought, tucking his chin to his chest. The crows have gone quiet in the trees.

'Come on.' Grace stands. 'Before you freeze to death.'

The Facts As I Know Them

- He didn't do it.
- He didn't do it.
- He didn't do it.
- So who did?

32

Tess wasn't the way I'd imagined her when the job came through. I'd pictured a small slim woman with a sweet sad face. The woman who answered the door was tall and broad-shouldered, *as broad as a man*, with pale hair tied back from a wide freckled face. She was young to be the mother of a teenager.

'Good morning. I'm the packer, Grace Maddox.'

'Of course, please, come in.'

Tears shone in her eyes. Later, I'd realize the tears were part of who she was. Elise's mum. The mother of my murdered girl.

To begin with, I stayed away from Tess, busying myself with my work. I packed the other rooms first, circling Elise's as I moved around the house. It had been explained to me this was a bereaved couple. I had expected the house to feel sad and empty but it didn't. Tess was too solid for that. She watched me as I packed, saw the care I took. When she was ready, she led me upstairs.

'This is Elise's room,' touching the door tenderly with her large hand.

The room felt full and happy as if Elise had just popped out, her gym bag bumping at her hip as she ran downstairs, out to the pickup, on her way to a lesson or a gymnastics contest. Her room smelt of pink chalky powder.

'I'll take good care,' I promised. 'Of everything.'

After that, we spent a lot of time together. Tess liked to make pots of tea and would invite me to sit with her in the kitchen, which was bright and cheerful, looking out onto a garden planted with hydrangeas. On occasion, she'd bake a cake. She missed baking cakes, for Elise.

'I kept waiting for her to say she was on a diet, or some new fitness fad like the others. But she was lucky, could eat cake and stay slim as a wand.'

We talked about her daughter all the time. It helped that I was a stranger, someone who wasn't grieving in the way her friends and family were. And that I asked questions. Most people didn't like to ask, Tess said, thinking it would remind her of her loss, as if that could somehow be separated from the rest of her, who she was now. She told me once she wished more people understood what a kindness it was to let her talk about Elise. What hurt was the idea of people forgetting. Who Elise was. How she died.

'It wasn't a sexual assault,' she told me over a pot of tea and a plate of biscuits. 'People keep getting that wrong.' She wiped her tears with her wrists, a clean sweep across her broad cheekbones. 'They think she was raped but she wasn't. Her clothes were torn and she was strangled. *Strangled.*'

Odd, the emphatic way she said it. As if being strangled were a blessing, as if she was saying, 'She didn't suffer.' It upset her, people thinking Elise's killer was a rapist. I understood she didn't want to think that particular horror had happened to her child but it seemed an odd thing for her to fixate on.

'Tell me about the Sheffield trophy,' I'd say when she was like that. 'What was it like, when she won?'

And she'd pull her stare back from Box Lane, and Elise would sit at the kitchen table with us, swinging her feet and laughing.

In this way, I did what I could to help. But what Tess needed was her husband. Clark was so rarely there; I don't think I saw him more than three times between the two moves. He was working, Tess said. 'And grieving, of course. I have to let him do that his way.'

His way, as far as I could tell, involved neglecting Tess until she was forced to turn to strangers for the peace and understanding she needed. I gave what I could of my company – my questions or my silence depending on her mood – but I wasn't her husband. I wasn't Elise's father.

Over the weeks when I was moving them between the two houses, I became intimately acquainted with Tess's grief in all its flavours. The tears she wiped with her wrists, the hardness forged from Clark's neglect.

Once she smashed a teacup in the sink. Deliberately. 'That's gone then,' her mouth and eyes set in narrow, wrathful lines. As she watched me tidy up the mess, she said, 'You're not what I expected.'

I smiled at her, inviting more, but she shook her head.

She was different with me after that, not standing as close as she had before, watching me when she thought I wouldn't notice. Thinking me odd. Everyone always thinks that, sooner or later.

Towards the end of my time on the job, I began to suspect her grief was turning in a new direction. Away from cherished memories of her child, towards resentment of her husband. His continued absences nagged at her, at the whole house. I could feel the empty space filling with her frustration.

Their marriage hadn't always been a happy one.

When you pack someone's house, it is inevitable you find things they have forgotten to throw away, or forgotten they had. I'd seen diaries and letters – tacky with the police's glove prints, discounted during the official investigation – which made me wonder. Even at the start of their marriage there was friction.

Clark proposed to Tess at the age of seventeen after getting her pregnant with Elise. They were in love, no doubt. But Tess considered an abortion. She'd planned to go to university. Clark talked her into being a mum. It made me wonder what else he might've talked her into. Also what resentment she might have carried, for what length of time, at the derailment of her life.

33

'Stop it,' Dan says. 'You do not know what you're talking about.'

'So tell me.' Grace eyes him across the kitchen.

She is relentless, segueing straight from suspecting him of killing Luke to this new suspicion of Tess and Clark.

'You think you know them because you packed their house. But people are more than the sum of their possessions. If you'd packed my house, you'd probably think I was a homicidal maniac. Oh, wait . . . you did think that.'

She nearly smiles but he is not going to distract her that easily.

'Tess found the pendant in the pickup. That is what you said out there in the garden. Did she take it to the police?'

'The police had already searched the pickup.'

It isn't an answer to her question but she pounces on it: 'Clark was a suspect? Was Luke?'

'Everyone was a suspect.' Dan gets up to put the kettle on. Perhaps she'll calm down if he makes tea. 'It doesn't mean what you think.'

'Tess knew the pickup was searched by the police.' Grace sits staring at the dark window. 'That means she knew the pendant wasn't dropped by Elise. And I'll bet she cleaned the pickup, from time to time. She's very tidy-minded. She'd have found the pendant if it had been there for any length of time. That means she knew the killer had been in the pickup recently.'

Dan sets the kettle on the hob, lights the gas, adjusts the dial. He is able to do these things without thinking but he can't remember what Tess told him about the pendant. Not in sufficient detail. He sees her face but it is twisted out of focus. *I know you did your best.* Did she say that to him? If so, why? What did he do and why wasn't it good enough?

'She knew Luke kept dragging you all out on that vigil. I heard her talking with Clark about it. She wanted him to stop but he couldn't. Luke wouldn't let any of you stop.' Grace narrows her eyes, conjuring pictures, her mind's eye hard at work. 'I bet it turned him on, going back to Box Lane. Where it happened. They say killers do that, return to the scene.'

Dan thinks of the animal smell in the pickup. He'd wondered if it was arousal. He doesn't want to believe it but she's right to say Luke was pushing all the time for them to commit to the vigil. Clark gave up his job because Luke wouldn't take no for an answer. Owen came out in all weathers in his split trainers, tapping his foot as he played on his console, stopping when Luke barked at him to stop. Dan opened a second can of lager when Luke threw it at him, and climbed out of the pickup into a fist fight with strangers on nothing more than Luke's say so.

'What if it was Clark?' Grace is saying. 'On the narrowboat? If he found out Luke killed Elise and was dragging you all back there week after week? Refusing to let Clark heal or move on, rubbing his face in what happened like he rubbed your arm on that tank—'

'You do not know what you're talking about.'

She shoots him a vehement look. 'I know exactly what I'm talking about. You told me what kind of an animal he was. He was out of control, the night of that fight. Blood lust got the better of him. He was sick of sitting still, wasn't getting the high he needed from terrorizing schoolgirls, wanted to hurt someone. *You* told me that.'

Dan bows his head, battered by her words. It's too easy, that's the trouble, too easy to see Luke as she describes him. Dan is balanced at the edge of a pit where vengeance and violence live, and she is tempting him to jump. He steps away from the stove, to stand between her and the window.

'Luke didn't kill her.'

'What makes you so sure?' Grace demands.

'I don't know, I wish I did . . . But it doesn't make sense. He was violent, yes. And he was angry. But I can't see him killing Elise. I just can't.'

Her gaze grows distant, grey eyes locked to his face but seeing straight through him to the garden and road behind, all the way back to where they came from. When she speaks, her voice is low, each word precise: 'Because you could have stopped him. If you'd reported him fifteen years ago. Told someone – anyone – what he did to you. If you had told Clark and Tess . . . They would never have allowed him near Elise. *Ever*. She'd still be alive.'

Each word is a blow, a hammer to Dan's heart. He is amazed he stays upright, on his feet. The pain in his hip is nothing in comparison.

'Now we're even.' He straightens in stages until he is standing under the light. 'Unless you'd like me down in the cellar for good measure.'

'I'd like you to *help* me,' she says furiously. 'If Luke killed Elise, then he's dead and that's a good thing. If Clark killed *him*—'

'He didn't. Clark isn't—'

'If Clark killed Luke, then Tess needs to know. They deserve to know who's responsible for what happened to their daughter.' Her eyes flash. 'You don't know what it did to them, Daniel. You weren't in those two houses with their grief. You have *no idea* how it changed them. They need answers. They need to know the truth about what happened.'

She is a grinding force. He doesn't know how to stop her.

'They need to *grieve*,' Dan says. 'They need the chance to get better.'

'Did *you* get better by doing and saying nothing? No. You got worse.'

'They're not like me. They have each other—'

Grace nods. 'Except one of them's a killer.'

'Will you . . . *stop*. Neither of them is a killer. I *know* them. I grew up with them.'

'You left them. You ran away and when you came back, Luke was in charge. Had been, for years. Clark lied to Tess for Luke. He gave up his job . . . If he found out Luke killed Elise after he'd lied to Tess, let her down . . . ? That would have been enough to tip him over the edge.' Her eyes narrow. 'Or Owen, he might have dropped the pendant in the pickup . . . Or Tess, if she lied about finding it there. If she hid it, kept it safe all that time . . .' She falls silent, thinking. 'I was in those two houses with them. I moved them from one place to the next and *everything* was stained by their grief. Like pollen. Grief and anger, too.' She pins him with her stare. 'Did you even know Tess had considered an abortion?'

Dan presses the knuckle of his thumb to the socket of his eye, trying to find the words to explain why she is wrong. Wrong to think because two people don't spend every second of their lives together happily in love it means they are capable of keeping secrets as deadly as the ones she is trying to uncover. They are hunting two killers now – Elise's and Luke's – when they shouldn't be hunting at all.

'Look, I'm sorry for what I did to you. I am but—'

'Stop saying *sorry* and help me.'

'Let the police do this. It's their job.'

'And they're doing it so well!'

She sounds like Luke, who nicknamed the lead detective 'Poundland Plod', saying he wouldn't trust him to pour piss from a boot if the instructions were printed on the heel.

'They'll have found him by now. The police. Found Luke's body on the boat. It's been more than three weeks. They must have found him.'

Grace looks at him, pityingly. 'If they were looking, maybe.'

'Why wouldn't they be looking? Someone will have reported him missing. Owen, or Shannon. He's too noisy to go missing for any length of time without someone sounding the alarm.'

'Not like you then.'

Dan props his fists either side of him, leaning the small of his back into the kitchen counter. He's so exhausted, it scares him. He wishes he'd stayed outside, in the cold. The kettle is coming to the boil on the stove, adding to the foggy heat in the kitchen. He shakes his head to try to clear it.

'They're looking for me, they must be. Chances are they think the two things are connected: Luke's murder and my disappearance. I'm a suspect, in all likelihood.'

'You're not a suspect. No one is.' She sounds impatient, as if she is waiting for him to catch up. Keep up.

'What're you talking about? There is a *body* on that boat.'

'It's why you kidnapped me.' Her face makes a new shape, exasperated. 'Isn't it? *Think*.'

He thinks. He says slowly, 'No . . .'

'*Yes*. You lured me here because you knew I had the key to the boat.' She spaces the words apart as if laying a trail of breadcrumbs for a dumb animal to follow. 'Someone – Tess or Clark – told you to go on that boat. They asked for your help. But when you got there, what did you find?' She waits. 'What did you find, Daniel?'

His mind is a blank, the fog in the kitchen crystalline by comparison. She is waiting for an answer. She won't stop waiting. *Torchlight moving across water, windows lit like eyes, darkness in the shape of a man.* Where do those pictures come from? He's outside, on the towpath. He's not alone. But the boat . . . The boat is empty. It's empty.

'What. Did. You. Find?'

'Nothing . . .'

'Nothing,' she agrees. 'Because of me. Because I did what I do. I tidied. I *packed*. His body, the blood. You knew it was me, that I was strong enough to do that. It's why you kept your distance when you had me down there in the cellar.'

'No, wait . . .' Shock crowds his chest, tunnelling his vision. 'You . . . packed his body . . . ? *Why?*'

'Instinct, I suppose. Or panic. Like yours, right now.' She crosses the kitchen to take his elbow. 'Sit down before you fall down.'

He does as he's told, folding himself into a seated position on the tiled floor, his back to the cabinets, his head on his knees. She sits beside him in silence for a short while before she starts speaking again. He has to look up and get her attention, can't hear over the thundering in his skull.

She raises her voice: 'There's another reason you're not a suspect.'

She digs her hand into the pocket of her jeans, takes out a phone. His phone. The sight of it sobers him. He pushes the panic down, reaching out a hand. She surrenders the phone without a fight. He thumbs the screen, finding multiple message alerts. He'd expected that. But not the replies.

Two days ago, according to the log, he sent replies to everyone asking where he is and whether he's okay. The replies sound like him. She's used phrases he'd use, signed off in the way he'd sign messages to the hospital, to Amanda Bowen, to Tess and Clark and Owen. *Two days ago*. When he was tied to a bed, fearing she had left him to die.

'What have you done?'

'You needed to tell them something.' Grace draws her knees up, resting her cheek there as she eyes him sideways. 'To explain why you're not home or at work, why no one can reach you.'

Dan re-reads the messages, waiting for the lurching in his chest to leave him alone. It doesn't. She has told the hospital, politely, that he has been signed off sick for two weeks. Dr Bowen has been told, less politely, that he is infectious and self-isolating.

She told Clark, 'Taking a few days to regroup.'

To Tess, she texted, 'I know you think I did my best. Speak soon.'

To Owen, 'Away for a bit. Take care of yourself, kiddo.'

Dan expects the panic to rush in but it's gone. Possibly because there is no room in his chest for anything other than fear. Sick, skin-clenching fear.

'What the *fuck* have you done?'

'That's the first time you've sworn at me.'

'Unlikely to be the last . . . *Why* did you do this?'

She points at the phone. 'No message from Luke. Not since the text luring you out of the pub that morning he threatened you.'

'Hard to message me when he's dead . . .'

Dan re-reads the texts a third time, setting his teeth to stop the shaking in his jaw. Yesterday brought new messages from Tess and Clark, wanting to know his whereabouts, needing to know he's safe. Grace hasn't responded to those messages. The kettle rattles on the stove, boiling over.

She gets up from the floor and starts making tea. He watches the smooth way her wrists move, the precision with which she measures water into the mugs. He thinks of Tess wiping tears from her face, Clark sitting in silence at the wheel of the pickup. They're worried about him but it's not him they need to worry about, or not in the way they think.

Grace makes tea neatly, the way she disposed of Luke's body on that boat. She thinks they're murderers, Tess and Clark. She is toying with their concern for him, plotting God knows what. *His friends.* How is he going to keep them safe from her?

Never Events

- He should never have unlocked his phone.
- He should never have turned his back on her, never let her out of the cellar, near the knives, loose in this house.
- Never have thanked her, or begged her forgiveness.
- Never let down his guard.
- She is going to hurt his friends, all over again. He won't be able to stop her.
- She'd never have come here without him. Never have sat in the cellar, starving in the stale air, losing her mind, plotting her revenge.
- He did that: drove her to this.
- Whatever happens next is his fault.

34

Daniel doesn't understand. I thought he would, by now. After everything we've been through, all the ways in which I'm helping him. We're in this together, I thought he knew that.

Cleaning the crime scene wasn't voluntary on my part, certainly not my first thought on finding Luke's body, seeing the mess made of his face. In broad daylight, I'd probably have run. The torch on my phone gave me snatches – red blood, white bone; don't give me *that* face – and the rest followed instinctively. Muscle memory, you might say. Daniel has his memories – lost and found – and I have mine. He was heavy but not as heavy as I'd expected. Adrenaline had a lot to do with that. I knew I needed something weighty to take him underwater and keep him there: a sack of coal from the aft, tarpaulin, rope. You can guess the rest. Over the side was tricky but he went down smoothly, the canal closing over him like a lid. I shone my torch across the water but couldn't see what the killer threw there, the splash of it landing like a ball. A phone, probably. That's what I'd have done with it.

The cleaning I enjoyed. A strange confession but I've always enjoyed cleaning. I went to town rather, because of the lack of light. You could have eaten your food off the deck and walls once I'd finished with them. That's what I told myself anyway. In all honesty, I don't remember every detail of the operation. Only that the rhythm of it soothed me, kept me from screaming or running. It is perfectly possible to stay calm and scream at the same time. You just put the two things into separate boxes, out of reach of one another.

By the time I'd locked up and walked back along the towpath to the allotment, the narrowboat was empty and the black pickup long gone.

35

The harder Dan tries to dredge the truth from his head, the deeper it sinks into sludge. Like Luke's body in the canal. Except this truth is weighted not with coal or rope but by doubt and the fear that tarnishes everything. The only thing he is clear about is Grace. She's dangerous, damaged, out of control. Why he ever imagined otherwise is a mystery to him. Where he got the idea from that he could hold her in a cellar until she gave up her secrets, why he thought she'd break . . . She broke a long time ago. When she was a child, he guesses. Growing up in what sounds like a madhouse. Abusive parents, impossible rules. He thought his childhood was difficult, but it had nothing on hers. She broke and then she mended the way a bone will mend – callused. Not stronger than before but harder.

Trapping her in the cellar was the worst thing he could have done, putting her back in a place of terror and isolation. Whatever shape her madness takes now, he is responsible for it. Grace was not this woman when she packed Elise's room. Then she was quiet, careful, respectful. Now she's a powder-keg. He's been a fool imagining common ground between them these past few days, since she let him up from the bed. They have nothing in common, unless it's an uncanny ability to create chaos.

In the bathroom, he peels the dressing from his hip, assessing the damage. The skin is inflamed but not alarmingly so. Had she punctured anything vital, left metal or dirt in the wound, he'd know it by now. Probably. The state his head's in, he cannot be certain. He cleans the wound, smears antiseptic cream, covers it with a fresh dressing. The mirror gives his face as smudges and hollows, dark evasive eyes. He reaches for a toothbrush. He can at least get rid of the foul taste in his mouth.

In the kitchen, Grace is making sandwiches. He marvels at her composure but of course it isn't really composure. It's dissociation, delusion, trauma. *We're two of a kind.* Two broken halves attempting to make a whole. Two graves to be dug. Elise and Luke. Did Luke kill her? And did Clark then kill him? Dan doesn't believe it. He doesn't *know* but at some fundamental level untouched by trauma, he is certain his friend is not a killer. Clark sought the vigil for the peace it gave him, not the prospect of vengeance, and yes, all right, Clark joined in that night, but so did Dan and Owen, and the three men who'd no reason to fight other than the town and the weather, the way it is hard to hold yourself in check all the time no matter how civilized you manage to be most days. *Animal.* Not Clark, though. Not enough to kill Luke, even for Elise. Surely? Dan thinks of his friend as he was all those years ago, making him laugh no matter how low he felt, and of Clark's child who was part of that sunshine, who *shone.* And he can imagine wanting to kill whoever did that – took that light out of the world. He feels the need for vengeance pulling at his skin, hot behind his eyes.

'I know you did your best,' Tess had texted.

Did you . . . ? Did I . . . ? Torchlight moving across water, windows lit like eyes, darkness in the shape of a man.

Where do those pictures come from, if he wasn't there?

'What is it?' Grace lays down the knife, watching his face. 'Daniel?'

He pulls out a chair and sits at the table, putting his hands in plain sight. He forces himself to relax, showing her the long spill of his fingers on the wood. 'We need to talk.'

'About Clark?' She wipes her hands. 'Or Tess?'

He waits until she's fixed her stare on him and only him.

'About me.'

36

Two days after the vigil turned violent, Dan came home to find Clark's pickup parked behind his Saab. When he drew level, it was Tess not Clark who leant across from the driver's seat to open the passenger door. 'Get in.'

Dan put his hand on the top of the door. He'd been running, could feel the chill of sweat between his shoulder blades even if he couldn't remember what route he'd taken or how long he'd been gone. The street was tilting, surrendering to his old/new enemy, vertigo. 'I need a shower . . .'

Tess said tightly, 'You need to get in.'

Dan did as he was told. When he was in the passenger seat, she said, 'Belt up,' and he did that, too.

It was no different to anything else he'd been doing since the Puddle Duck. On autopilot, following orders according to whichever set of rules he was meant to be obeying at any given time. The hospital's or the satnav's, or the Highway Code's. All night he lay awake watching the clock, waiting for the alarm to order him out of bed. The microwave told him when to remove the cup of coffee he'd trusted it to heat. The kettle baffled him. He didn't seem able to do anything for himself, by himself.

Tess drove in the direction of Box Lane.

She parked where Clark usually parked and switched off the engine, releasing her seat belt and turning sideways to face Dan.

'What's going on with you and Clark and Luke? And Owen, for fuck's sake. *Owen*. What've you been doing?'

'I . . . don't know.'

He didn't, his mind an obstinate blank.

'What happened to your face?'

'What?'

'Your *face*, Dan. What happened to it?'

Tess reached to drag down the sunshade. The mirror made sense of her question. His right cheek was grazed. He blinked, holding the memory at bay. Cold bricks, hot breath on the back of his neck. His reflection slid away, the pickup distorting. He put a hand to the dashboard to stop himself tipping forward, or passing out. Blood beat blackly everywhere in his body.

'What's going on?' Tess demanded. 'With you? With Luke?'

'I need to get home . . .'

'You *need* to tell me what the fuck is going on!'

Her anger filled the pickup like smoke. He couldn't breathe, wanted to put his fist through the window or the windscreen. He stayed where he was, letting the panic pack the inside of his chest.

Tess was breathing fast, hiccupping on her anger. 'Her pendant was in here. I found it. Right here!' She grabbed Dan's wrist, thrusting his hand down the side of the passenger seat until his fingers were rubbed by carpet fibres. He didn't fight, even when her nails dug into the scars on his forearm. The pain made sense, a solid thing, like instructions. When she let go, he left his hand where she'd pushed it, below the fastening for his seat belt.

'While you and Clark are playing vigilante, do you know what I've been doing?' She gripped the steering wheel. 'I've been going through pictures she drew when she was little. Notes she wrote to me, birthday cards. And I've been trying to decide what to say to the girls she stole those bits of jewellery from because it feels like I should say *something*, make amends. Except how can I make amends for my murdered child?' She spread her hands wide. 'Tell me how I make amends for her, Dan. Because I don't know. Do I write letters? It feels like I should say sorry but the only thing I'm sorry for is that *she's not here.*' Her shoulders shook. 'I want to *defend* her, not apologize. I'm her *mum.* I don't want to say sorry to anyone, I just want her back.'

'I know and I'm sorry.' He freed his hand from the side of his seat. In some remorselessly sane corner of his brain, he was shouting at himself to help her, stand the fuck up and be a man, but he couldn't move, couldn't think, could hardly speak. 'I . . . don't know what we're doing, not really.'

'It was Luke, wasn't it?' She wiped her eyes with the heels of her hands. When Dan didn't answer, she moved her mouth into a snarl: '*Wasn't it?*'

He looked to where Box Lane crouched.

Week after week of coming here. Waiting for girls Elise's age to turn into the shortcut that'd been a dead end for Elise. Luke's fist propped to the passenger door, Owen's foot dancing in the back,

Clark half asleep at the wheel, grief pulling his face out of shape, sleep smoothing it again.

'*Wasn't it?*'

'Yes . . .' Grit pricked at the pads of his fingers. 'It was Luke.'

37

'It was *you*,' Grace says. 'You told her Luke killed Elise.'

'What?' Dan recoils. 'No. *No*. I told her Luke insisted on the vigil, that it was his idea—'

'She was asking you if he killed Elise.'

'She was asking about the *vigil*.'

'For God's sake, Daniel! She'd just told you about the pendant. She was saying Luke killed Elise. "It was him, wasn't it?" And you said yes.'

Sometime in the past hour, night fell. It is dark in the kitchen, darker outside. He's lost track of time, again. Is it today, or tomorrow?

'The pendant was in the passenger seat,' Grace says. 'Where Luke sat.'

'It wasn't in the seat. It was down the side, on the floor.'

'Where his jacket pocket was, then. You said you took your coats off after the fight. The pendant must've been in his pocket. I saw that jacket on the boat, it was falling apart, the pockets hanging off it . . . After the fight when you took off your coats, that's when it fell out.'

He puts out a hand in protest but her insistence is a brick wall, unyielding. He drops the hand back to the table. How many meals did he eat here, as a child? Dad loading plates, Mum filling glasses, silver bangles at her wrist, smiling as she pours a glass of squash.

'You want it to be Luke,' he realizes. 'Because you got rid of his body and this makes that less of a crime, if he's a killer. Elise's killer.'

'Why're you defending him?' Grace demands. 'Of everyone in that friendship group, you knew best what kind of man he was.'

'We've been through this—'

'Not all of it.' She stands to click on the kitchen light. 'Not the part where you told Tess that Luke murdered her child.'

Dan flinches from the brightness, the bone-white of the sink, hot blue glass in the doors to the range. His parents' ghosts are gone. It is just him and her. He has an urge to eat spaghetti and drink a glass of wine, the first time in weeks he has had anything like a normal hunger signal. He wonders whether it means he's getting better, or worse. A functioning human being wouldn't suffer hunger pangs while debating violent murder. On the other hand, it's a relief to discover he's capable of basic survival instincts like hunger or thirst.

Grace is searching the fridge. Reading his mind, again. 'What did Tess do after you said yes, it was Luke?'

'I didn't say that but . . . she drove to the narrowboat.'

'That's it? She didn't say anything about the police or Clark?'

'What would she say?'

'That she was going to tell Clark or the police about Luke. Because if she wasn't going to tell them, then that means she was planning to deal with Luke some other way. Her own way.'

'How?' Dan watches her search the cupboards, taking out dried pasta and a jar of sauce. '*Grace*. In what way was she going to deal with Luke?'

'You're not stupid.' She sets the food down on the counter. 'How do you think?'

'So now Tess is a killer?' He gropes for a sense of outrage at her accusation but there is only exhaustion, soaking him like a sickness. 'Tess killed Luke, beat him to a bloody pulp with that helium tank?'

'She's big,' Grace says. 'Not like me. And she's strong. She moved a trunk of books when I asked for her help in the house. She's really strong.'

Torchlight moving across water, darkness in the shape of a man. Broad-shouldered, big – could that have been Tess on the boat? Dan tries to get a fix on the memory but it's impossible, all the details blurred, bleached out.

'Luke's name was in Elise's diary.' Grace shakes dried pasta into a saucepan, the sound like pellets fired from a gun. 'Tess will have seen it. She will have looked through those diaries again and again. She'll have found Luke's name and maybe it didn't ring alarm bells on its own. But with everything else in the mix? The vigil, the violence, the *pendant* . . . ?' She seals the packet of pasta by pressing her fingers along its neck. 'She'll have remembered seeing Luke's name in Elise's diary.'

'The police saw it, too. They didn't think it meant anything.'

'Or they couldn't make it stick. Tess asked for your help, and you gave it to her. Her text said, "I know you did your best." What did you do?'

'Nothing. At least . . . nothing I can remember.'

'You have to.' She dusts her hands. 'You have to remember. Someone told you to bring me here and put me down in that cellar.'

287

'No one told me.' He answers without thinking, resisting her efforts to rehabilitate his character. 'Stop finding excuses for me.'

'All right, so the cellar was your idea.' She adds water to the pan; her domesticity is alarming. 'But Tess was the one who left the negative reviews that led to the cancelled jobs.'

'What cancelled jobs?' He can't keep up with her.

'The ones that made me desperate enough to come here regardless of the risk.'

'You weren't desperate,' he counters. 'Not for work. You wanted to catch Elise's killer.'

'Nevertheless. Tess left the negative reviews. I learnt that from your phone. Her email address is on there, the same one used on the bad reviews.'

'That must have hurt . . . You thought she was your friend.'

'Your problem is too much empathy.' Grace eyes him. 'And not enough memory.'

'Maybe. But I'm sorry she did that. It's unfair, after the care you took.'

'She was upset. I don't blame her.'

'You lost work because of it.'

'In the scheme of things? So what.'

'Can you afford to lose work?' Dan asks.

'Am I financially independent? No. I bet you are. You live in your parents' house. Could you afford to lose your job?'

Could he? 'Financially, perhaps.'

'But not emotionally,' Grace says. 'Emotionally you'd be a wreck without your patients to look after.'

'Try that again,' Dan tells her, 'in the present tense.'

I have no patients. I am a wreck.

'Too much empathy, like I said.' She studies him. 'There isn't any way it was your idea to put me in the cellar, not without beating yourself up about it anyway. And you had other people to do that, didn't you? You had Luke.'

'Would you go back to your parents' house? If you had nowhere else, I mean. If you were looking at bankruptcy.'

Her eyes darken. 'I'd rather go back in the cellar.'

He is sick with self-reproach, has to look away.

'You're never going to forgive yourself, are you?' She is out of patience with him again. 'It's a waste of our time. I was hoping the catharsis would've moved things along by now. You've been weeping so much you must be dehydrated.' She runs her stare over him. 'How much catharsis is too much, Daniel? Did they teach you that at medical school?'

'They didn't and I don't know. But I've a feeling we'll find out, before this is over.'

'Advancing the cause of therapeutic medicine? Nice work if you can get it.' A single beat before she's back to business: 'What did Tess mean when she said, "You did your best"?'

'As a friend, Clark's friend. I tried to keep him away from the vigil.'

'At first. But you couldn't. Because of Luke.' She lights the stove, shakes out the match, soaking the head of it under the tap before dropping it into the pedal bin. 'He was the driving force behind all of it.'

Every action she takes is considered, controlled. He can see her at work on the boat, wrapping Luke's shattered head in tarpaulin, knotting rope around his body, zipping the flak jacket over the sack of coal used to weight him underwater. That's the trouble, he realizes. He is imagining too much without *knowing* anything. For all he knows, she lied about the boat and the body, about a second killer. For all he knows, she is lying right now with her neatness and domesticity, endless questions making *him* question everything. He's been trusting her for no good reason. He needs to stop doing that.

'You like Tess, don't you?' Grace sets the saucepan on the heat. 'And she likes you.'

'We're friends.' A sisterly kiss on his cheek. 'Since school.'

'She left you alone on the boat with Luke that summer.'

'She didn't know what would happen, any more than I did.'

'But you *did* know. You knew what happened the last time you were there with him, alone. You know Luke, better than anyone else.'

She looks at the high cupboard where the bowls are kept.

'What's your point?' Dan gets to his feet, reaching down what she wants. 'Or don't you have one?'

He sets the two bowls on the counter. They eye one another openly, the way animals will after getting the measure of the danger. Standoff. Deadlock.

'She asked for your help. After you told her Luke killed Elise.' Grace wipes the bowls with a tea towel, not breaking eye contact. 'And you gave it to her, or tried to. "I know you did your best" . . . You know what I think?'

'I know you're going to tell me what you think.'

'You went to that boat to clean up her mess. To help her clean up the mess she made when she beat Luke to death. Only I'd got there first.'

'Well . . . You think a lot of things.' Dan puts his hands in his pockets, shrugging himself narrow. 'Don't you? You make up stories in your head to make sense of the world. We all do it, to one extent or another.' He thinks of Jude. 'It's part of living. But you do it to avoid looking at facts that don't fit what you want to believe, what you *need* to believe. Facts like me being a kidnapper and a coward who should be in prison for what he did to you.'

Her face hardens. 'You were obviously in a fugue state.'

'I don't have answers to your questions. Too much of my head is *junk*.' He lifts his hand, raps its knuckles to the side of his skull. 'The only thing that makes sense is you leaving and calling the police. Let them deal with me and whatever else happened before.'

'We know what happened. Luke killed Elise. Tess killed Luke. She asked you to help her clear up the mess but I'd beaten you both to it.'

Arguing with her is like trying to dig his hands into a brick wall one finger at a time. His amnesia is her ally – colluding to convince her she is right, giving him no comeback, or none that counts. Giving no quarter.

Grace is studying the contents of the saucepan. 'There's too much pasta for the sauce.'

'Leave it. We'll put it in the fridge.'

There it is again: that uncanny, unnerving note of domesticity amidst the horror of what is happening. He doesn't know what to make of it, of them.

Grace folds the tea towel, lays it aside. 'You and Tess must have worked out who else had keys to the boat. One of you, probably Tess, remembered Elise's keys. When she realized those were missing, she thought of me. Who else had been in Elise's room lately? Not Clark, who was hardly ever home. There was only me. So now Tess is thinking I must know what she did on that boat.

She's remembering what I was like in her house, how tidy I was but also how odd. And she's paranoid because of the pendant and the lies you're all telling her – the vigil, Clark's job. She can't confide in him but she trusts you, Daniel. Only you're a bit odd, too. Just at the minute. She doesn't know why and she doesn't have time to get to the bottom of it so she decides to exploit it. Your oddness. The weird way you've been looking through everyone as if you're shut up, trapped.' She takes a wooden spoon, poking the pasta. 'One of you cooked up the kidnap plan. Unless you came up with it together.' She turns to consider him. 'No, you were in a dissociative state, barely functioning without instruction. It was Tess's idea.' She points to the cellar. 'Wasn't it? She left this for you to do. Maybe she decided her hands were dirty enough. Or she thought if the police knew you'd kidnapped a woman and held her prisoner, you might be capable of worse, of anything.'

'So now Tess is setting me up? I'm her fall guy for Luke's murder. That's your latest theory?'

'Can you prove you're not? That she isn't setting you up?'

Dan wants to break a cup in the sink, the way Tess once did. He wonders what Grace was doing right before it happened, whether *she* was what tipped Tess over the edge that day. Then he wonders why he is even bothering framing that as a question.

'You liked her.' He sets his palms flat to the counter. 'You wanted to bring her peace. You spent time together, in their house. Do you really think she is capable of what you're describing?'

'She's grieving.' Grace unscrews the lid on the jar of sauce with a twist of her wrist. 'And she's angry. At Clark and the rest of you for indulging your fantasies of vengeance. Because men can do that – run away, put their fists into things until they start to forget. She has to sit with her grief, every day.'

'We all sat with it.' Anger stirs a stick in Dan's stomach. 'That's what we were doing in the pickup—'

'Not Luke. He was waiting for the chance to scare another girl, or to punch someone. He didn't have to wait very long, did he? Meanwhile Tess is home on her own, sitting with all that silence, shouldering it alone.'

There is too much truth in what she says, these stories she spins. Tess *was* on her own when Clark should have been with her, when Dan could have been with her, lending his support instead of taking the coward's way out with that bloody vigil. He failed her and he feels guilty about that. Is that why he helped Tess, if he did?

'None of you were there for her. From what you've said, Luke and Owen were incapable of helping. Clark was fighting his own demons. Which left you, the medical man and her friend – since school, you said – but maybe that's how you treat your friends. It explains why the only ones you have are beating you up or having breakdowns while you bring cups of coffee, or soup in a Thermos so you can convince yourself you're not a monster.'

Dan focuses on breathing, on the taste of grit in his mouth and the pain in his hip. He is aware of her watching him.

'That was unfair. Daniel? I apologize for that.'

'No, it's fine.'

'It's not. You look worse than you did when I stabbed you.'

'Well, advancing the cause of therapeutic medicine isn't for everyone.'

Her mouth quirks in amusement. 'Sit down.'

He sits. That's all it takes for her to start up again.

'If it was me left alone like that, then discovering what the four of you had been up to . . . ? Finding the pendant, knowing what it meant . . . ? I'd have done something about it.'

Dan knows this is true. He remembers the woman she became in the cellar when he found her shoebox. All that time she knew who he was. Knew about Elise and Tess. She wanted to be here. And she wouldn't leave, didn't leave, even when she suspected him of being a killer.

'You must know what Tess did, Daniel. What did she do?'

'I can't remember . . .'

He is so sick of speaking these words. He's surprised she can stand hearing them again, that she hasn't reached for the knife a second time and carved the memories from him by force. She might yet do that, of course. He can't rule it out. Only a fool would do that.

'You *can* remember,' she says. 'You have to.'

He knows, more or less, how memory works. The tricks it can play in your head. Knows memory can be tricked too – made to do as you tell it. He used tricks like that to pass exams when he was fourteen, summoning data from scribbles in the margins of books he'd speed-read. Memory can be whistled up, brought to heel. But he is afraid of what he will summon, of whistling for a dog and bringing a wolf to their door.

The white smell of the pasta makes his throat clench.

The kitchen is filling with steam from the pan on the stove, windows fogging over. It tugs at him, the dark out there, the way he can't see through the glass, only shadows and shapes. The floor shifts under him as if the house isn't tied to the land, as if it isn't a house at all but a boat, narrow and low on the water, moored by the empty mouth of the lock.

38

Tess drove more easily than Clark, swinging her shoulders into the steering. Dan was aware of the pickup's weight and engine power in a way he wasn't when Clark was at the wheel. He'd so rarely been in the pickup when it was being driven, had come to think of it as stationary, a place to shelter from the weather while they watched Box Lane.

Tess hadn't uttered a word since he'd said, 'It was Luke,' in answer to her question about why the four of them kept returning to the site where Elise was murdered. With a length of thin cord he remembered, the information moving from the back of his mind to the front.

His head had been like this since the Puddle Duck: nothing as drastic as memory loss, not yet. Just a light remixing, a shuffling to the top of those things that felt safe: Mum smiling as she leafed through a book; Dad in the garden, burning leaves. Answers to GCSE Biology questions: the number of chromosomes in each cell of a fruit fly (8), a goat (60), a human (46). Line eight on the Snellen chart – D E F P O T E C – denoting twenty-twenty vision.

The cord that killed Elise was thin and plastic-coated like a charger cable. Dan knew this from the police report. She was strangled but not raped. Her clothes torn, possibly to make it look like a sexually motivated assault. Clark was a suspect in their investigation. Dan too, until they discounted him after checking his schedule against hospital records. Owen and Luke and Tess. Everyone who knew Elise was a suspect because the killer was statistically likely to be close to home, someone she knew. At the same time they all agreed it must have been a stranger. No one who knew her could've hurt her.

Dan could smell iron and earth. Dead water. Tess had parked at the allotment, close to the canal. He shivered in the clothes he'd pulled on to go running – yesterday? No, the burn in his calves was more recent than that. Today. This morning. What was left of the sun hung low in the sky, suggesting late afternoon. He spread his hands, seeing the pinched white tips of his fingers, the whorls of their prints echoing the spirals in his head. The vertigo was so familiar now, so constant, it would have been odder not to feel it.

Some part of him wasn't here, was still cringing into the bricks at the back of the Puddle Duck, or upstairs in his parents' house, picking mirrored pieces off the bathroom floor, fighting to catch his breath. He tried to work the clench from his right hand, rubbing at its fingers.

'I should never have let her come here. All this way, on her own . . .' Tess gripped at the steering wheel. 'But she loved it. The boat. Luke made it safe, that's what he said.' Her voice hardened: 'He made it safe for her.'

Dan expected her to demand answers, the way she had at Box Lane, answers he did not have. But she wasn't looking at him. He thought of his mother wanting a witness; he could smell scented bath oils and blood. He propped his head to the seat and listened as Tess talked and talked about her daughter and her husband, about Luke and Owen, who should never have been dragged into this, who was just a kid, one of Elise's best friends.

'You can at least put that right. Dan, are you listening? You can put that right. Get Owen away from Luke before it gets any worse. This vigilante crap, the fighting.' She pushed her hands into her hair. 'I'd like to burn it all down. The boat, this fucking truck!' She hit the wheel with her hands. 'All of it.'

Dan was gripped by a sudden fear she would ask him to drive; it wasn't safe for her to be at the wheel in this mood. They would have to switch places but he didn't know how to drive, hadn't learnt yet – Dad said when he was seventeen – and he knew that wasn't true or right and he was losing his mind, had lost it days ago, or weeks, or years. He should tell Tess he was losing his mind, at least try to explain what was happening, but he couldn't work out how to say it without making her pain worse. He'd lost his mind but she'd lost everything. Elise was everything.

'Come on.' She opened the driver's door, climbing from the pickup.

Dan forced himself to unfasten the seat belt and follow. Everything he did felt wrong, clumsy. He fumbled the seat belt, stumbled from the scuff plate to the ground. The cold air hit like a fist. He doubled up, out of breath. Tess was ahead of him, striding in the direction of the boat, her wide shoulders carving shadows. He followed, still stumbling.

By the canal it was face-numbingly cold, air hanging in wet ribbons over the water. The lock looked like the entrance to Box Lane: an open mouth of stone, tunnelling to nowhere.

Tess was in the well deck by the time he caught up with her. She banged on the door with a balled hand. 'Luke!'

She didn't have a key, Dan realized. Only Elise had one. And Luke. And Dan. Not Tess.

'Luke!' Banging with her fist. 'We need to talk!'

The boat looked deserted, windows frosted by the plastic Luke carved with his Stanley knife days ago – no, that wasn't right. Not days, *years*. Dan saw shadows inside. He did not want to go onboard but Tess did. She was searching the well deck for something she could use to break down the door.

'I've got it,' Dan said.

He didn't want to hear the noise of the door breaking. The noise of her fist was bad enough. He dug out his key and fitted it in the padlock, aware of her staring at him, wondering why he had the key with him, not knowing he always took it because nine times out of ten he ran up here, away from town. The key was with the others in his pocket and it opened the door and then they were in the boat and it was too late to do anything but watch as Tess went ahead of him, searching for Luke.

The boat looked different. Smelt different, too. Of coal dust and drain cleaner, a black and white smell that made the red all the more shocking – the blanket on the bed, the painted walls, the lampshades and the blood.

Tess said, 'Is that . . . ?'

Jackson Pollock, *Out of the Web*, 'Biomorphic, you see?' Mum's finger tracing the shapes in the book spread open on her lap.

Dan blinked and the blood on the boat shrank to a few dark freckles on the pillow, a thin brown stripe across the rug on the floor.

'I suppose this's where he came to clean up after that fight.' Tess nudged her foot at the rug, pulling a face. 'He couldn't go home to Shannon; Clark says she threw him out. He's not heard from Luke in days.'

She moved ahead of Dan, deeper into the boat. He followed, stepping wide of the helium tank that wasn't where it usually lived, under the sink. Someone had moved it. They'd moved other things, too. The table was in the dead centre of the room, curtains hanging straight. Everything was too neat, adding to his sense of being back in time – sanding woodwork as the sun burnt holes in the blind windows, heating the back of his neck.

Tess had reached the rear of the boat, Elise's tray of seedlings. Dan watched her lift a finger to touch a green shoot. He could taste vodka shots, feel the weight of an arm across his shoulders. Involuntarily his mouth smiled for the camera.

Tess narrowed her eyes at him. 'What's wrong with you?'

'I'm not . . .' He reached a hand for the wall but it was further away than he'd thought. His arm dropped to his side. 'I don't think I'm very well . . .'

'I don't understand you. Clark's depressed, he's gone to a bad place. And Owen does whatever Luke says, always has. But *you*? I thought you'd stand up to him. I thought they'd be safe with you. I thought you cared.'

'I do care . . .'

She shook her head. 'You're all the same. All you know how to do is fight. None of you knows how to *be still*.' She made fists of her hands and held them to her chest. 'How to hold her.'

She was showing him something she'd shown no one else, not even Clark. Her pain in all its colours. If Clark had seen her like this, he'd never have left her alone, not for Luke and the vigil, not for anything.

Dan could hear water booming and glass shattering, a noise like wind through a nylon kite.

'What can I do? Tell me. Please. What can I do to make this better?'

'You can make it stop,' Tess said. 'All this . . . *death*. The watching and the fighting, Luke and Owen and Clark – I want him back. I want this part to be over. Finished. Can you do that?' But she was shaking her head as she said it. 'Of course you can't. You're part of it.'

Back on deck, Tess stood for a long time looking across the water to the lock and the tunnel beyond. Dan turned as a spot of colour caught his eye, seeing the small round shape of a keyring lying in the well deck. Lost, or dropped. He bent to scoop it up, his hand closing around the cork buoy as Tess said, 'Where did you get that?'

'Here . . .' He nodded at the deck.

She took it from him, holding it in the curl of her palm. 'It's Elise's.' Her face was dark, unreadable. 'It was in her bedroom.'

Dan turned a slow circle in the well deck, searching for more. The police had been here, months ago. Here and at the house, in the pickup, at school – everywhere Elise had been – suspecting everyone who knew her. Making a list, checking it off. Clark was on that list, and Luke and Owen, Tess and Dan. All of them were suspects.

'You're sure it was in her room?'

Tess clenched her fist around the keyring. 'Yes.'

Footfall on the towpath made the pair of them look up. A runner, all in black, her hair in a plait that rose and fell between her shoulder blades. The sight of her held Dan in the present, more focused than he had felt in days.

'Who else has been in her room?'

'Only the packer. Grace Maddox. She took such good care of everything . . . Exactly as we asked.'

The words didn't match the expression on her face, which said Grace Maddox had taken more than care.

'Do you think she took that?' He nodded at her hand.

Slowly, Tess unfurled her fingers, staring at the key. 'She must have done. No one else was in her room.' She looked at Dan. 'No one except me.'

39

'You didn't clean the boat as well as you thought you did. And you dropped Elise's key. But that was deliberate, wasn't it?' Like a light coming on in Dan's head. 'You wanted one of us to find it.'

Grace shares the pasta between two bowls, placing the bowls on the table. She takes forks from a drawer and glasses from the draining rack. Dan watches her, still caught in the backwash of memories from that afternoon.

'Come and eat, Daniel. You need to keep your strength up.'

She sits at the table, waiting for him to join her. She has filled two glasses with water; he missed the precise moment when she did that. The holes in his head make her a magician, capable of more tricks than he can quantify. He doesn't stand a chance, he never did. He sits and drinks water, digs his fork into the pasta, eats. It is easier than thinking and he's hungry, properly hungry for the first time in a long time.

When the bowl is half empty, he says, 'You left Elise's key on the boat. You didn't just drop it, you don't just drop things. You wanted someone to find the key. Who?'

'Whoever had the most to hide.' She carries on eating. 'Or lose.'

'Whoever killed Luke, you mean.'

'Tess made an excuse for the blood on the boat, blamed it on the fighting. She took you there as a witness – someone to see how hard she was looking for Luke, as if she didn't know he was dead.' Grace licks sauce from her fork, pointing at him. 'You're her alibi.'

'She didn't know he was dead . . .' Dan turns his fork in his fingers, extracting the detail from his memory. 'Whoever killed Luke knew how to unlatch the door from outside. You said the killer was able to unfasten the latch *after* you'd hooked it. With a screwdriver, you thought. Close enough: you can do it with a credit card, in a pinch. But Tess didn't know that trick.'

'Who did?'

'Luke. Me. Elise, if Luke taught her, the way he taught me.'

'Clark? It's his dad's boat, isn't it?'

Dan concedes the point. 'Clark, maybe.'

'And Owen. You said he copies everything Luke does.'

'All right. That's all of us. But not Tess.'

They eat in silence for a short time. Then Grace says, 'No one has reported Luke missing. Why not?'

'He's always ducking out, from Shannon as much as anything. I said he was too noisy to go missing for any length of time but jobs do come up in odd places. We're used to him dropping off the radar from time to time.'

'Even on Fridays?' She wipes her mouth. 'Missing the vigil? Clark didn't think that was odd?'

'If he did, I don't remember.'

'Owen didn't wonder where his hero was?'

'Same answer. I don't remember.'

303

'They're wondering where *you* are.' She nods at his phone. 'Even Owen.' She frowns. 'If Tess helped you plan the cellar, why hasn't she come before now? To check up on us.'

'You tell me.' He wants her to reach the right conclusion by herself: that Tess has no part in any plan, that she's innocent.

But Grace sails straight past: 'She's counting on you to get it done. Whatever she had planned for me. She trusts you to do it.'

'Come on . . . She saw how useless I was on the boat. I doubt she trusts me to get myself dressed, let alone execute an elaborate plan for vengeance or whatever you think this is.'

'Not vengeance,' Grace says. '*Silence.* The killer knows I cleaned up on the boat. I expect they think I witnessed the whole thing.'

'But you didn't.'

She looks at him oddly. 'I told you what I saw.'

'You told me lots of things.' He eats the last of his pasta. 'Sorry if I can't keep up.'

Grace lifts her shoulders in a shrug. 'We'll find out sooner or later, even if we have to go back on that boat to do it.' She runs a finger around the rim of her bowl, licking the last of the sauce from it like a cat.

'You're not afraid of anything, are you?' he says wonderingly.

'I'm afraid of lots of things. I was terrified that night on the boat, thought for a second it was my old dad out there. Logically, I knew it couldn't be. But that sort of fear isn't logical, is it? Well, you know all about that.'

Dan studies her, trying to unpick the different strands of meaning from the statement she delivered. She does a good impersonation of a whole person – far better than his – but she's in pain. He sees that.

'Do you want to talk about it? Your dad . . . Your childhood. From things you've said, I know it wasn't happy.'

'My turn for the free therapy?' She sets the bowl aside, reaching for the phone. 'I'm not sure we have time.'

'As bad as that? Your childhood, I mean.'

'Bad enough. Besides, any more catharsis in here and you'll have to crank up that dehumidifier.'

He stands and goes to the stove, boxing up the leftover pasta for the fridge. 'I'd like to help you, if I can.'

'Yes, but that's because you're pathologically addicted to helping people, especially those who can't see properly.'

'You can see.' He is baffled by her, again. 'You were able to see in the dark down there. That's how it felt.'

'You said I make things up.'

'I didn't mean you can't see. If anything, you're more astute than most people. You saw through me, down there. And up here.'

She moves her thumbs on the phone's screen for a short time before stopping to look up at him.

'I see you, Daniel. That's true. You can't hide from me. I see how you care about Jude and Owen, and about your mum and dad and Clark. You miss his sunniness and want it back. It hurts you that you can't help him.' She considers his expression. 'Too much? You want me to stop?'

'Probably. Unless you want tomorrow's supper oversalted.'

'Cathartic carbonara? Yum.'

While she is making a joke out of it, he waits for his breathing to return to normal. Every word she spoke is true. Every word. She knows him better than he knows himself. And she understands him, more completely than anyone ever has. The connection between them is erratic, like a bad bit of writing, but when it works it illuminates everything.

'What you don't seem to appreciate,' she says next, 'is that you're in safe hands with me . . . Your car insurance is due, by the way. The premium's gone up but not by much. Want me to pay it?' She holds up his phone. 'You have online banking on here.'

'Not what I'd call the most pressing priority right now.'

'True. Anyway, you have me.'

'Excuse me?'

'Full breakdown cover.' She gives a small, satisfied smile. 'I never start therapy without it.'

'Right.' His head is pounding. He tries to remember how to breathe the right way to metabolize adrenaline.

'Relax.' Grace thumbs at the phone, flicking him a look. 'I'm not a complete maniac.'

True. Neither one of us is complete *right now.*

'Reassuring . . .' He finishes with the pasta, loading it into Tupperware and putting it in the fridge.

'You know your problem, Daniel Roake? You think because you can't remember what you did, it must be something monumentally monstrous.' She turns the phone screen towards him. 'But you're a good man. All the evidence points that way.' She is showing him the research he did into therapists for Jude, needing a replacement for Amanda Bowen.

'All the evidence apart from the cellar.' He collects their bowls, takes them to the sink. 'And what I did to you.'

'You survived what happened that summer. Your mum's suicide and Luke's assault. It didn't make you mean or weak. You studied for years so you could help people like Jude. Five years of medical school, another seven to specialize. You had a head start: gifted and talented. You're smarter than most people, that's obvious. But even so. That was twelve years of your life.'

'And look at me now . . .'

He rests his hands on the lip of the sink, standing with his back to her, shoulder blades chilled by her stare.

'Sorry,' he manages after a moment, 'self-pity getting in the way of the catharsis there. I'll try to stay on track.'

'This isn't self-pity. You're grieving. Worse, you're pre-emptively grieving. For Jude, for your job. Only one cure for that.'

'You have one cure for everything.' He straightens, turning on the taps. '*Remember* . . .'

'If you could at least *try* to remember' – she is on his phone, he can hear her thumbs at work – 'it would be a start.'

'You think I'm not trying?'

'I think you're afraid of what you'll find if you go back on that boat. Not literally onto the boat but in your head. It scares the shit out of you. I'm not surprised after what you went through but it would be good if you could get past that and help me figure this out.'

'You do know how trauma works? Look it up, if you don't.'

'That's exactly what I am doing.' She reads the phone screen, recites: '*Trauma causes your memory processing to malfunction* . . . What's a "declarative explicit memory system"?'

'Explicit memories are those we intentionally recall, like . . . revision for exams. Implicit is the other kind – getting dressed, brushing our teeth . . .' He doesn't have to make an effort to access this information, it is there on the tip of his tongue. 'Explicit memories are either episodic – personal experiences – or semantic – factual information. When explicit memories are affected by trauma they don't get logged in the right way. Instead, we encode them as pictures or sensations.'

'Well, now you're just showing off.'

'That's what dissociation is. Memories split into fragments like . . . shrapnel. Funnily enough our brains don't like having shrapnel embedded in them. Gets in the way of recovery. Gets in the way of everything, eventually. Emotions, making plans. Work, relationships, moving on with our lives. If we're not careful, we can get seriously physically ill—'

'Daniel,' she says softly. 'You are breaking my heart.'

He turns but she doesn't mean what he thinks she means: 'You can recall *textbooks* but you can't remember what happened with Tess on the narrowboat.'

'It's infuriating,' he agrees. 'But it's not personal.'

'Would you like to hear what Helen Keller had to say about it?' Grace holds up the phone. 'Or do you already know? She's a famous blind person, so you probably do.'

Jude would know, Dan thinks. She was learning about Helen Keller the last time he saw her. 'Tell me?'

' "Although the world is full of suffering, it is also full of the overcoming of it." I might print that on a T-shirt, just for you.'

He is trying to frame a response to this when she adds, 'That's what we're doing here, in case you didn't know. *Overcoming*. Getting you better so you can help find Elise's killer. Then Tess can *overcome* and Clark, too. You need to go back on that boat. You need to remember.'

Did he say relentless? She is remorseless. Nemesis, or Alecto.

'Maybe we could build a boat out there' – he points towards the garden – 'with the bits I smashed from the shed. Or – here's a wild idea – we get in your car and drive back to the canal. It's only an hour's drive or so. Wait until after dark obviously, for the full effect. Chances are I'll kick and scream a bit but if you bring a knife, I'm sure you can work around that.'

Grace doesn't look up from the phone. 'Sarcasm doesn't suit you.'

'Sarcasm doesn't suit *you*. I'm fine with it, in fact. I'm all for moving this forward.'

'We can't leave here. You said that yourself.'

'I said *I* couldn't. You can and you should.'

'I'm needed, in case you didn't notice. You need my help with the cooking and the washing and in case that wound is infected, which it probably is although you'll never admit it but anyone can see you're getting feverish.' She stops, frowning at the phone. '*Jag älskar dig*. What does that mean?'

'I love you.'

She looks up.

He's confused, blindsided. 'In Swedish. *Jag älskar dig*. It means "I love you" in Swedish.'

'You speak Swedish.'

'Apparently yes, I do.' He feels odd, as if he is seeing her from the other end of a long tunnel, miles away.

She looks back down at the phone. '*Jeg elsker dig*... What's that?'

'The same, in Danish.'

'Say it.' A smile curves her mouth. 'In Danish.'

'*Jeg elsker dig.*'

The words feel right in his mouth. How many more languages does he speak? An indistinct memory of textbooks, phone apps, wearing headphones in his bedroom, on the bus, in the street. Studying to fill his head, to keep busy and to shut out voices he didn't want to hear, thoughts he didn't want to have. Intrusive, destructive. Repetitive. How much more has he forgotten?

'Say it in French.'

'Everyone knows it in French.'

'Say it anyway.'

He reaches a hand for the lip of the table, partly to test his theory that it is a lot further away than it was a minute ago. But the table is right where it always was. He's the one who is out of reach. Out of touch. Out of his mind.

'What're we doing?'

'We're overcoming. And we're finding out how much you really know.' She thumbs at the phone. 'Bet you can't say it in Japanese.'

He has to clench his teeth to keep the words inside.

'You can!' She straightens, her face lighting up. 'You speak *Japanese* . . . Say it.' He shakes his head and her eyes harden. 'I'm doing all the work around here. You have *one job.*'

'Then let's talk about that.' His heart is racing in his chest. 'Because it doesn't matter how many languages I can speak, does it? If I can't remember what you need me to remember.'

'How many languages *can* you speak?'

'*I don't know. I've forgotten.*'

'Swedish, Danish, French. English, obviously.' She is doing that thing with her fingers again, folding each one into her hand. 'Japanese.' Her middle finger. 'Which is showing off again, frankly. Bet you speak Italian, too.'

Jude's T-shirt: *Nella notte buia.*

In the darkness of the night.

'Oh, Daniel Roake!' Grace has straightened to her full height of five foot four, 1.67 metres, and is looking at him as if he's an exotic animal in a zoo. 'You're a polymath.'

'Being multilingual doesn't make you a polymath. To be a polymath, you need –' He bites his tongue.

'No, please,' she says. 'Do go on. You were about to give me the textbook definition of a polymath, which, correct me if I'm wrong, is precisely the kind of thing a polymath would do.'

The more information in his head, the less room for remembering: Mum, Luke, the summer that changed everything. He can feel the weight of textbooks on his bed and on the shelves above it, his finger moving across the pages, headphones pressed against his ears: new words to take the place of the old ones. Everything wiped clean, put away, replaced.

'How is this helping? *How?*'

'It's interesting. You interest me. I interest you, don't I?'

You scare me.

'You fascinate me.' Grace comes closer. 'You're like a locked room in an empty house where someone has hidden something precious. I don't mean valuable. You're not a Fabergé egg –' She breaks off. 'Do you speak Russian?'

Nyet, pozhaluysta ostanovis. No, please stop.

He shakes his head at her.

'Not a Fabergé egg.' She's so close he sees the imperfections in her irises. 'Just a small, secret thing. A perfume bottle or a thimble with a chip in it . . . Something smooth and perfect and it's just one little crack, one tiny chip but now it's deadly. Now I could cut myself on it.'

Dan is going to pass out if she doesn't stop. The sink is hard and cold at his back, the only thing keeping him upright as the kitchen shrinks and tunnels in every direction and still she is coming, lifting her face to his. He can smell her skin. She smells of metal and water and she is beautiful, her cheekbones, her eyes, anyone else would call her beautiful if they saw her in the street, if she had never stuck a knife in them, if they hadn't lost their mind to trauma and fear.

'One job, Daniel. What is it?'

'Remember-what-happened-on-the-boat-with-Tess.'

He is out of breath as he says it.

'Preferably before she turns up here.' Grace retreats, back to the table. 'If she asked you to help her murder me and dispose of my body, that could make for a very awkward reunion.'

He presses the ends of his fingers to his forehead, half expecting to find blood, the fever painting everything red.

'She didn't ask me to do anything. No one did. It's just me and you. It has always been just me and you.'

'Touching. But I didn't kill Elise. Or Luke. And neither did you unless you're lying to me, in which case I'll find out so you're wasting your time worrying about that . . . You look like you're about to fall down.' She's back on the phone as if she never moved from the table, as if he imagined the whole thing. 'Stop getting upset and focus on remembering.'

'What happens if I can't? If I never remember?'

'Then we'll have to ask Tess. Maybe you'll text her and ask her to come out here . . .'

'No. *No.* She shouldn't be here – this is about you and me. Between you and me.'

'Say it in Japanese.'

'What?'

'*This is between you and me.* Say it in Japanese and I'll think about texting her, telling her to stay away.'

He needs his phone back. If he had his phone, he could—

'You're not getting the phone. I'll sleep with it if I have to.'

'*Kore wa koko dake no hanashi desu yo.*'

'Again.' She holds the phone out. 'Louder.'

'*Kore wa koko dake no hanashi desu yo.*'

She's using a translation app because the phone says in a robotic tone, '*This is about you and me.*'

'Now text Tess,' he begs.

But she won't, he already knew that. Her game, her rules.

'Do your friends know you're multilingual? I bet they don't. You'd rather break your own arm than have Luke find out. I expect that's why it was so easy for you to forget you speak them – because you've kept it to yourself. You learnt all those languages when you were away, or since you got back because you hate being in that house and it helps you feel less trapped. Fewer walls, more things under your control. Your brain's like a Japanese puzzle box. *Himitsu-bako* . . . I packed one, once. Antique, carved from a pagoda. It took one thousand, three hundred and sixty-six moves to open it, that's what they told me. How many moves to open yours, do you think?'

He shakes his head at her.

Then she says, out of nowhere, 'Do you ever wish you were dead?'

'No.' He is angry to be asked, the answer coming out more forcefully than he intended.

'Good. That's good. I'm glad.'

313

'Do you ever stop?' Dan is in serious danger of falling to his knees and begging her to stop. '*Ever?*'

'My old dad used to ask that.' Her voice is flat, thumbs working at the phone. 'I got sick of it, in the end.'

He turns away, unable to look at her any longer.

A second later, filling the sink with hot water, he remembers he only has her word for it that Luke was killed on the narrowboat, let alone by one of the few friends he has in the world.

When he turns back, she has put the phone down on the table and is staring dead ahead.

It is raining again, the sound of it strangely dry against the glass. The roads will be flooding. They will be cut off, stranded here. He should wish for that, probably. The best possible outcome for all concerned. But Grace would find a way around it. Build a boat, or an ark. A little thing like a flood would not stop her, not for long. He thinks of what he knows – all the learning he did for no reason other than to crowd out knowledge he never wanted and couldn't live with: Mum, Luke, that summer. What use is it to him now? None whatsoever. Unless he can find a way to stop this woman who is staring dead ahead, through the closed kitchen door and out into the night.

—

40

To understand the doll's house, you need to understand the Noah's ark. Like the doll's house, the ark was out of bounds. Unlike the doll's house, it was also out of my reach: on a high shelf in my mother's bedroom, display only, no hope of me getting up there to investigate what lay under its hinged roof. Animals carved from wood, I guessed, their toxic paint laced with lead. All in pairs from doves to donkeys. Lions and tigers and bears, in pairs.

Other childish things lived in my mother's room, also out of bounds. Behind a heavy brocade curtain on shallow shelves: a box of building blocks with pictures of balls and clowns, trumpets, dancers; a biscuit tin filled with pottery animals; a big book of nursery rhymes, its spine rotting, pages loose, *"Will you walk into my parlour?" said the Spider to the Fly.*

If I was ever caught in my mother's room, I was made to stand on a stool for hours. And other humiliations, petty and not. Daniel wants to hear about my childhood. *Quid pro quo,* you might say. But I don't need to be made to remember, I've not forgotten anything that matters. A glass jar filled with eyes, a doll with just one arm. Damaged things, all I was trusted with, 'Butter fingers,' since the harm had already been done.

I can make him smile, sometimes. Daniel Roake. When he smiles, it is like a boy raising a hand to ward off a blow. He said he loved me. Are you listening, Mum? A man said he loved me in three different languages. When you said no one would ever say it, ever, let alone in Danish. *Unlovable little madam.* But that was your doing. You saw to that. He was always at the threshold to my attic in his jauntiest clothes, peering in to where I was sitting with the one-armed doll, your jar of eyes at my elbow.

As a child, I ran away from home three times. On each occasion, I was brought back and made to understand why it must never happen again. I used to fantasize about *them* running away, leaving me alone in the house. I'd find a way into the attic where Dad laid mouse traps, sneak up when the stepladder was down, hide behind boxes until he went away, closing the trapdoor after him. They would look for me, for a short time. The police might come, or they might not. Eventually, they'd sell up and move on. I'd be free to come down. I'd have money from somewhere, enough to make a new home, far away from them.

That part of my fantasy came true. I'm here, aren't I? Tess and Clark might visit my new home. They're worried about Daniel but they needn't be. He is safe with me. I've made him well again. It will be nice to see Tess even if she killed Luke, which I think she probably did. Or else it was Clark. If it was Clark, Tess might forgive him for the vigil, for failing her and Elise. I'm not sure I could forgive him but Tess is different. Everyone is different.

Daniel is a good man. He speaks Swedish and Danish and Japanese, and maybe Italian and Russian, and probably French. He understands trauma, just not his own. He deserves to go home to his job, to Jude.

Luke deserved to die. He was a monster, a killer. I won't let Tess go to jail for that, or Clark.

I don't know what I deserve, exactly. But I'll find out soon enough. It won't be long now.

41

Dan can't sleep, despite the food and the fact he's able to turn on his side in the bed at last. Grace changed the sheets while he was showering, taking away the belts. Madness but he wishes she hadn't. He doesn't feel safe in the bed without them, as if he might fall. The shower was a bad idea. He kept the water away from the wound but it exhausted him – getting clean, getting dry, getting dressed. His body is worn out but his mind won't stop churning, trying to make sense of what he's learnt over the past two days.

It is tempting to take her word for everything. He's already relying on her for so much. But she is struggling with things he doesn't understand. He can just about make sense of what has gone wrong in his own head. Hers is different again. Darker and more dangerous.

He knew she was dangerous, right from the start. He must have known. Why else would he keep his distance when she was in the cellar? Not because he was afraid of what *he* might do but because he knew she is capable of terrible things. Those half-memories of Luke watching him, rapping out instructions whenever his resolve faltered. Except all that time, Luke was dead.

How sure are you, he asks himself in the night, *that you didn't kill him?*

He imagines the heft of the helium tank in his hands, the satisfaction of smashing it down. And again. There is no sleep, after that.

He sits by the window in the chair where she sat when he was her prisoner. He is free to go now. In theory at least. His car is outside, parked out of view, but he'll find it if he looks. Keys, too. He knows this house, its hiding places. She is sleeping in the room upstairs, in the bed where he slept as a child. He can hear the small sounds of her settling. Sleeping? He doubts it. She trusts him but not that much. As far as she can throw him maybe, which is further than he could throw her right now, despite her smallness. He recalls the slight weight of her in his arms. What was he thinking? What was it he thought he could fix by putting her down in the cellar?

'You can make it stop,' Tess said. 'All this . . . *death*. The watching and the fighting, Luke and Owen and Clark – I want him back. I want this part to be over. Finished. Can you do that?'

Is that what he was trying to do? Stop Luke and the vigil? By using violence against a stranger he suspected of stealing Elise's key to the narrowboat? He remembers being certain Grace knew something crucial; if he kept her in the cellar long enough, she'd tell him. He remembers fearing she was savage, strong. Did he suspect her of cleaning a crime scene? What memory he has is like a length of broken pipe, serving no purpose without any way of connecting it to anything else, anything definite.

He props his head to the window, forcing himself to breathe slowly, steadily. What does he really know? What are the facts and what can he extrapolate from them?

Luke is dead. This feels like a fact but he only has her word for

319

it. Her word and his memory of mess, the aftermath of an atrocity. *Fire, flood, explosion.* Broken bits of pipe. No use.

Elise is dead. That's a fact. The police failed to find her killer. She was strangled, her clothes torn, her body left in the mud of Box Lane a year ago. Her pendant was missing. Her killer is at large.

Tess found the pendant in the pickup after the vigil turned to violence. Clark, Luke, Owen and Dan stripped off their coats after the fight. One of them dropped the pendant. Tess found it down the side of Luke's seat.

Or did she? He only has her word for it. How sure is he of Tess, really? Grief changes people, he knows that. Tess could be anyone at all now.

Elise wrote Luke's name in her diary, surrounded by stars. He only has Grace's word for that. But she's protective of Elise; he can't believe she would invent a diary entry of that sort. And if Grace saw Luke's name in the diary, then so did Tess.

Tess blamed Luke for the vigil, the fighting. That's a fact. She asked Dan to end it, to get Owen and Clark away from Luke's influence. She said Dan was different: 'I thought you'd stand up to him. I thought they'd be safe with you, Owen and Clark. I thought you cared.'

He cares. That's a fact.

Tess took him to the boat to look for Luke. Because she didn't know he was dead. Or because she wanted Dan to witness her pretending not to know.

Grace is a fantasist. That's a fact. She pretended to be Gwen Leonard. He doesn't know why, not really. He suspects a dissociative identity disorder.

Grace left the cork keyring on the boat for him to find, or for

Tess or Clark to find. She is obsessed with them, with Elise. Dan lured her here but she was in control the whole time. She is still in control now.

Her childhood was a horror show, full of abuse and power games. Was it? That feels like a fact. All the evidence points that way, to her parents being bullying monsters. She was programmed from an early age to pack and clean and to keep quiet. She isn't a bad person. Her field of vision has been distorted, that's all, by everything she has lived through until this point in time.

In the cellar, she was two different people: Gwen and Grace. But he is different people, too. Daniel, Dan, Danny boy. If only he can remember which of them put Grace in the cellar and why. She is trying to help him figure it out. She believes she can fix broken things. She is fixing him. Is she?

—

42

'I wasn't very nice to you yesterday.' This is how Grace greets him the following morning. 'I'd like to be better today. What can I do for you? Would you like a sandwich or a hot drink? Would you like to go and sit outside again?'

I'd like you to leave and call the police. I'd like you to stop accusing my grieving friends of being murderers. Failing that, maybe you'd like to stick another knife in me, only properly this time, finish the job.

She is waiting. He can't tell her he doesn't want anything so he says, 'I'd like my watch back.'

She's pleased, leaving the room to return with the watch. 'Here.'

'Thanks.' He straps it to his right wrist without thinking.

'You're not left-handed.'

Her voice is spikier than a mace. He keeps his head down, polishing the face of the watch. Under its leather strap, his pulse beats so hard it hurts.

'I am, actually.'

'No, I've been watching you. And that was on your left wrist when I tied you to the bed.'

He climbs to his feet. She is momentarily distracted by the sight of his T-shirt. 'You're bleeding again.'

'Yes, I need to change the dressing.'

'I'll do it.'

'I'd rather do it myself.'

'All right.'

She steps away. He can tell without looking at her that she is furious. She stalks to the window, turns her back, stares out at the garden.

'It's just that I'd rather—'

'Do it yourself. Yes, I heard you. Here.'

She tosses a wound dressing at him without warning. He doesn't duck, catching it reflexively in his left hand.

'I knew it,' she says. 'You're ambidextrous.'

What I am, he thinks, *is an idiot.* School taught him nothing, clearly, about keeping his head down and not drawing attention to himself. He has been ambidextrous all his life but this is the first time it's landed him in trouble. Yesterday, Grace seemed pleased to discover the extent to which he was different to the average kidnapper. But that was yesterday.

'Is there no end to your talents?' The way she looks at him suggests she'd like to put an end to a few of them before breakfast.

'I can't remember what I was doing three weeks ago. That counts, surely. It should count.'

'You *can* remember.' Her face knots. 'I'll make you remember.'

'I don't know why I brought you here. I don't know what I thought I was doing. I know I've lost my mind—'

'You only *think* you've lost it. You don't *know.*'

'All right.' He tries to ignore the wet from the knife wound, focusing all of his attention on her. 'Well, I know I've broken the law and for that I'm going to prison for a long time. For kidnapping and false imprisonment.'

'How long will you get, do you know that?'

'Anything up to fifteen years.'

Her stare is razored. 'How do you know that?'

'How do I know anything? I read it somewhere, or I heard it.'

'Fifteen years.' She curls her lip. 'That'll give you the chance to learn a new language. Must be one you don't speak yet.'

He looks at her in silence until she says, 'What?'

'Nothing. I need to change this dressing.'

'That wasn't you thinking about telling me to *piss off* in Arabic then? It's what it looked like from where I'm standing.'

'Well,' Dan says, 'thank you for the wristwatch. It was nice of you to want to do something to make up for yesterday.'

She smiles, making the room lurch. 'Sorry, wrong side of the bed.'

He needs to use the bathroom but to do that he has to get past her and from the look of her there is a good chance she will punch him if he gets close, or stab him; he can't be sure she isn't hiding a knife in the back of her jeans or up one of her sleeves.

'Don't look like that,' she says.

'Like what?'

'Like you're scared of me. You need to stop being scared of things, Daniel. People, places, the past.'

'All right. You're right. I'll work on that, after breakfast.'

She comes away from the window as if this is a first, free lesson. Crash course in not being scared. Can he do it? She moves like a cat. A small, grey-headed cat with fists and a kitchen knife stashed up its sleeve.

'Who gave you the watch?' she asks. 'And when?'

'Dad. When I left for university.'

'When you ran away.'

'If you like. But you did that too, didn't you? It's what we're meant to do. Leave home, move on.'

'You came back,' she accuses.

'For work, yes.'

'You speak eight languages; I have your phone, I've seen your emails. *Eight languages.* You could work anywhere in the world. Instead, you return to that shithole where men like Luke thrive and men like you, Daniel, don't. What was there, for you? Clark? Or Tess?' Her mouth curls into a new, savage shape. 'Your *friend since school.*'

'If this is a fresh theory, can it wait until we have coffee? I'll find some marker pens, we'll use the fridge as a whiteboard. Thrash it out.'

But she won't be distracted. 'Your best friend's wife . . . Are you that much of a cliché?'

'I'd hope not.'

'Gifted and talented . . . How many languages do you speak when you're with her? What *talents* have you shared?' She blinks, refocuses. 'What's the matter with you?'

'I'm bleeding on the carpet. But carry on. You were talking about my talents?'

She stands aside, lets him go past her into the bathroom. He is about to close the door when she puts her foot in it.

'What happened to giving me my dignity?'

'That wasn't working out for me. Anyway, I've seen you naked. Stripped you that first day, in case you don't remember.'

'After you stabbed me.'

'After I stabbed you,' she agrees.

Dan turns his back to empty his bladder while she stands and watches and, '*Do* you speak Arabic?' she asks.

'I don't speak Arabic.'

'One for when you're in prison, then.'

'When I'm in prison' – he flushes the toilet – 'I'm keeping my head down and not saying a word more than I need to, to anyone.'

'That's a pity. You've such a lot to say, once you get started.'

He washes his hands the way he would before surgery. She goes quiet, watching him. The silence is such a gift he keeps washing, turning his wrists under the water until she says, 'You have beautiful hands,' when he turns off the taps and reaches for a towel, hiding his hands as he dries them. When he looks up, there is an expression on her face he hasn't seen before. In another person, he would call it sadness. Her eyes are clouded, her mouth crooked. It makes him feel tired and old. 'Look . . . let me change this dressing and I'll make breakfast, if you like.'

'You can't help yourself, can you?' She straightens, wiping her expression as if she is using a cloth to do it. 'One sad look and you want to be kind to me. You *have* to be kind. Even after everything I've said and done. The fact you're bleeding again and I won't let you have your dignity. You're sorry for me, even so. It's who you are. Who you will always be.'

Dan tunes her out. Changing the dressing requires all of his attention. The wound is a mess. He's not sure why. It doesn't smell infected and the skin isn't inflamed, no swelling or pus. There is blood, quite a bit of it. He is running a temperature but no worse than yesterday's fever. He applies the fresh dressing, washes the blood from his hands, watches the water take the red away. When he next looks up, she is still standing there, still speaking.

'I saw a couple dancing in the bandstand in the memorial park. An old couple. They were waltzing, I think it was a waltz. He was wearing a fedora and she was in a red dress with an astrakhan coat. Do you know what astrakhan is, Daniel?'

'No.'

'Liar. They didn't have any music but they waltzed anyway, smiling into each other's eyes. What do you think of that?'

He runs through his options. It is like trying to pick a poison for his own execution. 'It sounds . . . romantic.'

'No. Not *what-do-you-think-I-want-you-to-say*. What do you – *you*, Daniel – think of that?'

He drops the soiled dressing into the bin. His hip hurts, his head hurts, he'd kill for a cup of coffee. 'I think it sounds like a set-up for tourists. I think you're making it up. I think this has gone on long enough . . . What do you want me to think, Grace?'

'Did Tess kill Luke?'

'I'm certain she didn't. I don't even think you think she did. She hurt you and you're angry with her so you've made up this story. Not even made it up – you don't consciously make things up – but there is shrapnel in your brain from your godawful childhood, whatever your parents did to you, as a result of which your hippocampus was reduced and your amygdala function compensates by increasing your creativity and capacity for storytelling.'

The long speech forces her to be silent. For now anyway. Next time she is just as likely to accuse him of being an arrogant know-all

327

and who is he to argue with that? He is sick to death of the sound of his own voice.

She frowns at him. 'Is any of that true?'

'I don't know. Maybe. Or I'm making it up. What do you think?'

Her gaze softens. '*Aishiteru . . .*'

I love you, in Japanese. Her pronunciation is perfect. How long was she practising that? Upstairs in the room where he slept as a child, speaking to herself in Japanese while he tried, and failed, to sleep down here?

In the kitchen, she watches him make breakfast. He takes two pain-killers, washes them down with water.

'Lazarus,' she says.

Pandora, he thinks. 'All gifts', the first woman, punishment by the gods for Prometheus stealing fire from heaven.

'Have you ever been to Japan, Daniel?'

'No. Have you?'

'What about Sweden? Or Denmark? Or Italy?' She draws out the last word, exaggerating an accent: *eat-a-lee.*

He shakes his head. 'It's black tea, I'm afraid. Or coffee?'

'Tea. You speak eight languages but you've never been to any of the countries where you'd use them. Too busy working, I suppose. Bet you don't even take proper holidays. Until this one anyway. Your off-grid getaway.'

'Yes, some people have all the luck. Ham sandwich? No butter but there's mayonnaise.'

'The bread's stale. I'll have toast. Does the hospital know you speak eight languages? You should tell them. They might send you to an overseas conference. Big ophthalmologist pow-wow with a podium and a party in the evening. Room service anyway, a mini-bar in your room with those doll-sized bottles of booze. No point being exceptional if you're keeping it a secret.'

'I'll bear that in mind. Plates?'

She takes them from the cupboard, hands them across. 'You are exceptional, Daniel, you do know that.'

'Not that exceptional or I wouldn't be standing here with a hole in my hip eating stale toast for breakfast, would I?'

'Still,' she says, 'must be nice to spend time with someone who knows exactly what you're capable of. For whom you don't need to dumb down, or mask. You mask all the time, don't you? For everyone else. But not for me.'

'Like I said, some people have all the luck.'

'I'm a gift, Daniel. Admit it.'

What she is is a grenade wrapped in barbed wire. Once the pin is pulled, he will have between two and six seconds to reach minimum safe distance and how he even knows that fact is both mystery and misery to him.

Through the window, the day is iron-clad, no chink of sun. Even so, he wants to be outside, sitting in silence on the stone wall with only the rooks for company. Grace was different out there, gentler with him and with herself. It's the house, being near the cellar. He did this, turned her into this person, this Grace. He needs to work harder to understand her. Maybe then—

'What's your house like?' she says. 'Describe it to me.'

'It's just a house.'

'Nothing's *just a house*. How many rooms? Start there if you like. Square footage. What's it worth?'

'I don't know.'

'Liar. It's worth seven hundred thousand. I looked it up on your phone. Four bedrooms, Edwardian, gabled ends.' She crunches toast. 'Very nice, Roake. Lovely bit of real estate.'

'Grace . . . Has anyone ever gone mad, do you think, just from therapy?'

'Debatable. Very chicken and egg, I'd say. Why?'

'No reason . . . Can I ask you something else?'

'Go ahead.'

'Do you have a diagnosis?'

She finishes the slice of toast. Sits pushing crumbs around her plate with her index finger, looking at him as she does it.

'You told me to stop being scared,' he reminds her. 'I'm just doing what you told me to do.'

'You're the medical man. What's your diagnosis?'

'Complex PTSD exacerbated by acute trauma.'

'Is that your diagnosis, or your best stab at mine?'

'Both,' he admits.

'Told you' – she wets a finger to collect crumbs – 'we're a match. Lonely hearts one-oh-one. Broken hearts.'

He is silent, watching her clear crumbs from her plate until it's empty, as spotless as if it has been washed.

'And your prognosis, Roake? For the pair of us?'

'Expensive . . . Therapy until the end of time.'

'Or we could team up and solve the murder of our friends' child. Cash out on the catharsis and start over.'

This isn't the start of anything. It's the end. Can't she see that? Or is he the one missing the bigger picture? She sees it; she planned for it. He thinks of the fire pit Dad dug in the garden, red layers of heat laid down.

'I know I'm responsible for at least some of this.'

She gives him her flattest look.

'Putting you in that cellar made you worse.'

'*You made me . . .* ? All right, Dr Frankenstein. Guess I was wrong about you. You studied for twelve years so you could feel superior to the rest of us. Nothing as interesting as *trying to be a good man . . .* Just a straightforward Messiah complex like every other surgeon on the planet.'

'Actually, I chose ophthalmology because it guaranteed I'd be away from home for twelve years. The longest possible absence. That was what I wanted, what I thought I wanted.'

Mum gone, Dad pretending it never happened. And Dan joining in, keeping secrets of his own until it was too late for anything else.

'Tell me about the day of your dad's funeral.' Grace is reading his mind, again. 'I'd like to know about that.'

'It's done. And it has nothing to do with this.'

'In real time.' She curls her feet under her in the chair, her attention rapt. 'If you don't mind.'

He has only been awake for an hour but it has already been a really long day. He wants to go and lie down. He does not want to summon the ghost of his grief to dance for her entertainment.

'Hang on.' She uncurls herself and crosses the kitchen, digging in the dresser before bringing a carrier bag to the table.

For one sickening moment, he thinks it's the bag he pushed there at the start of this nightmare, the one he vowed never to open. But the only thing in this carrier bag is a half-empty bottle of Smirnoff. Left behind by a holidaymaker presumably. He doesn't remember seeing it before but if he is making a list of what he doesn't remember, they will be here all day.

'Vodka for breakfast,' Grace says. 'Now you know you're on holiday.'

Dan does not have the strength for this particular battle. He takes two tumblers from a shelf and sets them on the table. Grace pours two measures neatly, chinking the glasses together before handing one to him. Whoever said vodka has no smell was a liar. It stinks of metal and perfume at least as bad as gin, and it tastes worse. His teeth ache after the first mouthful.

'Tell me about the funeral.' Grace curls in the chair facing his. 'Tell me, specifically, what it was like going home after you'd finished shaking hands with everyone and it was over and you were alone in the house.'

He blinks. 'It was miserable.'

'Liar.' Her eyes are bright across the rim of her glass.

'Tell you what.' He drinks another mouthful of vodka, holding hard to what is left of his endurance. 'Why don't you tell me how it felt, since this is clearly not about me. None of it is really about me, is it? I'm just the Japanese puzzle box. *Himitsu-bako.* You're the one who knows how to solve it. So you tell me what it was like going home to that house after I'd finished shaking hands with my dead dad's friends and I was alone.'

'You're a mean drunk,' she says. 'I was not expecting that.'

'I'm not drunk yet. Hang around, see how bad it gets.'

'I think . . .' – she tips her glass at him – 'you were exhausted. You'd been doing that *sad-but-accepting* smile we're expected to do at funerals. Your face had been hurting for hours and you were still doing it when you got home because you couldn't switch it off straightaway. Or' – she considers him – 'you didn't know you were still doing it and when you went to wash your hands – because we both know that's the first thing you'll have done – you looked in the mirror and saw it was still on your face.' She gives him a perfect facsimile of the smile she means, her eyes empty and unseeing. 'Bet you couldn't turn it off even then, not right away. You had to wash your face to get rid of it. But when the smile was gone and there was just you and the house, alone and quiet, Daniel . . . ?' She leans in. 'I think it felt good. Really, really good.'

He must have been holding his breath because his chest staggers as he sucks air into his lungs to compensate. Every word of it is true. Again. As if she removed a portion of his cranium, rummaging around in the mess before extracting these truths.

'You *made* yourself feel miserable, later. Because you knew that's how you're supposed to feel after a funeral, especially your dad's and if your mum's already dead. Or maybe' – she refills their glasses – 'you really did feel miserable because you have too much empathy. But even so, I bet I'm right. There was a moment when it felt good to be alone in the house with all the noise gone and life going on elsewhere but not in there, not in you.'

He touches his fingers to the rim of the glass before lifting it and emptying it, setting it back down for her to refill a third time. He is curiously calm, breathing normally now. She has sidelined him from the emotional scrum of his life a year ago. It feels good. Then he remembers: he is not here to feel good. He points his glass at her. 'Tell me how I felt the following day.'

She gets comfortable, her tumbler held to her chest. 'Oh, then you were definitely miserable. Beating yourself up about having felt good the day before. *Self-reproach bullet . . .*' She mimes firing

333

a gun into one side of her skull, mimes her brains exiting on the other. 'You were inconsolable but not with grief. With guilt.'

'You're wrong, in fact.' He watches the way the light falls into the glass she's refilled. 'I was miserable but we all were. That was the day Elise died. The day Clark called to say she'd been found dead in Box Lane.'

Grace uncurls herself alertly. 'The day after your father's funeral?'

'Check it, if you don't believe me. It's in my calendar on that phone, but if you're thinking that's significant—'

'I'm not thinking that. Daniel . . .'

He doesn't want to play this game any longer. Not from the sidelines. He wants to go home and grieve. For his parents and his friends, for Elise.

'*Daniel.*'

He raises his eyes, blinking at her expression. Pity and a brand of tenderness he has never before seen on anyone's face, let alone hers.

'I'm sorry. I'd no idea it happened so soon after your dad died. I thought months maybe, weeks at least. That must have been horrible. Impossible for you to grieve.' She stops, studying his face. 'What? I can't be kind to you for one minute, without you suspecting me of an agenda?'

'Yes, what am I thinking? Considering you've never done anything like that before.'

'You *are* a mean drunk.' She tops up their glasses. Then she sits back to study him again. 'I do care, you know. About you. I'm not totally consumed by the quest for her killer.'

'My mistake.' He lifts his glass but the smell turns his stomach and he sets it back down. 'I'll file it with all the others.'

'Who was at the funeral?'

'Which one? Oh, you mean Dad's. People from his work, friends. I didn't know most of them.'

'Was Clark there?'

'Yes.'

'With Tess?'

When he looks at her, she shrugs. 'I'm multitasking.'

'They were both there, yes.'

'But not Elise.'

'She was in school, so no.'

'Was Luke there?'

'What do you think?'

She narrows her eyes for a long moment, looking through him to the wall behind. 'She was killed on her way home from school . . . What time did the funeral finish? The wake – whatever – the party afterwards? Sandwiches and vol-au-vents?' She mimes eating entrées. 'Where was that?'

'At his favourite pub.'

'The Puddle Duck?'

'Good luck getting entrées at the Puddle Duck . . . No, it was the Hope and Anchor, outside town.'

'The pub near the narrowboat?' Her gaze widens then refocuses on his face. 'That was your dad's favourite pub?'

'Grace—'

'How often did he go up there?' She is on the edge of her seat. 'Was he the one who gave you a lift that summer? Did he go on the boat? What about when Elise was ten and started hanging out there, did your dad—'

'Don't,' he warns. His hand is spread on the table, his palm and all his fingers pressing there. '*Do not* say it.'

'Say what? That it was your dad who—'

He shoves upright, grabbing at the table for support because his head is spinning but it's not vodka – it's her.

'Just once. As a favour to me. Can you *fucking* not?'

She looks up at him and she is so still and small in the chair it drains the anger out of him before he has processed the fact he's on his feet.

'Daniel. Obviously I do not think your dad killed her. He was dead days before she died.'

He has to turn away from her. He can't do this any more.

'What I was going to ask was did your dad know Luke and Elise used the narrowboat and if so, whether they spent time on there alone together?'

He reaches for his coat, pushes his feet into the deck shoes.

The door isn't locked. He pulls it shut after him, striding around the side of the house to where his car is parked alongside hers.

He puts his hand into his coat pocket and of course his keys aren't in there, of course she has taken them, but he tries the car door and amazingly it opens and then he is sitting in the Saab with his hands on the wheel and his head on his hands and when he shouts it's loud enough and long enough to send rooks rattling from the trees.

Get her legs. Dan, get her feet.

Build it slowly, start with the small twigs.

Good lad.

You'll learn.

He breathes in and breathes out and the rooks return to the trees one by one and the world tips back the right way, slowly.

He is still sitting there when Grace comes out into the garden. He hears her footfall on the gravel. She stops at the side of the open car door with his phone in her hand.

'*How to hotwire a car.*' She reads from the phone. 'One: remove the plastic cover around the steering column. Two: locate the ignition switch plug. Three—'

'You can't hotwire a car with keyless ignition and an immobilizer.' He keeps his thumbs on the steering wheel as he straightens, unlocking the stressed joints of his shoulders. The car smells of antiseptic wipes and coffee, his old life. 'I'd have to hack the immobilizer then use a relay amplifier and transmitter within a hundred metres of wherever you put the key fob.'

He waits for her to ask how he knows that. He has the answer pre-prepared: *I don't know, I've forgotten.*

But, 'I'll put the kettle on,' she says. 'Then we'll talk. I have a new plan.'

'Great. Good. I'll be right in in that case. Can't get enough of your plans.'

'Here.' She passes him a long-handled screwdriver. He recognizes it as the one from the carrier bag he swore he'd never open. 'It was for hotwiring the car but you can keep it. A weapon.'

'Why would I want a weapon?'

'Why wouldn't you?'

She stands a moment longer looking at him then walks away, back to the house where his parents brought him when he was six and where if he turns quickly enough, he'll see them standing at the windows, watching him.

Grace is in the kitchen with two cups of black tea and his phone.

'Take a look.' She is pleased with herself. That cannot be good. 'Check sent messages.'

Dan picks up his phone, calculating the chances of holding on to it this time. He stops calculating when he reads what she's written to Tess and Clark.

'We need to talk,' she's told Clark. 'You know where to find me.'

To Tess, she has typed the same message as before: 'I know you think I did my best,' to which she's added, 'but we need to talk.'

Dan puts the phone down on the table. He is distantly aware of how much his hip hurts but honestly? So what.

'I think they'll come,' Grace says. 'Or one of them will. Whoever has most to lose by staying away.' She nods at the chair next to hers. 'Sit down.'

He does as she says, reaching for the cup of tea so he has something in his hands, a place to put his anger and his alarm. There is a second when he thinks of throwing it – hot tea is a weapon – but it wouldn't do any good. She is waterproof, bulletproof, foolproof. Screwdriverproof, in all probability. He sits in silence, listening to her present her new plan.

'I'm right, aren't I? About Clark knowing where to find you. They know about this house. You offered it to them as a holiday home. I overheard Tess telling Clark.'

He digs for the memory of this, comes up empty-handed. She is waiting for his approval, expecting him to congratulate her on this cunning ploy to lure his friends into her trap.

'You want them here. A killer and his accomplice – that is what you've decided they are. So you issue an *invite*?'

'It's time. You said it yourself, this has gone on long enough.'

'What are you going to do? What are *we* going to do when they turn up? Your killer and their accomplice?'

He needs to know how far ahead she's planned. He has to keep his friends safe from her, this nightmare of him and her. *His friends*. Who have lost their child, their happiness, their way. He cannot let her do this, not this.

'What are you going to do?'

'I'm going to give them the chance to explain. Confess, if you prefer. And then I'm going to help them.' She spreads her hands, lets him see how small and neat and clean they are. 'The way I helped you.'

The Facts As I Know Them

- He speaks eight languages but he can't say 'thank you' in any of them.
- I've given him every chance. I have helped him but now he has to help himself. If he can't do that, we're done here.
- We're done.

43

Dan is pretending to read but the book may as well be in Russian or . . . Not Russian, since he knows how to read that. Alien Sanskrit. He is using the book as a prop because Grace is pacing and when she's pacing she is even more alarming than when she is sitting in a chair like a coil of barbed wire. She's been restless since sending the texts. Dan's phone is in her fist. She won't stop firing questions. You'd think he'd be used to it by now but it is hard to focus on her questions at the same time as trying to figure out how to keep his friends safe. None of his gifts or talents is of any use to him here. He can tell her to stop in eight languages but she won't listen, in any of them.

'Only two photos on this phone, Roake. Of a leaking gutter. Who has photos like that on their phone?'

'Someone asked by a roofing specialist to supply photos of his leaking gutter.'

If Tess and Clark come here together, she will assume it means they are in it together. She has already made the assumption Dan will side with Grace. Is there leverage in that, an element of surprise? Could he pull it off? His hip is wet again. He should change the dressing but he is wary of interrupting her pattern. The pacing is alarming but at least it is familiar.

'You don't have Jude's phone number on here. Why not?'

'She's a child. It wouldn't be appropriate.'

His friends have met Grace already, or Tess has. That might help when it comes to explaining what is happening. Or it might mean Tess misreads the situation and walks in here thinking she can reason with this woman. Or walks in here angry with Grace, which is unlikely to improve Dan's chances of keeping Tess safe. Or Grace safe, for that matter.

'What's . . . *Blick Aare abwärts bei der Fähre Muri-Belp*?'

'What?'

'*Blick Aare abwärts bei der Fähre Muri-Belp*.' Grace reads the German phonetically, her expression skirting impatience.

'View from the Muri-Belp Ferry down the Aare . . .'

'Why would you pay five thousand pounds for that?'

'Why would who pay five thousand pounds?'

'*You*. You were watching the auction.' She waggles the phone in her hand. 'You were going to place a bid. Lot 414. A year ago.'

He remembers. *Pen and ink on paper. Signed Klee and dated 1909 (lower left). All four edges deckled. Scattered areas of pale discolouration, possibly related to historic restoration of small areas of paper skinning.* He can remember that but not what he needs to remember, to keep them safe.

'Daniel?' Grace prompts.

'A sketch by Paul Klee. I was buying it for Mum's room.'

'Did you?' She stares at him, her expression unfathomable.

'No . . .'

How is he going to keep his friends safe? She gives no quarter;

no secret is safe from her scrutiny. Nowhere is private, not even the places in his heart or stomach, or in his hip, which hurts like nothing on earth. Nothing is allowed to be hidden, not from her. Not grief or guilt, or loss or hope.

'Why not, Daniel? Why didn't you buy it and put it in her room? Or at least bid for it?'

'My father was dying. I ran out of time.'

Like I'm running out of it now. If Tess and Clark are on their way here, separately or together. How am I going to keep them all safe?

'Were you with him, when he died?'

Was I? Did I hold his hand and ask his forgiveness for the distance I put between us when I left home because I didn't understand his need to take comfort from the lie he told about her death, even though I was lying too, about the scars on my arm, about Luke?

Dan keeps his eyes down on the book. 'Can I ask *you* a question? Just to shake things up.'

'As long as it's one I can answer.' She is still on his phone, refreshing his inbox, he imagines, hoping for a reply from Tess or Clark.

'How did you construct the compartments in your shoebox?'

She swipes at the phone, not looking at him. But he has her attention. Danger signals sweep from her, the way a lighthouse warns of rocks. *Fresnel lens,* his brain offers, *glass prisms that change the way in which light travels until all of it exits in the same direction, refracting and reflecting at once.* His brain needs to mind its own business.

'That's none of your business,' she agrees.

'Really? I thought we were in this together. You're going through my phone but I can't ask a simple question about your shoebox.

343

Not about the contents, just how you made it. I like what you did with it. Very neat.'

She thumbs at his phone. '*Bastardo condiscendente*. Do you know what that means?'

'I can guess.'

'I'll bet you can. How about this?' Her thumbs move; she's using the translation app, typing in whatever she wants it to say. When she holds it out, the phone recites, '*Dra åt helvete.*'

She is telling him to *fuck off* in Swedish.

'Arabic,' he says, 'would at least be a challenge.'

'Remembering what you did three weeks ago is a *challenge*, Daniel. This is an instruction.' She fires the phone at him again: '*Dra åt helvete.*'

'I saw the scarab. And the poison bottle.' He keeps his eyes down on the book he's been pretending to read. 'I saw the intaglio.'

The pause that follows is the most threatening thing he has listened to in his life. He hears blades being sharpened, rope being knotted, the long drop of a dead body into water.

When she speaks, her voice is threaded with ice and menace. 'Is that a good book, Daniel? I didn't have you down as the classic crime type. Silly of me since I was in your cellar for days being starved, imagining you meant to bury me in the garden. Or leave me down there to rot.'

'You were asking for it.' He closes the book, meeting her gaze. 'Sorry, I thought we'd established that? You came here knowing what would happen. You left your phone at home on purpose and all your ID, said you were Gwen Leonard. Who is she, by the way? Someone you pretend to be when you're trying not to be Grace? Because Grace was your parents' favourite, or their least favourite.' He tilts his head, the way she tilts hers sometimes, trying for a better perspective. 'No, she was their favourite. The one who cleaned and tidied and packed away whatever godawful mess they'd made. Grace was their good girl. You were trying not to be her when you were first in the cellar. You held out a long time, which means you don't like being Grace. She leaves a bad taste in your mouth, like soap. Or drain cleaner. But you knew you had to be her to survive this. She's the survivor. Gwen only knows how to live, she doesn't know how to fight.'

He stops, sitting in the silence his words have carved from the kitchen. Even the fridge has stopped humming, holding its breath on his behalf.

'This is new, Daniel.' Grace puts the phone into her back pocket, freeing her fists, her face lit with interest. 'Don't stop. Gwen doesn't know how to fight?'

His brain shouts at him in eight languages to shut up, stop baiting her. *You'd better have that screwdriver, you madman, you're about to need it.*

'There are other names too, I suspect. Other ways you tried to stop being Grace. Interesting you chose the same initial.' He holds the book in his hands as she strolls towards him. 'I'm thinking . . . Greta, Gisela, Gaia.' He points at her with the book. 'Gaia, born of Chaos, obsessed with vengeance.'

She stops directly in front of him. They consider one another for a long second before she lifts her hand and hits him flat across the cheek, an open-handed blow that lights every nerve in the left side of his face. Her pupils dilate as she does it; his brain gives him 'psychosensory pupil response (PPR)'. She balls her fist, swings it at his left hip. He sees it coming and twists enough to save himself from the contact she intends. Her fist grazes the base of his ribs. Before she can try again, he grabs her wrists and holds them, hard.

The pair of them are on their feet now. He is holding her and she is baring her teeth but it's a smile, she's smiling at him and his face is still lit where she slapped it and her pupils are still dilated.

'So you're not just made of empathy . . . Come on, then!' She's panting a little. They both are. 'What happens now?'

'Now you text my friends and tell them not to come here. Because it's better if it's just the two of us. Don't you think?'

'Just you and me.'

'You. And me.'

It is a waltz on a razor blade but he thinks he has her, there is a moment when he is certain of it. Then she thins her mouth and—

'Take your beautiful hands off me, Roake.'

He lets her go immediately and steps back, glad of her instruction; she's stopped him, again. It was never going to work. Nothing is ever going to work with Grace.

She rubs at her wrists, her stare bright on his face. He feels sick but not scared, not any longer, which is strange and almost certainly stupid given the look in her eye.

'You really thought that would work? One touch of your magic hands and I'd be swept off my feet?'

He reaches for the book he dropped, putting it on the table. She is so close he feels her breath coasting the side of his neck as he straightens.

'At least now I know what you're made of. I was starting to think it was compassion and stale toast. Would you have hurt me, do you think?'

'I hurt you before, didn't I?'

'That was different. You were out of your mind.'

'Try that again in the present tense . . .' He props his good hip to the table, trying not to think about the other one. 'So what does happen now?'

'Now . . . you're in trouble.'

'Clearly. But some parameters would be helpful.'

'I'll bet. Hard to draw lines when everything keeps shifting.'

'Honestly, Grace? I've had complex cataract surgeries that were easier than holding a conversation with you.'

'Well, that hurts.' She hasn't stopped smiling. 'But at the same time, fair comment. It takes two, though, doesn't it, to have a conversation?'

'A sane conversation, certainly.'

Her smile widens. 'Are you calling me insane?'

'No. Because apart from being suicidal on my part, it would be clinically inaccurate. You're not easy to talk to, that's all I'm saying.'

'Funny, I find you very easy to talk to. Even easier to slap.'

'Yes, I got that message. Thanks.'

His attempt to navigate this with humour isn't working for whatever reason. It's worked before, about the only thing that has, but the way she is looking at him . . . He's in trouble. He was in it before but this is different. Even so, it feels a thousand times better than the no-man's land of this last year – after Dad's death and Elise's, while the vigil was dragging on – a place where pain pretended to be his friend and he slung his arm around its neck, imagining he was warm, that he was anywhere but here in this trench, this pit he dug for himself, smiling as he did it. Better to be where he is right now, in the immediate orbit of her fresh interest in him than back there.

'To answer your question,' Grace says, 'I made it myself.'

He remembers they were talking about her shoebox. 'I didn't look through much of it. Only the first few compartments.'

'You stopped when you saw it was private.'

It isn't a question. She's decided this for herself.

'I stopped because it started raining.'

She rolls her eyes at that. 'Your honesty is a compulsion, isn't it? Even when it lands you in trouble. Given how much you're suppressing the rest of the time, I guess it's a safety valve, the only thing stopping you from exploding.'

'Look, I'm—'

'Say *sorry* again and I'll punch you in that hip. I don't want your apologies, preferred it when you were standing up to me. That was proper honesty. *Useful* honesty.'

'Right. I'll work on that.'

'It is, isn't it? An *absolute compulsion*. You couldn't lie to save your life. Or anyone else's for that matter.'

He rolls his neck, rubs his cheek. 'Shall we get some fresh air?'

Outside, the rooks have deserted the trees. The day is even bleaker than before. They sit on the low stone wall, Dan shivering in his coat, Grace impervious in her flannel shirt. She has his phone in her hands. He wishes – not for the first time in the past fortnight – that there was no phone signal or Wi-Fi here. When he was a child, the house was properly off-grid. Board games, card games, picnics in the garden, hot water rationed between baths. He feels ancient. *We made our own entertainment in those days.*

'What's so funny?' Grace asks.

'I was remembering the time I nearly set fire to this garden when I was seven and Dad left me in charge of the fire pit.'

'That's a big responsibility for a seven-year-old. But I expect you were a very serious child.'

'I wasn't, actually.'

He sees his seven-year-old ghost turning circles on the lawn before falling down dizzy, laughing at the sky. Madness to think it was ever him. Or not madness. Sadness. He feels sorry for that boy, the way he does for Clark, his once-sunny friend, and Owen, who should be far away from the destruction of these last twelve months.

'Serious enough to be left in charge of fire.' Grace holds his phone like an injured bird in the cup of her palms. 'That's a big responsibility.'

'Too big for me. Luckily Dad had the garden hose connected at the time, otherwise we might not be sitting here now.'

She gives him a level look. 'That *is* lucky.'

'Sarcasm doesn't suit me? That was closer to irony, though. I think I got away with it.'

'Roake,' she says.

'Yes, Maddox?'

'Are we insane? To be sitting here, doing this?'

Dan is surprised to discover he doesn't instinctively answer in the affirmative. Instead, he considers her question in the light of what just happened in the house. For some reason, that's changed things between them. He doesn't know why exactly, or how. But they are not the same people they were before. He is reluctant to examine what it might mean.

'I think . . . we're a bit broken. But we're not insane. We want a better outcome for our friends. And we don't want a child's killer to go free. That's not insane. In some ways it should be the definition of sanity.'

Grace makes a fist and raises it like an activist at a rally. 'Justice for Elise.'

'Justice for everyone.' He shivers. 'Wouldn't that be nice?'

'How's that hip?'

'It's been better. How's that head?'

'Hard. Like a pig's.' When he looks at her, she shrugs. 'It's what my old dad used to say. *Pig-headed little madam.*'

Dan pushes his hands deeper into his coat pockets. '*Dein Vater klingt wie ein verdammtes Arschloch.*' He shuts his eyes at the sky. 'Your dad sounds like a fucking arsehole.'

'*Danke.*'

Into the silence comes the sound of traffic but it is distant, way off west, not coming their way.

He has the strangest feeling he has known this woman all his life, that the pair of them grew up together. The world is filled with strangers – the same as it always was – but he and Grace have more in common than not. '*I'm stranger. You're stranger. Together, we are . . . strangers.*' Who said that? The Cheshire Cat in Wonderland. He's regressing, still seeing his seven-year-old self spinning on the lawn. He wants to watch out for that.

'Would you like to see the shoebox?'

Dan brings his head down to look at her, surprised to find her smiling. 'Of course. Yes.'

'Come on, then.'

She stands, pushing his phone into the back pocket of her jeans. He won't try again to get his hands on the phone or to stop this from escalating, to keep his friends away or derail her plans. He can't stop her and maybe he shouldn't. Elise is dead. If Clark or Tess killed her killer, then maybe it's right they're coming here, to Grace. Right or wrong, he can't stop it. Time to accept that. Time to move on.

He waits in the kitchen while she goes up to the bedroom where he slept as a boy, returning with the shoebox cradled in her hands. He remembers how she fought him for it that day in the cellar. It feels like years ago, time playing its usual trick with his memory.

Grace places the shoebox on the table and eases off the lid, laying it aside. 'Go ahead,' she says.

Dan straightens, leaning forward in the chair. 'Isn't it . . . ?' He hesitates then sits back. 'I don't want to invade your privacy.'

'Says the man who locked me in his cellar for days on end.' She checks the phone, sets it aside. 'Tell you what, we'll bargain for it. You teach me a fact I don't already know. For each fact that is new to me, I'll let you open a compartment. No foreign languages allowed and no surgical jargon.'

'Those are the only rules?'

'The only rules.'

'And will you tell me about the contents? Where it came from and what it means to you?'

'Greedy.' Her grey gaze fixes on him. 'I might, yes. Depends how fascinating your facts are.'

'How many items in the box?'

'Thirteen.'

'So thirteen facts you don't already know. And make them fascinating.'

'Should be simple enough for you, Roake. You're what – one rung away from a genius?' She clicks her fingers. 'Impress me.'

He looks at the shoebox, feeling the fascination it exerts, as if she has laid her heart and soul on the kitchen table.

'In Greek mythology, Pandora was the first woman, meant as punishment for Prometheus stealing fire down from heaven—'

'Pandora's box?' She rolls her eyes. 'Try harder, genius.'

'Except it wasn't a box. It was a jar. It is widely believed Erasmus, writing in the sixteenth century, mistranslated the Greek.'

'New rule.' She yawns. 'No showing off.'

'The jar contained all manner of misery and evil. When Pandora opened it, the misery and evil had a field day. Only hope was left inside the jar. I think we're meant to puzzle over whether hope is an evil or a balm for evil.'

'So which is it?'

'Within the narrative rules laid down by Hesiod, it is obviously an evil. The jar contains "all manner of misery and evil" so—'

'For a genius, you're not very smart, are you? What did I *just say* about showing off?'

'Do I get points for the jar-not-box at least?'

She nods, nudging the shoebox nearer to him. He's as careful as if he is handling an explosive device, or a wild animal. Opens the first compartment, takes out a tightly wrapped package the size of a fridge magnet. He already knows what it is. An amber glass intaglio. Its size suggests it was once mounted in a signet ring. Old, early nineteenth century. When he turns it to the light, the engraving is thrown into sharp relief: two doves in a birdbath. The birdbath is chipped. The amber is red in places, orange in others. He smooths his index finger to the damage, feeling the small sting of sharp glass.

'Will you tell me about it?'

'For Pandora's jar? No. Try harder, Roake. Give me a properly fascinating fact.'

He returns the intaglio, carefully, to its compartment.

'When glass breaks, the cracks move at three thousand miles per hour. That is five times faster than the average aeroplane.'

'Now that's a fact.' She nods her approval, offering him the shoe-box. 'Pick wisely, wise one.'

Dan knows what is inside the compartment to the left of the one he just opened: a scarab beetle. He pushes past it to the next compartment.

She stiffens in her seat. 'What are you doing?'

'You didn't say I had to open them in any particular order.'

'I thought you'd work that out for yourself.'

He wonders what is hiding at the bottom of the box, what she's reluctant to let him touch, or to talk about. Hope, like Pandora's jar?

Wishful thinking, Roake, at this late stage in the day?

He backtracks to the scarab. It is an extraordinary colour, changing from brackish water to pale gold under the light. He is very aware of how still Grace is sitting, as if she might be holding her breath.

'This is glass?'

'Libyan desert sand. Gold tektite. Do you know what that is?' He shakes his head. 'But you know how glass is formed.'

'From sand.'

'And you know what a scarab is. What it means.'

'It's a beetle. That's all I've got. Tell me?'

'The scarab is a symbol of protection and strength. Scarabs can carry six hundred times their own body weight. They're associated with the Sun God Ra . . . You'd better not be pretending not to know this shit, Daniel . . . It's believed a deva spirit resides inside the scarab.'

'Diva?'

'With an e – deva.'

Her scarab has a minuscule chip in its thorax. Like the intaglio, the damage turns a smooth pebble of glass into a sharply stinging stone.

'Where did you find it?'

'Where did I steal it? From a house in Henbury. Do you know Henbury?'

'I've driven through it.'

'Then you've driven past the house I stole it from. His wife died.' She rolls her eyes again when he glances up. 'Take it easy, brainiac. She died of natural causes. I don't just pack houses where killers lurk.'

'Have you ever packed a house like that?'

'We'll find out, won't we? When Tess and Clark get here.'

She holds out her hand for the scarab. He places it lightly on her palm, watching as she touches her thumb to the chipped thorax. The glass is warm from his fingers; he tries to read her face but could be seeing pleasure or its opposite. He looks at the shoebox, wondering about the rest of its contents.

'Is there a crack in everything?'

'Duh. It's how the light gets in. Thought you'd know that one.'

She returns the scarab to its bubble wrap and lays it aside, nodding at the box. 'Go again. Feed me a new fact.'

The fridge hums behind them. Otherwise the kitchen is quiet, the whole house is. As if she is casting a spell, setting them afloat, apart from the night and whatever is out there in the darkness.

'Like all living things, we're bioluminescent. People, I mean. We glow brightest in the afternoon, our lips especially. But we glow in the dark, too.'

'*Our lips especially?* Damn, Roake.' She props her chin in her hand. 'You're good. How do we glow in the dark?'

He shakes his head. 'You said no showing off.'

She nudges the shoebox towards him with the ends of her fingers. 'Whatever you want. Dig deep.'

He doesn't trust her smile, not quite, choosing the third compartment according to her original rule. But the little square of bubble wrap is empty. Whatever was inside has been removed.

'The caterpillar?'

'You tell me.'

Her chin is in her hand, eyes soft as she studies him. In this mood, she is phenomenal. As if she is made of wisdom, focus and peace. He wants to lean into her stillness, into her spell, and rest.

'It was a seventh birthday present. Tess said she was obsessed with caterpillars so I bought half a dozen in different sizes, packed them into boxes to make a game of it at her party –' He stops when her expression changes, her eyes achromatic. 'What?'

'*You* gave her the caterpillar?' Her face is fierce, her voice full of splinters. 'That was you?'

'I gave her lots of caterpillars.' His pulse slams in his left side. 'Like I said, it was a game—'

'Was it chipped when you gave it to her?'

'No. That happened when she was unwrapping it. I wasn't careful enough with the packing.'

She reaches both hands for the shoebox and pulls it from him, starts fitting the contents back together again.

'Maddox?'

'Tell me about this party, *Daniel*.' She speaks his name through her teeth. 'Since apparently you were there.'

'It was Tess's idea. Fairy lights in the garden, balloons . . .'

'And boxes. You gave her *boxes*.' Her fingers push the compartments shut inside the shoebox. 'How many caterpillars?'

'Seven.'

'Seven boxes, one inside the other. But you didn't wrap the glass one properly. It fell out and broke on the patio.'

'Yes.' His body rings with alarm. 'What did I do? Grace, tell me what I did. Please.'

She gets to her feet, stands over him. 'What happened with Tess on the boat that night?'

He shuts his eyes, pushing his fingers there, willing the images to come, praying to the deva spirit, to gods he doesn't believe in, to anyone. 'I can't remember.' He drops his hands to the table. 'I'm sorry. I'm seeing Tess and the boat but nothing else. Only what I've already told you.'

'You're protecting her.' All the peace is gone from Grace. Her eyes are wild with anger. 'From me.'

'I'm not. If I could remember, I'd tell you. I owe you that.'

She keeps packing the shoebox, thrusting her fingers, punching her precious treasures into the slots.

'What did I do?' Dan asks again. 'If you don't tell me, I won't know and I won't learn.'

'You said you packed a fragile object so badly it broke. Don't think I'm letting you touch anything more of mine after that admission.'

That is part of it but not all. She's angry because he spoke about Elise and the birthday party, because he was there with Tess and Clark and Elise, part of their celebration. It is meant to be the two of them – him and her – but like an idiot he put pictures in her head of him with the family she loves but to which she doesn't belong and never will. 'I'm sorry . . .'

'What did I *just* say,' she hisses, 'about apologies?'

'That you're sick of them. I know. You never want to hear another apology out of me no matter how many weeks and months we spend together in this house trying to solve the murder of a girl who was loved. Who *shone* and had a happy life and who should be here right now living it, not gone out of the world, away from everyone who loved her and who would have happily given their lives for hers if the world worked that way, if it was fair.'

She has her fists on the table, her head down, face hidden. Very slowly, Dan gets to his feet. He moves to where she's standing and when he's close, he puts out a hand and lays it on her left shoulder. A shudder passes through her, coming up from her feet until he feels it quivering in the palm of his hand.

'For what you went through,' he says, 'I'm sorry. And for not being able to remember. But I will help you, in whatever way I can. I want to help. Not just because I owe it to you, for what I put you through in the cellar. Because what you are doing matters. It matters.'

'You think I'm insane.' Her shoulder is clenched under his hand. 'You tried to leave this morning. If you'd had your car keys, you'd have gone.'

'The moment passed. I'm not going anywhere.'

'I've heard that before. Don't think you're the first to say it.'

'I bet I'm not.' He smooths his thumb at the point of her shoulder, unsure which of them he is trying to comfort. 'But could the others say it in eight languages? I'm exceptional, or so I'm told.'

'Nothing wrong with *my* memory.'

'*Himitsu-bako* . . . How many moves to unlock me? One thousand, three hundred and sixty-six, wasn't it? Must be some we haven't tried yet.'

She is quiet for so long he is starting to lean into it – the silence and the stillness of her.

'Better take your beautiful fingers off me, Roake, before I get the wrong idea.'

He steps back, putting his hands in his pockets. She reaches for the lid of the box, fits it over the contents she has repacked.

'Ask me about the poison bottle,' she says then. 'I know you've seen that. You said you'd seen it. Ask me.'

Dan has the certain feeling he does not want to know about the poison bottle. 'I didn't give you a fourth fact, did I?'

'You said you'd have given your life for Elise's, if you could. That was a fact, wasn't it?'

'Yes . . .'

'So ask me.' She turns to face him. 'Can you remember what it looked like? The bottle?'

'Yes, I think so. It was about the size of my little finger.'

'Show me this finger.'

He takes his hand from his pocket and shows her.

'Correct. What else do you remember about it?'

'It's very pale blue. More like water than blue . . . There are narrow ridges running down it. The word 'poisonous' is embossed on one side.'

'Those ridges tell you the bottle contains poison, even if you're blind or can't read. But I suppose you knew that. What else do you remember?'

'The lip of the bottle was chipped.'

She is watching him more closely than she ever has before. 'How many ridges, do you remember that?'

He shuts his eyes, feeling the slim chill of the bottle in his fingers as he stood beside her car, the shoebox open in its boot. He can smell fibrous carpeting, the metallic scent of rain as it spots down from the winter sky.

'Five ridges?'

'What happened on the narrowboat with Tess?'

He tries the same trick, summoning the memory of the smell of iron and earth. Dead water. Tess thumping her fist on the cabin door, calling Luke's name. The creak of the canal, pinched white tips of his fingers. Tess saying, 'I should never have let her come here. All this way, on her own. But she loved it. The boat. And Luke made it safe, that's what he said,' the hardness in her voice as she said it. Her hand unfurling to show him the keyring.

'I've told you everything.' He opens his eyes. 'There isn't anything else. I'm sorry but there isn't.'

'You're lying,' Grace says. 'Ask me where I got the poison bottle.'

'Where did you get the poison bottle?'

'From a box in my mum's bedroom.' Her expression doesn't

change, all her attention fixed on his face. 'On a high shelf behind a curtain. I wasn't supposed to go looking there. But it's what I did, what I do. I look in the places people keep hidden. I poke and I pry and I take things sometimes, and sometimes I put them back but not always.' She measures him against her stare. 'Sometimes I keep them and never let them go. Do you understand?'

'I understand.'

'You don't. But that's all right. We're not alike, you and I.' She drops her gaze, finally. 'We've talked about your mistakes but that's mine. Thinking you are like me, that we belong here together. You don't belong.'

'Grace . . .'

'It's all right. You just . . . don't.'

'If not here, then where?'

'Back there.' She nods towards the door, the road running away from the house, down into town. 'Where you came from.'

Dan waits a moment in respect of how quiet she is, all her anger out of sight again. 'I can't go back. We've talked about this. When we leave, if I leave, it will be for prison. But that's all right. It's where I belong for what I did to you. I think . . . Not enough people have paid for what they did to you.'

She dips her head to the shoebox before raising it again, fixing her bullet-grey stare on his face.

'It's all right,' he says again. 'I've made my peace with it.'

'It's not all right. And your peace is only part of it. What about mine? What about when I have to think of you rotting in a prison cell when you could be helping people like Jude?'

'I won't rot. I'll read. And I'll write to you.'

'You won't. No one's ever written to me.'

'I will. I'll write to you in Arabic, if you like. That's a promise.'

But she shakes her head. 'You won't last a week in prison. Anything up to fifteen years, you said. Well, you've already spent fifteen years in prison in case you didn't work that out for yourself. You've served your time. I won't let them do it to you, in any case. I'd keep you here before I let you go to prison.'

He lets that rest for a while before he asks, 'What if it's what I want? What if it's justice?'

'Not justice for Elise. And if you deserve to go to prison, so do I. For disposing of evidence, perverting the course of justice. Conspiring, entrapment, assault with a deadly weapon . . . What else?'

He has no answer to that, other than one she won't want to hear.

'We should eat,' he says instead. 'Keep our strength up.'

She shrugs. 'Cold carbonara? How can I resist?'

'Let's eat it outside. I'll light the fire pit.'

'Not you, you pyromaniac. I'll do it.'

She takes the shoebox from the table and heads upstairs.

Dan divides cold pasta between two bowls. He searches the cupboards for another bottle of vodka, or one of wine, but there's nothing so he takes mineral water from the pantry, sets the whole lot on a tray, pulls on his coat.

His hip isn't happy but it hasn't been happy in hours. He tells it to shut up, tells his brain to switch off. This new mood between them feels as fragile as spun glass; he doesn't want to spoil it. Doesn't, in any case, have the energy for another fight, not tonight. He fetches blankets from the cupboard under the stairs. To do this, he has to pass the door to the cellar. The door is shut. When he tries the handle, he finds she's locked it. He wonders where she put the key. She is coming down the stairs, empty-handed. He doesn't ask her about the key, a question for another time.

It's dark in the garden but there is light enough from the house for Grace to locate the fire pit, filling it with pieces of dried wood taken from a basket in the kitchen. She adds screws of packing paper from the boot of her car, before dousing the whole lot with lighter fluid.

Dan watches without comment, hearing Dad's voice in his head: 'Build it slowly, start with small twigs.' But she knows what she's doing, waits for the fumes to dissipate before she strikes a match. The pit dances with flame.

They sit on blankets and eat the pasta. Her eyes are silver in the firelight. Owls patter in the trees. Wood spits and splits in the flames.

After they've eaten, Grace draws up her knees and lays her cheek there, watching the fire. A sound like a cat crying brings her head up but Dan says, 'Buzzard,' and she puts it back down. He pushes his left hand into the sleeve of his coat, out of sight of her peripheral vision, tracing the scars on his forearm before taking his pulse, which is no worse than he thought it would be.

'I'm tired of therapy,' Grace says after a long while. 'I'm thinking of giving meditation a go.'

He studies her before shaking his head. 'Sorry, Maddox. Can't see you as a Buddhist. I'm trying but something doesn't fit.'

'The rage, maybe? Because I'm working on that.'

'Must be something else then. Too easy to picture you with knives, perhaps.'

'No lotus flower without mud,' she says serenely. 'I read that somewhere.'

'Well, that does sound very wise. Perhaps you could pull it off.'

Something stirs in the trees above them, settling in for the night.

'You're clever, Roake. Can't you think of a way out of this, for us?'

'Not one that avoids prison. Sorry. At least you'll get a window this time. And no maniac chucking soup at you at odd hours, demanding you answer questions he can't ask.'

'I had a window . . . How long will I get?'

'With mitigating circumstances? A couple of years, maybe less.'

'Two years? For dumping the body of a child killer?'

Dan reaches for a stick, stirs at the fire. 'Luke has daughters. Taylor and Ashleigh. Ashleigh's expecting Luke's first grandchild. Taylor is just twelve, thirteen at Christmas.'

Grace narrows her eyes. 'He'd have started on her next.'

'They deserve to know their dad's dead. Not just gone and never coming back. They deserve the chance to bury him and to grieve.'

The fire sends up sparks, thin and red as blood.

'Damn you, Daniel Roake.' Her voice has a crack in it, like the glass treasures in her shoebox. 'Damn your good heart to hell.'

He accepts this in silence. They sit together, in silence.

'Do you want to know what else is in the shoebox?' she asks then.

'Only if you want to tell me.'

'Bet you're imagining all kinds of horrors. All the evils and miseries of the world. Teeth and blood and bones . . .'

'No. Everything in the box is beautiful. The scarab, the intaglio, the poison bottle . . . Damaged but beautiful.'

'You're wrong, in fact.' She reaches for her own stick. 'There *are* teeth in there. Baby teeth. For some reason, people can't bring themselves to throw those away. Just one of the things I cannot fathom about other people ...'

The fire stirs, flames circling.

'Even my old mum kept my baby teeth. I took them from her hiding place and planted them in stony ground. Take a guess at what happened next.'

'A skeleton army sprang up to battle Jason and the Argonauts?'

She laughs then stops, poking her stick at the fire. 'Baby teeth, and eyes. In the bottom of the shoebox.'

'Eyes?'

'Glass eyes and button eyes. They lived in a jar in my room.' Her gaze is distant, fixed in the past. 'Dad could never look at the jar. Mum put it by my bed. As a charm, I suppose you'd say.' She props her chin on her forearm. 'Here's the thing, Roake. My dad liked little girls and my mum blamed me.'

Dan straightens slowly, blinking the fire's heat from his eyes.

'Keep your thoughts to yourself,' Grace warns. 'But you can listen, if you like.' Then she repeats, as if speaking words she has never before said aloud: 'My dad liked little girls and my mum blamed me. I wasn't neat enough or clean enough or nice enough ... He never touched me. But he touched lots of other little girls. Nicer little girls. He'd bring home gifts for them. Dolls, usually. Rag dolls because they were cheap, easily hidden. Mum always found them, cut them to pieces. If the dolls had sewn-on eyes, she'd snip them off with scissors and put them in the jar. I suppose she was saying, "I see you." Her way of keeping watch . . . The jar lived near my bed. I didn't mind, didn't have a lot of things I was allowed to play with. Sometimes she'd let me have one of the dolls, if she hadn't done too much damage to it. The jar was . . . an evil eye. Her way of keeping him away from me. Of course, it didn't feel like that to me. I thought she was warning *me*, not him. I was so afraid of her . . .'

She shoves the stick into the burning wood, holding it there until it catches fire. 'I was a very clumsy child. It was their excuse for not letting me play with anything nice: I was always breaking things. *Butter fingers.* But it was her. She made me afraid with her rules and punishments. Even the stories she read to me. *The Snow Queen*, little Kay with her chip of ice lodged in his heart . . . I was nervous the entire time, always shaking, dropping things.'

She draws the stick from the fire. 'I haven't broken anything in years.' She blows a soft breath at the burning stick, making its end glow and spark. 'Well, nothing I didn't mean to break.'

'Grace, I'm so sorry.'

She nods then squints at him sideways. 'You're too young to have seen *Jason and the Argonauts.*'

'It was one of Dad's favourites. We must've watched it together a dozen times.'

'Do you forgive them?' The fire's reflected in her eyes. 'Your parents.'

'Yes.'

'And do you forgive yourself, for not forgiving them when they were alive?'

'Yes.'

He thinks she'll call him a liar for that but she doesn't. She says, 'Tell me how you did it. Forgave them. And when.'

'Here, with your help. In the past few days. They have been in this house the whole time.' He glances across his shoulder to where the windows throw back stray snatches of the fire's glow.

Grace hugs her knees, resting her cheek back there. 'Tell me.'

'When Dad died, there was so much guilt in the mix, the grief was like a cliff face. I suppose . . . I ran the other way. It's why the vigil made sense, to start with. It was a place to hide, somewhere to put my guilt and shame. I never told Dad about Luke, what happened that summer Mum died. He'd have helped me, had I told him. I never gave him the chance.'

Grace is so still she might be carved from stone. Only the fire is moving, shifting its shadows and light over her face and hands.

'Those fifteen years between then and now . . . I've been hiding. In my studies, or my work. It's true what you said about his funeral, how it felt going home to the house alone. There was a moment when it hit me that I didn't have to lie to him any more and it felt good. I'd been lying for fifteen years. About who I was, the damage done to me on that boat . . .

'It was like living underwater.' He studies the empty palms of his hands. 'When I surfaced, which I did from time to time, I liked to look in the mirror and not recognize myself. It's how I measured my success; the less I looked like myself, the better I liked it. It was masking, like you said. Even in my sleep, I was masking. And I loved it, the buzz of *not being me*. Mum would not have recognized me, that's what I dreamt. What I wanted.'

He leans into her silence, what he takes to be her acceptance. She won't judge him. He can tell her anything, everything. None of it will change what she thinks of him or wants from him.

'Work helped. Being good at what I did, able to make a difference. Sometimes. But all the time' – he closes his right hand on his knee – 'I was becoming *less*. That was good, too; I called that good. Less of me meant less of the guilt and the grief. It's hard to live like that, of course. Work helped. And the vigil, for letting off steam or keeping it in check. You asked why I stayed friends with them, Clark and Owen and Luke. I think perhaps it is because I've never moved past it, what happened that summer. The vigil was . . . where I felt I belonged. With that violence and grief. The only things that made absolute sense to me.' He keeps his eyes on the fist he's made. 'I hadn't the courage to hold out my hand and ask for help. You cured me of that, this last week.'

'Crash course, full breakdown cover?'

He nods, looking towards the ruined shed. 'After Dad died . . . it was as if I'd lost whatever small claim to honour I once had. And to honesty, too. I'd missed my chance to tell him the truth. He died thinking I was someone else. Not his son, not the son he raised. Who helped him pull Mum from the bath and went with him in the ambulance with his books . . . I hid in those books and then at university, just as you said. And when I came home, I was a stranger. A stranger who lived in his house for the last years of his life.'

He is aware of her watching him with tears in her eyes but his own eyes are clear, unclouded.

'The more I learnt and the harder I worked, the less there was of me. And the less of me, the safer I felt . . . Masking kept me going, or mirroring. But the trouble with mirrors is that sooner or later everything gets inverted.' He seesaws his hand to demonstrate what he means. 'So . . . the less I was, the more I was. That was my delusion.' His right hand is still a fist. He studies it as he says, 'I called myself a coward, and I was. I am. But everything was inverted. I thought . . . strength was weakness, and vice versa. Rest was weakness. Love was weakness. *I* . . . was weakness.'

Slowly, he opens his fist, fingers unfurling in the firelight.

Grace says softly, 'But look at you now.'

'You did that,' he tells her. 'You're a Fresnel lens. You change the way light travels until all of it exits in the same direction . . . You helped me see how upside down everything was.'

'I mean . . .' – she props her chin on her arm – 'that does *sound* like me.'

'Very on-brand, Maddox. Advancing the cause of therapeutic medicine in spite of yourself.'

'In spite of everything . . .'

'Therapists will weep for the money they could've made out of me had I not had you on the job these last two weeks.'

'Maybe. Probably.'

She looks sad. He wants to make her smile, so he points at the night sky. 'Galileo had rotten eyesight. Jude taught me that. He saw ears, not rings, around Saturn. They call it creeping angle closure glaucoma. The night sky was a carnival of colour for Galileo.' He waits until Grace is looking at him. 'You remind me of her. Jude. The way you see things so much more clearly than I do. Like . . . how to make peace and when to wage war.'

What to do with anger and loss and a returning love of life.

'Will she be all right? Jude. Will she be all right without you?'

'Yes. She'll find a new counsellor, someone who will help. She's too smart and too strong to stay down where Dr Bowen tried to put her.'

A wash of moonlight touches the walls of the house with white. The night sky is shredded by cloud, its shadows like a hand folding and unfolding.

She stirs at the fire. 'How bad is it? Really.'

His hip, she means. He knows that's what she means.

'It's been better,' he admits. 'How's your head?'

'Like a bullet passed through it, a long time ago. Like I went away to war and never came back.'

'No one ever comes back from war, do they? Not really.'

'Deep, Daniel, deep . . . I keep thinking of Luke in that flak jacket, those boots. *He* was a coward. Luke fucking Hooley. He knew it, too. It's why he went looking for war. Not like us, who found it without even trying.'

'And yet here we are. Overcoming.'

She offers her fist to his, bumping knuckles. 'Overcoming.'

'We'd better put this fire out. Before we go in.'

She climbs to her feet and reaches a hand for his, pulling him upright. 'Let it burn.' She snaps their sticks in half, adding them to the pit. 'It'll burn itself out. Fires always do.'

44

'Daniel, wake up. They're here.'

He is on his feet, half-dressed from another restless night, in T-shirt and chinos. The window wavers with daylight. Early, first light. Grace is in her flannel shirt and jeans, boots laced on her feet. She looks like a soldier, bullet-headed, deadly. She nods and turns from the doorway to his room, light flashing from her hand. The knife. She has hold of the knife again.

'Wait!' He shoves his bare feet into the deck shoes. When he lifts his head, the room swarms. 'Grace, wait!'

By the time he reaches the kitchen, she is at the back door.

'Let me talk to them, they're my friends. *Grace*. Let me talk to them.'

She is closer to the door than he is. She can see outside what he can only hear. Loose gravel grinding underfoot.

'No,' she says in disbelief. '*No . . .*'

Dan snatches up the tea towel and winds it round his right hand, taking two steps towards her, but he is already too late.

The door bangs open, everything dazzling for a second. Broad shoulders, long legs, a fist swinging at the end of a long arm . . .

Grace meets it halfway, her knife flashing up in a burst of brightness as it collides with the light from outside.

Then a bolt of black, the slam of sound and fury as she is struck, flung from the doorway into Dan's path, an armed missile in a flannel shirt.

He rolls with the impact, his arms around her, holding her down, his back to the door – some idea of shielding her, or them – until a second slam puts paid to that, pain erupting like a landmine at the base of his spine, so much of it he fears for a second his back is broken as he sprawls, face smeared into the floor, weight pinning him down. Impossible to breathe, his lungs on fire, blood in his mouth, eyes screwed shut. A mouth, hot against his ear.

The words, when they come, freeze his blood.

'Time's up, Danny boy. You're fucked.'

45

Grace is a banshee, shrieking, hauling at Luke who is burying Dan in the tiled floor, putting his fists into him repeatedly, hissing obscenities in his ear.

Her knife is gone, out of reach.

He's half aware of it winking under the table where they sat looking through her shoebox as all the time Luke was coming closer until this.

Landing like a tiger on Dan's back.

Not dead, not dumped in the canal. She *lied*.

Grace lied and it is going to kill them both.

46

Daniel isn't moving. Blood spills on the floor from his head and his hip where my stab wound has been opened by Luke's fists. His neck's at an odd angle, broken-looking. He is a dark smear at our feet, Luke's and mine.

He hit me until I fell to the floor but I wasn't there long. He didn't leave me there the way he's left Daniel. Dragged me up, dumped me in this chair, hitting me again when I tried to stand. He hits hard. Blood in my mouth like the blood on the floor. Daniel's reflection is in the steel caps to Luke's boots.

'You're dead,' I say.

I last saw those toecaps on the narrowboat. Workman's boots, green flak jacket. But this Luke is bigger, broader, taller than the one I wrapped in tarpaulin, tied with rope. 'It wasn't you . . .'

'No shit.' He wipes his knuckles on the flak jacket, newer than the one I zipped over the sack of coal to weight him under the water. That jacket was faded and patched, its pockets hanging loose. This jacket is new.

'Who was it?'

He looks at me, curling his mouth. His eyes are bottle-green like the glass in my cellar window. His hair is black-blond, sweat-streaked. He hasn't slept in days by the look of him, has the air of an animal, cornered. Smells like an animal too, of sweat and musk and blood.

'Who was it?' I have to know. 'On the boat?'

Who did I put in the water? Whose skull was smashed with the tank this man used to score Daniel's arm, scarring him for life? And who did it – lifted that tank and smashed it again and again until the man on the ground had no face, only the same clothes Luke is wearing.

'You stupid bitch. It was my brother. It was Owen.'

Owen. Wearing Luke's hand-me-downs. Daniel told me about the split trainers, old clothes. Luke promised him a new Switch, too. It was *Owen* on the narrowboat. It is Owen at the bottom of the canal.

I want to howl. '*Why?*'

He points a finger at me. 'Stay in the chair or I'll break your legs.'

He hauls Daniel from the floor, using his foot to drag out a second chair before dumping Daniel into it. He has to put his fist in Daniel's chest to keep him from pitching back onto the floor.

'Where is it?' he demands. 'Where d'you put it?'

He's insane. He's killed him and he expects him to speak. Even as I'm thinking it, Daniel's head comes up. He blinks blood from his eyes, gathering it in his mouth before spitting it to the floor at Luke's feet.

'Where's . . . what?' His voice is broken, in the back of his throat.

Luke snarls, 'The fucking kit I gave you to sort her out. The hammer and nails. You didn't do it, did you? *Little bitch.* Now I'm going to.'

Daniel straightens slowly in the chair, setting his shoulders back. He is wearing the T-shirt he slept in, his scars in plain sight on his forearm. His right hand is closed over his left hip. He's shaking from shock and the damage Luke's boots and fists did. But something is happening, in his head. He looks changed. Damaged but whole. *He's remembering.* What happened that night, what brought us here, to this.

'I told you to take her to the fucking boat! Instead you hide the bitch all the way out here? Thought you could hide her from me, Danny? Thought she'd be safe from me here?'

Luke circles him, staring down at the damage he's done – fifteen years ago, five minutes ago – dreaming up new damage to do. He leans in close to Daniel's left ear, hisses, 'I told you. To bring her. To the fucking boat.'

Daniel was keeping me *safe*. In the cellar. Safe from Luke, from this war in Luke's eyes and fists. He wasn't holding me prisoner. He was saving my life.

'I told you,' Luke says. 'I needed her *on the boat*. That's where she did it, that's where I wanted her. Lost your fucking nerve, did you? Again.'

Daniel gathers more blood in his mouth, spits it to the floor. *There's your answer,* I think, *that's how scared he is of you.* But Luke doesn't seem to see Daniel is spitting at him, at who he is and what he's done. Only I can see Daniel Roake. Who lured me here to rescue me from a killer. To save my life.

Luke slams a hand at the table, the sound like a gunshot. 'Where is it?'

Daniel takes his time answering. 'I threw it out. I didn't need it.'

Luke's face flickers as if there's a bad connection, a misfire. He glances at me then back at Daniel. 'She told you?'

'Yes.' His voice is steady and his stare too, despite the blood glazing his eyes.

'Yeah?' Luke doesn't believe it. But he wants to. I see him wanting to believe it. 'So why the fuck didn't you call me?'

Daniel must be scared. I'm scared and I've not suffered at the hands of this man the way he has. But right at this minute he does not look afraid. He looks deadly. Dangerous. 'You said no phone calls,' he tells Luke.

'Didn't stop you texting, did it? Clark. *Tess.*' His teeth close on the last name, shredding it. ' "I know you think I did my best. But we need to talk." You little bitch!'

Daniel wipes blood from his face with the crook of his elbow. Under the blood, he is worn and white with pain. And he's lying. About the carrier bag with the hammer and nails, which is *right there* in the dresser, exactly where he left it. He's lying about me telling him whatever it is Luke wants from me. I've not told him anything, nothing to satisfy this maniac. Daniel is lying to Luke about what he's done and what I've done, and I said he couldn't lie to save his life, but here he is doing it to save mine, to save the pair of us if he can. It's going to get him killed. *Roake*, I think, *don't do it. I'm not worth it.*

'So where is it?' Luke demands.

Daniel doesn't say, 'Where's what?' He says, 'In my car.'

'The Saab?' Luke flicks a glance at the door, holds out a hand. 'Keys.'

When Daniel doesn't respond, Luke slaps at his shoulder like he's swatting a fly. He thinks Daniel is weak, pathetic. He hasn't seen what I've seen, doesn't know what Daniel is capable of. Or me, for that matter. He doesn't know anything at all about me.

'I have the keys.'

I say it to get his attention and before he hits Daniel again. Both men look at me. Daniel moves his mouth into a warning shape, wanting me to be quiet. But I won't be quiet. Not for him and certainly not for Luke.

'I have the keys,' I repeat.

Luke was leaning into Daniel but now he steps back, swinging his body to face me, showing the power in his chest and torso, his thighs. He could snap me in two without breaking a sweat.

'This bitch. Why's she not at least in the fucking cellar? This house has a cellar, right? Why the fuck isn't she in it?'

'She was.' Daniel wipes blood from his eyes. His fingers shake. His right hand is red and wet, still holding the stab wound together. 'Until she told me what you wanted to know. Then I let her out.'

'Yeah?' Luke runs his stare over me. 'Fancied a bit, did you? Full of surprises, Danny boy.'

'You have no idea.' Daniel says it in a voice that agrees with Luke: he is full of surprises. There is something else in his voice, something for my ears only. A caution or a plea. It tugs at me, wanting me to look at him.

I don't look at him. All of my attention is on Luke Hooley. This is the man who put me in the cellar, who wanted me trapped, wants me hurt. Daniel was his instrument but it was Luke's will. Because of what I did on the narrowboat, what I saw, what he thinks I saw. He bought nails and a hammer, a long-handled screwdriver, throwing in a first aid kit as an afterthought. Then he went off radar, waiting for Daniel to do his dirty work. He's only come out of hiding now because he needs whatever it is he thinks I have, whatever Daniel is lying to him about.

'What's in his car? If I'm giving you the keys, I'd like to know.'

Luke swings his stare between the two of us, slicing a smile with his mouth. 'Getting comfy here, were you? Was this little bitch making you feel at home? Were you, Danny?'

'What's in his car?' I repeat.

Daniel's voice thins, razored with warning. 'Owen's phone.'

Luke is staring down at me. I think fast, 'So that's where you put it,' covering my tracks, but I'm a beat too late because Luke is suspicious, looking between the pair of us again.

'Exactly how much have you told her?'

'She was there,' Daniel says tiredly. 'She knows more about it than I do. She can't tell anyone, though. Because she cleaned it up. The boat. The body. She cleaned it all up.'

'Yeah, she did. And I want to know why.' Luke folds his arms. Daniel's blood is on his knuckles or maybe it's mine; I can taste blood. 'Tell you that, did she? Why she fucked about on the boat. *Cleaning.*'

'She panicked.' Daniel draws a breath. 'She put him in the canal. He's gone. This was never about blackmail.'

Luke takes a step back. He seems to see Daniel's hand for the first time, fastened over his left hip, blood running through its fingers. I see the question take shape in his face, the demand to know how the hell Daniel has a knife wound and is bleeding out. His stare swings back to me.

'Why did you do it?' I ask him. 'Why did you kill Elise?'

There is a long second when the air is thick with his fury and I cannot breathe because of it. If I put out my hand, I'll touch it – the wall of his rage.

His fist, I think, *here it comes.*

But it's Daniel he hits, a backhanded blow that knocks him from the chair to the floor again. Luke raises his eyebrows at me as he does it, daring me to try to stop this. I fight to stay down, gripping the chair with my hands to stop myself surging at him. I cannot win this fight, not with my fists.

On the floor, Daniel curls in on himself, coughing. The sound of his pain makes my head spin.

'Say that again,' Luke challenges.

Grit shifts under his feet. He walked it in here in the treads of his boots, smelling of seared stone and carpentry glue. The kitchen is smaller because he's in it. He makes less of everything, crowding in and taking over, no room for anyone else. I have come to know this house over the past fortnight. An hour ago, I'd have known if someone was hiding in the cellar or in the rooms above me, instinct telling me the second someone stepped inside. Not now. It belongs to Luke. The house and us. We belong to him.

A hammer and nails. He expected Daniel to do that – torture the truth out of me. He believes Daniel belongs to him, that they all do: Clark and Owen and Elise. The vigil was about binding them to him. Feudal, brutal. He wasn't helping Clark, certainly not to get better or find closure.

There is no peace in Luke Hooley. No wholeness. Just a jagged line, a fault line, familiar. Like the one under my skin, buried so deep no warmth can reach it. Only Daniel made it better. When he was fighting me, or trying to make me stand still with my fight-ing held inside. When he was joking in eight languages to keep me from drowning in my own rage, telling me about Elise and this maniac's daughters, how they deserve peace. He said I fixed him but he did the same for me, or tried to. He wasn't to know I can't be fixed. He lied for me and he is going to die for me. Luke will never understand. He isn't capable of anything but violence. He came here to kill me. To kill the pair of us. He wants us dead.

On the floor, Daniel lies still, blood seeping from his head and side. He remembers now what happened on the boat that night. Not with Tess, never with Tess. He told the truth about her. We were searching in the wrong place.

One thousand, three hundred and sixty-six moves. *Himitsubako.* My Japanese puzzle box, bleeding into the tiles. Luke opened him with a hammer, smashing him to pieces. I'll never forgive him, as long as I live.

47

The narrowboat lurched as the well deck took Luke's weight.

Dan waited by the cabin door, the taste of stagnant water in his mouth. Rain had puddled in the corner where he'd found Elise's keyring the last time he was here. With Tess. Earlier today, or yesterday. Or last week. Time is playing its trick again, folding in on itself, swallowing him. *Earlier today*. It was light then; it is dark now. Luke shone his phone's torch across the water, lighting the boat's windows like eyes. At the mouth of the lock, darkness crouched in the shape of a man. *Night*. It is night.

'Key.' Luke held out his hand. He had his own key but he wanted Dan to be the one to unlock the cabin door, or he fancied ordering Dan around.

Dan felt like telling Luke it didn't make him special – anyone in the world could order him around right now. When Luke had pulled up outside his house, driving Clark's pickup, he'd been grateful for the chance to do as he was told, afraid if he sat in his parents' house any longer, he'd lose what little was left of his mind. He didn't question why Luke was driving the pickup, assuming it was with Clark's approval, to get him to the vigil faster. The journey itself was lost somewhere between the cracks in his head. He'd blinked when he found himself looking at the allotment. Even then, he didn't ask questions, just followed Luke from the truck to the boat. It should have scared him to be back on the boat with Luke but it didn't, the numbness sealing him against emotion of any kind.

Inside, the boat was the same as when he was here with Tess: dark red like the lining of a lung. He looked for the blood spatter but the freckles on the pillow were brown now, could have been rust or scorch marks left by an iron.

He's ironing Dad's shirt collar because it's Sunday, his share of the chores. Mum's upstairs, running a bath.

'Tell me exactly what Tess said. Every fucking word of it.'

'You're the one I love the most.' The bath water's brown, sucking at her, she's too heavy for him to hold.

'Oi.' Luke flicked fingers at his face. 'Danny boy, get your head in the game. Exactly what did Tess say? About the pendant and the pickup? She found it in the footwell, yeah?'

'No. Down the side of the seat.'

'Which seat?' Luke folded his arms, propping his shoulders to the wall. 'Which fucking seat, Danny?'

Dan kept his breathing shallow, forcing himself to focus on the detail in the paintwork, woodwork, brasswork. If he could hold on to the detail, the pictures in his head might start making sense. More than anything, he wanted things to make sense. To be able to answer Luke's questions, be present in this moment even if it meant Luke's fists or his fury. The past . . . The past was worse.

A storm's coming. He's built a fire, opened a can of lager so Luke won't think he's a kid. The hem of his T-shirt's stained with paint.

'Front seat. Passenger side.'

'*My* seat.' Luke thinned his mouth, frowning. Not at Dan, at the truckle bed. He wasn't seeing it any more than Dan was seeing cans of lager or a storm rolling in. Luke was seeing the inside of the pickup after the fight with the three men. 'That's definitely where she found it? The pendant?'

Dan tried to work out what Luke was doing here, what he wanted from him, what he was plotting. But the storm kept getting in the way, rain rocking the boat, Luke's elbow pinning him in place, pain in his armpit. He couldn't breathe because of it, not properly, not enough.

Luke pushed off the wall, started pacing. When he reached the sink, his foot kicked the helium tank and he stepped back, standing for a long moment staring down at the tank until Dan's arm began to throb, his vision blurring.

'Who else has a key to this fucking tub?' He turned on his heel, his stare landing like a punch on Dan's face. 'You. Tess . . . ?'

'She doesn't but –' The cork buoy, Elise's key dropped in the well deck. 'There was a key here. When Tess was looking for you, earlier.'

Luke was avoiding Tess. And Clark too, for some reason. Dan was a last resort. He wondered about Owen but the thought didn't stay in his head, crowded out by party balloons and a banner, paper plates, Tess serving vodka shots, clinging to his arm, laughing. The flash of cameras, crash of music.

'What's up with you, Danny boy?' Luke was in front of him suddenly, searching Dan's face with his sniper's eyes. 'You look like shit . . . Are you high?' He drilled his thumb into Dan's shoulder with a wolf's grin. 'You're fucking high, aren't you? Getting your hands on all sorts of shit at that hospital of yours. Fuck, Danny! Guess you're not such an uptight prick after all.'

Dan didn't argue with him. He hadn't argued with anyone since the Puddle Duck. Hadn't argued, hadn't eaten, hadn't slept.

'Tell me about this key then, when Tess was here earlier.'

And Dan did. He told Luke about Grace Maddox, how Tess had said she was odd, how long she had spent in the two houses, packing and unpacking, recreating Elise's bedroom like a shrine in the new house.

And Luke said, 'Shit,' and the next thing Dan knew he was being handed a carrier bag from a hardware shop, heavy because it contained a hammer and nails, a screwdriver and a Stanley knife like the one Luke used to cut the opaque sheeting to make the windows on the boat blind, the summer Dan's mum took her own life.

48

'Why did you kill Elise?' Grace demands.

Luke's fist knocks Dan to the floor, stuffing his head with the bright sound of shattering glass. He's been in freefall since the night at the Puddle Duck. Hits the ground so hard his teeth shake, so hard he breaks, but it's a good break, the kind that knocks everything into place. He is in the kitchen of his mother's house with the sound of Luke's threats ringing in his skull. *Make her tell you what she did.* Nails and a hammer. *Grace.*

Luke is up there, all the way up at the top of the floor and the floor is a mountain, a cliff face, if Dan could only get to his feet and climb. If he can just stop lying here, leaking life.

Luke's saying, 'You should've picked a better hero,' and there's a wet sound that Dan knows is Grace spitting at him and he tries to get up the cliff face but he cannot find a foothold and his hands ... His hands are useless. His left hand is out of his reach, its fingers twitching thinly. He blinks, a slow slide of syrupy red light all around him. His heart beats irregular time, his body wasted, all the energy and momentum slammed out of it. A crushing pressure crowds his chest as if he is under bricks, as if the house has exploded, burying him under rooms he has known all his life, making him part of the rubble.

'Don't you fucking dare!'

He can't tell if it is Luke or Grace speaking. When he tries to look up, his head slips in his own blood, his vision falling sideways, cutting out.

'I'll fucking kill you!'

He has to climb. He doesn't need to see to climb. That is not how the human eye works. He just needs nerve endings and a functional memory. Of the kitchen and his own anatomy: what is hard and what is soft, what can be damaged and what can with-stand damage.

A bullet passed through it, a long time ago.

Something dark and hatched, made of parallel lines, to the right of him. *A chair.* The chair Luke knocked him from.

He reaches for it – *ballast* – climbing up from the floor. Then he reaches for it again – *weapon* – swinging the chair at Luke.

Now Luke is the one down there and Dan is standing, bringing the chair down a second time until Luke stays where he is, until everything in the kitchen stops moving and there is silence finally, broken by birdsong. He staggers then but only for a second, finding his balance.

'Daniel.' Grace's hand is on his arm. 'You're bleeding.'

'I'll sort it in a minute. Get the belts.'

He doesn't trust the slack roll of Luke's neck, knows he is in no shape for a return match. This was his one shot at stopping it. He keeps hold of the chair, ready to use it again if Luke is faking. But when Grace returns with the belts, he is still unconscious. Dan crouches to assess this new damage he's done. No blood from where he hit Luke, just a lump coming up behind his left ear. Like the night he hit Grace. Luke's pulse is strong under his fingers. He works fast, with Grace's help, to fasten Luke's wrists to the table legs. It's a good table, solid oak. Luke might be able to shift it a foot or so across the kitchen floor but no further than that. Even so, Dan hesitates. Will it hold him? What if it doesn't?

Grace has a better idea: 'Put him in the cellar.'

It's a great plan, the best she's had so far. But . . . 'We'll never get him there.' Dan rests a hand on the table. 'He's sixteen stone.'

'We can do it. Between us.'

She is right, as usual. They unfasten the belts from the table legs, using them to secure Luke's hands behind his back. Then they drag, shove and roll him to the cellar door. Grace is about to empty him down the stone steps when Dan says, 'Hang on,' going down into the cellar to move the mattress so Luke's skull has a soft landing.

While he does this, Grace waits at the top, standing guard over Luke with the kitchen knife in her hand. Dan's hip is not a fan of the workout with the mattress or for that matter a fan of him staying upright when what it wants is a stretcher and a strong sedative. He climbs to where Grace is waiting and between them they roll Luke down into the cellar.

He lands on the mattress, more or less. Or less.

'Hang on . . .' Dan goes back down the steps to put him into the recovery position, unfastening the belt from Luke's wrists.

As he straightens from doing this, a beam of light blinds him, hitting the cellar walls like a spear.

Grace, with her knife. Coming down to join him in the darkness. Light keeps hitting, from the top of the steps but also from behind.

He turns to see dozens of bottles of water and stacks of cans, each throwing the reflection of the knife's blade. He is down in the dungeon he built but he didn't put this water here, or the canned food. That was done after he freed Grace. Grace who is coming towards him with a fist full of knife.

'Maddox . . .' She doesn't stop. He takes a step back. His heel hits the edge of the mattress where Luke is lying. 'Grace?'

Her eyes fix on his face. 'Move out of my way.'

'What are you going to do?'

She cocks her head. 'What do you think I am going to do?'

You're going to stick a knife in him, and in me if I get in your way.

'I didn't put those down here.' He points at the rations. 'Did I?'

'They were for you. I was going to shut you in here for twelve days to teach you what it's like. But I changed my mind.' She nods at Luke. 'Now move. Out of my way.'

'What happens if I don't?'

'We find out which matters more to you. His life or my alibi.'

'Your alibi?' His head is spinning.

'Daniel, if you pass out, I'll have to leave you down here.' She is wiping the knife clean on her shirt, getting rid of her fingerprints. 'I'm not strong enough to get you up those steps by myself.' She adjusts her grip, holding the tip of the blade in a section of her shirt's hem. 'Not right now.'

He steps aside.

She crouches to put the knife's handle into Luke's slack right hand, closing her fingers around his until he is gripping the knife tightly. When she straightens, she wipes the blade on the hem of her shirt to make certain the only prints left on it are Luke's.

'I'm going to clean this house,' she says then. 'Forensically.'

'Don't . . .' Dan's brain is catching up with her. 'It'll look suspicious. No one's house has no fingerprints in it.'

'Our prints are all over this one, Roake. And mine are in the system.'

'Are they?' He blinks, battling dizziness. 'Well . . . I expect I'll have a better idea in a bit. Give me time.'

She helps him climb the steps out of the cellar, saying, 'Wait here,' when they reach the door. He waits, leaning into the wall.

She takes the knife to the kitchen, returning with the cellar key, which she turns in the lock, pushing her hand against the door to test its solidity. The key smells of coffee grounds. She must have hidden it in one of the jars. Dan wonders if she hid the car keys in the same place.

Afterwards, she wants to examine his stab wound, 'You didn't bleed this much before,' but he tells her it's okay, he's got it.

In the bathroom, he sorts himself out with the first aid kit Luke dumped into the carrier bag the day Dan became his accomplice. He washes the blood from his face before leaning into the lip of the sink to consider his reflection. His pupils are blown. His skin is white and clammy. He's very thirsty. His wristwatch was a casualty of the fight: a crack runs across its glass. He unstraps it, puts it on the shelf above the sink. He doesn't take his pulse because there isn't any point. The adrenaline will tank soon and then he'll be in trouble but for now he's coasting on it, like fumes. He fills his palm with water from the tap, swallows it with paracetamol, taking the rest of the strip to where Grace is tidying the kitchen, putting the chairs back around the table.

'Let me look at you,' Dan says. 'He hit you pretty hard.'

She stands under the light while he runs his fingers over her skull, vigilant of the swelling under her left eye. Her eye socket is sound, and her cheekbone. He smooths it with his thumb. 'You're good.'

'Are you?' she asks.

'I'm great.'

Birdsong, outside. From the cellar: silence. Grace fills the kettle, sets it on the stove. Dan fetches mugs, teabags and a teaspoon. He fills a glass with tap water and drinks it. Refills the glass and stands it next to the mugs.

'If he didn't kill Elise, who did? Roake?'

He aligns their mugs on the counter as if this symmetry is what matters most right at this minute. Hesitating because he doesn't want to say it, does not want to believe it. The thought tears a hole in his heart. He sees the tidy two-year-old trying to keep his clothes clean at Elise's christening, and the boy playing on her games console in the hospital, kicking the frayed heels of his trainers at the linoleum floor. Then he makes himself remember the young man standing with his fists balled by the side of the pickup, face smeared sideways with emotion: *They need telling! They need to know!*

'Owen,' he says at last. 'It was Owen.'

'Luke told you that?' Grace demands.

'He didn't tell me anything. Just gave me orders, instructions.'

'To bring me to the boat. But you didn't. You brought me here. You were keeping me safe, Roake. Saving my life.'

'I was stalling for time.' He swallows drily. 'I'm the one who gave him your name, Maddox. That was me.'

'But you didn't take me to the boat. Or do any of the things he told you to do. You lied about the hammer and nails. You lied to save my life.'

'Well . . . honesty wasn't working out for me.'

'And you remember what he told you,' Grace insists. 'What happened on the narrowboat. You've got your memory back.'

'I think so. I mean . . . I don't know what I don't know.' It makes sense in his head. And to her, presumably. He doesn't fancy trying to explain it to anyone else, though. The police, say. 'But yes. I think so.'

She turns back to the kettle. 'Who killed Owen?' She is tense, afraid of his answer. She got rid of the evidence. Owen's body. That was her.

Dan says, 'It's why he's so angry. Why he wanted to hurt you. Because you tidied it all away. He couldn't face up to what he did. Worse than that, he didn't know what you'd done with the evidence. Or what you might do.'

'Luke,' she says on a long sigh. 'Luke killed Owen.'

He has an impulse to hold her. It's madness. Apart from anything else, he is bleeding, inside and out. The pair of them are covered in bruises. Not the moment for physical contact. He wants to comfort her nevertheless.

What happened three weeks ago with Luke is crystal clear in his head, 4K, digitally remastered. But his time spent here with Grace is like the canal bed: a place of mud, broken bricks and glass. He pictures Owen's body resting there, wrapped in tarpaulin, tied with rope. Dan's conversation with the police is nothing compared to the one Grace is going to have with them.

She repeats it as if to herself: 'Luke killed Owen.'

'I think he must have done. Don't you?'

'I thought it was Tess.' She fills their mugs from the kettle. 'Because she found the pendant.'

'Tess isn't a killer. You were right the first time – Luke was always the violent one.'

'And Owen.'

'I can't believe he meant to kill Elise. I doubt he knew his own strength; he was growing so fast and he was clumsy . . .'

'He could have confessed,' Grace says tightly. 'If it was a mistake.'

'Maybe he would have done if the rest of us hadn't kept insisting it was a stranger who killed her. "No one who knew her would've hurt her . . ." He must have heard that a hundred times. I bet he started to believe it. It probably made more sense than the truth, in his head.'

Dan pulls out a chair and sits at the table. His body is burning with the damage Luke did but he is so grateful to have his mind back he wouldn't care if he had a ruptured spleen. *Be careful what you wish for, Roake.*

'I'll tell you what I know and what I think. Luke didn't share much of it with me, only what he needed to get me to play along.'

He relates what he remembers of the night on the narrowboat when Luke's anger made about as much sense as the landslide in his own head.

Grace listens in silence, sipping at the mug of black tea. 'He thought you were high – that was his explanation for why you went along with it?'

'He saw an opportunity, threatened to report me to the hospital. If I'd had any sense, I'd have let him. Then none of this would have happened.' Dan listens to the silence from the cellar. 'I was out of it, no idea what was wrong with me. But the hospital would have known . . . I'm sorry. Again.'

She shrugs his apology aside. 'He didn't tell you about Owen and Elise?'

'No . . . He said *you* knew who killed her. You'd stolen from her room, tricked Tess into telling you details of the murder. Maybe you were even the killer – he put that idea in my head. I was supposed to keep you in my house for a couple of days – not this house, the other one – while he covered his tracks in town. Then he wanted you back on the boat.' Dan rubs his thumb at a stain on the table. 'He wanted to know what you'd done with Owen's body.'

'How did he find out Owen killed Elise?'

'It can only have been the pendant in the pickup. He knew he didn't drop it but it was near his seat. Owen always sat behind him, always did everything Luke did. Warned the girls, threatened them. And he loved Elise. You were right about that. Her killer loved her. But I think . . . Owen didn't know how to do that without being violent. He saw Luke treating Shannon like a punchbag, heard how he talked about women. If Luke figured that out – realized he was the one who gave Owen the idea that if a girl says no she doesn't mean it – it will have made him sick. With himself as much as Owen.'

Dan drinks a mouthful of the sweet tea. 'He must have given Owen his key to the boat. It's why he didn't have it when he took me there. I imagine he told Owen he was going to sort it, maybe he thought he could. But then Owen said or did something to tip him over the edge. He loved Owen, I'm certain of that. He wouldn't have gone there to hurt him.'

'Wouldn't he? Everything he did was about finding Elise's killer and punishing him. The vigil, the checks at the hospital . . . All of it was about vengeance for Elise's murder. I'll bet it wasn't that hard for him to kill Owen.'

393

'Maybe. But that doesn't mean he wasn't grieving afterwards. Where else did that rage come from? At me because he made me a part of it. At you for disposing of the evidence.'

'He should've disposed of it himself,' Grace says. 'Why didn't he?'

'I imagine he was going to. It's possible he didn't have everything he needed; if Owen told him about other evidence, things he'd kept . . . The cable charger that killed her – the police never found that. Owen might have told him where it was. Luke will have wanted everything together to deal with at the same time. Or perhaps . . . he was in shock at what he'd done. Went to clear his head and when he came back to deal with it, Owen was gone.'

The gaps in Dan's knowledge are more defined now, nothing like the fog of the amnesia. Even so, he is aware he is attempting a diagnosis with insufficient data. The police are unlikely to be impressed by that. Unless Luke volunteers the information, Dan is going to look like an accomplice or, worse, a suspect. His amnesia will be written off as a convenient excuse, given the evidence in this house and his car.

Grace is thinking the same thing: 'Tell me about the phone in your car.'

'I was an idiot. He said it was a burner to contact him in an emergency. Warned me not to use it otherwise, said it could be traced. But of course it's Owen's phone. He was setting me up, like you said.'

'I thought he threw a phone in the canal. That splash . . .'

'I've thought about that.' Dan shifts his shoulders in the chair. 'I think it was the games console, the one Clark gave Owen.'

'Are you still bleeding, Roake?'

He lifts the hem of his T-shirt, checks the dressing. 'The console belonged to Elise. That might have been what pushed Luke over the edge – seeing Owen playing on it after he'd worked out he was her killer.'

'If you're bleeding, I need to know. We have to get our stories straight.'

'I don't need an ambulance.' He ignores the second half of her statement. 'Luke gave me Owen's phone as part of his alibi, like you said.'

'He tried to make you believe I was a killer.' Grace thinks about this. 'He was buying time, is that it?'

'Part of it, yes. If I believed you were a killer, I'd keep my distance, be less likely to listen to you if you tried telling me what you'd seen on the boat. He'd no idea how much you'd seen, or why you hadn't simply gone to the police. But he was also buying time, you're right. He'd told Tess he was taking Owen off on a job up in Hebden Bridge – that would explain why no one was going to see Owen for a bit, while Luke was figuring out what to do next. He was desperate to know what you'd done with the body: "Make her tell you what she did." I thought he was talking about Elise, insofar as I was capable of thinking at all. But he meant what you did with Owen's body; the clean-up on the boat freaked him out. He couldn't come up with a rational reason for why you did that, other than blackmail. He was afraid of you, I know that much. It's why I was so nervous around you myself.'

'There's a third reason he was buying time,' Grace says. 'To implicate you in all this. As his fall guy.'

'Three reasons,' Dan concedes.

'Wait.' She reaches for his phone. 'Owen texted you – two days ago. And before that, too. Three texts. Look.'

The texts sound like Owen, enough to be convincing. More evidence; Dan's word against Luke's. He hands back the phone.

'Luke sent these, another part of his alibi. That's a guess but I'd put money on it. He was always giving Owen new phones, old phones . . .'

'We should look at the phone in your car.'

'I think we've looked at enough. We should avoid touching anything else. My prints are probably the only ones on that phone but just in case . . .'

She is holding his phone, thumbing at its screen. He wonders if she's looking at the texts she sent when she was pretending to be him. Between her and Luke, Dan is going to need a really good lawyer. He is going to prison, that's just a fact. For years, if not life. Kidnapping, unlawful imprisonment, conspiring, perverting the course of justice . . . Murder. He finds himself thanking God his parents are no longer alive.

'He'll never confess.' Grace puts the phone down. 'You do know that.'

'Shame about the evidence.'

On the narrowboat, he means. Evidence she washed away, wrapped and weighted, sunk to the bottom of the canal. Her eyes gleam for a second as if she is appreciating his joke. He wasn't joking but he doesn't pursue it.

'What're you planning on doing?' he asks her.

'I'm not making any plans.' She drinks tea. 'Everything's secure, for now. He's here. You're safe. You have your memory back, and your life.'

'My memory, yes.' He makes himself smile. 'Come on. If we're getting our stories straight . . . I'm going to prison. We both are.'

'I've been in prison.' She stands, collecting their mugs from the table. 'I don't recommend it. Certainly not for someone like you.'

Dan is still processing the first part of this when she adds, 'I don't mean the cellar.'

'When?'

And why? Her fingerprints, she said, in the system.

'Fifteen years ago.' She runs the hot tap. 'For arson.'

'What did you burn?'

She shakes her head. 'Concentrate on getting your own story straight.'

'Come on. You've got secrets written all over your face.'

'I hope not.' She wipes a hand there. 'Better?'

He wonders who she was when she committed the arson. Whether she was Grace or Gwen, or someone else entirely. There is an image in his head of a big house burning, buckets of sand fired to glass by the heat.

'We should call the police while we both look like this.'

Bruised. Battered by Luke.

'And that?' She nods at his knife wound. 'Luke's prints are on the knife but they might still figure out it was me. The wound's not recent.'

'Self-defence, then.'

'Attempted murder,' as if she is bidding against him in an auction.

'Self-defence,' he repeats.

'You opened the door. Told me to leave.'

'I kept you in a cellar for days. Starved you—'

397

'You forgot about me. I suppose in a way that was unforgivable . . .'

She isn't taking this seriously. Why? She said she wasn't making any plans but he finds that hard to believe. She is probably working out how to deep-clean his car, Luke's car – all of it. The pain in his hip tightens a notch.

'He'll never confess. His word against ours. Against yours.'

'Grace, we need to call the police.'

'Daniel, no, we don't.'

Deadlock, again. You'd think he'd be familiar with it by now but it sets his head spinning all over again. He doesn't know her. Just because they have lived through this does not mean he knows anything about her.

'No one knows he's here,' Grace says. 'He won't have told anyone. We're the only ones who know.'

Dan watches her, watching him. She is waiting to see which way he'll land. As if he is still falling, or clawing his way up from the floor.

'We could leave him down there,' she says next. 'He'll last a good while with the rations. Maybe he'll even figure a way out, in time.'

'And meanwhile we do what? Go back to our lives as if nothing happened?'

'Why not?'

'We'd be murderers. We would have murdered a man.'

'Not a man. A monster.'

'I don't believe in monsters,' Dan says. 'And neither do you.'

She fixes her cool grey gaze on his face.

'We haven't killed anyone,' Dan insists. 'Not yet. That was Owen and Luke. Neither of us is a killer.'

Still she looks at him, unblinking. His mind's eye puts two figures in the upstairs window of the burning house: a woman with a jar of eyes, a man in a velvet tie standing at the threshold of his daughter's attic bedroom. His face must have betrayed him because—

'They live miles away,' she says stonily. 'In retirement housing, no children allowed. No little girls. My mum moved them there as soon as they were both over fifty-five. I haven't seen them in years.'

'Good . . . Let me call the police. Please. Let this be over.'

'It is over. For you. Go home, Daniel. Start over. You'll do better this time, you know you will.'

He drops his eyes. She's too much, like staring at the sun.

'Buy a Paul Klee for your mum's room. Take flowers to their graves. You've made your peace. You went to war and you came back, and making war is easy, but making peace? It's why you're remarkable, Daniel Roake.'

'I don't believe that. I don't even think you believe it.'

'You're wrong, in fact. But if that's not hitting the spot for you, then Jude needs you. Tess and Clark need you.'

'I was out of my mind . . .'

'So get help,' Grace says. 'Just not from Amanda Bowen.'

Thudding from the cellar.

'And Luke?' Dan asks.

'Leave Luke to me.'

The Facts As I Know Them

- He is bleeding inside, my knife wound made much worse by Luke's fists. He is lying about how bad it is. His face gives him away, all the colour gone from it.
- He left his wristwatch in the bathroom, a gift from his father. There's a crack across the glass. He left it for me. A new treasure for my shoebox. A souvenir of our time spent together, which is over now. Finished, done. But if Daniel is done, what's left?
- Only Luke who won't have forgotten what I told him while Daniel was unconscious on the kitchen floor. That I'd never forgive him. That I'd hate him as long as I lived. That I would kill him if I could.
- In my mind's eye, he is spending the rest of his life locked up. A prison cell is a sort of box. Too big for him, though. He rattles in there.
- I'd like him in a far smaller box, his height and width, no more. Six feet under. He does not deserve to be safe.
- Tess is in a box, too. The one Luke and his brother put her in when they killed her child.
- I do not want Tess in a box. I want her to stand in the sunlight where Elise once turned cartwheels, shining.

Never Events

- They will never get away with it.
- Luke will never confess. She's right about that.
- Owen is at the bottom of the canal. Clark and Tess may never know peace. They may never know peace.
- The rations she put in the cellar will last for weeks. Luke will last for weeks. But Dan won't. This bleeding won't stop without surgery. He's dying, essentially.
- How much of this was preventable? *You'll never know.*
- Focus on what matters. Damage limitation. He's meant to be the clever one. *You're meant to be the clever one.*
- He will never get a better chance to prove it.

49

The knife is back in play. Wrapped in a tea towel to preserve Luke's prints but back in Grace's fist. *She is still made of knives.*

'You have to trust me,' Dan says again. He's been saying it for the past seven minutes. Sitting in the kitchen, facing Grace across the table where they ate and argued and ended up here, with time fast running out.

'Trust you to do what?' she says. 'Get in my way?'

'To come up with a better way out of this for us. I couldn't do it before. Insufficient data. But I can now, with help.'

'Whose help?'

'It's already on its way. Thanks to your text messages.'

'You mean Tess and Clark? They won't help. Tess hates me.'

'She doesn't. She just doesn't understand you. If she understood you, she'd love you.'

Her mouth crooks. 'Is that a declaration, Roake?'

'It's a fact. You did all this for Elise.'

'It won't matter. Tess thinks I'm odd. She won't help, not in the way we need. And Clark listens to Luke before he listens to you.'

'I'll make him listen to me. I can make them understand.'

'You've not told the truth to anyone in years.'

'That's why they'll listen. Call it . . . the element of surprise.'

She shakes her head at him. 'You're dead on your feet. And anyway, how can they help? What is it you imagine they'll do?'

'They'll call the police, explain what Luke did. Tess has the pendant. I'll give Owen's phone to Clark. We know Luke threw the games console into the canal, maybe they'll find the murder weapon with it. The charger cable. The police will dredge the canal—'

'And they'll find Owen. How will Tess and Clark explain that?'

'Luke killed him. Luke got rid of the body.'

'Occam's Razor,' Grace says slowly. 'The simplest explanation is the most likely explanation.'

'*Yes.* And damn, Maddox. Now who's showing off?'

'The principle of parsimony: one of my old dad's favourites . . .' She flexes her fist around the knife. 'So Luke gets the credit for that clean-up job on the boat, does he?'

'Who else would have done it? You wore gloves. None of your prints are there. And Luke's mess, Luke's job to clean it up. Not the first time he's washed blood from that helium tank, remember? He has form.'

She studies him. 'You'd tell them about that – what he did to you, all those years ago?'

'If it gets him put away? Yes, of course.'

'And when he says it was you? And me? What then?'

Dan takes a moment to breathe. He is running out of breath. And he's thirsty, no matter how much water he drinks. 'Luke can say what he likes. No one is going to believe you were involved.

You'd never even met him. If he tries pinning the blame on you, he is going to look insane.'

'I have a police record, Roake.'

'So we'll stay low until the investigation is over. I'll keep you safe until the court case, a conviction. We can go anywhere. Blackstone Edge or . . . Bellagio. Saddleworth or Stockholm. Higher Shelf Stones or Hokkaido.'

He reaches for the glass of water, his vision dimming. He can hear a clock ticking. There is no time left to argue with her. No time for anything.

'We can go wherever you want,' he says again. 'Anywhere.'

'A road trip?' I picture it. The open road, the two of us. But wherever we go, there I am. 'Tess will back Luke up. She hates me. She hated me when she left those reviews.'

'She won't when she understands what you were doing and why.'

'This whole plan rests on you talking them into trusting me? I've made better plans in my sleep.'

'No doubt.' Daniel is white, like his fingers around the glass he can't stop drinking from. 'But I'm working with what I have. They're on their way here, I'm sure of that. You made sure of that. We're going to have to tell them something. Why not the truth?'

I move the knife back and forth as I consider this. 'And the chair-shaped lump on the back of his head? The fact he is locked in a cellar in your mother's house?'

'That's trickier,' Daniel admits. 'It'll require lying on Clark's part and Tess's, too. But they'll do it, if I ask them. If I explain what's at stake.'

'Keeping you out of jail, you mean?'

'Not just me, Maddox. We're a package deal at this point. I can't explain what I was doing here without implicating you.'

'So you're going to ask Clark and Tess to lie, for our sake? Why would they? For you, maybe. But for me?' I start to climb to my feet.

He holds me still with his stare. 'Think about it. Who did you do all this for? *Elise.* Who deserves the truth about her death more than Tess and Clark? They need answers; you can give them that. You can bring them peace.'

'The peace of knowing the boy you all loved strangled their child?'

'Like peace after war. Hard won, altering everything, but still peace.'

'And what do you think they will do, Daniel, when they find out the man responsible for so much of what happened is locked up here, at their mercy?'

'Grace . . .' He doesn't have the strength to keep arguing with me, barely has the strength to stay upright.

'It's a serious question. You're trying to talk me out of killing him. Because I want to kill him. What makes you think they won't?'

'I know them. They're my friends.'

'You *knew* them. You grew up together, went to school together . . . But I was in those houses with them, for weeks. I saw their grief, how it changed them. It changed everything in their lives. *Everything,* Daniel. Your version of them doesn't exist any more.'

405

'You're wrong. Of course they're grieving but that doesn't mean they're different people, capable of—'

'That's exactly what it means. You don't understand, Daniel. You're very clever and you care very much but you're not a parent. You don't have any idea what they're capable of. Tess, especially. When she finds out what Luke did, the part he played in Elise's death? She *will* want to kill him. Maybe I should save her from that.'

I wrap my fist more tightly around the tea towel that is preserving Luke's prints on the knife. My solution is violent but clean. This way it's done. Finished. Only Daniel doesn't want this to be done, not like this. He doesn't want an ending where any of us are monsters.

'Grace . . . let me at least try. To make them understand, to ask for their help. Give me that chance. If I cock it up, you can deal with it your way.'

'You'd never let me hurt them . . .'

'You wouldn't hurt them. It's Luke you're thinking about killing, not them. But yes, I'd try to stop you. For your sake, not his. You're not a killer, Grace. You're the one who is going to bring them peace. You have to trust me to make them understand. Can't you trust me, after all we've been through?'

When Tess and Clark come, Daniel takes them into the garden, to the place where we built the bonfire last night. I stay inside the house, watching the three of them from the window, seeing the triangle they make as they stand around the blackened circle of the fire pit. Mum's voice echoes in my head: 'Stand up, don't slouch,

406

straighten your skirt.' It is her fault I cannot make sense of people, the strange shapes they make. But it is my fault, too. Not everything fits in a box. A jumble of eyes in a glass jar; I should forgive her for that, for trying her poor best to keep me safe.

In the garden, the three of them stand close together. Clark is listening, at last, to his better friend. Daniel is so gentle with them. He is bleeding but you wouldn't know it. All his focus is on his friends. Their pain and their grief. Tess is stitched together with it, with anger and loss and the need to know peace. When she reaches a hand for Dan's elbow, I know she is asking if he is all right. She sees his pain, as clearly as I see hers.

Daniel shakes his head. Clark reaches for his shoulder. They are holding him, Clark and Tess. Even through their grief, with every-thing he is telling them, they are worried for him. He puts his hands over theirs and their shape shifts as they lean towards one another.

My heart must have a chip in it but not of ice. I'm not numb or cold or carefree. I am aching all over. My eyes are hot, the bridge of my nose tight with tears. It hurts. Everything hurts.

I'm still hurting when Daniel brings them back into the house.

Tess reaches to take my hands. She holds my hands, not speak-ing, or not words, just her eyes saying she understands and *thank you* for what you did, for Elise. Is that what she is saying? I want to believe it. And it is peace, Daniel calls it peace, this violence spreading in my chest, clawing its way up my throat, scratching at my stomach and behind my eyes. *Peace.*

'Tess and Clark will wait here, for the police.' Daniel is ashen. 'I need you to drive me to a hospital, Maddox. Can you do that?'

I don't want to leave them alone with Luke but I cannot let Daniel get any paler. If he gets any paler, he will be dead.

My car starts first time, its tyres spitting gravel as I turn it towards the road. The house behind us looks empty, gutted by the day's grey light. I watch it shrinking in the rear-view mirror, swallowed by trees.

'They're going to stay there? With Luke?'

'Until . . . the police come.' His breath is short, close to gasping. 'Yes.'

'A vigil?'

'A vigil.'

In my mind's eye, Luke is taken from the cellar by the police. No power, no friends. Standing on the other side of that line he drew years ago when he put Daniel beyond the reach of help, with no one to turn to or believe him. Now Luke is the one out in the cold. Or else he is dead, Tess standing over him with the knife I used on Daniel, dripping red across the cellar floor, blood running to fill the initial I scratched there all those days ago. G for guilt, for grief, for gone. Next to me, Daniel closes his right hand over his hip.

'Roake?'

'Just . . . keep driving.'

'We should've called an ambulance.'

'This's . . . quicker.' He opens an eye at me. 'You drive . . . like a lunatic.'

'I'm saving your life.'

'Yes, you are . . .'

His voice fades but it's all right. He will be all right.

I've never yet lost anything precious in transit.

Acknowledgements

Sharp Glass first entered my head as the splinter of an idea about captivity. That splinter did what all writers hope an idea will do: it obsessed me. The more I wrote, the more I wanted to write. The characters whispered (and occasionally roared) in my head until I was done. With the help of my brilliant publisher, Vicki Mellor, my tireless agent, Veronique Baxter, and a host of champions in Pan Macmillan, that splinter became this book. I'm grateful to the friends and family who tolerated my absence, silence and strangeness as I was writing *Sharp Glass*. Special thanks to Jane Casey and Julie Akhurst, who read an early draft. Imran Mahmood supplied sentencing advice; Chris Merritt, psychological insights. Victor was my Japanese consultant. Any mistakes are my own. Ray Kahn won the Good Books auction in support of Young Lives vs Cancer and has a role in this story as a result. To the booksellers, librarians, reviewers, bloggers, festival organizers, interviewers, podcasters and everyone who presses books into the hands of readers – thank you. And to readers, dear readers, I hope *Sharp Glass* finds a place in your heart.

About the Author

Sarah Hilary's debut, *Someone Else's Skin*, won the Theakston Crime Novel of the Year Award and was also a World Book Night selection, a Richard & Judy Book Club pick and a finalist for both the Silver Falchion and the Macavity Awards in the US. *No Other Darkness*, the second in her DI Marnie Rome series, was shortlisted for a Barry Award. The series continued with *Tastes Like Fear, Quieter Than Killing, Come and Find Me* and *Never Be Broken*. *Sharp Glass* is her third standalone novel, following *Black Thorn* and *Fragile*.